PRAISE FOR *[...]*

". . . a pull-no-punches tale o[f...]
residents, urban versus rura[l,...]
Mitchell gives as balanced a glimpse of the issues, the politics,
and the spirit of the West and Kenya in this novel as one will
find anywhere . . . He shows how all sides will often find themselves in a different cut of the 'emperor's new clothes.' A good
read."
 —**Mark Lehnertz,** Tattered Cover Book Store,
  Denver, Colorado

PRAISE FOR *The Height of Secrecy*

"An engaging mystery with strong characters and a wonder-
fully authentic setting in the Southwest. Keep your eye on this
nascent series."
 —**Colorado Authors' League**
  2015 Award for Mainstream Fiction

"Loved it! A mystery with strength and realism. Mitchell's
background leads to blended masterpieces of plot, setting
and characters, complete with insider authenticity. He's got a
good series going."
 —**Betty Palmer,** op. cit. books, Taos, New Mexico

"This was a fun read. The characters are believable, the rescue
and fire scenes ring true, and Mitchell worked in the agency
long enough so that he knows how things can go bad. . . ."
 —***Ranger: The Journal of the Association of
  National Park Rangers***

"What Grisham does for law and the courtroom drama,
Mitchell does for national parks and the politics of land

and preservation. His behind-the-scenes knowledge of the subculture creates a believable setting that blends seamlessly with the story."

    —**Isaac Mayo**, Developmental Editor

PRAISE FOR *Public Trust*

"In *Public Trust,* J. M. Mitchell brings a richness to the wilderness mystery that's not to be missed. Fire starts the novel and it burns fast and furious, but pales to the political firestorm that becomes a battle for nature herself."

    —**Nevada Barr,** *New York Times* best-selling author

"[S]o real you think you're reading nonfiction. . . . This is a good read."

    —***Ranger: The Journal of the Association of National Park Rangers***

KILLING GODIVA'S HORSE

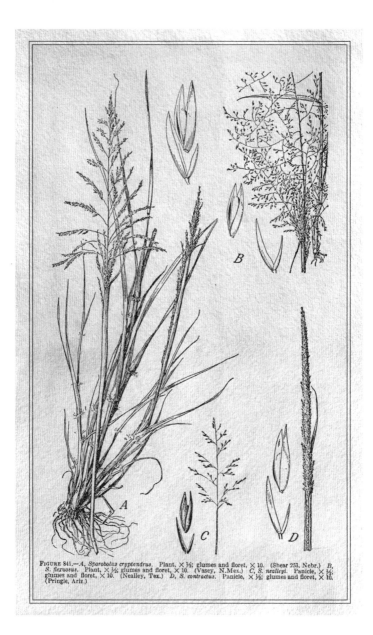

FIGURE 841.—*A, Sporobolus cryptandrus.* Plant, × ½; glumes and floret, × 10. (Shear 253, Nebr.) *B, S. flexuosus.* Plant, × ½; glumes and floret, × 10. (Vasey, N.Mex.) *C, S. nealleyi.* Panicle, × ½; glumes and floret, × 10. (Nealley, Tex.) *D, S. contractus.* Panicle, × ½; glumes and floret, × 10. (Pringle, Ariz.)

KILLING GODIVA'S HORSE

—

J. M. MITCHELL

PRAIRIE PLUM PRESS

DENVER

ALSO BY J.M. MITCHELL

Public Trust

The Height of Secrecy

Copyright © 2018 J.M. Mitchell

PRAIRIE PLUM PRESS
P.O. Box 271585
Littleton, CO 80127
www.prairieplumpress.com
Email@prairieplumpresss.com

Printed in the United States of America

First Printing, 2018

Print edition ISBN 978-0-9852272-7-2
Digital edition ISBN 978-0-9852272-8-9

Library of Congress Control Number: 2018930650

Sand dropseed *(Sporobulus crytandrus)* illustration: USDA-NRCS PLANTS Database / Hitchcock, A.S. (rev. A. Chase). 1950. *Manual of the grasses of the United States.* USDA Miscellaneous Publication No. 200. Washington, DC.

Book design by K.M. Weber, www.ilibribookdesign.com

*Dedicated to the rangers of Kenya and
elsewhere in Africa who have died fighting
to preserve their heritage, and to the memory of
Esmond Bradley Martin, investigator, who fought
the trafficking of rhino horn and elephant ivory.*

CHAPTER
1

The ranger turned onto a dirt track and saw it. Reflection off tail lights. A Land Cruiser. No light or movement. Not a good sign.

He slowed, then turned off his headlights.

Only a hint of morning invaded the dark.

Eying the other vehicle's dark silhouette, he brought his to a stop, took hold of his rifle, and slipped out. His partner moved the opposite direction. If what they feared, they did not want to walk into a trap.

A few feet into the bush, the ranger stopped, held his breath, and listened. Nothing.

He inched forward. Closer to the vehicle, further from the road. Again, he stopped and listened. Nothing.

Working his way around, he crept deeper into the bush, both hands on his rifle.

He edged past an acacia. On the ground, darkened outlines. He approached, knowing. Rhinoceros. He stopped alongside and saw the stump. Horn, gone. Sawn off. Clotted blood covered the ground. He touched the carcass. Cool. This happened hours ago.

He clicked on his flashlight, stepped past two other carcasses —a cow and her calf—and headed straight for the Land Cruiser.

There he found them. Two rangers, one a scientist, both on the ground in front of the vehicle, dead, cold, one bullet each, straight through the heart.

Gabriel Kagunda finished writing an entry. Enough for today. He picked up his quadrat of PVC pipe and cotton string and disassembled it. Turning away from the setting sun, he let his eyes wander across the savanna as he stuffed the pieces away. He threw on his pack and began the walk to the vehicle. There, another ranger waited.

He approached, and the ranger—David Ole Nalangu, in camo uniform and brown beret—stood staring to the left, his service AK-47 hanging from his neck by its strap, his arms folded over it.

Gabriel turned to see what he was watching.

Black rhino—a bull following a cow that picked at leaves in the brush, a two year old calf at her side.

He stopped beside Nalangu and leaned against the grill of the Land Cruiser. He took in the view. The rhinoceros. The long stretch of horizon. The shadows of fever trees, sent reaching across the savannah.

He smiled to himself. "David, this is the reason I am so happy to be home."

Nalangu nodded, his eyes still on the rhino. "Even with the ministry trying to stop your research?"

"The minister will learn that he needs it," Gabriel muttered. "You have no idea how much I have missed being here."

"You were not happy at university?"

"I was happy. Oxford was a privilege, but it was time away, years committed to study so far from home. I carried a void for this place. All I could do was remind myself I would someday bring everything I learned back to Kenya, to benefit my home and my heritage."

David nodded. "Are we finished for today?"

"Yes. Let me enjoy this view a few moments more."

"Of course. Your wife and son . . . did they enjoy England?"

"Njoki endured. She's happy now, knowing our son will grow up here, as we did. We have so much to show him." He paused, watching the young calf. So good to be home. "Our son will . . ."

Something whizzed past. He heard a dull thunk. Nalangu slumped to the ground.

Eyes wide, Gabriel Kagunda could not make himself move. Then, he heard the same dull thunk and felt the bullet dig into his chest.

— · —

With the click of a mouse, a page began to print. A letter, without letterhead, dropped into the tray.

Just a little request. My wife is pestering me to support her favorite cause. (What is it with women and horses?) Enclosed is information on something she's worked up about. Feds being stupid, saying they're protecting wildlife when they're really wanting to shoot horses somewhere in New Mexico. Your involvement would help. Though not really a priority to me, it is for my wife, so I'd appreciate you doing something to give this organization some traction. That'll go a long way toward making the little lady happy and getting her off my back. My man will be in touch. You can count on my support when you need it. Keep up the good work.

The page was laid alongside another, the top of which held the banner, "*Action Alert, Wild Horse and Burro Babes,*" and below it, "*Stop the killing of wild horses in Piedras Coloradas National Monument.*" With an illegible flourish of a signature on the first page, both were folded, then stuffed into an envelope, marked personal, and addressed to an occupant of the Hart Senate Office Building, Constitution Avenue, Washington, D.C.

— · —

DAYS LATER. CANNON HOUSE OFFICE BUILDING,
INDEPENDENCE AVENUE, WASHINGTON, D.C.

Congressman Brent Hoff closed the file on his latest polling numbers. Not bad. Not bad at all. If advisors are correct, they'll get even better.

Coat off, he sat back and ran his fingers through blond, wavy hair. The numbers supported everything advisors had told him so far. He opened a second file, and read the list of issues projected to get him through the primaries to secure the party's nomination. After that, the general election, and the rules would change. For now, the focus had to be on this list. At the top: *perceived government overreach.*

Hoff heard a knock at the door. He looked up from the page.

"How was your trip?" asked an aide, standing in the darkened hallway, loosening his tie.

"Productive. What's up?"

"We're getting emails, Congressman." He stepped inside and gave a stroke to his beard, pulling at the dark brown lines framing his chin. "Constituents. Well . . . not constituents, donors. Major donors. Unfortunately, I don't like the issue. It could be trouble."

"How so?" Hoff dropped his eyes back to the list.

"They want us involved in an issue in New Mexico. It concerns a rancher grazing on public land, refusing to pay his fees. He says he doesn't recognize the authority of the Bureau of Land Management, or any fed, for that matter. Suffice it to say, the agency claims his cattle are in trespass. Courts agree. BLM plans a round-up, intending to sell his cattle at auction to cover fees and fines. Meanwhile, this guy's being called a hero for standing up to the feds."

Hoff closed the file and pushed it aside. "Interesting."

"Yeah, but it's complicated. By horses. Wild ones, which BLM wants to shoot or capture. That has horse lovers up in arms, pointing at the rancher, saying get rid of his cattle, that everything would be fine if his cattle were gone."

Hoff smiled. "So why do you think it'd be trouble?"

"First, the rancher hasn't paid grazing fees in years. He makes lots of noise, justifying his actions, but bottom line, suffice it to say . . . he's a freeloader. Other ranchers pay their fees. He doesn't. Second, the agency's caught in the middle, between horse lovers and this Manson character. Third, it's not your state. You'd be sticking your nose in another delegation's business."

"Interesting take on things, Alex." Hoff sat back and rested his hands behind his head. "Are you aware the Senate may take up legislation on this issue?"

"To do what?"

"Make horses priority." Hoff shook his head in disgust. "Someone's calling in favors. Pulling strings. The little guy loses." Hoff turned and stared out the window, first at the capitol dome, then at the marble-clad wing of the Senate. "I won't bore you with my usual diatribe, but this country has problems. Real ones. Across the way, the Senate's playing games, messing with horses."

"You're sure?"

"I heard it this morning. Chatter before conference committee. Talk of putting staff on it." He leaned over his hands. "This rancher . . . Manson. He may need our help."

"That's not a good idea, Brent. He's everything you've worked against, your whole legislative career. He's a welfare case."

"Maybe, maybe not. Making him a hero might serve the greater good. We might need a poster boy to drive the upcoming election. At least for our base."

"He'd be a distraction, Brent. I can't risk letting you crash and burn over something that could turn into an ugly fight." He sighed. "You've got too much to offer. I can't let you jeopardize your chances. Not on this. If a partisan fight, hell, I'd push you to do it, but that's not what this is."

"Do not worry."

"Horse lovers . . . they're passionate. In a mud fight it's hard not to get dirty."

Hoff laughed, and set his hands on his cherry wood desk. "Alex, let's talk horses. Metaphorically speaking." He waved his aide to a chair.

Alex Trasker sat, his lanky frame sprawled in the chair. A

cocky smile grew on his face, as if he knew which story he was about to hear.

"Remember Lady Godiva?" Hoff waited for a nod. "Her horse did the work. Carried her all over town, but who remembers the nag's name? Do you?" He paused and awaited a response. Seeing none, he continued. "Thought so. That's because Godiva took the risks. Not the horse. Godiva. She was the one with the cause." Hoff paused and drummed his fingers on the desk. "Not a criticism, Alex, just a metaphor. You are my most trusted aide. Like Godiva's horse, you do the work. All of it on some issues. But like Godiva, I'm the one with the cause. The one who moves causes forward. Important causes. To do that, I have to be willing to take some risks."

Trasker sighed and stroked his beard. "But, this cause is . . ."

The congressman cut him off. "Alex . . . remember, I'm taking the risks. I'm Godiva. You're Godiva's horse."

CHAPTER
2

Scattered clouds gathered over parched earth. For two years, they gathered but brought no rain or snow. Nothing. Not here. The headwaters of the river saw plenty of snow, but clouds passed by the high desert and plateaus of northern New Mexico, waiting to reach Colorado before releasing their moisture. The dusty range held little for deer, pronghorn, cattle, horses, or any surviving animal. Those that remained stripped the land of leaf and stem. If they could jump the fences in search of food, they had done so long before now. If their search brought them here, they had put themselves on the wrong piece of range.

Year one brought concern. Year two, panic. Most ranchers gathered their stock and took them to pasture elsewhere, or sold them to wait out the drought. The animals remaining picked at desert scrub, searching for anything that could provide a little energy.

Cumulus clouds floated over the plateau, somehow appearing a little more numerous, a little taller, a little bluer along the edges, but the cloud cover was not complete. Just wandering clouds, as had been the case for two years.

One cloud settled over the plateau, seemingly held there, possibly by thermals rising up to meet it. Other clouds slowed to wait, only teasing the earth with virga—their rain drops evaporating before reaching the ground—but this cloud, as if defying an established plan, let go and poured. The San Juan Mountains, visible only moments before in the distance, now lay hidden behind a veil of rain draping from the cloud.

The ground, splattered by raindrops, sucked up what it could. With few plants to help with the task, soil was soon overcome. Trickles formed and streamed downslope. Those trickles joined others, then sheets, then water marching toward drainages, coming together to form creeks, and those came together in a rush to the river.

With parched ground for miles in all directions—except here, under one cloud—no one downstream expected what was coming. A wall of water.

—·—

"Here we go," Jack Chastain said to himself.

He let the kayak drift, pulled by the current toward the tongue feeding into the rapid. With long arms, he dipped one end of his paddle, held it, and turned the kayak across channel. He studied the boiling water below.

Seems different than a minute ago.

What do you expect? Scout a rapid from the hillside, it always seems different. Have some faith.

He pointed the bow forward and let the kayak slip into the tongue. Slow, calm waters turned quick. Waves crashed over the kayak's deck. Only one option now . . . to see it through.

Current pushed the kayak toward boulders, nearly submerged, a swirling hole in between. He paddled left, through foam and splash. The river fought back, not letting go, pulling him right. He paddled harder. The hole grew large. Water slipping over boulders, calm, then turbulent.

Keep away from that hole.

He glided onto the rim—water plunging. He paddled hard, fast. Again. Again. Again.

The kayak pulled away, into the current flowing past.

Now, only the small stuff.

He sucked in a breath, and let the paddle skim the surface, holding the kayak on line. He cut through the last of the waves and settled onto flat water, soaking wet, water shedding off his life vest and Park Service uniform. Paddling into the eddy at river left, he slipped around, then raised the paddle with both arms.

Paul Yazzi, waiting above the rapid, returned the signal. Slipping into the current, he let his kayak float forward. He entered the tongue, picking up speed. Waves crashed over him, obscuring all but his helmet. The ends of his paddle appeared in alternating flashes, in and out of the water. He pressed for river left. Gliding toward the boulders, he worked one end of the paddle, stalled on the lip, and slowly pulled away. Free but balance lost, he slipped over, waves crashing over him. The bottom of the orange kayak bobbed in and out of whitewater, then up-righted. Yazzie dashed through the last of the rapid. Hitting flat water, he steered into the eddy.

Jack let out a holler. "And we call this work."

Yazzi smiled and pulled off his helmet. He ran fingers through wet, black hair, then over his face, shedding the water streaming between wide-set cheeks.

"C'mon Paul, even men of few words gotta cut loose on a day like today."

"I am avoiding paying for a helicopter," he said, his words heavy with Navajo accent. "We finish reading veg plots. You go back to your project."

"Can you believe it? Middle of a drought, all this from the headwaters."

"Confuses things. Range beat to hell, much water in the river." Yazzi let his paddle balance on the deck of his kayak. "I appreciate your help. I am sorry to pull you away from the report to agencies and Congress."

Jack turned away.

"You want me to keep you from your work?"

Jack let the thought settle over him. "It's done. Mostly."

"Good. What's next?"

"The Congress part."

"Good."

"Not sure it is. I'm starting to think we should limit our actions. Do what we can without dealing with politicians."

"Why?"

"Because . . . of their games."

"We need new authorities. To do the things to keep ranchers and environmentalists working together. And why would Congress care? Unless they're from New Mexico?"

Jack furrowed his brow, and let out a long, seething breath.

"You're angry. This is not like you."

"Sorry, Paul." He pulled off his helmet, loosened the strap on his sunglasses, and slipped them off. He gave his head a shake. Wet, brown strands settled over blue eyes. He swept them away from his face. "It's just . . . ." He scowled. "Never mind."

"Famous white man saying—all politics are local. Let our members of Congress earn their keep." Paul skimmed the water with his paddle. "You've done much good here, Jack. Three years ago, the president created the national monument. Afterwards, hell. Everyone fought. Now, they work together. They remember they're part of the same community. You made that happen. Don't stop now."

"It was your work, too, Paul." Jack sighed. "As much as I want us to do what we can to help preserve this little part of the world, keep people together, help them save what they value . . . the next phase scares me."

Yazzi laughed. "You white guys. You think too hard. Do this. You're good at it."

Jack shrugged, and slipped on his helmet. "Where to now?"

"Next drainage, on the right. We'll climb out to monitoring sites. Important ones."

Jack paddled into the current, then waited for Paul to come alongside.

The gorge grew wide, its walls pulling back from the river. Around a bend, on river right, two rafts came into view, beached on the sand. Paddling close to shore, they approached the rafts.

Half a dozen men sat under a cottonwood, alongside a creek feeding into the river. River guides—one male, one female—hunkered over a table, picking at food and packing it away.

Chastain and Yazzi came ashore, upstream of the rafts.

The male guide, in river shorts and white Grateful Dead T-shirt, looked up. "Rangers!" he hollered, "hide the contraband."

"Contraband?" a client hollered back, sounding confused.

The guide laughed, and tossed back his long, sun bleached hair.

"Hey, Stew." Jack crawled out of the kayak, stood, and stretched his tall, lanky frame. He took hold of the webbing on the bow of the kayak, and dragged it onto the sand. "Who's your partner? New guide?"

Stew, lean and muscled, let out a yawn. "Sorry, I need a nap. This is Lizzy. Lizzy McClaren. Not exactly new. She started last summer."

"Haven't had a chance to meet," Jack said, extending a hand.

The woman looked up through locks of curly red hair, her green eyes piercing. Equally lean, shoulders muscled, she wore a sleeveless sun dress, threadbare and sun bleached. She set down the knife, shook the hand, and finished chewing. "You are?"

"Jack Chastain, Park Service. This is Paul Yazzi, Bureau of Land Management." He gave her dress another look. Typical river guide. Squeaking by. Doing whatever it takes for a life on the river.

She glanced at Yazzi and took another bite. "We still in the park?"

"You left the park a few miles back. You're in the national monument, one of the reaches managed by BLM."

"I figured as much." She backed away. "No time to chat. If we wanna good camp, we gotta keep moving." She lugged a stack of plastic containers to the downstream raft, reached over the tube, opened an ice chest, and tossed them in. She turned back. "Unless you're doing inspections, we'll see you down river." She waved her clients over. "Load up," she shouted.

"Inspections? No." Jack glanced at Stew, then back. "This is a science trip."

"I see," she said, unfazed. She held a garbage bag open to the clients as they climbed into the raft. Following them over the tube, she stashed the bag, and pointed to life vests. "Get yours on first, then someone hand me mine." She plopped down and took hold of the oars. Stew untied her line, setting her adrift.

As Stew's clients boarded, he turned to Jack. "She's good," he whispered. "Sometimes a little distant. She's from back east. New York."

"No worries. Catch you over beer at Elena's."

"Deal, we'll . . . " Stew paused. He cupped an ear.

Jack heard it. Low. Rumbling. Growing by the moment. Rising over the sound of the river.

Paul turned to listen. "That cannot be."

The sound. Rock against rock, water pounding walls.

Willow and cottonwood leaves rustled. Breeze turned to gust.

"Smell that?" Jack said, turning to Yazzie.

He nodded.

"What?" Stew asked.

"Dirt." He glanced at the sky. Blue, scattered clouds. But, . . . "Get your people upslope. Now." He pointed upstream. "There. Do it fast."

Stew rushed his boat. "Get out. Quick!" Clients jumped from the tube and ran, feet fighting sand.

Jack waved the other boat to shore, an eye on the side canyon. The sound grew loud, a freight train barreling toward them, hidden by serpentine cuts through the rock.

Lizzy pushed the oars. The raft lurched forward, bumping the shore. Two men jumped, already running. Lizzy started after, but stopped. A third man tugged at a river bag lashed to the boat frame. She clutched the man's arm and pulled, jerking him back. His glasses flew off. He fought as she pulled.

Ready to move, Jack glanced from boat to side canyon. The rumble changed. Air shook. He watched as water exploded from the canyon. Dark, filthy water, laden with debris, tens of feet high.

"Run."

"Leave 'em!" Lizzy shouted.

The man ripped his arm away and reached for his glasses. He put them on. His eyes grew wide.

Paul dashed toward talus, dragging his kayak. Jack waited seconds, then followed, grabbing his in a tenuous hold as he moved away from the surge.

It hit. Water, debris, the surge scooping up the rafts, flipping them over, pushing them into the current, belly up. The rafts floated downstream, through a bend of the river.

Jack lost sight of them. Two people. Gone. Possibly dead. He exchanged glances with Paul, then Stew, then the others.

Questioning looks. None with answers.

He tugged on his splash skirt, and caught a look of concern from Paul. "I know. Bad idea," Jack said. "What else can we do?"

"Do not do this," Paul said.

"Surely, there's not another wall of water coming."

"You do not know that."

"Right." Jack studied the dark tongue. Dirty water slithered downriver, carrying limbs, whole trees, and debris. He moved upstream and pulled the kayak to water's edge. Paddle in one hand, he slipped in and pulled the splash skirt over the rib of the cockpit. "The next mile's flat water, right?"

"Normally," Paul shouted, over the roar. "In a flood? I do not know. Do not get yourself killed!"

Jack gave a nod. "See if you can get someone on the radio." He plunged one end of the paddle.

Crossing the river, he skirted past the inflow, avoiding debris, pushing limbs away with the paddle, working toward open water.

At the bend, one raft sat eddied out, river-right, going nowhere. No people. None he could see. He floated past, into a straight stretch, water fast and turbulent. Ahead floated the second raft, upside down, one person—a head and an orange vest—bobbing in and out of sight in the midst of debris. No way to tell if they're okay. The second person? Nowhere to be seen.

Plowing forward, he closed the gap. The second person? Where?

There. Alongside the raft.

Arms flailed, slipping, attempting to climb on. No hand holds. Who first? Which?

A log floated at the raft. He cut left, toward it.

Red hair. The Lizzy woman. He overtook the log and pushed off with the paddle, propelling the kayak alongside the raft. "Take hold of the grab loop. I'll pull you to shore."

"No. Gotta save Maynard," she screamed. "Gotta save the boat."

She took the grab loop and hefted herself onto the bow, pitching Jack forward. He lay back, countering the weight. "You'll never . . ."

She wriggled her way onto the tube, giving a kick, pitching the kayak back.

He rolled. Warm, dirty water. Debris. He thrust the paddle, rolling himself upright.

"Where's Maynard?" Lizzy hollered. She paced, corner to corner on the belly of the raft, water dripping from her, feet slipping. "Where? Under the boat?"

"Downstream," Jack shouted.

A swell hit the raft, throwing Lizzy on her face, washing over her and sending her willowy body sliding along the rubber. She managed to stay on.

Jack steadied the kayak, and glanced up river. Another swell.

He caught a look on Lizzy's face. Fear.

He followed her eyes.

A boulder, mid-river, split the stream, collecting debris. A cottonwood bole bobbed in the water, trapped against it, it's leaf-covered limbs pushing back the current. Water boiled.

Maynard, his head nested in orange, floated toward it.

"Swim, Maynard!" Lizzy screamed. "To shore. Swim." She stepped forward, onto the tube.

"Don't!" Jack shouted. "Let me get . . ."

She dove.

Surfacing, she plunged her arms in and out of the water, swimming toward the orange vest.

A swell hit the raft, floating it over her. She disappeared.

Pushed by the swell, Jack paddled toward the man, closing the distance. "Maynard, look at me!" Jack shouted. "Look at me!"

The man's head turned.

Jack reached under the splash skirt, found his throw bag, and hurled it toward him. Line fed out. The bag splashed down behind the man, rope splatting on the surface. "Grab hold!"

The man flailed, fumbling for line, managing a grasp. Jack clipped the end to his vest and made a quick right, paddling toward shore. "Kick!" he ordered, feeling the drag of the man.

A swell hit the kayak, broadside, capsizing him. A thrust on the paddle and Jack kept it rolling, losing his sunglasses but up-righting the kayak, keeping it pointed to shore. The man, still kicking, came aground. Grasping willow branches, he pulled himself out of the water.

Jack spun around, catching sight of Lizzy upstream of the raft. It slammed into the cottonwood pinned to the boulder.

The next swell hit, pushing the raft into the crown of the tree. Limbs held the bow, as the force of the water stood the raft on end, flipping it onto the shattered mass. Lizzy, bobbing in the water, rose with the swell, hefting herself onto the log. A wave carried her up the bole, dragging her over splintered branches. Her movement stopped. She reached down, tugged, then stood, leg bleeding, dress in shreds. She stumbled up the log, working her way toward the raft. As she approached, the raft broke free, spinning in the current, scraping past the boulder. Stunned, she watched it float away. A wave washed over her. She scooted toward the boulder, holding onto branches as the next surge hit.

Jack pulled in the line, stuffing the throw bag. Upstream or down? Current's too fast. Has to be up.

He paddled upstream along the bank, then kicked into the current. Floating toward her, he took hold of the bag. "Be ready to swim!" he shouted. He tossed it. Line fed out.

She caught it one-handed.

The log shifted. He tried a hard turn. A limb cut him off. A swell picked up the kayak, floating it over the log, dropping it against the boulder. The bole shifted, pinning the kayak. Jack ripped off the splash skirt and squirmed out of the cockpit, crawling onto rock. The kayak shattered.

He scrambled up the boulder.

Lizzy stood watching, blood dripping from a gash on one thigh, her dress in tatters, a spaghetti strap gone, long rips exposing her thighs and side. She gathered the tears in one hand, and held out the rope with the other. "So, now," she muttered, "what am I to do with this?"

CHAPTER
3

The river rolled and rumbled, red and soupy, the current shoving debris. Gusts bit their faces, the air thick with the smell of dirt.

Water inched up the rock.

Jack turned, looking for options, saw none, and caught sight of the raft, river bags and pieces of kayak floating into a wide reach of the river, settling into an eddy on river-right. Maynard, eyes wide, stared, everything passing him by.

"River's getting higher," Jack muttered, fighting the urge to run with nowhere to go. He cleared his throat. "When's payday?"

"Huh?" Lizzy forced her eyes from the torrents. "Why?"

He knelt. "Let me see that." He reached for her leg and wiped the blood from her thigh. He ran a finger along the wound. Not deep. Good.

She grimaced. "What about payday?" she shouted, fighting the roar of the river.

"Your dress has seen better days." He ripped a strip of fabric from along the hem.

Shivering, she gathered shreds of cloth. "Stop."

He tore off another strip. "Hold still."

"Hey, it's all I've got on."

He squeezed out the water and began wrapping her leg. "Imagine that."

"Keep going, you won't need to. Don't you have something else to think about?"

He glanced at the river. "Yes, I do, but can't do a thing about it." He knotted the bandage. "I'm done. That'll protect the wound, help stop the bleeding. If the river keeps rising, it might not matter . . . but if it doesn't kill us, we'll need a first aid kit. Need to clean and put something on that. So . . . why a dress?"

She took her eyes off the river and glared. "Now why is that any of your damned business?"

"It's not." Jack eyed the surge lapping the rock, only feet below, sloshing through cottonwood branches. "Sorry."

Lizzy sighed. "Simple. Comfort. It's cool in the heat." She gave a rub to her thigh. "We're gonna die." She let out a sad little laugh. "All I've been thinking about lately . . . a big purchase I want to make . . . seems rather petty when facing the prospect of dying."

"We might make it to shore."

"You don't sound confident, and the water keeps rising, getting worse." Eyes on the river, her shoulders dropped. "If we're swept to our deaths, Jack Chastain, what are you going to regret? . . . If that's possible . . . regretting something when you're dead."

"Pain, for those who'll miss me."

She nodded.

"And . . . the work I didn't finish. This time, I thought . . ."

She gave him another glance. "This time?"

"You don't want to know about the other . . . but this time, I hoped to protect folks . . . from those who play games with their lives, confuse 'em, make 'em go to war with each other."

She cocked her head. "I just realized why I've heard your name. You're the guy . . . that made people listen to each other."

Jack shrugged. "I'm not sure that's what . . ."

She cut him off. "No, you're the guy." She crossed her arms and glared at the river. "That settles it. We're not dying here. Not today. You have unfinished business."

Jack sighed.

They watched in silence. Minutes passed. The river crept

higher, splashing their feet. Jack scooted back, taking the last inches. Cottonwood limbs scraped toward them. They teetered at the tip of the rock. Then, water seemed to recede.

Uncertain, they watched. A few minutes more and Lizzy raised a hand. She pointed at the waterline. "Told ya. We're not dying today. Not to some fluke storm."

He exhaled, then felt her studying him.

She brushed a red, sun-lit curl behind an ear. The wind blew it free. "I owe you."

"You don't."

"I do, and I'm sorry, I was a jerk back there. I thought you were hitting on me."

Jack stared into the distance. "I'm taken."

"Obviously. I'm half naked, you're worried about a little flood." She laughed. "I didn't notice before . . . you have nice blue eyes, even if you are taken. Your sunglasses . . ."

"Lost 'em."

"Then I owe you twice."

"You don't. Comes with the job."

"No, I owe you. Big time. Maybe you don't keep track of favors, but the world does. I want karma on my side, my debts paid."

"Then buy me a beer. After you buy a new dress."

Piece at a time, sticks, brush, and—last—the uprooted cottonwood, dislodged from the jam and floated downstream.

A kayaker appeared, paddling through riffles at a bend in the river. They watched Paul Yazzi navigate the edge of red, muddy strands marking midstream. The river straightened, and he paddled nearer to shore.

Upstream, on the opposite bank, a band of people appeared, picking their way through boulders along the fringe of debris-draped willow at river's edge.

They moved quickly, likely having seen the first raft eddied out on their side of the river. A man in white T-shirt, probably Stew, reached the eddy, dove in, and returned with the rope. Forming a line, they pulled the raft to shore, then began their efforts to upright it.

Yazzi approached. He pulled into a rocky shallow, and steadied himself with his paddle. "Any sign of the other man?"

Jack pointed. "He's okay."

Paul glanced that way, then back. "I cannot get anyone on the radio. Dead spot. For now, we are on our own." He paused. "You okay? Where's your kayak?"

"In pieces. We're okay. We can wait for the raft."

Paul beached and walked upstream, lugging his kayak, following the river's edge.

"Stew's got his oars," Lizzy muttered. "Pins and clips held. Hope I've got mine." She chuckled self-consciously. "This is gonna be embarrassing when the clients see me."

"You're lucky to be alive."

"I know, but those guys." She nodded upstream. "Old frat bros. Together, first time in years, behaving like they're back in college. Unbearable. Now . . . look at me." She flipped a strip of cloth.

"Everything's fine. Act normal. You're a river god."

"Does that speech usually end with, *you're a ranger*?"

He let out a chuckle. "Maybe."

She laughed. "River god . . ." She lay back and relaxed. "Everything's fine. Normal." A sparkle came to her deep, green eyes. Then she closed them. "I might see a bump in tips. Might even pay for a new dress."

— · —

The two rafts sat in an eddy, tied to a cottonwood. Assessments were made of damage and losses. A few river bags missing. Might be found downstream. One of Lizzy's oars, gone. Her spares, still lashed to the tube. Seemingly oblivious to the rips in her dress, she sorted through gear, found her river bag—still tied under the frame—and slipped into shorts and a T-shirt. She proceeded to reassemble her oars and began the process of repacking.

Jack and Paul turned to assess their own losses.

One kayak destroyed. PVC quadrat for assessing plant cover, gone, probably no chance of finding it. Jack's lunch and change of clothes, gone. Data logger and radio, found, and—most important

—dry, both in a dry bag that had been lashed to a strut on the kayak, and found floating in the eddy.

"Not bad," Jack muttered, eyeing the gear. He ran a hand over his face.

"You okay?" Paul asked. "You look shaken."

"Shaken? I'm okay. You?"

"Frustrated." Paul looked upstream. "That drainage. Those veg plots. They were important. The ones I needed most."

"We've been out since sunrise, hauling ass down river. Why the urgency?"

"Because of what happens today. Agency chiefs . . . I'm not sure they have the political will, but if they do . . ."

"Are you serious? Regarding veg plots?"

"No, not plots. A permittee. This reach of river runs along Moony Manson's allotment."

"Manson?"

"Rancher. He hasn't paid grazing fees in years. His cattle are in trespass."

"So because of the drought . . .?"

Paul shook his head. "More complicated. Wild horses. From Colorado, searching for food. Horse advocates want them left alone, no matter how much they beat up the range."

"They can cause lots of damage."

"Yes. And when we act, we will get politics. Ugly politics."

"Horse lovers or Manson?"

"Action on horses is difficult if we do not deal with Manson. I told the chief we need to impound his cattle. I want veg plots monitored before, not after." He sighed. "I needed those plots."

"We could hike back from on top."

"That would take more time than I've got," Yazzi muttered. "I need to finish today. There are two more sets of plots on his range. I'll figure something out and do them alone."

"Why?"

"Because, you have to go down with the rafts."

"These guys have another overnight. I have to be in town tonight for the meeting."

"You rest. Blow off the meeting."

"I'll help on the first plots, hike out from there, get picked up at the road."

"Why would you do that, and what do we do for a quadrat?"

"Cut some willow. Lay 'em out. If we're off a few inches, so what. We want percent cover. We can assess that with all the precision we need."

Paul nodded. "Why bust your butt to get to the meeting? You said the report's mostly done."

"Mostly." Jack sighed. "Because, it's unfinished business."

— · —

The raft approached the sand bar.

"Sure it's safe?" Jack shouted, watching Paul on the shore, his kayak already stowed.

"The creek is dry," Paul shouted back.

The raft bumped the sand and Jack jumped from the tube. He waved his goodbyes and turned up-creek, following Paul, carrying only a radio and a water bottle borrowed from Lizzy McClaren. Paul moved out quickly, his pack on, carrying a handful of willow branches.

A half mile in, they climbed out of the drainage. Paul consulted the GPS on the data-logger, then led across open range. After another quarter mile he stopped. "The pin should be here," Paul said, head down, searching the ground. He kicked, then dug with his fingers. "Found it." He dusted around the pin, and slipped a tape measure over the head. He consulted his notebook. "Eight meters north." He walked the tape out and stopped. He looked down.

Jack stopped beside him. Dirt. Ground devoid of grass. Not devoid of hoof prints. "This won't take long. Won't even need the quadrat. Not for this one."

Paul nodded, jaw clenched. He punched on the data logger. "One hundred percent dirt." He looked up. "Next plot, sixteen meters." He walked upslope. "Here."

"Same. Dirt," Jack said.

Paul nodded.

"No wonder the creek flashed. Nothing to hold the rain."

Paul read off the next location, and moved to the next plot. "No grass."

"But three percent cover," Jack said, laying the willow sprigs on the ground. "Snakeweed, on the line."

Paul moved on. On the next, sagebrush. Only a small percentage of cover.

When done, Paul dropped the data logger into his pack. "Big difference."

"Didn't need me on these."

"No, but it helped on the others." He set a hand on Jack's shoulder. "You will be okay?"

Jack keyed his radio, and listened for the hit on the repeater. It popped. "I'll be okay. You?"

"The last plots are also on range Manson uses. If like these, I will easily get to the takeout on schedule. If going according to plan, trespass cattle are being rounded up now."

"So the data aren't really a factor?"

"No, his cattle are in trespass, a policy matter. But I want the data. It is best we have it."

Jack nodded.

"We should have acted years ago. The state office would not sign off, until now." He pointed. "Because of that."

Jack turned. On a distant knoll, horses picked at what looked to be more dirt than browse. He squinted, counting. Six, maybe seven, maybe more beyond the rise. Some gray, some sorrel, some white. Even at a distance, he thought he saw ribs. "Bad shape."

"Like the range. But, horse advocates are ready to take us to court."

"Must have a good bloodline. Skinny, but otherwise might be nice horses."

"An old rancher in Colorado put his stud out with the mustangs. He'd push 'em into a box canyon, take the best colts for himself. Old man died a few years back."

"And now they're here."

"Caught in the drought. Moved south searching for food." Paul threw on his pack.

"Before you go, let me look at your map," Jack said. "What'll happen with Manson's cattle?"

Paul turned, giving him access to his pack. "Auction. Five hundred cows with calves. Proceeds to pay fees and fines. It won't cover it."

Jack unzipped a pocket and pulled out the topo. "What's the schedule for the horses?"

"Later in the week. Then off to adoption."

Jack opened the map and slid a finger across the contours, studying terrain, then roads. A range road meandered across the desert, veering through a saddle between a mesa and a smaller knoll, and ended at a graveled county road. He looked up and scanned the horizon. Mesa—there, to the west. The knoll—south of it. He refolded the map and stuffed it back in the pocket. "Careful on the river, Paul."

"You, too, my friend. Sorry I won't make it to the meeting tonight."

"Got it covered."

Paul took off for the drainage.

Jack turned, put his eye on the distant mesa, and set out walking toward it. At the top of a rise, he keyed his radio. "Dispatch, this is Chastain."

"*Dispatch, go ahead Jack.*"

"Molly, I'm gonna need a ride. Anyone who could pick me up on the BLM part of the monument? Back side of Spanish Skirts Mesa?"

"*Standby.*" The repeater clicked off.

Jack dropped his arm and continued walking.

"*Chastain, this is Dispatch.*"

He raised the radio. "Go ahead."

"*Luiz Archuleta's on the plateau. If I can reach him, he could circle back to your location. Could be two hours. Three at the most.*"

"Might be tight but that'll work. I've got a meeting tonight in town."

"Copy. I'll see if I can find another option. By the way, the superintendent's looking for you. He couldn't raise you on the radio."

"About what?"

"Questions. Your friend from the regional office is here."

"What friend?"

"Erika Jones. She's here with a congressional aide."

Jack stopped. He took a breath, and raised his eyes to the sky. Friend? Yeah, right. "Tell Joe, I'm in a good location to talk. Got plenty of time. Otherwise, I'll call from Luiz's phone."

"Copy."

Why the hell is Erika here? He stepped around sagebrush and reset his direction. Let Joe Morgan worry about her.

Late summer, skies blue, light cumulus on the horizon. Hundred degrees in the shade. Hell of a day for a hike. He glanced west. Dust devils danced across the desert. He looked north. None. In places, the dirt looked red. Dark from rain. He reset his eyes on the mesa. Gonna be a bitch of a hike.

"Chastain, this is Dispatch."

"Go ahead Molly."

"Change of plans. Jones and the congressional aide will pick you up. Be aware that it was not you they wanted to see. In fact, . . . how do I put this . . . it was you they hoped to avoid. Apparently, the superintendent insisted you're the best person to answer their questions."

Why is she telling me this? "I copy. I'll be at the pickup location in about an hour."

"Copy."

"Tell 'em to bring water. And something to eat."

CHAPTER

4

Once he'd crossed through the saddle—Spanish Skirts Mesa to his right—Jack looked downslope and saw the road, a two-track swath through the sagebrush.

Off the road sat a white government pickup, Park Service markings.

Jack veered toward it, wiping sweat from his brow.

The driver's door popped open.

A woman got out. Tall. Lean. Erika Jones. "About time you got here," she shouted. Her blonde hair—longer than when last he saw her, and closer to its length when he first knew her years before—blew in the breeze. "It's damned hot sitting out here." She slammed the door and marched toward him, wearing a field uniform, one neatly pressed.

The passenger door swung open. Another woman exited, and stood at the door. Brown hair, light skin, slender, tan pants, blue camp shirt. She looked like any park visitor.

Jack slowed and watched Erika approach. "Why the uniform? What, no Stetson?"

"Give me a break." Erika stopped, and put her hands on her hips. "I've got Claire Prescott with me," she said, under her breath.

"From Montana?"

"Washington. Do not mention Montana, or Senator Tisdale."

"Why not? He's about the only member of Congress I ever felt I could trust."

"Do not mention him."

"Why?"

"Let's just say, according to rumor, it didn't end well."

"She's no longer a staffer?"

"Sh-h-h-h." She turned and started back for the truck. "Claire's a survivor," Erika whispered. "Now a committee staffer. She may've called in some favors, who knows?"

"I need water."

"It's in the truck. What took you so long?"

"Only fifteen minutes late. It's further than it looks."

"Prescott's in a hurry. You made me look bad. Wipe the sweat off your face."

He glared, and left the sweat where it was. "Don't wanna make you look bad. Especially with someone influential."

"Shut up." She waved him to follow. "You are not who she wanted to see. She doesn't trust you after Montana, so be nice. Answer her questions. No editorial comments."

"Editorial comments are your department. Why no trusting me?"

Erika dropped her head. "Sh-h-h-h." She looked up, flashed a smile toward Prescott, and shouted, "Ripped him a new one for holding us up."

Prescott's expression remained unchanged. She continued leaning against the truck.

Jack offered a hand as they approached. "Been a few years."

She shook his hand. "Yes."

He stepped past, looking into the cab of the pickup. "Excuse me. I need water."

"My side," Erika said. "In the bed. Ice chest."

Jack went around to the back.

Erika followed. "You're making a bad impression," she whispered.

"Why are you here, Erika?" he whispered back, sliding the ice chest toward the tailgate. "And why are you in uniform? Thought it was decided it gave the agency a bad rap."

"Very funny." She popped open the ice chest, grabbed a bottle, and pushed him toward the front of the pickup. "Here's your water," she said, voice raised, then whispered. "Behave yourself."

"For you?"

"Sh-h-h-h." She dragged him toward Prescott. "Okay, Claire. Jack's time is yours."

"Your superintendent believes you know the issues here better than anyone."

"Maybe."

Prescott crossed her arms. "Like you knew the issues in Montana?"

Jack and Erika traded looks.

"Well, yes," Erika said.

"What's this about?" Jack twisted the top off the bottle.

"Horses," Claire said.

He took a swig. "What about 'em?"

"Saving them."

"You mean wild horses?"

"Of course, and I'd like to see some while I'm here. I'd like to gain an understanding of the issues surrounding their welfare."

Jack gave her a once over. She's serious. "Have you talked with BLM?"

"I have. It wasn't productive."

"Got to be more productive than talking to me. BLM lands are where you'll likely find 'em."

"They don't come into the park?"

"They will, I'm sure, if they're here long enough. The park is fenced, but it might be hard to keep 'em out. Not so of the monument."

"Why keep them out?"

"They're non-native. They can cause lots of damage."

"They're more native than cows."

Jack glanced at Erika. She gave her head a subtle shake.

"Let's drive up to a place where we might see 'em," Jack said. "We'll talk about it there." He turned to Erika. "Bring any food?"

"Cheese doodles. In the truck. You take the middle." She waved him toward the door.

He followed her around. "You don't have real food?"

"Sh-h-h-h. Getting here was more important. Eat later."

"Haven't eaten since breakfast."

"Good, you need to lose some weight." She glanced at his belly. "Never mind, you're skinny as hell."

Jack slid to the middle, knees against the dash.

Erika climbed in, grabbing the chips off the floor. "Here, food. Which way?"

He pointed north and ripped open the bag.

Claire Prescott settled in, crossed her arms, and frowned, her eyes on the landscape.

Erika pulled the pickup onto the road, headed north.

"All this is managed by BLM, so again, it'd be best to talk to them," Jack said.

Claire nodded. "Are you sure we'll see horses?"

"No guarantee, but I saw some an hour ago."

She nodded, brow furrowed.

"How far?" Erika asked.

"The next high point with a view. Should be able to see for miles."

The road climbed higher. Erika took a couple of bends and Jack pointed to a turnout. She pulled to a stop and killed the engine. In the foreground, an ocean of sagebrush. Scattered outcroppings and buttes. In the distance, the plateau, rising up to meet the sky. The mouth of the canyon, to the east, only a sliver from this angle. The river, emerging from it, sweeping through a bend, flowing east. Its confluence with another river—from this angle, possibly larger—beyond the hamlet of Las Piedras. Other creek beds cut paths toward both.

"Where do we look?" Claire asked, distracted by the view.

Jack gestured west, across the entirety of the landscape.

"I see a band," Erika said, pointing left. "There. Not too far."

A scattering of cattle, and beyond them a knoll, and on it, horses, more than half a dozen. A big grey stud, three or four mares and their young, juveniles and foals. They picked at the ground, moving slowly, the stud watching over them.

Claire stared. "Beautiful. Anything significant about this location? Water?"

"Not much," Jack said. "We're in a drought."

"That's terrible," Claire said. "Are they suffering?"

"Remember they're wild. This is wild country."

"What does that mean?"

"They're not livestock. No one's taking care of 'em."

"What about the cattle?"

"Unfortunately, the same may be true for them. Most ranchers pulled their cattle, but not that guy." Jack shook his head. "Even range improvements, stock tanks for example, don't help much at times like this, but most ranchers are responsible. They take care of their cattle. Horses? . . . uncontrolled populations . . . can cause lots of damage. In a drought, they can die, but maybe not until after they've caused their damage."

"How do you know they'll cause damage? Didn't they just get here?"

"Yes, but . . ."

"So you haven't studied their effects?"

In the distance, a horse—ears back—nipped at another, causing it to back away. It ducked a charge, then stopped outside the group.

"What's happening? Males challenging each other?"

"I think those are females." Jack said. He pointed. "The stud's the big grey over there, but the mare with her ears back, she's established her dominance over the others. She's dishing out reminders."

"Will that one leave?"

"Not likely. She'll stay with the band. She'll cope. They're social, gregarious animals."

"Beautiful," Claire said.

Jack exchanged looks with Erika. "Yes," he said. "But, they have to be managed. Otherwise, they can cause lots of damage."

"You've said that, but I'm told I should take agency arguments with a grain of salt," Claire said, not looking his way, but twisting a brown strand of hair. "We received advice from a new advocacy group, Wild Horse and Burro Babes. They seem to have money and clout, and to have their act together. Frankly, some of their arguments are hard to ignore." She pointed. "I'd like to go down there."

"They won't stick around."

"That's okay. I'd like to get a sense of what this land's about." Prescott headed off road, into the desert. She slipped on a cap, casting shade over pale, delicate skin.

Jack and Erika followed.

Twenty minutes later, walking toward the breaks of a creek, they came to an outcropping of sandstone. Slick rock, sloping toward the drainage. Claire veered across the rock.

"I thought you said there's a drought." Standing on rock still wet, Prescott pointed at solution holes brimming with water, some several feet wide. "Drought looks over to me."

"Maybe, maybe not, but we did have rain in here somewhere," Jack muttered. "Caused a flash flood. Maybe this very creek. Hit the river with a wall of water."

"Any damage?"

"Coulda killed a few people."

"I see," Claire said, dismissively. She spun around, looking. "So, I don't see reason to be convinced there's a problem. Horse population. Drought. Any of it."

"Look at the range," Jack said. "No grass."

She appeared to study the ground, then something in the distance. "Let's move on."

Beyond a rise, they came to a stock pond, one possibly dry a few hours earlier, now full. Just off the slickrock, hoof prints punctured the mud at the edge of the water. Cattle and horse. Manure piles, some old, most above the water line, wet from rain. The fragrance of freshly wet rabbit brush, growing at the edge of the rock, dampened the smell of urine and manure.

"I want a picture of this," Prescott said, pulling a camera from a cargo pocket. She approached the water. "Can the two of you stand in the picture? It'll give me scale and perspective."

Jack glanced at Erika. Why not?

They stepped onto the mud, avoiding manure, stopping a few feet from water. They spun around.

"That's fine," Prescott said. She snapped several shots.

Erika crept forward, mud clumped to her feet. She stopped. Jack tried stepping past her. She grabbed his arm. "Wait," she muttered, standing on one foot, trying to scrape the mud from the other. She slipped, flailing, her weight on Jack's arm. He slipped. They landed, flat on their backs, splatting into green sloppy goo.

Claire Prescott doubled over, laughing. "Sorry. I really didn't plan it that way."

Erika jumped up, and tried to see her backside. Green covered her bottom, back, and hands.

Jack got to his feet, knowing he looked even worse.

"Two things," Prescott said. "One, cattle are your problem, not horses. And two, do I have to ride with you two back to the park? You're gonna smell awful."

Jack and Erika looked at each other, then at Prescott.

"I'm serious. Do I?"

Erika stepped onto slick rock and stopped. "I'll take this one. You go that direction. Back over there," she said, pointing for Jack. "Claire, we'll catch up. That, or meet you at the truck."

Prescott looked at the depressions in the rock, brimming with water, some several feet wide and deep. She nodded and started up hill. "Please do. I'll try to get shots of the horses."

Jack shook his head and continued after Prescott. "Not gonna worry about it."

"Get back here, Jack Chastain."

Jack stopped, and studied where she pointed. "There's nothing over there."

Erika waited for Prescott to disappear beyond the rise. "I know, but she doesn't. She does not need to know what rangers have no qualms about doing." She loosened her laces and kicked off her boots.

"What are you talking about?"

"Strip," she ordered. She unbuttoned her uniform shirt.

He laughed. "That's the stupidest thing I ever heard. That's what you think rangers do?" He let his face turn serious. "And, qualms? I've got qualms."

"It's a hundred and five degrees. Your ass is covered in cow shit. There's water, and this is a beautiful place. Sometimes it's just the right thing to do."

"Not taking a bath."

"You are." She pulled off her shirt and tossed it in a solution hole. She turned around. "Any green on my bra?"

"What do you think?"

She undid the clasp. "Strip. I've seen you before." She tossed the bra into the solution hole. "Use that one for clothes." She pointed at a larger tank. "That one's mine. You've got your choice of the others."

"It's as if you plan these things. How do I let you talk me into this?" He started on his shirt buttons. "Why are you here? After the last time, I was sure you'd be fired, demoted, or locked in a broom closet." He slipped off his shirt and dropped it in the water. "Why you? Why here?"

Her smile grew, bringing a sparkle to grey, predatory eyes.

"Surely the new regional director knows what happened here. She has to know you were involved. With everything. Her predecessor, his dealings with Mike Middleton. Almost giving away part of the park. How did she let you out of Denver?"

Erika slipped a rubber band off her wrist and pulled her hair into a pony tail. "How is my ol' buddy, Mike Middleton?"

"I don't know. Frankly, at this point, I'm more worried about the other guy, Harper Teague. The man with Montana connections."

"Montana? You don't say?"

"I do say. He was not what he presented himself to be. What do you know about him?"

"He wasn't a face I remember from Montana, but I thought we were talking about the regional director." Erika unbuttoned her green uniform jeans, and let them drop to the ground. She stepped out of the legs, jerked the belt from the loops, and tossed the pants in the tank. "The new RD didn't trust me at first. In time she realized Nick was responsible for his own actions. Made his own bed. Me? I'm a peon, doing my job. I'm also adaptable. I'm creative. I know how to become indispensable." She spun around, her backside toward him. "Any green?"

"Kinda goes with the blue, don't you think?"

She gave a dismissive shake of her head, stripped off her undies, and tossed them in the tank.

He turned away.

"C'mon Jack, if you're not looking, how can I tell you not to?"

He unbuttoned his river shorts and dropped them to the ground.

"You are skinnier than last time. Somehow looks good on you. You know . . . that weathered, withered, wildernessy guy kind of way." She laughed. "You can look. I'm in the water."

"Shouldn't you wash your uniform first?"

"Go ahead." She lay back against the rim and closed her eyes. "I don't do laundry."

He shook his head. "If it'll get us out of here faster . . ." He knelt over the tank. Pulling out her pants, he worked the soiled spot. "This is stupid. Why suck up to her? This was her fault."

"Shut up and keep washing."

"What the hell can Prescott do for you? What are you hoping to get from this?"

Erika opened her eyes. "Jack, it's you that needs to be sucking up."

He stood and laid her clothes on a sun drenched rock. "I'm not concerned about her, or horses. Science will prevail."

"It's not that, Jack. She doesn't like you. She's in an important position. Staff for the Senate Interior Committee. Anything you have that needs to go through committee is gonna be touched by her. Kiss of death, if she doesn't buy what you're saying. And right now, she doesn't."

"Why?"

"Because of what happened in Montana. Maybe your association with the senator, who knows?"

"You're kidding. He was the only politician I ever trusted."

"She knows that. Shortly after that, whatever game she was playing came back to bite her. She was history. She'll hold it against *you* . . . unless you learn to suck up to *her*."

"Why?" He worked at a spot on his shorts. "Why should I?"

"To make her forget how well you got along with Senator Tisdale."

"Didn't help much."

"No, it didn't. You and the proposed park, both, political

piñatas. Hit from every direction. Prescott could make that happen again. A good time for her, at your expense."

He sat and fell back against the rock. "Why's she interested in what's happening here in New Mexico?"

"Horses, stupid, and if you don't appease her, she'll remember that little screw-up of yours at the hearing in Missoula."

"It wasn't a screw up, and it didn't have anything to do with this."

"It affected your credibility. You defended a grad student, who didn't have the decency to show up for a hearing."

"Defended him because that was my job."

"It made you look stupid."

"Why do you say that?"

"I don't know. You just get stupid seeing someone being attacked. All sorts of things can be directed at you—call you a bum, attack your lineage, whatever. Never fazes you visibly. But attack someone else, like that grad student . . . What did we call him?"

"Kid. He was a local. The Kid was his nickname in high school."

"Yeah, right, The Kid. Someone attacks The Kid, you go stupid."

"They didn't understand his research. Locked onto rumors. Misunderstood its purpose."

"What's to misunderstand? He went after fracking. He came up empty."

"He did not go after fracking. He was simply doing a survey of water sources. His methods would not've told him anything about fracking. No idea where that rumor started."

"That was the word on the streets, and people wanted to know, because they were scared. They wanted answers, and all they got was industry rhetoric. Then they heard about The Kid's research, that he was focused on fracking, and then he wasn't. You tried to defend him, but you should've left him hanging out to dry."

"Couldn't do that." Jack paused. "We had methane we couldn't explain, but The Kid's methods would not've allowed us to point fingers at fracking. Then, later, our data were changed. Inside job."

"All I know is . . . you looked like an idiot. A man with a hidden agenda."

"What does any of that have to do with Prescott?"

"If she questions your credibility, she'll accept what any bozo has to say. You've got to get on her good side. Politic her a little." She closed her eyes. "Now finish my clothes. We can't stay here all day."

"They're done, and wet," he said, tossing his shirt on the rock.

"Good. I could use a little excitement. I can't seem to muster any watching you."

He ignored her. "I will not play politics."

"Such a Boy Scout," she said, her eyes still closed. "But you did politic Senator Tisdale." A corner of her mouth turned up. "You did, didn't you?"

"No."

"You had briefings. Just you and the senator. Some kind of connection. You put all your eggs in that basket. I think you politicked the hell out of him."

"I gave him a few briefings. One with The Kid."

Her eyes popped open. "Remember that hearing? I can still see the look you shot Tisdale's direction, afterwards, like you'd failed him." She laughed. "And frankly, in the burning ruins of that hearing, you're lucky he didn't . . ."

"Stop," Jack shouted, cutting her off. "No more." He tossed his shorts on a rock, and settled into a tank. He closed his eyes.

"You're thinking about getting whacked."

"What?"

"Whacked. That's what you're thinking." She stood, water up to her knees. "I can see it on your face." She stepped out of the tank. "You don't even see me, do you?"

"Huh?"

"Nothing." She found a spot in the shade. "Here I am, as if alone, naked as a jaybird, enjoying the scenery. Like the shadows on that butte . . . which are really beautiful, by the way."

He heard her words, and let their meaning escape him.

How had that hearing gone to hell? The Kid. Why didn't he show? When his data would have cleared everything up. And The

Kid's phone call that morning, saying he'd found something new. Something he'd share at the hearing. What happened?

"Stop thinking about that," Erika muttered. "Think about schmoozing Claire Prescott."

A shudder shot through him, recalling his testimony. Approved and polished by Interior. All of it, fodder for one particular congressman. Every word, prey to a pat response. *Bureaucratic double talk.*

Other testimony seemed loaded. As if tested, played out, and known to work on the psyche of anyone who heard it.

Members of the public, long supportive, grew confused.

Facts withered on the vine. Truth died.

People had worked so hard. People who loved the place so much. Who fought so hard to preserve it. How disappointed they were. And the senator, listening in the galley. The look on his face.

"Jack!" Erika shouted. "We've got to go."

"That congressman at the hearing. The one from Indiana. It was as if he knew more about The Kid's research than I did. Almost. He knew just enough to turn it into something it wasn't. Lies. And the family of that sick little girl . . . who died. What they were put through. When in reality, The Kid's research had nothing to do with her. How that started, I do not know."

"It started. You failed to control it." Erika picked up her uniform and began to dress. "This is a beautiful place, if it wasn't so damned hot."

Jack watched her without seeing.

"We don't have all day. It's later than you think."

He nodded.

"See you back at the truck." She turned to leave, then stopped. "Tell Kelly—you know, your girlfriend, my dear old friend— remember to tell her we used separate tanks."

—·—

Jack trudged uphill, Erika ahead in his sights, Claire Prescott already at the pickup, leaning against a fender.

Erika arrived, then Jack, their uniforms already dry. Without words, they climbed in.

Erika pulled the pickup around and headed back the way they came.

"Could you drop me at my vehicle?" Jack asked.

"Where?"

"River takeout."

Erika nodded.

"Does that take us by any more range?" Claire asked.

"It does."

"Good. We can talk. I have more questions. First, really, why do you government biologists oppose wild horses on the range?"

"Not native. Virtually no natural predators. Have to be managed. If not, populations explode, causing lots of damage."

"That's not what I'm hearing from scientists who work on these issues more than you do."

"Who would that be?"

"Well, ones working for Wild Horse and Burro Babes. Their briefing statements dispute the assertion they're exotic. In the evolutionary record, they arose here. This is where horses came into being."

"True, but they died off. Assemblages of plants and animals changed. When the Spanish brought them back to the continent, it was to a different ecosystem. Sounds like their scientists are more likely advocates than scientists."

"Of course you'd say that. I was told you would. I've had a few calls from the director of the Babes. She's got more confidence in their guy, than they do in the scientists advising BLM. BLM's policy sucks. Same for yours in the Park Service."

"I might say the same about theirs," Jack said, then felt a knock in the knee from Erika.

"What Jack's trying to say is, this issue's not as simple as the Babes put it. It's complex. We're willing to help you understand our position, and we're willing to listen, to see if there's anything we need to reassess in terms of our own policy."

"Good," Claire said.

"I don't think I was trying to say that," Jack said. "Turn here." He pointed at an approaching road.

Erika slowed and made the turn. The road aimed at a slot between hills.

"What were you trying to say, then, Mr. Chastain?"

He sighed. "Never mind. Talk to Erika."

"I won't let you off the hook that easily."

"How long will you be here?"

"I leave tomorrow."

They cleared the rise. Vehicles came into view. Some parked near the river—the river user's take out. Some parked on the other side of the road, near a BLM enclosure. A corral, filled with cattle. Riders on horseback. Some inside the enclosure. Some outside. Tractor trucks with stock trailers. One backed to a loading chute. Other trucks in line. People. Some in uniform. Others not. Movement, only from cattle. No movement from people, even the riders.

"What's going on?" Jack muttered, studying the crowd.

Outside the corral, a black-haired man in BLM uniform—Paul Yazzi—stood facing a circle of people. And something else. Video cameras, on the edge of the crowd, pointed at Paul. And, more troubling, men with rifles. Pointed at Paul and others. And men, between the corral and the road, blocking departure. Inside the crowd, a circle of women, on the ground, sitting, facing the government rangers.

"Turn here," Jack ordered.

Erika steered onto the side road, then slowed as reality seemed to settle in. "We better stay out of this." She stopped the pickup, short of the ring of cameras.

"Let me out," Jack said, scooting toward Claire Prescott.

She opened the door and climbed out.

Jack exited and worked his way around, past the first row of cameras. He stopped.

Among the crowd stood a woman with a video camera, shouting at the BLM men and women, seeming to record as she spoke. Between her and Paul—and two other rangers, firearms drawn—stood a ring of men carrying rifles. Not just rifles, assault rifles. AR-15s and other semiautomatic weapons. They wore desert camo, no two the same. Dark sunglasses covered eyes on icy faces. One man, not in camo, stood in a face-off with Paul. In jeans, a white western shirt, and straw cowboy hat, he looked to be in control.

Jack worked his way around to see the man's face. Is this Moony Manson?

"Move," the man shouted. "I'm not letting you take my cows."

Paul, brow furrowed, held his stare.

Jack slipped to the side.

"I'm gonna give you one last chance. Get out of my way."

Paul stood motionless.

"Why are you taking his cows?" the camerawoman shouted. "They're his cows."

Paul glanced at the woman, then back at Manson.

Jack studied the woman. Camo. Hair pulled back. Not likely a reporter.

"Don't you have answers?" the woman shouted. "You don't, do you? Admit it, you're stomping on his rights. You're stealing his property. Admit it."

Paul made no effort to speak.

Behind them, real reporters watched, their cameramen filming and exchanging glances, keeping track of the militiamen, as if wondering if they were in the wrong place at the wrong time.

"Move, damn it!" Manson shouted. "I'm not telling you again."

A ranger shifted nervously on his feet.

Militiamen snapped toward him.

Paul's eyes followed their movement.

"You have no goddamned business stomping on my rights," Manson grumbled, stepping toward Paul. Militiamen inched forward.

"Stop!" Jack shouted, kicking up dust as he moved past the outer ring of people. He raised his arms. "Get back. These men are federal officers. You're breaking the law."

"The Indian guy said that already," the woman shouted. "Who are you? Why is Park Service here?"

"Doesn't matter who I am. You are obstructing federal officers."

She laughed. "Not in our book. You have no right to be here.

This is Manson's land. They're stomping on his rights. Government overreach."

"Hell they are," Jack shouted, glaring at Manson. "You're on public land. Everyone's land. You're not paying your grazing fees. Haven't in years. And there's a drought going on."

"There is no drought," Manson said. "Not anymore. Rained today. God's message. He's on my side."

"Yeah, right," Jack said. "Because of range conditions, people almost died in a flashflood."

"I don't know what you're talking about, and I'm not gonna listen to government lies. Fabrications to kick me off my land. Land I've got more claim to than you do."

"Bull. And the Hopi say Paul's people are newcomers." Jack glanced at Paul, and flashed a grin.

Paul looked his way and back.

"What does that mean?" Manson shouted.

"Means you're full of it." Jack stepped forward, raising his arms. "Get out of here. Leave."

Manson looked to his right, then his left. The militiamen at his sides took one step forward, leveling AR-15s at Jack's chest.

"My friend," Paul said. "Stay out of this."

Jack stared into the face of a militiaman. "He won't shoot."

The militiaman pointed his rifle skyward, fired a round, then leveled it back at Jack's chest. Other militiamen took one step forward.

Rangers, gripping pistols, hands tense, glanced between faces behind dark, un-telling sunglasses.

A woman on the ground stirred.

A ranger flinched.

"Paul," a voice shouted, from a vehicle among the stock trucks. He turned.

"Let 'em go," the voice said. "Orders. Let the cattle go. They said not to let this escalate further."

"Who gave the orders?" Paul shouted back.

"Washington. Let 'em go."

Paul gave Manson a hard stare, signaled the truck at the chute to pull forward, then gave a signal to rangers at the corral.

Gates swung open. Cattle burst through, fanning out, trailing away from the corral. They topped the hill and were gone.

Manson smiled. "Cowards."

A militiaman stepped forward, his nose in Jack's face. He grinned, and spat, "Bang."

CHAPTER
6

Jack walked up the road toward the river takeout.

The government pickup sat parked off the road, Erika in the driver's seat. Through the windshield he saw Claire Prescott, wide eyed, watching the humanity at the corrals.

Jack veered toward the driver side window.

Erika scowled. "That was stupid."

"You didn't have to wait," Jack muttered. "My ride's over there."

"I said, that was stupid. What's with you?"

"I did what I had to do."

"Even if it's stupid?"

"No one ever said I was smart."

———·———

It all replayed through his mind as he drove. Paul. Moony Manson. Militiamen with guns.

Yes. It was stupid. Erika was right.

Call the superintendent, let him know. Don't use the radio. Use the phone.

He reached for the glove box and pulled out the cell phone he'd stashed before dawn. Pulling up Joe Morgan's office number, he pushed call. It rang without answer, rolling over to voice mail.

Try his cell. He called, listened to the ring, then the recording of Joe's gently commanding voice, saying to leave a message.

"Joe, this is Jack Chastain. Need to tell you about something. Sorry. Involves BLM, a rancher, and trespass cattle. Call when you can." He tossed the phone on the passenger seat.

Turning off the gravel road onto the highway, Jack checked his watch.

Coalition meeting starts in twenty minutes. No time to get home.

On the outskirts of town, he drove past scattered houses. Most of them simple, square, adobe. Some newer. Some ornate. All with pastel hues. Some with gardens behind low walls, accessed through adobe passageways with timber gates.

On the edge of Las Piedras, he turned onto Calle Vicente, drove past the plaza and the more recent nineteenth century store-fronts lining the streets around it. The centuries old adobe church sat at one corner. The bell in the tower began to ring, and Jack checked his watch. Seven. Late, but not by much.

In the plaza, a young Hispano troubadour played for a small crowd enjoying the summer evening. Passing Elena's Cantina, the parking appeared full. Carne asada sounded good, but time did not permit. Maybe later. Maybe tomorrow.

He turned left off the square, took the next right, and entered the grounds of the Inn of the Canyons, parking near the porte-cochere. He ambled in, feeling the dull buzz of the fade of adrenaline, and a lack of focus from the events refusing to stay at the back of his mind.

Erika's right. But they threatened Paul.

He stopped, looked across the lobby, and shook off the confusion.

The day's listing of meeting rooms showed the Piedras Coloradas National Monument Coalition to be meeting in the Coronado Room. He headed down the hall, and stopped at the door.

Inside, a room of people, facing off across a conference table.

"We cannot go backwards," said Dave Van Buren, one of the environmentalists on the coalition.

"This drought has made some things abundantly clear," said Ginger Perrette, still in her chore clothes. "We need assurances. We need water. We have to have it. Cattle need water."

"But we've got to protect the river and the range. Especially now. Wildlife are as affected by drought as cows. If cows destroy the river, what's left?"

Ginger turned to Kip Culberson.

Culberson sipped from a glass of water, looking his usual self, the graying statesman of the West. Sturdy build. Western-cut sport coat. Old pair of jeans. Mustache, the same gray as his temples. He frowned and cleared his throat, considering his words.

"Jack, come in," said Karen Hatcher, the director of the Trust for the Southwest, and Kip's counterpart from the environmental community. She waved him in. "We weren't sure you'd make it." A strand of blonde hair lay matted to her forehead. She looked fresh off a hike. "What's wrong?" She eyed him closely. "You're pale."

"Tired."

"You sure?"

"Yeah." Jack moved around the table to an open seat, nodding first at Helen Waite, the county commissioner, then the hotel proprietor, Mack Latham, representing the chamber of commerce, then Thomas, his friend and the representative from the pueblo, then Daniel Romero, another rancher. "Sorry I'm late. Having some sort of trouble?"

"Ranchers are talking like all bets are off," Dave said. "The drought's bringing out their true colors. Cows are more important that protecting the river." He glared across the table.

"I didn't say that," Ginger responded. "I was saying . . ." She turned back to Kip.

Again he cleared his throat.

"Hold it," Jack said. He took in a breath, and turned to Ginger. "I do not want you having to defend yourself." He turned to Kip. "And not you either." He looked across the table. "Karen, I would ask you. Do you mind?"

She gave him a twisted smile. "Uh, sure." She turned to Van Buren and looked him in the eye. "Dave, you're jumping the gun, being unfair. Ginger's a steward of the land. She's proven that. Well before now, she and her husband took their cattle off the range, put 'em on pasture in Colorado and Nebraska. They put their money where their mouth is. It'll cost them dearly. They'll be lucky if they squeak by. The drought has her thinking about their future and she wonders if they can make it. Short-term. Long-term. Everything about their operation. Their BLM allotment is important to that operation. All she's saying is, work with her, help her make sure the path we're on doesn't cripple her and other ranchers." She looked at Ginger. "Is that fair?"

"Yes. Very fair."

Dave shifted nervously in his seat. "All I'm saying is . . ."

"Stop," Jack said. "Turnabout's fair play. I won't let you defend yourself either. Kip, would you please?"

Kip nodded and cleared this throat. "I believe Dave's saying we can't lose sight of the things we value. We all value the land, the river, water, our connection to all of it. Times like these are hard, but we still value those things. We want to come up with practical measures, but we can't throw the baby out with the bath water. It's tough all over. Other critters are suffering, too. We want to come through this. Ginger, if you can help protect those things, he'll work to help ranchers in their plight." He turned to Dave. "That fair?"

"Yes, diplomatic. Something I'm not good at." He looked across the table. "Sorry."

"Times are hard," Ginger said.

Faces turned to Jack.

"Do we need to discuss this further?" He looked around the room. No response. "Good. Anyone else coming?" he asked, taking attention off Van Buren and Perrette.

"Might just be us tonight," Kip responded. "People are busy. They've read the report. I've gotten comments, but otherwise, they think it's ready to go."

"Same for enviros," Hatcher said. "Everyone feels good. They trust us to know what to do next."

"I'd like to talk about that." Jack stood and poured a glass of water. "Been thinking. I worry about going to Congress. Who knows what we might end up with."

Kip laughed.

"No, I'm serious. Maybe we should scale back on what the coalition initially asks the agencies to do. Do what we can, without additional authorizations. Wait till we get a Congress that's less political."

"I'm sorry, son," Kip said, laying large, weathered hands on the table, "but Congress is always gonna be political. Time won't change that."

"Yeah, but this Congress turns everything into a fight. A political statement."

"Yes, but we have to think about holding the coalition together," Hatcher said. "Think about the discussion we just had. If we don't seek new authorities, we lose the ranchers. If we don't protect the river, we lose the enviros. If we lose either group, if the battles start over, the business people freak out." She looked across the table at Mack Latham. "Right?"

Latham gave a nervous tug at his button-down collar. "Business people don't like uncertainty."

"I know, it's just . . . ." Jack paused, looking at eyes around the table.

"What's wrong?" Culberson asked.

"Old ghosts. Nothing more than that."

"Let me worry about Congress. Karen and I can take that. In fact, I know just where we can start. Senator Baca."

Hatcher's eyes lit up. "Think so?"

"I do. He's busy, but I think he'll have an interest in making it happen. He's respected. His staff can corner counterparts from the House, get bills coming through both chambers."

Karen turned to Jack. "Ever work with Baca?"

"Only his staff, but I've worked with politicos I trusted and it didn't help. We still got caught up in political games. Crucified. When the horse trading stopped, nothing was left."

"Relax," Kip said. "But we need to keep moving. If we don't, we risk impatience, and falling apart."

"I agree," Hatcher said, tapping her dimpled chin. "I've spoken with national enviros and reps from stockman's associations. I'm told this needs to happen now. The closer to the election, the greater the chance someone will politicize it. Then, it might be hard to support us."

"That's what I'm hearing," Kip said. He turned to Jack. "What's it gonna take to wrap this up? Can we finish this week?"

Jack sighed. "Got comments, let me have 'em. I'll finish in the next day or two."

"Very good," Kip said. He sat back, locking his fingers behind his head of salt and pepper hair. "I'll make a few calls, make plans for Karen and I to pay a visit to Baca's field office in Santa Fe."

— · —

Jack turned off the highway, onto the road to his cabin.

Rounding the bend, he saw a woman sitting on his porch. A beautiful woman, dark hair pulled back, brown Hispano eyes, piercing even from the end of the drive. She wore a cotton skirt and sleeveless blouse. Kelly Culberson stood as he brought his Jeep to a stop. He sat watching her, thinking how much easier hard times had become since encountering her at Caveras Creek three years before.

He got out.

"How was the meeting? How was the river? How's Paul?"

"That's more questions than I can answer in my condition. My lunch washed away in a flood."

"Flood. Very funny."

He stooped, kissed her, then slipped past and unlocked the door. "Do I look like I'm joking?" Going straight to the kitchen, he picked an apple from a bowl on the counter. He came back and sat, bit off a chunk, chewed and swallowed. "Need calories." He took another bite, then picked up the remote, turned on the television, and flipped through the channels.

"You relax. I'll cook. Were you serious . . . I mean . . . about a flood?"

"Flashflood, one of the creeks. And relaxing might not be possible." He settled on a channel and scooted to the front of the chair.

"What's going on?" She eyed the television.

On the screen, an unmistakable background—the broken canyon and plateau country of northern New Mexico.

"I was afraid of this."

"What?"

The scene cut to a studio and trio of commentators, then to an on-scene reporter. The reporter ended his update as the network cut away to a clip of an angry rancher, ranting about his refusal to recognize the authority of the feds. Armed militiamen stood on either side of the rancher, on guard, as he preached into a microphone. The camera zoomed in on a militiaman in camo, stoic as he faced a crowd. He held an AR-15 across his chest, a finger resting on the trigger guard.

"I heard about this," Kelly said. "Heated up while you were on the river." She gasped.

On screen, Jack Chastain stood with Paul Yazzi, confronted by reporters, their bevy of microphones in Jack's face. "*Because he hasn't paid his fees. He's overgrazing. We're in a drought and he's got five hundred cows on the range, plus calves. No other ranchers are doing that. Why? Because they're taking care of their cows, and they know what it means to be stewards of the land.*"

Jack flipped to another channel. Same scene. Himself in the middle of his rant. "*. . . he's got five hundred cows on the range, plus calves.*"

Jack cringed and clicked over to a third news channel, same scene. The network cut away to a panel of commentators. "*Right there,*" said a paunchy man with light-colored hair, stopping the video. "*This has nothing to do with a drought. They had rain today. This is all a fabrication by the government to go after this guy. He's a hero for standing up to the malarkey.*"

"*Excuse me, Barnes,*" a host said, bringing attention back to himself. "*I need to cut away for a moment. We have Congressman Brent Hoff at his office in Washington. Good evening, Congressman. Good of you to join us. What do you think of all this?*"

The studio scene dissolved away to an office setting. One man, crisp gray suit and blond wavy hair, neatly combed. After salutations, the smile left his face.

"*I agree with the last comment. This man may be a hero for standing against the odds. One man, against the tyranny. Classic example of government overreach, and he's willing to take them on.*"

"*Congressman, are there merits to what's being said by the government?*"

"*I doubt it. An investigation is warranted, but from what I can tell, it looks like a case of bureaucrats overstepping their authority, not being accountable to anyone. A classic situation where mid-level bureaucrats, not elected by or accountable to anyone, are trying to rewrite the laws. I encourage Moony Manson to fight.*"

"*Am I hearing you correctly? Fight, you say?*"

"*Absolutely.*"

"I know that face," Jack said, eyeing the screen.

"The congressman? You should've. He's everywhere. If they're talking politics, he's there."

"I don't pay attention to talking heads, but I've encountered that guy."

"Jack, that's Brent Hoff. Odds on favorite for the presidential nomination."

He gave her a double take, then turned back to the television. "I remember that expression. Hallway in the federal building, Missoula, four years ago."

"You've dealt with Brent Hoff?"

"A couple of dealings. First in the hall, then at a hearing a day later." He paused, to catch the words of a commentator. Contrivance. "His aide tracked me down, said he wanted a briefing. Right then. I didn't have time. People were waiting. Public meeting. Next day, at the hearing, he knew almost as much about our research as I did. I don't know how. But, he lied his ass off. I defended the work of a young scientist but the congressman ripped me to shreds."

"Today, I thought you were on the river," Kelly muttered. "Monitoring, of some kind."

"I was. . . . about this."

"Manson grazes BLM land. Why were reporters talking to you?"

"Because, I couldn't keep my mouth shut. Manson and his

wanna be soldiers . . . they attacked Paul." Jack slammed a hand onto the armrest, then sucked in a long, slow breath. "I may've screwed things up for the coalition."

"People know what Manson's about. He's a separate issue."

"He's not."

"Why would this have anything to do with the coalition?"

"Because, we need legislation. We have projects we can't do without it. Water projects. River protection. Without legislation, we can't hold the coalition together. We go to war with ourselves."

"But that doesn't have anything to do with Moony Manson." Kelly said. "People here know him. They know he's a deadbeat."

"But grazing on public land, on part of the national monument. I'm less concerned about people here than I am about Congress."

"Then work with Congress."

Jack pointed at the television. "You saw that. The congressman told Manson to fight. He called for an investigation. He won't exactly pave the way to giving the coalition the legislation it needs."

"Other members of Congress . . . they can help."

"Kelly, it's Congress. They play games. They play politics. Look what happened in Montana. Even with the local senator by our side, people like Hoff got involved. Everything went off the rails."

"I thought Montana happened because a Park Service higher up messed with a research report."

Jack sighed. "Nail in the coffin. Things were going south before that. Maybe my fault. I had no idea this congressman was powerful. Maybe I should've given him what he wanted."

"Stop thinking like that. That's the past."

"Now it's the future. The road to protecting what this community values . . . the road to implementing recommendations of the coalition . . . goes through Congress." He sighed, and ran his fingers through sweat-matted hair. "Maybe, if I stay out of the way, your father and Karen Hatcher can work their magic, carry things forward."

The house phone rang.

Jack snatched it up. "Hello."

"Jack, this is Joe Morgan."

"Hold it, Joe." He cupped the mouthpiece. "The superinten-dent." He waited as Kelly turned down the television, then took a deep breath and composed himself. "Sorry. Get my message?"

"Yes, and several others," Joe said, his voice deep and solemn. "Some from on high. I'll make this short. You and I have been summoned. To Washington."

CHAPTER
7

Joe Morgan pushed the button for the floor. The elevator jolted, then moved smoothly. Jack watched the lights ascend, then stop. The door opened.

Third floor, Main Interior Building, Washington, D.C.

They exited, turned right, then left, into the National Park Service wing.

"I'll catch up," Jack said, slowing at the bathroom door. He watched Joe continue up the hall. Joe—average height, grey hair, and dressed in a navy blue suit—still had a ranger's presence for a man his age. Jack took notice of his own attire. Similar, with dress shoes he only remembered wearing in this town.

He ducked into the bathroom, wet a paper towel, and wiped the sweat from his brow. Damned humidity. He slipped back into the hall, the towel folded and concealed in his hand.

Continuing into the wing, he stopped at the plaque for employees who died in the line of duty. He scanned the columns and paused at a name. "Hello, old friend," Jack whispered. "Here, again. Trouble. Again." He chuckled, a nervous laugh among friends. "Not simple times. Not like the old days. You would've handled this better than me." He stared a moment more, then turned. "Water under the bridge. Wish me luck." He headed down the hall.

He joined Joe at the receptionist's desk. To the right, the Director's office. To the left, the Deputy Director's. The receptionist, a young woman, African American, in a black wool suit.

"We miss you around here, Mr. Morgan," she said.

Joe smiled. "Thank you, but it's good to be back in the park."

"I'm sure. Can I go with you?" She flashed a smile.

"Love to have you, but your first job would be human shield. Protecting me from the director."

She laughed.

Jack pointed at the open door behind them, the director's meeting room. "We in there?"

"No." She gave a nod toward the director's office. "In there. It'll be moment. He's in a meeting."

The door sprang open. A silver-haired woman, in a blue pastel suit, stepped out and stopped, looked at Joe, did a double take at Jack, then stepped back to the office door. "You did not tell me you had them coming to Washington. And today, no less."

The director appeared, and walked her back into the hall. "Goodbye, Nancy." He stepped around her. "Come in, Joe." He locked eyes on Jack. "You, too."

The woman watched as they entered. The director, in shirt sleeves and tie, closed the door. His suit coat lay thrown over the arm of a chair against the back wall. "Have a seat." Hair mussed, he went around his desk and sat.

Joe chose the seat to the left.

Jack took the one to the right, glancing around the room as he sat. Big desk. Plaques on the wall, things engraved on them that didn't seem to matter at the moment.

Benjamin Lucas sat back, ran a finger across his brown and gray-tinged mustache, and stared across the desk at Jack. "Well," he said, finally. "You sure managed to become the center of attention. Today, you're a big name in town." He dropped his hand.

"That good or bad?"

"It's not good." He let out a sour chuckle. "I take that back, a bit. I spent the morning with my counterpart from BLM. The director of BLM is your biggest fan. He knows that today, he and his agency would have been tarred and feathered by one particular side of the political spectrum, except for one Mr. Jack Chastain."

"Director," Joe said. "Give me a minute to explain the background."

The director laughed. "Joe, I know the background. The Secretary and I heard it all from BLM. Whole story. I could recite details. Court records, everything."

Jack raised a hand and wiped the sweat from his brow. A headache began pounding between his eyes.

The director turned back to Jack. "What do you have to say for yourself?"

"I screwed up."

The director sighed. "Actually, I don't know if you screwed up or not. My question is, why was my employee standing in front of the cameras, opening his mouth about something that didn't concern him? On an issue I knew nothing about."

"Long story."

The director glanced at his watch. "Interesting thing . . . I've got time. And I should tell you, as of this morning I thought I'd be dragging both of you to the White House for twenty questions from the Chief of Staff. I've settled those waters a little, but when I say I want to hear the whole story, I think you owe me the whole story." He rested his arms on his desk. "Was this guy in the park?"

"It's not easy to explain," Jack said. "Turns out, the rancher's cattle have been known to trespass on park land."

"But we weren't taking corrective action. BLM was."

"Correct."

"Then why is the face of my employee all over television? In Park Service uniform?"

"They pointed guns at my friend. A trusted colleague from BLM. Native American. A man of few words. Manson didn't understand that, or didn't care. They were pushing, attacking. Paul came through for me on a fire, years back. I had to come through for him. To protect him."

"By stepping in front of crazies with assault rifles?"

"Seems stupid, doesn't it?"

"Very."

"Didn't seem that way at the time."

"I'm not sure why."

"Well, . . . no one ever said I was smart."

Lucas held his tongue.

"You were angry, because Manson threatened Paul?" Joe asked.

"More to it than that. This rancher Manson acts like it's his land, not public land. He's spreading discontent, when BLM's only doing their job. He's overgrazing the range. We're in a drought."

"It supposedly rained yesterday," the director interjected.

"And Paul and I were nearly killed in a flash flood. Doesn't mean the drought's over." Jack twisted in his seat. "I have no data supporting what I'm about to say, but I believe because of his grazing, the runoff was more severe than it would've been."

"No data, but you're sure?"

"Fairly certain." Jack sighed. "Haven't had time to talk to a hydrologist, but I will. I was on the river when the wall of water came down, nearly killing two raft-loads of people. All because nothing's on the ground to slow the runoff."

"That fueled your rant?"

"That and AR-15s pointed at Paul."

"Well, people may not know your name, but today, yours is the second-most seen face in America, after our rancher friend's."

"I was not trying to bring attention to the agency. Especially not bad attention."

"I know," Lucas said, leaning back, massaging the back of his neck. "Unfortunately, your actions played into the hands of others. Gave 'em opportunities. It's a game this town plays very well. It's what they do best." He scowled. "You're getting both bad and good attention, but, son, you're gonna become a target." He turned to the window and raised a finger to his mustache.

Jack glanced at Joe.

Joe shrugged.

After a long moment, the director turned to Joe. "Things aren't like the old days, back in Yellowstone. Things have changed.

Even more political. I don't want him sent back to New Mexico. Not into that mess. Not right away." He settled his eyes on Jack. "I want you to lay low. Let things blow over."

"What're you saying?" Jack asked.

"I need to hide you, at least for a while."

"I can stay in my office. I've got things I need to do."

"Like what?"

"The coalition report. Finishing touches, before it goes to Congress."

"It's not a good time for that."

"If we don't keep moving, the coalition could fall apart. If it does, they go to war with themselves." He paused. "You have been briefed on this, haven't you?"

The director nodded. "Yes, two weeks ago, by legislative affairs." He shook his head. "I don't buy that only you can make finishing touches." He stood, looked out the window, then turned back. "Don't take this the wrong. What I'm about to say is for your own good. Your protection. You could become a pawn. A chess piece in someone's political game. You're too valuable to the agency. I won't let that happen. I'm not gonna let your reputation be tarnished. I'm not letting you go back till this has blown over. If, at all."

"Director, I'll quit before you put me anywhere else. Piedras Coloradas is now my home. I'll stay out of sight, anything, but I want to go home to New Mexico."

Joe cleared his throat, pulling attention his way. He turned to the director. "What've you got in mind, Ben? Maybe a short detail in another park?"

"Maybe," the director said, giving it thought. "Wait . . ." He reached for a notepad and flipped back a few pages. He tapped a finger over an entry circled in yellow. He read, then raised his eyes, letting them settle on Jack. "Got a passport?"

"Yeah."

"Government or personal?"

"Uh, . . . both, I guess. Unless one's expired."

"Government passport downstairs?"

"I think so."

"Good." Lucas gave him a crooked smile. "Jack, you're going to Africa. Kenya, to be exact."

Jack shot a confused look.

The director picked up a pencil and tapped his notepad. "I've got a technical assistance request from Kenya, for two people. I'm sending you."

"I'm not two people."

"No, but you're a biologist. It's complicated. They've requested a biologist and a manager, a senior executive. I think it best that we send only a scientist. No manager."

"What kind of scientist?"

Lucas leaned over his notes. "It says, either a large ungulate biologist, or an ecologist, or a range scientist."

"Why?"

"I don't know for sure. All I know is, a couple of rangers were killed by poachers. They're afraid one's work will end if no one keeps it going."

"Poachers?"

"I don't like the sound of this," Joe muttered. "Before now, who were you sending?"

"I wasn't." The director flashed another crooked smile. "Sounded too dangerous. But compared to political crucifixion, it suddenly sounds manageable."

"Not sure it does to me," Jack said.

The director cocked an eyebrow. "This is an order." He paused, letting the words settle in. "Do not leave headquarters, at least not alone. This is to be an intellectual exercise. Train someone to do the work. No field work for you. No going to dangerous places. Got that?"

"I'd like to talk you out of this. I'd prefer to go home."

"Not a chance. Answer me. You will not leave headquarters."

"Uh, . . ."

The director stared back.

"Uh, . . . " Jack sighed. "I will not leave headquarters."

"I'll get your passport sent up from downstairs. Make travel plans. Leave as soon as you can." He slid the pad across the desk. "Here's your point of contact."

Jack studied the information.

Samuel Leboo, Senior Warden. Nairobi National Park, Nairobi, Kenya.

He slid it back to the director. "Why only me? Why not two, like they requested?"

"I'm not sure many in Kenya want this to happen. They seem suspicious."

"Then why the request?"

"It doesn't appear to be their idea. It was pushed by powerful interests in the wildlife conservation community. Politics are involved. Politics I don't understand. Politics, I want no part of. But, scientists . . . ?" He smiled. "Scientists, regardless of politics, they get along. They find ways to work together. They collaborate. They achieve things, even with egos involved. They're focused on their science, so that's what you are. A scientist, nothing more."

"I guess I kinda resemble that remark. At least I used to."

"Don't let anyone think you're more than that. You might hear things—I'd be interested to learn what—but show no interest. Soak it up. Stay out of it. Stay a scientist."

Jack nodded.

"Give 'em two weeks, maybe three. That should be enough to let this blow over. Brief me when you get back."

Jack stood.

"One more thing," Lucas said, walking them to the door. "Do not get yourself killed."

CHAPTER
8

In the dark of night, KLM Flight 9964 circled on approach to Jomo Kenyatta International Airport. Staring out the window, Jack Chastain saw the lights of a vast and variable cityscape. Nairobi.

So this is Kenya?

The jet landed and taxied to the terminal.

Upon disembarking, in cargo pants and tan cotton shirt, he walked the concourse, made it through immigration with little inconvenience, strolled to baggage claim, then customs, then past the last of security. Near the exit, he stepped around other travelers —many in clothing suggesting imminent safaris—and began looking for signs of someone or something there to collect him. What will it be? A placard? He saw none. He scanned the concourse, then noticed a slender, graying, somewhat crusty looking African man, a scar on his chin, wearing a camo uniform and brown beret. Jack veered toward him. "Here for an American?"

"Indeed, I am, sir."

Jack extended a hand. "Jack Chastain, U.S. National Park Service."

The man shook the hand, uttering something, followed by what might have been, ". . . Senior Warden, Kenya Wildlife Service."

Accent. Almost British, but . . . "I'm sorry, I didn't catch the name. My ear's not yet adjusted to . . . ."

"I understand," the man said, his bearing disciplined, almost military. "My name, Mr. Jack, is Samuel Leboo."

He let the pronunciations rattle around his brain a moment. "Good to meet you, Samuel. Sorry I took a late flight."

"There is no problem. Day or night, I work them all." He glanced at Jack's bags. "Your luggage? Has it arrived?"

"This is all I have."

"You travel light."

"Spur of the moment. I might pick up a few things later, unless you're taking me to the middle of nowhere. In that case, it'd be good to buy a few clothes."

"You will not be in the middle of nowhere. You are in the only capital in the world that is also a wildlife reserve. If you need, I can provide clothing items. I can dress you like a ranger."

"I'm accustomed to that."

"You're tall, but not as tall as Maasai. If I can find trousers for them, I can find trousers for you."

"I'll try not to need them."

"Follow me."

They exited the terminal, into hot night air. Leboo led him past lines of vehicles picking up passengers for various accommodations, some advertising safaris. Crossing the road, a strangely striped vehicle whizzed past, swerving to miss them.

"If I'm killed by a zebra, please let it be a real one," Jack grumbled.

In the dimly lit parking area, Samuel found his vehicle, a dark Toyota Land Cruiser with agency markings. He opened the left side door and waved Jack over.

Jack came around, and stared inside. No steering wheel. Passenger side. He threw in his duffle and climbed in.

Samuel circled to the driver's side, climbed in, started the Land Cruiser, and backed out of the parking space. "Mr. Jack," he said, glancing toward the exit. "How long will you be with us?"

"Two, three weeks. As long as you need me. If we could wrap this up in a couple of days, that'd be okay, too."

"You did not wish to come to Kenya?"

"Uh, . . ." Jack felt Leboo studying his face. "Always wanted to, but . . . it's just . . . I have other things that need to be finished." He turned to the window. "But that's irrelevant. I'm here. My time is yours."

"I see." Samuel gave a slow nod and accelerated onto the road. "How much do you know about Kenya?"

"Not much, really." He gripped the armrest as Samuel steered onto the left side of the road. "Learned I was coming only yesterday. Or maybe it was today. I'm . . . uh . . . little turned around about what day it is. I did some reading on the flight, but my options for study were limited."

"Not to worry. I can provide materials." Eyes on the road, he seemed settled in for the drive. "Kenya Wildlife Service manages national parks and wildlife reserves. People come from around the world to safari in Kenya. This is Africa as the world imagines it to be. Our wildlife are our heritage. To preserve that heritage, our rangers carry AK-47s and AK-103s. Do you know why?"

"Poachers?"

He gave a slow nod, then pulled into traffic, seemingly ignoring the others on the road. "Yes. Do you know what they poach?"

Eyes straight ahead, watching darting cars, Jack said, "Elephant?"

"Yes. Big game animals. Especially elephant and rhinoceros. Do you know why?"

Jack braced himself against the dashboard. "Elephant for ivory, rhino for horns?"

"Correct, and do you know who does the poaching?"

"Not really. Not something I understand very well."

"Maybe it's not important that you do. You are a scientist, not someone hired to stop poaching . . . but unfortunately our rangers are. They must carry automatic weapons to do their job. And to survive."

Cars screamed past, horns blaring.

"Scientist . . . true," Jack responded. "But we, too, have law enforcement rangers." He put a hand on the dashboard. "Is traffic always like this?"

"No. During the day it is very busy." Leboo turned into a roundabout, steering across the lane. Horns blasted behind him. "Do your law enforcement rangers carry AK-47s?" He turned onto another road, this one just as busy.

"Well . . . some train with automatic or semiautomatic weapons—I'm not exactly sure which—but most carry hand guns. Pistols."

"Here, carrying a pistol would simply make you a target."

"Is there a reason we're discussing this? Did you need someone proficient in automatic weapons? If so, they sent the wrong guy. Send me back . . . ask for a different skill set."

"I do not presume to know what proficiencies you should have as a scientist. I simply want you to understand the risks we face."

"I'm not sure what difference this makes, but I'm only here because two days ago I was staring down the barrel of an automatic weapon. Several actually. But as you say, I'm a scientist, not someone who carries one. So, why am I here, Samuel?"

Samuel took his eyes off the road. "This incident . . . were you in danger?"

"I suppose. Felt like it. Could've been posturing. Not something that happens every day."

"For our rangers, being ready every day is something to which they're accustomed. You are here because a week ago, two of our rangers were killed by rhinoceros poachers. One, a biodiversity ranger."

"A scientist?"

"Yes. An accomplished one. He had recently finished his Ph.D., and returned to Kenya because this is where he wanted to be. He did not want to work at university or in the science office. He wanted to be in the bush."

"That, I can understand. Where'd he do his studies?"

"Oxford."

"England?"

"Is there another?"

Jack laughed at himself. "Why turn to us? Why not Oxford?"

Samuel sighed and fixed his eyes on the road.

Jack tried to read him. "Why not Oxford, Samuel?"

"I did contact Oxford. They are in shock. They knew Gabriel quite well. They knew how much he longed to return to Kenya. The news of his death was difficult for them, and . . . they don't want professors or students put at risk."

"I see. So, . . . the Americans . . . it's the Wild West over there. Go get one of them."

"What do you mean?"

"Americans like playing with guns."

"No. It was not that at all." He swerved around a vehicle, then back into the lane.

Jack bounced against the door. "Then, why us, and why the urgency? Why not wait? Or find another university, maybe here in Nairobi?

Samuel's face turned stone. Not even a flinch.

"Simple questions, Samuel." Jack gave him a moment, then, "Never mind. Sorry to pry."

"My usual avenues for seeking collaboration and support were closed. By the Ministry." He flashed a subtle smile. "But, I have connections. Here and there, people with appropriate levels of influence. My connections put me on a path to your International Affairs Office."

"Okay, but why the urgency?"

Samuel drew in a long, slow breath. "Some in the Ministry think Gabriel's research should be ended. I and my connections believe that would be a mistake. We must continue Gabriel's research. We must not let them push us aside."

"I don't understand. Why would the ministry not support it?"

"Discomfort. Lack of political will. The prospect that Gabriel's research would yield inconvenient findings." Samuel turned and seemed to study Jack's face.

"Hey, don't worry about me. I'm a scientist. Always big on research." He raised a brow and smiled. "Tell me about his work."

"Multi-faceted. Some of it similar to what I'm told your agency calls, *vital signs.*"

"Indicator species and systems?"

"Precisely. But the more controversial aspect of the work focused on habitat fragmentation. The relationships between intensity of human activity and the health and viability of wildlife habitat and populations. Wildlife corridors, and eventually, through collaboration, ecological economies."

"Tough nuts to crack," Jack said. "Is that why he was killed?"

"I do not believe so. I believe it simply an unfortunate encounter with a poacher."

"But you're not absolutely certain."

"Not entirely. The investigation continues."

"When will they know?"

"There is no they. It is I conducting the investigation."

"I see. Back to Gabriel's work. The things he focused on. They take time. There are no quick, easy answers, and I can't be here forever."

Samuel appeared to consider the words. "There is seasonal migration of wildlife into and out of Nairobi National Park, even as it exists on the edge of Nairobi. Fences surround the park to the north, west, and east, but not to the south. Not entirely. But Maasai lands, and even more so, the private ranches owned by individuals and land brokers, and corporations intending to cash in on appreciating land prices due to population increases ... these are strangling the migration corridors. If we do not do something now, or soon, the migration corridors will be gone. The beauty and rhythms of nature subdued. The park will become little more than a zoo."

Jack nodded, watching the road, noticing traffic becoming lighter as Samuel skirted what seemed a different part of the city. Industrial. Large buildings alongside a rail line. "Where are we going, and who am I working with?"

"We are going to the south of the park, where we have a ranger outpost for you to stay. And it is me with whom you'll be working."

"Are you a scientist?"

"I am not a scientist. I am ranger, a warden."

"Who also happens to be investigating two murders."

"Do not concern yourself with that," Samuel said, steering

into a roundabout, taking the third turn. "Teach me to do Gabriel Kagunda's research, and I will assure that it continues."

Jack studied him a moment. "Did you know him well? Did you know either of them?"

"Very well. The other ranger—David Ole Nalangu—had been under my command for many years. He was Maasai, a good man, a good ranger."

"I'm sorry for your loss."

"Thank you." Samuel raised a hand to his beret in salute. "And thank you for coming. Do you know why your government sent only one?"

"Is that a problem?"

"Maybe just as well."

"Why?'

"It might make things easier. I wasn't exactly following protocol."

"Interesting. Care to share?"

Samuel chose not to answer.

"Sorry. None of my business."

The cityscape became something less, yielding to a fence and an entrance sign. East Gate, Nairobi National Park.

Within minutes of driving past a cluster of buildings, they were on open expanses, a moonlit picture of Africa. Looking back, lights of the city. Looking forward, grassland, scattered fever trees and acacia. After several turns and road junctions, they came to an encampment. A cluster of small buildings. Samuel steered through, stopping at a solitary building, small and unmarked. He killed the engine and climbed out. Jack followed him in.

The house held a small, functional kitchen, and a room with a desk and what was little more than an army cot. Jack dropped his duffle on the bed.

"Will this be adequate?" Samuel asked.

"It'll do fine."

"If not, we can try again to find a room in Nairobi, or at one of the lodges or safari camps. I was not expecting such a rapid response from your government."

Jack laughed. "Impressive, wasn't it? Doesn't happen very often, I promise." He looked around the quarters. "This will work."

"I've stocked the kitchen, but maybe not adequately."

"I'm sure it's fine. What do you people eat?"

"Less meat than Americans. Some of us like curries."

"Love curries, I think. Coffee?"

"In the pantry. Tomorrow I'll take you to get supplies to your liking."

"I'm sure what you've gotten is fine. Experience the local cuisine, I always say. So, what's the plan for tomorrow?"

"We begin." Samuel pointed at the desk. "I assume you'll want to read Gabriel Kagunda's research plan. It is there, in the top drawer. You will find the key in the kitchen cupboard nearest the stove. I will permit you to read, then I will pick you up here at ten."

"Oh, I forgot. I promised my director this would be a headquarters exercise. Training. No going into the field."

Leboo stared at him a moment. "I assume you'll want to see what the national park has to offer?"

"Very much so, yes."

"Good. Two things, Mr. Jack. First, I can easily make my headquarters a mobile one. Second, do you always follow orders?"

CHAPTER

9

Jack woke at sunrise, made his way to the kitchen and figured out the stove. After making a pot of coffee, he slipped on cargo pants, took his first cup to the porch, and sipped staring out over the savanna.

Scattered fever trees, tall and wispy, floated above the grasslands, their canopies seemingly held in check by the sky. Birdlife welcomed the morning. Chatters and songs rose from acacia surrounding the enclave.

He went for a second cup, and when finished, forced himself to go inside. No more time to enjoy this. Need to wrap it up and get home, before the coalition falls apart.

First things first. Email.

He pulled out his laptop and hurried to draft a message to Karen Hatcher and Kip Culberson, with the latest version of the coalition's report to Congress, and changes he'd made on the flight from Washington. After attaching the document, he noticed no signal for wireless. Seriously? He checked the outpost for phone lines. Nothing. No place to plug in a modem.

He dug his phone from the top pocket of his day pack and turned it on. Signal, fair. But who the hell is the carrier, and what's this gonna cost? He checked email. Nothing new. Not since yesterday. No data transfer. Electronically, stranded. He noticed the charge on the battery—nearly dead—and glanced at the nearest electrical outlet. No way the charger's gonna fit that thing. Not without a converter.

The emails aren't going anywhere. Not now. It's the middle of the night in the states. A few hours won't hurt.

He turned off the devices and put them away, then sauntered into the kitchen, poured another cup of coffee, and opened the cupboard to look for the key to the desk. He found it under a bag of rice.

He opened the desk and found the research plan alone in a drawer.

The plan was thorough, and, as Samuel said, multi-faceted. Gabriel Kagunda had all the hallmarks of a good scientist. His sampling protocol and statistical design were well defined and likely had been well before he ever went into the field. Nothing reeked of pre-determined conclusion, but his work would help them understand how the ecosystem worked, and serve as a basis for decisions and monitoring conditions over time.

His initial phase of work focused on grass and browse species for rhino, zebra, gazelle, wildebeest, and giraffe. He also intended to look at those same plant species in areas used during seasonal migration, and for what would be prime and sub-prime years, for habitat utilized in and outside the national park, for wet and dry seasons. His purpose appeared to be that of defining the values— the plant species and their distributions, the water sources and connectivity factors—that held the migration corridors together. Ambitious, and hardly something easily tackled in two to three weeks. After a morning of hard study, Jack had a sense of what he could do to help kick start Kagunda's work.

Promptly at ten there was a knock at the door.

Jack reached back and swung it open.

Outside, Samuel stood, almost at attention. "Good morning. If you are ready, Mr. Jack, we will begin with a tour. We will go only places where tourists go on safari."

"Sounds great." Jack reassembled the sections of the research plan he had scattered around the desk. "I think I'll bring this."

"Very well. Were our preparations for your arrival adequate?" Samuel remained planted a meter from the door.

"Yours were great. Mine sucked."

"Pardon me. I do not understand."

"American colloquialism. Not worth explaining. The provisions are great, thanks. My preparations, not so great. Need some sort of adaptor for the electrical. I need wireless, or some way to send email. Got a report I need to send home. Soon, or things go to hell."

"Your research?"

"No, other duties as assigned," Jack muttered. He stuffed the research plan in his pack. "Politics and deadlines."

"Politics and deadlines? For a scientist?"

"Everyone has deadlines, Samuel."

"Yes, but politics? Gabriel Kagunda spoke of science being best when sheltered from the influence of politics."

"Yes. That's wise, but . . ." Jack paused, remembering the director's words. *You're only a scientist.* "Never mind." He gave a flippant wave of his hand. "Just work. Something I need to pass off to someone while I'm here."

"I see. I will get you what you need."

Rubbing his chin, Jack said, "Forgot to shave." He threw the pack over his shoulder, backed out and closed the door.

Samuel led him to the Land Cruiser.

Climbing in, Jack noticed something on the floor. A rifle. Stock, wooden. Magazine, curved, and long enough for a not unsubstantial number of rounds. "Tourist route? Do tourists have guides carrying AK-47s?"

"No. Rangers only. I promise, this is not the time of day to be worried. Poachers prefer the night. In the day they know rangers are about, watching and ready."

"How about at night? Rangers, I mean."

"We are there at night, but the odds are less in our favor."

"Why?"

"Some poachers are better equipped."

— · —

Wildlife in abundance. Not quite everywhere, but the sight of giraffe with a cityscape background made it seem as though they were, the two seemed so incongruous. Herds of gazelle moved gracefully through the savannah, while the occasional rhinoceros plowed about, picking through forage with, what seemed, all the time in the world. When there were rhino, Jack—if he bothered to look—could typically spot rangers nearby, toting automatic rifles, eyes searching the bush. "What about cheetah and leopard?" he asked.

"You will see both, in good time."

Driving south and west, Leboo pointed at zebras on the move up a draw, grazing as a unit. "This is dry season. Zebra and wildebeest have moved back into the park. Their wet season ranges are to the south."

"Beautiful thing to see. These the only zebra in the park?"

"Many are here. More will come."

To the west, across the grasslands, lay distant upland forests. Species Jack had no clue about. He pulled a notepad from his shirt pocket and wrote two entries. *Plant book. Plant key.*

The radio crackled, then words, none in English. Samuel seemed to turn an ear, listening. When the talk died away, he said, "Did you form an opinion about Gabriel Kagunda's research?"

"I did."

"And?"

"Very thorough. Are you sure you have the background to help, Samuel?"

Leboo held his eyes on the road. "Are you saying I cannot contribute without being a scientist?" He gave the radio a look, as more chatter came over the speaker.

"What language is that?"

"Maasai. You will also hear Swahili and English. I wish for you to teach me how to do his work. I do not expect to learn enough to call myself a scientist, but I hope to keep the project moving forward. To not let it suffer a sudden death."

"Samuel, no offense, but Gabriel's study plans are not exactly basic. They require both a good knowledge of the local flora, and a detailed understanding of sampling methods and statistics. Have you thought about turning to the local university? Finding a grad student. Someone to help."

"I have. I had believed two students from university would join us today. They did not come. Their professors are concerned."

"Same response as Oxford? Concerned for their safety?"

"Yes. I promised protection, but still, they did not come." A look of resolve formed on his face. "For now, it is only I to assist. You are here for only so long. I must learn what I can, while I can."

"Maybe you should rethink this. Put things off a while. Find someone with credentials to do this permanently. Send me home, bring me back when the fear has blown over."

"Are you afraid?"

"No, it's just that . . . "

"I will find someone. I hope it is while you are here. For now, you have me to teach."

"This may be tougher than you think. Plus, I need some things. Basic supplies."

"What?"

"Three-quarter inch PVC pipe, or whatever it is in metric used here, and cotton cord. I need a plant key. If there are plant books published for the park, that'd make things easier."

Samuel steered the Land Cruiser off the road and stopped. He climbed out and returned with a well-worn day pack. From the top of the pack jutted four pieces of three-quarter inch PVC. Samuel took hold of the pipe and pulled, sliding them out of the pack. One meter long. Small screws set at intervals. Elbows for forming a square. He handed them over, then dug into the pack again, finding white cotton cord wrapped around a stick. Opening the pack wider, he stared inside, then pulled out two books. *Plants of Nairobi National Park*, and *The Plants of South Central Kenya*.

"That's responsive." Jack took one book and flipped through the pages. Dichotomous key. Perfect. "I'm impressed. You have everything we need to get started."

"They are Gabriel Kagunda's. I intend to return them to his wife, but not until I have cleaned the blood from his pack."

Jack glanced over. Reddish black stained the nylon. "Should we be using this?" Jack whispered.

Samuel looked up. "I think he would want us to do so, to continue his work. I will ask his wife, but for now, show me what this is for."

Jack exited the Land Cruiser, PVC in hand. He plugged the long pieces into the elbows, then strung the cord between screws. "Nine equal squares. Three by three, defined by the cotton cord. This is a quadrat. Basic tool of the plant ecologist." He let it drop. It lay over grass and forbs. "Gabriel prescribed using what are called Daubenmire cover classes. Common methodology in rangeland studies. Very commonly used in the United States and, I suppose, elsewhere. Two days ago, I was helping a colleague, using this very methodology."

Samuel nodded.

"Daubenmire used half a dozen cover classes, from as small as zero to five percent . . . the mid-point of which is two point five percent . . . to as large as complete coverage . . . ninety-five to one hundred percent for the class. So, these grasses, are, uh, . . ." He reached for the park plant book.

"*Themeda triandra* and *Bothriochloa insculpta.*"

Jack glanced over. "Serious?" He opened the index at the back of the book, found *Themeda triandra* and turned to the page. He studied the picture, then looked at the grass. "Very good, Samuel. You know your grasses."

He smiled.

"If we assume this species covers almost all of the quadrat, we'd give it ninety-seven percent cover, midpoint for the cover class. This little forb in the corner . . ." He pointed, giving Samuel a questioning look.

"I do not know. Is it not inconsequential, as small and as few as there are?"

"Maybe, but that's not for us to decide. We'll let the science—the analysis—determine that." He pointed at another plant. "How about this one?"

"I do not know that one."

"Okay, what about this one?"

"I do not know that one."

"We were going strong there for a moment. I'll key them out later. Each would get listed with a small amount of cover." He picked up the quadrat, and tossed it a few meters away. "Now, those plants, those species are entirely different. By randomly locating the quadrat, and doing enough quadrats to deal with the variability between quadrats, you sample the population—and compile information to use in statistical analyses. Those analyses are used to make inferences about the entire ecosystem. Looking at impacts, and levels of utilization by wildlife species and humans, and comparing those results over time, to controls—or places where you do not have utilization—you can actually draw inferences about system resistance and resilience."

Samuel nodded.

Jack turned to face him. "So, Samuel, you obviously know some plants, but not all. More importantly, you're not a scientist. You don't strike me as a foolish man. Even with the risk of losing the research, it'd be better to put it on hold than do it poorly, dishonoring the reputation of Gabriel as a scientist. Take the time. Find someone with credentials to carry on his work."

"I will find that person. But first, we must show that Gabriel's work has continued. That it must continue." His radio crackled with voices. Samuel turned away and listened. When the exchange ceased, he turned back.

"Do you understand Maasai?" Jack asked.

"I am Maasai."

"All the rangers are?"

"No. We are a small tribe compared to others."

"Was Gabriel Maasai?

"No. He was Kikuyu."

"I see," Jack said, watching his eyes, wanting to ask more questions, deciding not to probe. Not now. Not without knowing what questions were right or wrong.

The radio popped. Incomprehensible words. Samuel pulled the radio from its holster, and spoke. When the exchange was over, he said, "I must go. Poachers."

"In the daylight?"

"I will return when I can." Samuel bolted for the vehicle.

"I can stay in the truck," Jack shouted. He tucked the plant book under his arm, and picked up the quadrat, disassembling as he jogged. He climbed in, as Samuel started the Land Cruiser.

Samuel hit the gas, steering onto the road. At the next crossroads, he turned south, then abruptly onto a lesser road. At the sight of another Land Cruiser, he lifted the radio to his mouth, spoke a few words, listened to the response, then drove past, slowing at a bend in the road.

Ahead, two rangers—one male, one female—lay prone on the ground, aiming AK-47s across open grassland toward a fringe of acacia. Samuel grabbed his rifle and slid out the door.

Samuel moved quickly, then diving as bullets pinged the length of the Land Cruiser. With the vehicle's shell perforated, sound rang through the cab. Jack froze. Another burst. Glass shattered. He yanked the door open and rolled into the grass, crawling for the front wheel well. Sheltered behind the wheel and engine block, he drew in an excited breath. Another shot, and the vehicle sank, one tire gone.

Stay or run?

Another shot.

Jack twisted around, unable to see. Where's Samuel? He started to yell, then stopped. Don't. You'll get him killed.

The rangers in front of the vehicle, wearing camo, returned fire from behind a berm, in bursts directed across open ground. Another burst came from behind. Maybe Samuel.

Shots popped in the distance. Dirt erupted at the top of the berm. Rangers lowered their heads. One raised a Kalashnikov and returned fire. The other crawled toward a larger, grass-covered mound. She peeked over the mound, sighted in and waited. After a moment, she raised binoculars and scanned.

Jack sat watching, listening, tucked behind the wheel.

A ranger fired off another shot, then looked over the berm.

Jack cringed as he watched the man raise his head.

Nothing happened.

Peering through grass, they scanned for movement.

After a few minutes, and exchanging words, they crept forward.

Jack watched, staying low, losing sight of them as they advanced. Stay put. Don't be a disruption.

Minutes passed.

No more shots.

More minutes, then, "Mr. Jack?"

Jack jumped.

Samuel stood clutching his AK-47, sweat dripping from his brow, his shirt soaked.

"You okay?" Jack asked.

"No harm done."

"Your rangers?"

"No one hurt. Poachers are gone. Your director was right. We shall stay at headquarters. I am sorry. I put you in harm's way."

Jack let out chuckle. "My idea, and . . . hey, happens all the time."

"You are attempting to jest, I assume."

"Yes, I'm joking." He stood and followed, as Samuel walked around the vehicle, surveying the bullet holes in the rear door and quarter panel.

"Poachers are getting bolder. I did not expect this to happen during the day." He sighed. "It is wise that you chose not to stay in the vehicle."

"Needed some air."

Samuel ignored the humor. He stared hard. "Regardless. After today, we stay at headquarters."

CHAPTER
10

Weeds. In abundance.

Jack stood, hands on his hips, staring out at the ground surrounding headquarters. Anything but pristine. Not unexpected. "Okay. This certainly collapses the effectiveness of our training, but . . ."

"Will it not require the same methodology?"

"It will, but I'm not sure how applicable it feels." Jack shook his head. "Uh, . . . before we get started, I'd like to send a few emails."

"Perhaps later." Samuel shrugged. "The internet connection is not functioning properly."

"Seriously?"

"These things happen. Service will be restored. At times patience is required."

"Okay, but . . . I have emails I need to send, pronto."

Samuel rubbed his eyes.

"You look like hell, Samuel."

"I did not get much sleep. I was up late, following leads. Leads that did not play out."

"No help?"

"Correct, no help. Shall we continue the lessons from yesterday?"

It wasn't long before Samuel understood the concepts behind the cover classes. "The most difficult thing for most people," Jack said, after watching Samuel make several quick, almost flippant judgments, "is precision. Developing your eye to make accurate calls. Doing it the same every time."

"Am I being inaccurate?"

"You're fine. Consistency comes with repetition."

"And you will make me do it correctly?"

"Yes."

"Will students at the University of Nairobi know this methodology?"

"They should. How long will it take for the shock of Gabriel's death to blow over?"

Samuel shook his head. "I do not know."

— . —

After a few hours of training, Jack stood upright, stretched his back, and pulled his watch from a cargo pocket. "Can we check the internet?"

"It is not yet working. I left word with my office manager to let me know."

"And they haven't."

"Correct."

"Then, it's time for lunch. I grabbed a few things from the cupboard this morning. We can drive south, eat in the southern part of the park."

"I will not put you in danger. Not again."

"We can stick to the main roads."

Samuel held his tongue.

"I'd like to understand these migration corridors. I'd like to understand why you have connectivity issues."

"No."

"Samuel, you can take care of me. What happened yesterday will not happen today."

"It could. Your director . . . "

"I know what my director said, but I can't get a sense of how I can help unless I understand the issues you face. I want to understand these connectivity issues."

Samuel scowled, and rubbed the scar on his chin. "On one condition."

"Anything."

"Follow me." Samuel led him into a building, past a counter, into a back room. On the back wall, in a rack, rifles stood upright.

Jack stopped at the door. "Whoa." He shook his head. "I do not do automatic weapons."

"I will take you only if I believe you can protect yourself."

"Hell, I'd probably shoot myself."

Samuel pulled a rifle from the rack. "This is an AK-47. Standard issue." He opened a drawer, took out a magazine, checked to see if it was loaded, slipped it into its slot on the rifle, and pulled back on a lever. "It is now loaded and ready." He held it out.

Jack stepped back.

"You will take it, or we will not leave headquarters."

Jack eyed the well-worn rifle. "Never used one of those. No interest in starting now."

"You have never used a rifle?"

"Not one like that."

"It is not difficult."

"I'm sure it's not."

"Unless you do, we stay at headquarters."

Jack scanned the length of the rack. Rifles, most being AK-47s. At the end, a few different kinds. He pointed. "What are those?"

"Carbines, from the great war. Old. I wish we didn't need to keep them."

"Got anything like a thirty-aught-six?"

Samuel sighed and stepped over to a door, opened it—a closet—and pulled out a padded case. He slid out a rifle with scope and strap. "Taken from a poacher."

"Just my style."

"In terms of fire power, little different than those." Samuel nodded at the carbines. "I would suggest the AK-47."

Jack took hold of the rifle and ran an eye down its length. "This will be perfect. Can't get in much trouble with this."

"You will look like a poacher. A poor one. If I were you, I'd want the best rifle I could get."

Jack reached into the pocket on the padded case. He pulled out a box. Springfield shells. "No one ever said I was smart."

— · —

Driving south, the savannah gave way to breaks in the terrain. The vegetation grew dense. Samuel steered onto a rise. "Mbagathi River. Southern boundary," he said, turning off the road onto a smaller track overlooking the drainage. "This location is popular with those on photo and bird safari." He followed the track, stopping where they had a view of the more broken terrain to the south. He turned off the vehicle, took hold of his rifle, and climbed out of the cab.

Jack followed.

"Your rifle, Mr. Jack."

"Here?"

Samuel nodded.

He turned back and retrieved it, slinging it over his shoulder. "Expecting trouble?"

Samuel offered no answer. He led to high ground, stopped, and pointed. "The park boundary follows the river. Migration corridors cross the river. Nairobi National Park is made up of lands that were once Maasai. Maasai then moved south, into what is called the Kitengela." He swept his hand across an expansive scene. Houses, fences, gardens, livestock, cultivated lands. "Many Maasai remain. Those with the small protected gardens are likely Maasai. Some lands have been sold and divided into group ranches. Farmers, corporate farms, and developers. It is these farmers and group ranches that are most likely to fence their lands to hold in their cattle, sheep and goats. Migration corridors are becoming filled with these farms, the corridors cut off. Wildebeest and other wildlife move between the park and the Athi-Kapiti Plains to the south." He pointed. "It is on the plains that they feed during wet season. Then, they return to the park in dry season." He pulled off his beret and ran a hand over his sweat-covered brow. "Fences now limit options for migration. In many places, they block access to water courses, which are already limited in this part of the world." He squinted, scowling, as if seeing something he'd not seen before. He seemed to shrug it off. "Wildebeest numbers . . . a mere fraction of former abundance. Range compression and truncation affect eland, buffalo, giraffe and Thompson's gazelle, but some of those are not migratory. Wildebeest has been replaced as the dominant herbivore by zebra. Even they are at risk."

"What do you see in a wildebeest migration, numbers wise?"

"Thousands, now. Tens of thousands, before. Now, in some years very few migrate into the park. Fences are to blame, not just for their influence on the migration corridors. Poachers and dogs drive them into the fences and kill them. Populations are not what they used to be." Samuel sat.

Jack plopped down, laying the rifle beside him. "Gabriel's study plan looked at factors related to migration corridors. He also hoped to map and document the decision variables with common range science methodologies. A question is starting to form in my mind. It seems those grazing pressures were already here, if those kinds of herbivore numbers were common. Migration corridors are but one factor to manage. Are there other factors that shape the ecosystem?"

"Fire."

"Explain?"

"Fire was not uncommon on the grasslands. The Maasai use burning to maintain the land for their herds, but those practices are hard to continue, in light of the newer practices of the pastoralists. In the park, grass now grows tall. Some animals want the green re-growth. Others, however, want the tall grass. What would be best would be both, tall grass and green re-growth."

"A mosaic. Wonder why he didn't address fire in the plan?"

"As a phenomena, it is well understood. By researchers at the University of Nairobi. Gabriel's colleagues."

"I see. So Gabriel's work is intended to yield bigger picture data. Something systematic. To leave no doubt?"

"Gabriel believed in science. In many ways, Gabriel was a naïve young man. He would often quote great men, like Hippocrates. Science is the father of knowledge, but opinion breeds ignorance, he would say." Samuel paused, and dropped his eyes to the ground. "I will remember Gabriel more for his own words. He once told me that science is a light. That light cannot be counted upon to shine where you think it will. It will shine only upon the path of evidence. If you stick to that path, he said, you will learn something. Something that will guide you, he said." Samuel stared north, over the expanse of savannah. "I suppose we should go."

"So, you're looking for that light? That path?"

"He deserves to have his work completed." Samuel started toward the Land Cruiser. "Do not forget your rifle, Mr. Jack."

— · —

"Stop," Jack said.

Samuel stepped on the brakes. The Land Cruiser slowed to a stop. He stared out the windshield at savannah. "Why here?"

Jack grabbed the backpack and rifle. He opened the door and slid out. "Next lesson."

"I think we should return to headquarters, Mr. Jack."

Jack slammed the door. Slinging the rifle over one shoulder, he dug into the pack as he walked. Pulling out the PVC, he began assembling the quadrat, veering toward a distant margin of acacia. Nearing its edge, Jack stopped and dropped the quadrat. It settled into the grass. He turned to Samuel. "There. Is that random?"

Samuel looked down, then up, then spun around, eyeing the surroundings as he rubbed the scar on his chin. "It appears random."

"It's not."

"It is not?" Samuel looked confused.

"I chose this spot. I could do this all day. Selecting sites that appear representative, but my bias would affect the results. If we were only studying impacts, we could start at places that show those impacts, but we still need inferences about the larger ecosystem. We need random study sites, and sampling repeated with enough frequency to deal with the variability in the ecosystem." He looked into Samuel's eyes.

He stared back.

Clueless. "Samuel, are you really prepared for this? To go on? You can send me home, I can come back when things blow over."

"Show me. How do we achieve random?"

Jack slipped off a pack strap and pulled Gabriel's plan from the pack. Then, a booklet. "We can achieve random the old way or the new way. The new? Random numbers generators. The old?" He held up a booklet. "This." He flipped through the pages. "It appears Gabriel was rather traditional, maybe because of who he studied under at Oxford. These are random numbers tables. Fortunately for us, he's generated a list of random sampling locations. Places to start. We'll go to those locations, then use the tables to place the quadrat. Make sense?"

Blank stare.

"Okay, let's do this. Assume this was one of Gabriel's study sites. We could lay out a one hundred meter tape, and stake it out, running north." He pointed, then opened the book and turned to a 4 digit table. "The first number is 4139." He stood. "We could be random by following our tape north for forty one meters, then east for thirty nine meters. Then, we'd drop our quadrat, see what we get."

Samuel nodded.

"We'd repeat those steps using the sequence of numbers on the table."

A loud chattering rose up from the east, beyond the line of acacia.

Jack turned. "What's that?"

"Birds. Long-tailed fiscal." Samuel pointed toward a patch of tall grass. "There. Secretary bird."

Streams of plumage. Feathers flowing from yellow eye patches. A terrestrial raptor, stalking on long legs, picking through grass, snapping at the ground. It stood upright, a lizard in its beak. It quickly devoured its prey.

"Uh . . . and . . . uh, that's how we achieve random." Jack stared, amazed. "I have never seen anything like that."

"Follow me," Samuel said.

"Where we going?"

"To water. To see birds. People come thousands of miles to see this."

Jack picked up the quadrat, slung the rifle over his shoulder, and followed.

"We must be careful. We do not want to encounter hippopotamus. If we do, we must avoid threatening their access to water. They are faster than we, and dangerous."

Seemed unlikely, but Jack didn't dispute it.

Beyond the veil of acacia, Samuel stooped and waved Jack over. He pointed. Near-shore, long-legged, black and white birds, standing in a cluster. "Marabou storks," he whispered.

Jack watched as one opened its wings. Huge. Tremendous wingspan.

"Black-winged stilt. Egyptian goslings," Samuel said, pointing to birds near shore.

The stilt pecked in shallow water, the goslings floating nearby.

"And across the way, African spoonbill."

"Too much to take in."

Samuel pulled off his pack, dug out binoculars, and scanned along an arc. "No sign of hippopotamus. Not yet." He pointed, and whispered, "Black rhino. Far end, in the water." He offered the binoculars.

"I see him," Jack whispered back. He watched the beast slog forward, head down, drawing from brown water. "Big guy."

"Yes." Samuel ducked his head, and moved right. He stopped, stared, then turned back. He raised a finger to his lips.

Jack froze.

Samuel waved him to follow.

They crept right, staying behind acacia.

Samuel knelt. Squinting, he stared past thorny branches, scanning the shore.

"What is it?" Jack whispered.

"Sh-h-h-h. I saw something."

Jack turned and looked. Trees. Shadows. A hippo? No. Another rhino? No. "What? A lion maybe?" he asked.

"No," Samuel whispered. "Potentially more dangerous." He continued scanning the shore, then gave a slow nod and pointed. "There."

"What?"

"A man."

Jack searched—in the shadows, along the edges of the trees—seeing nothing.

"He's moving toward the rhinoceros," Samuel whispered.

Through the leaves, Jack could see the outline of the rhino, knee deep, head down, slurping up water.

Samuel dropped to all fours and crawled forward. He stopped and readied his rifle.

Jack fell back, then followed, stopping beside him. "What are you doing?"

Samuel parted the grass with his rifle. "I would try scaring him away, but there may be others. I think he will wait, let the animal return to shore. But is he alone?"

"What if he isn't, and what's wrong with a guy out here watching a rhino?"

"He is not simply watching. He is a poacher."

"How do you know?" Jack turned, disoriented by the ruckus of sound, of birds in abundance. He noticed a head, bobbing in and out of view, moving laterally. "Are you sure?"

"He carries a rifle. He is not a ranger."

The rhinoceros turned, lumbering toward shore.

The man stepped behind a tree, stopping or disappearing in the brush below it.

Samuel stared over the gun sights. "When next he shows himself . . ."

"Samuel, wait!"

Samuel scanned the shore. He reached, tapping Jack on the arm. "There are two." He pointed. "Maybe more."

Jack followed his point, spotting a profile in the brush.

"Can you use that?"

"The rifle?"

"Of course."

"Yes . . . but . . . it's a man."

"Yes, and if he sees you, he will shoot you first."

Jack picked up the rifle and slipped the caps off the scope. What if it's not sighted in?

"Take the one to the right. He's further away," Samuel said. "Okay, this one has shown himself." He leaned into the rifle, peering over the sights. "Quickly, Mr. Jack. He's preparing to shoot."

Jack chambered a round, shouldered the rifle, and put his eye to the scope, aiming where he'd last seen the poacher. Where'd he go?

"Quickly," Samuel repeated.

He searched the shadows, then saw him. Dark skin. Red shirt, sweat drenched. "I see him." Jack set the crosshairs on his chest.

"On two," Samuel said. "One."

He's a kid.

"Two." Rounds pulsed from the AK-47.

Jack lowered the crosshairs and squeezed off a shot. He watched the poacher go down.

Birds took flight, thousands escaping, all directions, the beat of wings horrific.

The sounds died away, leaving only screams of pain.

"The rhinoceros is gone," Samuel said, sounding relieved. He craned his neck. "I do not believe they got off a shot."

Jack lay staring through the scope. The boy rolled in agony.

"I know. It is difficult," Samuel said.

Jack nodded.

"I am sorry to ask you to do that, but the rhinoceros lives."

"How long? How long have you been doing this job?" Jack muttered.

"Twenty years. A long time for a warden." He dug his radio from his pack, exchanged words with someone, then put the radio away. "It is easier for me," he acknowledged. "But I have seen rangers killed. I have seen what is left of rhinoceros after slaughter. I have seen the population of rhinoceros decimated." He got to his feet. "Do not let down your defenses, Mr. Jack. One lives. Scared men are dangerous."

Jack stood, ejected the spent cartridge and chambered another round.

Samuel negotiated his way through the brush, circling the waterhole. No wildlife to be seen, the waters sat dark, no sound other than the moan of someone in extreme pain.

They neared the tree where Samuel's target had stood. A man lay crumpled on the ground, having collapsed where he stood. The man, poor, likely in his twenties, maybe his teens. Old T-shirt, now blood soaked. Holes, not all from bullets. Pants, tattered. Sandals, worn.

Samuel kicked the man's rifle away. An old one. A carbine. He prodded the body. No movement. He stooped and lowered a hand to the poacher's neck. Without words, he moved on, toward the screaming.

Waving Jack to slow, Samuel raised his rifle, slipped past a tree, and stepped forward. He shouted, words Jack could not understand, and kicked the poacher's carbine from reach. He gave the young man a once over, and abruptly looked at Jack. "His leg? You shot him in the leg?"

Jack shrugged. "Sorry. Couldn't do it."

Shaking his head, Samuel turned his attention to the boy. In terse words, he spoke. The poacher, writhing in pain, unloosened his belt and pulled it from its loops.

Samuel placed the belt around his leg, above the knee, then stood and put in a call on the radio. When finished, he turned to Jack. "I have rangers coming to get him."

The boys eyes grew wide.

"His name is Ojwang," Samuel said. "Interesting name. Infers having survived despite neglect."

"Does he speak English?"

"He should. Ojwang, do you speak English?"

"Yes," he said, cringing in pain.

"You are a lucky boy, Ojwang. You could be dead. This man chose to shoot you in the leg. You live. Your friend did not."

He stared at Jack. Scared, hate-filled eyes, appreciation the furthest thing from his mind.

—·—

Two rangers arrived, both extremely tall. The bleeding now slowed, they dressed the wound, put the boy on a stretcher, and loaded him into the bed of their Land Cruiser.

Samuel and Jack stood watching as the vehicle pulled away, the boy screaming.

"Two more rangers are en route," Samuel said. "To protect the rhinoceros, wherever it has gone." He sighed. "The poachers are getting bold."

Jack Chastain sat staring at the white walls of the emergency room lobby. The uncomfortable plastic chair, the intermittent sirens, and the pulses of people coming and going—all seemed minor distractions. With Samuel called away to other duties, Jack sat thinking about the condition of the young poacher, wondering why he would take those kinds of chances, against rangers with AK-47s. Made no sense.

"Mr. Chastain?"

Jack jumped, startled at hearing his own name. He looked up to see a man in the aisle, a big man, nearly filling the space between rows of chairs. He wore a suit and green striped tie, his white shirt glistening against his skin. "That's me," Jack said.

"I know, Mr. Chastain."

"How is he?"

"I am not a doctor, Mr. Chastain."

Jack stood. "Obviously not a nurse."

"No, I am not a nurse." He crossed his arms and glared. "I am Under Secretary Mwangi, Ministry of Environment, Water and Natural Resources."

"Samuel Leboo had to leave. Called away to other business."

"I am not here to speak to Samuel Leboo, Mr. Chastain. I am here to speak to you."

"Something wrong?"

"That depends. Should I be sending you home, Mr. Chastain?"

"Maybe. I've done things I promised my director I wouldn't. And now, there's a kid in a hospital because of me."

"You shot him in the leg, Mr. Chastain."

"I've never done anything like that before."

"It is his leg. He is a poacher. He lives to poach another day."

Jack shrugged. "I suppose, but why would he after this?"

"Let us talk, Mr. Chastain." He swung an arm, gesturing toward the door.

Jack followed him through the door, down the hall, and out through an exit. Heavy traffic filled the street. Mwangi found a sidewalk and slowed to a stroll, locking his hands behind his back. "You asked why he would do that, Mr. Chastain. He is a poacher. That is what poachers do."

"Why face off against rangers with automatic weapons?"

"You make it sound as if the odds are in the ranger's favor? Do you understand what motivates the poacher, Mr. Chastain?"

"Not really. Rhino for its horn, elephant for ivory. That's about it."

"Rhinoceros horn sells for more than sixty-five thousand dollars per kilogram. That makes it more valuable than gold or cocaine, Mr. Chastain."

"Why?"

"Demand. And superstition. The largest demand is from Asia. China and Viet Nam. Rhinoceros horn is used in traditional medicine and—more recently—as a cancer cure, despite the fact that research has shown it to have no medicinal benefit."

"But this is Kenya. Why would Kenyans fall for someone else's superstition?"

"Yes, this is Kenya. What is your point?" He waited, then continued. "Big money, Mr. Chastain. That is the reason. The Asia market is willing to pay big money. Rhinoceros horn and elephant tusk are also trophy. Long they've been valued in the middle east and other parts of the world, and we can only do what we can. The poachers are the little people. There is an endless supply of them. They do it for money, but it is those higher up the chain who benefit most. They are the ones who manage the flow to the markets, and reap the benefit of the big money. If they have people willing to provide a supply, and take all the risk—and there's an endless supply of boys like the one that you shot willing to take that risk—then they can use their operation to generate big money. Some find ways to fund terrorism." He paused. "Al-Shabaab and the Lord's Resistance Army—terrorist organizations—use poaching to bring in millions to support their activities. Do you understand now, the difficulties we face?"

"Is the boy a terrorist? Can he be educated?"

"No, the boy is but a peasant. One of the little people," Mwangi said, impatiently. "He would have no ideological connection whatsoever. And you did not hear me, Mr. Chastain. Our bigger concern is the market for Asia's traditional medicine. Markets are powerful forces. Those in Asia do not want to be educated. Not by us. They want Kenya to provide. Product. Rhinoceros horn and elephant ivory."

"Then, . . . what about . . . laws?"

Mwangi stopped and scanned the cityscape. He pointed. "What do you see there, Mr. Chastain?"

Jack looked down the road. "Uh, . . . a road . . . a traffic light . . . cars."

"What color is the traffic light?"

"Red."

"And what does that mean to you?"

"Stop."

"Yes, and in your answer is the difference. In your country, red means stop. In Kenya, red is . . . maybe stop, maybe go. It is the same in other parts of the world, including parts of Asia."

"Why would it mean both?"

"It doesn't, Mr. Chastain. The difference is, in your society you have rule of law. In our country, we do not have the same rule of law. It is something very different. In your country, people stop when they see a red light. If they don't, if they are caught, they go to traffic court. They pay a hefty fine. Your society understands its norms and accepts the consequences of not abiding by them. Here, that is not the case. If you drive through a red light, you may be stopped by a policeman, but you are more likely to pay a bribe than ever be forced into court or suffer a significant consequence. That is just the way it is."

"That explains the roundabouts." Jack chuckled to himself. "Sorry. That was a joke."

"So, Mr. Chastain, what am I to do with you?"

"I'm here to help with a research project. I'm not here to fight poaching. I screwed up. I will stick to research."

"You see, it's not that simple."

"Did I break the law?"

"Possibly, but I'm not concerned with that, although it could provide leverage." He smiled. "No, in my eyes, you did not, quote, *screw up* by shooting the poacher. You screwed up by shooting him in the leg. You caused me work, Mr. Chastain. Had you killed him, that would have been the end of it, forgotten by tomorrow. But now, if word gets out, there will be questions. People will wonder why I allowed an American to remain here after shooting a native Kenyan." He crossed his arms and scowled. "Or, they will wonder if rangers now shoot poachers in the leg."

Jack stared forward. "I don't deny, I screwed up. But mostly because I should not have been there. And, I had no business being armed."

"So, back to my previous question. Should I send you home?"

"Mr. Mwangi, I'm not finished with my work. I made a commitment. I'm not leaving till I'm done."

"Mr. Chastain, I am not invested in your research. It is of little consequence to me. In fact, I think it best that we avoid useless academic exercises."

"It's not useless. It's important, and it's not finished."

"Mr. Chastain, I am not going to send you home. I simply want you to understand that I can. I want you to realize that someday I could chose to delve into the question of whether you broke the law. Why?" He smiled, big teeth glistening. "At some point, I may look to you for . . . what is known in your country . . . as favors."

Jack stopped walking. "I don't understand."

"It's not important now that you do. And I may not even need such a favor. That is the beauty of it." He laughed. "As I recently heard, only days ago from one of your own, 'tis far better to be owed, than to be the one who owes. My power will come not from calling in the favor, but from you fearing I might." He let the thought settle in. "Remember. I am not indebted to you for coming here to do your research. You are indebted to me for allowing you to stay."

"What'll happen to the boy?"

"Ironically, he'll feel the full weight of our court system. He's a poacher. He matters little to society."

"I want him patched up and sent to me."

"Why?"

"To help. We need assistance carrying out Gabriel Kagunda's work."

"What can he do? He is a peasant."

"If he can't read and write, he can carry things."

"Not very well, Mr. Chastain. You shot him in the leg. He will become a burden. He might even try to kill you. You may wish your aim had been better. And why do I suddenly feel it is you who thinks he can call in the favors?" He allowed himself a bit of smile. "Is the concept of favors something you do not understand?"

"I don't play in quid pro quos. I carry burdens. I shot a young man, for doing something he may not've understood."

"He is a poacher. Some day he may successfully kill a black rhino, or a ranger. Are you willing to carry that burden?"

Jack nodded. "Understood. But unless Samuel disagrees, I would like him patched up and sent back to me."

Mwangi laughed. "Be careful what you ask for, Mr. Chastain."

They reentered the hospital. Inside the waiting room, Samuel stood at the desk, talking to a nurse.

"Warden Leboo," Mwangi said, his voice filling the room.

Samuel turned. He looked straight ahead, his posture almost military, no expression on his face.

Mwangi crossed the floor, stopping his mass just feet from Leboo. Speaking not in English, he used raspy irritated words.

Jack watched as Samuel listened, nodding at moments, appearing to offer no more than maybe so, maybe not.

Abruptly, Mwangi turned. "Goodbye, Mr. Chastain. It is late. Get some rest." He marched himself through the door and was gone.

"Did I get you in trouble?" Jack asked.

"No, Mr. Jack, you did not." Samuel smiled, flashed a look through the corner of his eye, then set them both again on the door. "I did." He appeared to relax.

"What was that about?"

"You do not understand tribal culture, do you?"

"Apparently not. Apparently there's much I don't understand."

"That, my friend, was a reminder. Of my place."

"That he's your boss?"

"Deeper than that, but yes. And to remind me I did not have his permission to forward the request to bring you here. Now, if the poacher boy kills us both, it's my fault. My responsibility."

"He told you, huh? Bad idea?"

He shrugged. "Bad or good, either way, it is going to happen."

Arrangements were made to pick up the boy the next morning, at the hospital.

— · —

After a short night of sleep, Jack woke, brewed coffee, and waited for Samuel, who arrived at sunrise, the agreed upon time. Jack locked up and climbed into the vehicle. "Morning," he said. "You look like hell. Late night investigations?"

"Yes, unfortunately."

"Learn anything?"

"No. Whispers have gone mum. I'm hoping the boy might have something to share."

They drove, sun rising off to the right, the cityscape forward, appearing to sprout from the savannah. In Nairobi, Samuel drove through busy streets to the hospital, parking near the ambulance entrance. He put on his beret, went inside, only for minutes, returning to wait for the boy to be delivered.

A nurse rolled him out in a wheelchair. Leg extended, splinted, and heavily bandaged, and wearing a clean white T-shirt and shorts, the boy appeared nervous, squinting in the sun, looking in all directions, appearing uncertain of what to expect.

Samuel pulled forward. He climbed out, opening a rear door.
The boy's eyes grew wide. "No," he pled to the nurse.

"He is still in considerable pain," she said, handing Samuel a plastic vial. "This should help. Instructions on the bottle."

The boy's eyes moved between the two men.

"Ojwang, you are lucky to be alive," Samuel said. He pointed. "This white man is Mr. Jack Chastain. He is a guest in our country. He is from America. The United States. You will treat him with respect. You will also speak in English in his presence. Understood?"

He nodded.

"Mr. Jack purchased the clothing you wear."

He glanced at Jack.

"I am Senior Warden Samuel Leboo. You will also treat me with respect. For now, you work for me. I am your boss. Understood?"

He nodded, his eyes wide with fear.

"You have nothing to fear."

His eyes moved between them as they helped him into the vehicle, and grew wider seeing the rifles on the floor in the front. For a moment, his pain seemed to capture little of his attention.

"If you even think of touching those, I will shoot you. Do you understand?"

"Yes." He nodded, in violent shakes. He settled into the back, his leg outstretched.

"We are going into the national park," Samuel said. He went around to the driver-side and climbed in. "You have work to do, Ojwang."

"Like this?"

"Like that." Samuel turned to Jack. "If the boy disobeys me, shoot him, and not in the leg."

"I will not disobey you. Please, do not let him shoot me."

"So, you understand me?"

"Yes, but what work can I do? I cannot walk."

"You can carry a rucksack. We will give you crutches."

Jack twisted around to the boy. "Can you read and write?"

Samuel let the vehicle lurch forward.

Ojwang grimaced at the movement. "Yes. I am very smart. I completed my schooling."

"So, if I spelled something and asked you to write it down, you could do so?"

"Yes," the boy said. His eyes turned suspicious. "What am I writing?"

"Science. Consider it all under the broad heading of science."

— · —

Hobbling on crutches, Ojwang followed, wearing a rucksack, in it only a small assortment of gear—the disassembled quadrat, tape measures, and a few other things. Just enough to give him an understanding. In the days to come, his load would grow heavier.

Samuel, in camo uniform, and Jack, wearing a wide-brimmed straw hat he found while looking for clothes for the boy, carried notebooks for recording observations, the plant guides, a GPS unit, enough food and water for three, and the rifles—as much out of respect for the wildlife as a precaution against poachers.

As he walked, Jack studied the map marked with starting points and directions for transect locations, taken from Gabriel's study plan. Consulting the GPS, they arrived at the first location, dropped their bags, and helped Ojwang settle onto the ground, enduring considerable pain. Rifles were laid out of his reach.

Jack took a pencil from his cargo pants pocket and scribbled a few notes in a field book. Date, time, weather conditions, and location. He handed the book to Ojwang. "Be ready to write what I tell you." He tapped on the page. "Right here."

Jack pulled six inch pins from his pack. "Found these in an outbuilding."

"Do they meet our needs?" Samuel asked.

"They'll do." Jack pounded one into the ground with a rock. "You'll need a magnetometer."

"Why?"

"So whoever repeats the measurements can find the pins.

Measuring change over time." Jack pulled a GPS from a cargo pocket. "Write this down, Ojwang." He stood over the pin and read from the GPS. "South, minus one, point three, seven, zero, eight, zero, zero. East, thirty-six, point six, seven, four, nine."

Ojwang wrote.

"Get it?" Jack asked.

He read them back, his expression uncertain. "What are these numbers?"

"Coordinates." Jack turned to Samuel. "You'll want a data logger with a GPS, but this'll do. Learning, the best way to do things is the old way, field books and pencils." He pointed at the tape measure. "This line runs north. Connect to the pin."

Samuel walked out the tape, as Jack consulted the random numbers table, dictating locations.

Jumping into their work, Samuel started naming plants. When he thought he knew the scientific or common name of the plant, Jack would accept it as gospel. When he did not, Jack collected a voucher specimen to key out later. Standing over the quadrats, the two men read off cover classes. Ojwang wrote.

When finished with one plot, they moved to the next, Ojwang hobbling behind them.

After the third set of quadrats, and a twenty minute hike to reposition, they broke for lunch, Samuel digging containers of food from his pack. "Ugali . . . maize and rice," he said, dishing it out. "And, sukuma wiki, which means stretch the week . . . made of collard greens, onions and tomato."

Jack plopped down. He felt the boy staring. "What?"

Ojwang said nothing.

"Boy," Samuel muttered, passing a plate. "Have you never seen a man with blue eyes?"

He shook his head.

"Do not be rude."

"He's okay," Jack said. "I'm sure I'm a strange sight."

"That's where you were yesterday," Samuel said to Ojwang, to divert his attention, pointing at distant trees and a shrub-covered mound.

Beyond the mound, distant chatters of birdlife.

"My leg hurts." Ojwang drew in several breaths. "My possessions. Are they there?"

"We did not take them. We did not see them either. Where do you live, boy?"

He shrugged.

"Where?"

"I have no home. Could we get my bag? I own nothing else."

"Why not?" Jack said, scooping rice with a piece of flat bread. Samuel nodded.

When finished, they packed up and started for the mound.

Approaching, they stayed behind cover and checked for hippo and lion. They saw neither. Again, birds in abundance. Samuel craned his neck, straining to see the furthest end of the waterhole. He waved the others to follow, and worked his way around. He stopped. In the water and moving deeper, a large rhinoceros. "King George," he whispered. "Bull rhino. We do not want to get his attention."

Beyond the bull, lying in shallow water, another rhinoceros and calf.

"Small herd?" Jack asked.

"You rarely see George with other rhinoceros, unless he's following a female. Typical. A herd of rhino is called a crash but rhinoceros are not gregarious. If you see them in numbers, it is in a place such as this, a watering hole." Samuel pulled out his radio and made a call. A brief exchange and he put it away. "Rangers are nearby. They know we are here. We do not want them thinking we are poachers."

Jack glanced at Ojwang. He looked away.

"When rhinoceros leave the watering hole, they go off by themselves. Calves stay with their mothers."

King George dropped and rolled, sending waves across the water.

"George is one of the old bulls," Samuel whispered. "Many of the calves here are his."

"This his harem?" Jack asked.

"Rhinoceros will defend a receptive female, but they are not like other ungulates. They do not have harems."

The female moved toward shore, her calf following. On dry land, she stopped, snorted, and looked about, alert, ears raised.

Samuel backed away, signaling the others to follow. They repositioned themselves behind an acacia.

The rhino approached a shrub and picked at the limbs, pulling off leaves.

Samuel turned to Ojwang. "Where are your possessions?"

His eyes grew wide.

"I will get them. You stay here," Samuel said. "What am I looking for? Where is your bag in relation to where we found you?"

"It is a green Adidas bag. I put it on the ground where we first saw the rhinoceros. Then it moved. I followed." He pointed, left. "So, my bag would be that way." He pointed right.

"I will return shortly." Samuel ducked between acacia and slipped away.

They watched, catching only quick glimpses of his slender profile as he circled the water hole.

After a moment, Ojwang asked, "Are you a ranger?"

Jack nodded. "Yes. In the United States."

"What is that like there?"

"Different wildlife. Deep canyons. We have acacia, but not of the same species."

"Do you like it there?"

"Very much."

"Then, why are you here?"

He laughed. "I was invited. To help with this work."

"Why did you shoot me in the leg? Why did you not kill me?"

"Never killed anyone. Didn't intend to start."

"Do rangers in America only shoot you in the leg?"

"No, but . . . things are different."

"How are they different?"

"Several ways, actually. Being a ranger isn't as dangerous as here, usually." He glanced at the boy. "Second, a thing we call due process."

"What is that?"

"I'm not sure you'd understand." Jack squinted, checking for Samuel at the densely vegetated far end of the waterhole. No sight of him. Only King George. "Look at that creature. Big, strange, intriguing. Why would you want to kill an animal like that, Ojwang?"

"Money. For food. I was hungry."

"Guess it's hard to understand that unless you've been there." He watched the bull rhino take a roll, sending another wake across the water. "I've never been really hungry, but I can look at ol' George there and marvel. Look. Look at that beast. He's part of your heritage, Ojwang. He represents something Kenya is known for."

"I was hungry."

"I understand that. Today, Samuel and I will feed you. Every day we work together, Samuel and I will feed you. But I've got a question. If you were not hungry, if I gave you this rifle, would you want to shoot ol' George?"

"Rangers might shoot me first."

"True, but I'm talking about King George. Look at him. Big, battle scarred. Seen his share of intruders for food and water, intruders hoping to replace him with a female. He's dealt with drought and lack of water. He's learned to deal with heat of the day. He's faced challengers, even predators, and survived. I can't imagine much of anything willing to take on ol' George there, but they have."

The boy watched.

"For an ugly ol' guy, I'd have to say he's quite beautiful in his own way."

Squinting against the sun, the boy's eyes followed the old rhino.

"What if there were no more rhino?"

He flashed a confused look. "There will always be rhinoceros."

"No, they're gone in many places."

"I didn't shoot them."

"I'm talking other parts of Africa. They're gone." Jack let the thought settle over him.

Through the brush they could see the female move toward them, then away, ears turning, listening. Her little eyes searched. The calf stayed close.

Ojwang raised himself upright, braced on his crutches.

She reacted to the movement.

"Be still," Jack whispered.

She stepped toward them.

Ojwang spun around, eyes on the beast, hobbling, grimacing every step.

The rhino reacted, breaking into a trot.

Too late now. Jack dashed toward him. "On my back, quick." Jack caught him, throwing his arms over his shoulders. The crutches fell. "Hold on." Hunched over, Jack dropped the rifle and ran.

The boy screamed with pain, each jarring step.

The female ran, her horn huge—long, looking sharper by the moment.

"Gawd!" Jack shouted.

"It . . . it . . . hurts. Oh . . . oh . . .

He veered toward a tree.

The rhino closed on them.

"Oh, oh . . ."

Jack ducked behind an acacia, buying a second.

She circled, hardly slowing.

Ten feet. A sycamore. Unsubstantial, but . . . The boy began to slip. Hurry. Get there.

"Oh . . . oh . . ."

Jack rounded the tree.

The rhino dug in, sliding to a stop. She snorted, stepped back, then pawed the ground.

"Ha, ha, ha."

That sound? Jack let the boy slide off his back. He peeked around the tree.

"You run pretty well, Mr. Jack," Samuel shouted, the green, nylon bag in one hand, his Kalashnikov in the other. He bent over in laughter. "Like a camel."

The rhino glanced between intruders, ready to charge.

Jack remained quiet.

Her head moved in jerky movements, searching.

Can she see us? Bad eyesight? "This way," Jack whispered, backing away, keeping the tree between them and the rhino.

"My crutches."

"Sh-h-h-h. You'll have to do without. At least till it's safe."

"I can't . . ."

Jack stopped. "Okay, we'll wait."

They stood, no movement.

The rhino pawed the ground, nose to the air, ears moving, then turned and made her way to the calf.

Samuel trudged through tall grass toward them, holding back a laugh. He handed the green bag to Ojwang. "American ranger, praying like a missionary."

"I was not."

Ojwang unzipped the duffle and looked inside.

"You would not be the first to say Hail Marys when chased by a rhinoceros."

"I am not Catholic."

"You appeared a likely convert." He laughed, holding his gut, eye on the female now standing at the edge of the pond.

Ojwang zipped his bag, appearing somehow relieved.

"Funga safari," Samuel said. "Where is our gear?"

"Packs, still by the acacia. Ojwang's crutches, over there." Jack pointed. "What safari?"

"Funga Safari. Swahili for pack up equipment and march. The regimental march for the Kenya Rifles, formerly, the King's African Rifles."

"You in the military?"

"I was, yes."

That explains some things. "Okay, then. Funga Safari."

— · —

At the ranger outpost at the end of the day, they unloaded the equipment from the Land Cruiser, putting it away in the quarters for safe keeping. Ojwang should stay, Jack insisted, and sleep on a mat on the floor. Though concerned about the arrangement, Samuel didn't have a better option—Ojwang last lived in a cardboard shanty on the far side of Nairobi. Inconspicuously, Samuel slipped the thirty-aught-six out to the Land Cruiser, then returned to prepare dinner. His specialty. Pilau. Rice, meat, vegetables and spices. When done, Samuel set the pot on the table, with three tin plates. "Dinner is served."

Jack helped Ojwang into a chair, then settled into his own. "How's your leg?"

"It hurts. I need a pill."

Samuel dished up the meal.

"Did our little run open your wound?"

Ojwang ran his hand over the bandage, stained with blood, now dry.

"How bad is it, by the way?"

He slurped down a spoonful of rice. "Doctor said I was lucky. Three inches lower it would have shattered my knee. The bullet cracked bone and tore muscle."

"Is that where you aimed?" Samuel asked, picking at his food.

Jack gave a nod.

"Then, you're not lucky, boy, you're fortunate. You are lucky I was not the one looking through the sights."

Ojwang dropped his eyes.

"Was the other man your friend?" Samuel asked.

"I guess."

"I am sorry you have one less friend."

"We all die sometime." He shrugged, continuing to eat.

"Hell of an attitude," Jack said. "What's your story, Ojwang?"

"I don't have a story."

"Where are your parents?"

"My mother lives in a village a day from Nairobi. She is poor. It was hard for her to find the food to feed me and her both, so I left to take care of myself."

"Common story," Samuel said.

"She's very proud of me. I am very smart."

"That's good. You say you finished your schooling?" Jack asked.

"Yes."

"Enough schooling to attend university?"

He shrugged.

Jack thought he heard the sound of a vehicle pulling up outside. "We expecting someone?"

Samuel stood. "Gabriel Kagunda's wife. I invited her here, hoping to ease her pain." He turned to the boy. "Either stay inside, or, if she asks, do not mention the reason for the bandage."

He gave a quick nod.

They stepped out into the night, stars shining, the glow of the city to the north.

A ranger opened the door to a Land Cruiser. A woman stepped out. She held a child. A small boy. Bashful. Clinging to his mother. She wore a long dress, brown. She held her eyes down as she approached.

Samuel stepped forward and led her onto the porch.

"Njoki, this is Mr. Jack. Jack Chastain. A scientist from America."

Struggling with emotion, she fought to raise her eyes.

"I'm pleased to meet you. I am sorry for your loss," Jack said.

"Thank you." Close to tears, she bowed her head.

"I've read the things written by your husband." Jack touched his hand to the boy's arm. "Your father appears to have been a very fine scientist."

"Thank you." Njoki wiped her eyes. She turned to Samuel. "Do you know who killed Gabriel?"

"I do not. Not yet."

"Will you ever?"

He didn't answer.

She held her stare. The moment grew long.

"Mrs. Kagunda," Jack said, to break the tension, "as we start on his transects, we . . ."

Her eyes shot over, then back to Samuel. "You are continuing Gabriel's work?"

"Yes," Samuel said. "I promise, I will return what belonged to him."

"Why would you? It is not safe."

Samuel dropped his eyes.

"Gabriel so wanted to return to Kenya," she said, to Jack. "He had so prepared himself for his work. That's all he thought about. Coming home to work. To raise our son. I thought I wanted to return as well." She looked into her son's eyes. "Now, I find myself wishing we had not. My son would still have his father." She looked up. "I'm sorry, Mr. Chastain. You have come so far, but go home. There are dangers here. Go home. Do not deprive your sons and daughters of their father. Go home."

"I have no children."

She looked away. After a moment, she turned to the young ranger beside the truck. "Take me home." She faced Samuel. "Do not let them kill him," she muttered, pointing at Jack. She moved toward the vehicle. "I do not want Gabriel remembered for having gotten him killed." She climbed inside.

The three watched the vehicle pull away.

Ojwang leaned against the building. "Does she want us to not do what we did today?"

Samuel stared at the tail lights. "This is a difficult time, but why wouldn't she want her husband's work to continue? This was his life. His purpose. It's what he will be remembered for." He sighed. "If people do not remember him . . . then, . . ."

"I will build a monument," Ojwang said. "Where should it be?"

Samuel shook his head. "He would not want a monument. He would want his work to be completed. Carried forward."

"Then I will do his work."

"Unfortunately, Ojwang, neither you nor I can do much."

"Why?"

"Because we are not scientists. Mr. Chastain is a scientist. We can only help."

"I will become a scientist," Ojwang said. "I can finish his work. How do I become a scientist?"

"Boy, I am afraid the fates are not on your side." He turned to Jack. "I will see you in the morning. Get some sleep."

CHAPTER

13

"Where's the boy?" Samuel asked, barging in the door.

Jack stepped aside, coffee in one hand, the other rubbing the now dark stubble on his chin. "There, sleeping. Needed pain pills in the night. Conked him right out."

Samuel put his hands on his hips and let out a sigh. He pulled off his beret and ran a hand from forehead to neck.

"What's wrong?"

"Nothing. I was worried for your safety."

Jack took a sip. "I'm fine. He's harmless, but you look awful. Worse by the day. Midnight investigations?"

"No. Maybe I should have. There is a rumor about, concerning one of the poaching rings, but no, I was not investigating. I simply was struggling with what to do."

"Because of her reaction? Gabriel's widow?"

"Yes."

"In time, she'll feel differently."

"And if she does not?"

"There's a reason you supported his research. That hasn't changed. You have to do what you have to do."

"It is not that easy. And what are we to do with Gabriel's possessions?"

"Give 'em back. We can copy the study plan, go to a bookstore, get 'em to order the plant key and guide. Get me to a hardware store, I'll make a quadrat and get you a tape measure."

Samuel stared, eyes uncertain.

"In time, she'll be glad you did this." He waved Samuel into the kitchen. "Come. Have a cup of coffee. Let the boy sleep."

"I do not drink coffee."

Jack poured himself another cup. "African coffee's pretty good. You should try it." He sat. "So, what's this about a rumor?"

"A major poaching ring is supposedly being pushed to get out of the business."

"That's good."

"Yes and no. Others want the boss man's turf."

"But if there's one less . . ."

"This man, apparently a vindictive son-of-a-bitch, is getting everything he can, trying to burn the intruders. Leave them with little to supply their markets." Samuel sighed. "It is a dangerous time. This man is taking risks, scoring big, planning to disappear." He clenched his fists.

"What can you do?"

"I do not know."

Jack saw Ojwang standing at the door, braced on his crutches. "Good morning."

Samuel turned.

"I am ready," Ojwang said. "To do science. To complete Gabriel Kagunda's research."

— · —

"Funga safari," Ojwang said, having packed away the quadrat and slipped on the rucksack. He hobbled off.

"The other way," Jack said, pointing east. "Toward the road, then north." He and Samuel began to hike.

Ojwang followed.

A line of wildebeest worked a dusty trail across the savanna. Jack walked and watched, studying the curve of their horns, their rangy conformations. Gazelle, small by comparison, trailed alongside.

In the distance, zebra grazed, scattered about a hollow.

An impala darted into view, stopping, then starting. From nowhere, a cheetah appeared, circling. The predator burst into a run, diving onto the back of the impala, digging fangs into its neck, dragging it down. The impala lay motionless. The cat dragged the kill into the brush.

"What a show!" Jack said, in awe.

"Yes," Samuel said.

"All this wildlife. Amazing."

"Before the farms came to the south, you would see thousands of wildebeest migrating north from the Athi-Kapiti Plains. Then, during the rainy season, they would migrate south, again by the thousands. They may soon be gone. At least here. Zebra and other animals will continue seasonal migrations, but for how long? When will it cease for them?"

Jack noticed Ojwang listening. "Samuel, you're beginning to master this methodology. Enough to keep it going."

"What are you saying?"

"Big picture, the most important work may be the latter phases. Where Gabriel hoped to isolate variables related to migration corridors and ecosystem connectivity. Data to objectively tackle the issue."

Samuel nodded. "Are you proposing we stop this phase of the work?"

"Not yet, but I'll review the study plan and be ready to dive into that part of the study."

Samuel nodded.

"Check the GPS. We may be close."

Samuel read the coordinates, and veered south. They found the location, nailed in a pin, and stretched out the tape. Ojwang settled onto the ground to record.

The radio squawked. Samuel listened. Excited voices died away. "I must go."

"Where?"

"Funga safari?" the boy asked.

"You stay. I must go," Samuel said.

"What's wrong, and where's the vehicle?"

"Over that rise." Samuel pointed. "I cannot wait."

Jack helped Ojwang to his feet. "Get started. Go. You too, Samuel. I'll pack up and run."

Samuel grabbed his pack and started walking, quickly catching the boy.

Jack reeled in the tape, disassembled the quadrat, and ran for the Land Cruiser. He reached it just before Ojwang, got him settled inside, and threw everything into the back.

Samuel punched the gas, accelerating onto the road, speeding south.

Another Land Cruiser fell in behind.

They pulled off the main road, onto dirt track, bouncing over ruts and rock.

Around a bend, another Land Cruiser came into view, parked alongside the track. They pulled behind and stopped.

"Stay inside," Samuel said to the boy. He picked up his rifle and slipped out. Standing in the door he turned to Jack. "A ranger did not make it back to post, and did not check in on schedule." He slammed the door and took off, into the bush.

Jack watched, then grabbed his rifle and followed.

Samuel crept past scrub, into an opening. Eighty meters ahead, maybe less, a carcass lay in the grass. A rhino.

Samuel moved toward it, then walked past, his eyes searching for signs.

Jack stopped. A massive rhino, on its side, pools of blood on the ground. Horn, gone. Saw marks, jagged. Nothing left but a stump. A bloody head. King George.

Samuel turned. "You should not be here. Go back." He reached for his radio, spoke a few words, and listened to the response. He broke into a run.

Jack followed.

At an opening between trees, Samuel raised his rifle, stepped forward, then spun around. He noticed Jack, then held up a hand. He inched forward.

Two rangers broke into the clearing, rifles ready.

Samuel pointed them toward an opening to the left. He went right.

They slipped through a break in the acacia. A ranger sent out a holler.

Samuel bolted toward them.

One ranger stood staring at the ground, face contorted. The other dropped to his knees.

Samuel slowed, stopping beside the body. He stooped closer.

A woman, in uniform, lay flat on the ground, blood pooled beside her, a rifle a few feet away.

"She is alive," Samuel muttered. He turned to the ranger backing away, fear on his face. "Bring your vehicle. Go."

The young man took off in a run.

Jack slipped closer.

Samuel held his fingers to her carotid. "Marsha. Can you talk?"

She swallowed, and tried to speak, making only guttural sounds.

"Rest. You will be okay. We will get you to hospital." Samuel turned to the other ranger. "Have you bandages?"

He pulled a kit from a cargo pocket.

Samuel peeled away the paper, and pulled back her shirt, placing the gauze gently over the wound. He pulled back his hand, now bloody, and wiped it off on his pants. "You will survive this," Samuel said, leaning over her ear, forcing an encouraging tone. "You are a brave woman. A good ranger."

He stayed beside her until a vehicle arrived.

They loaded her in.

"Be quick. Do not throw her around. I will be behind you."

—·—

An ambulance sat waiting at the park entrance. They surrendered the ranger to the care of a medic. He transferred her to the big, boxy vehicle. They watched it speed away, lights flashing.

Samuel shouted something in Swahili, and pointed at Ojwang.

The young ranger dashed over and escorted Ojwang to his vehicle. "Leave him at the outpost," Samuel said.

"Me, too?" Jack asked.

"You, come with me." Samuel got into his truck and started the engine.

He drove without speaking. Eyes set, brow furrowed, he stared at the road, sharing nothing.

A sign came into view, arrow to the left.

Jomo Kenyatta International Airport.

Samuel took the turn, then a roundabout. He locked his arms on the wheel, "I am sending you home, my friend." He glanced over. "Someone is preying on rhinoceros and rangers. He has grown bold, and I have been Nero, fiddling while Rome burns, pretending I can be a scientist. Pretending I can continue something a widow now begs me to cease. I have been a fool."

"You're no fool. It's important work. Work that must be finished."

"Maybe so, but no, we will not finish. I need to concentrate on finding a poacher. A killer. I need to attend to the welfare of my rangers. I have failed them, and I risk getting you killed. Njoki is right. Today, poachers could have been hiding in the bush, crosshairs on you. The bullet would not have been aimed at your leg."

"I should have stayed in the truck. Sorry, but . . ."

"Your things are being brought from the outpost. Thank you for coming all this way. Thank you for trying to help. It was all foolishness. I apologize."

"I don't need an apology, Samuel. I don't need to be sent home. I can work on Kagunda's project alone, while you focus on bad guys."

"Gabriel's project will have to wait, until it is safe. Until real researchers from university feel it is safe to return. If we lose ground, if politicians deny me the chance to restart his work, so be it. I need to focus on catching a poacher before he kills more rangers."

"What'll happen to the boy?"

"I will try to find a way . . . a way to take care of him." He paused. "To keep him from going back to being a poacher."

Samuel slowed, pulled out of traffic, and stopped alongside the road.

"Why are we stopping?"

"This is a hotel. Very nice. Posh. Five-minute shuttle to the airport. You can fly out tomorrow."

Jack glanced out the window. Multi-story building. A sign. *Nairobi Skies Hotel.* "No, Samuel. I'm not running out on your project."

"You told me yourself, you have priorities that require your attention. You are free to go." Samuel raised a hand, dismissing him. "Go, take care of your business."

"Those things can wait."

"Tell the desk clerk to expect a call from Kenya Wildlife Service, regarding payment."

Jack climbed out and offered his hand, but Samuel's eyes were on the mirror, watching traffic. He closed the door.

Samuel sped off, swerving wildly onto the road. The Land Cruiser turned into a roundabout, then onto a side street, disappearing in the traffic of Nairobi.

CHAPTER
14

Jack stood watching cars speed by, his pack on the ground at his feet.

Now what? What options are there? None but going home.

He slung his pack over his shoulder, and sauntered toward the hotel.

A blue-coated doorman snapped to attention, took hold of the door, and swung it open.

"Thanks." Jack plodded in and approached the registration desk.

A young man, in a crisp, pressed suit, glided up to the counter. He smiled. "May I help you, sir?"

"Guess I need a room for the night?"

"Yes, sir. How many in your party, sir?"

"Me."

"If you would like, sir, we have a suite with a courtesy bar, stocked with the best liquor from Great Britain and America. And, if you have special requests, I'm sure we can accommodate them, sir."

"Smallest, cheapest room available. I'll give you my credit card, but Kenya Wildlife Service will supposedly call to pay for the room."

"Very good, sir."

"Do you have wireless?"

"Yes sir. It works best here in the lobby, or in the lounge, sir. Your credit card, sir."

Jack handed it over.

"Passport or other identification?"

He dug it out of his pack. "My bag will be delivered sometime tonight."

"I will be working all evening. I will assure that it gets to your room, sir." He finished the paperwork and slid it across the counter. "Your signature, sir."

Seeing the nightly rate gave him pause, but he signed on the dotted line, took the key, and headed for the elevator. On seeing the lounge, he veered toward it and peeked inside.

Mounted heads and pith helmets. Safari theme down to the wall hangings. Drinks and loud patrons. He stepped in and wove through the tables, passing a group recounting stories, and another laughing and telling jokes. At one table sat a young Germanic couple gazing into each other's eyes. A woman seated by herself nursed a cocktail. A pot-bellied Anglo—in maybe his fifties—sat hunkered over a laptop, punching keys, staring at the screen. Jack slipped past him, taking a table in the corner. He pulled out his phone and switched it on, first time in days.

A waiter in short coat and tie stopped at the table. "May I get you something to drink, sir?"

"Beer. Stout."

"Very good, sir." He left for the bar.

The phone cycled through its processes. Charge on the battery, not a lot. Phone signal, adequate. Wireless? He checked the options. *Nairobiskieshotel.* He clicked to connect, and watched as email flooded in. When finished, over two hundred new messages sat waiting. Among them, several from Karen Hatcher and Kip Culberson, both asking first for the report to Congress, then for an update, then for any information at all. The clock is ticking. Supporters of legislation are growing nervous.

Sorry folks. Things didn't go as planned. He checked his watch. Nearly six p.m. Nine hours earlier in New Mexico. Until I get my laptop, you'll have to wait, but you'll have it soon enough.

Molly should be in dispatch by now. He typed a quick email.

"Molly, could you book me a flight for tomorrow, Nairobi to Washington, D.C.? Let's wait on the leg back to New Mexico. Need a room. Rosslyn's easy. Thanks."

He pushed send. *Not exactly the way I expected to leave Nairobi.*

The waiter arrived with a pint of Guinness. "Will this be adequate, sir?"

"Very much so, yes." He set the phone aside and took a sip. *Starting to talk like Samuel.*

Samuel. Sitting in a hospital, praying his ranger will survive. Poor guy.

And now, another dead rhinoceros. A survivor of so many battles, but not the poacher's bullet. One country's heritage, put on a timeline to extinction because of another culture's silly traditions and unsubstantiated cures—the availability of which will end when the one country's heritage is gone.

Ironic, and stupid.

And not Samuel's only worry.

Encroachment. Migration being choked off. The need for research. Politics. And, of course, being the one to assign rangers to work that can mean maiming or death.

Tough job.

Is he being foolish? In over his head? Out gunned? Unsupported? Living in a society with a different set of rules?

Jack picked up the phone and checked for email. *No response from Molly, but it's early. She's just starting her day.* He took another sip.

A ring sang through the room. The man at the next table fumbled for his phone. "Bubba. You here?"

American. A loud one.

"Good. . . . Still at the airport? . . . You're kidding. . . . How long will that take?"

Accent. What is it? Louisiana? Don't people in Louisiana know how to whisper?

"This is a wild-ass place," the man said. "You don't wanna drive here. . . . No. . . . You thought those ol' boys in mud trucks down on the bayou were crazy. Wait till you see 'em driving here at rush hour." He laughed, nodding, as though Bubba were sitting across the table.

Ignore this guy. Jack picked up his phone and checked again for an email from Molly. Still nothing. Why is everyone in here so damned loud?

"We're in luck," the man whispered. "No. I found a guy. Yeah."

Better.

"Has to be tonight," the man said, his voice even lower. "After tomorrow, he's out of here."

Now, his whispering is hard to ignore.

"Yeah. Both."

Both. Both what?

"Yeah . . . yeah."

The man turned.

Jack looked into his glass, feeling the man study him. He picked up his phone.

The man cupped his hand over his mouth. "No, I told him that's not sportin'. We need to do it ourselves." He paused, listened, then, "It's not cheap, and he says it's hard to guarantee more than one. Says they're solitary, but he'll see what he can do."

Jack took a sip, eyeing the blank screen on his phone.

"Come to the hotel, but we're changing plans. Our guy suggested a safari camp a few miles away. Says it's a better place to work from. Our guy will have 'em send over a vehicle. He'll meet us here."

Jack took another sip.

The man dropped his hand. "If your bags are lost, you'll be fine," he said, no longer whispering. "They've got bush clothes in the hotel shop. We can have a beer and head over."

The man ended his call. He looked around the room.

Jack felt the man's glare as he feigned a few taps on his phone, took a sip, and gave it two more taps.

The man ordered another beer. When it arrived, he took a long, slow swig, and turned back to his laptop, punching keys and staring at the screen.

Jack let a few moments pass, then raised his glass and stared over the rim, noting everything he could about the man. Every feature, head to toe. Brown hair, chubby face, knobby nose, yellow shirt, tan polyester cargo pants, cheap boots from an American outdoor outfitter.

He set down the pint and stood. "Which way to the loo?" he asked, faking a hint of an accent.

The waiter pointed into the lobby.

Jack slipped into the hall and walked outside. He pulled up the number for Samuel Leboo, given him by the director and saved on his phone before leaving the States. No answer. It rolled over to Samuel's recorded message. On it, Samuel gave an emergency number.

Jack called the number. It rang into dispatch for Kenya Wildlife Service. "Can you reach Samuel Leboo?"

"I can try his radio? Why? Who is this?"

"Jack Chastain, the ranger from America. Tell Samuel, I think I've found him a poacher. One who hopes not to be here much longer."

"Standby, please."

He listened to the call go out over the radio. Voices alternated in conversation—the woman in dispatch, and Samuel, his voice shifting from withdrawn to alert.

The dispatcher came back on the phone. "Where should he meet you?"

"The hotel. Tell him to wait nearby. When they're ready to go, I'll call you. You, then, can call him. He can pick me up behind the building."

He listened as the dispatcher relayed the information.

Samuel agreed. He was on his way.

— · —

A zebra-striped Land Cruiser pulled under the porte cochere. The driver exited and rushed inside. In a seat in the bed of the vehicle, under a fringed canvas awning, sat a man, white, relaxed or three sheets to the wind, one foot on the gunnel and an arm over the seat back. He wore sunglasses, a battered felt hat, khaki pants, and a linen shirt.

Jack made mental notes, watching from a window in the lounge.

The blue-coated doorman swung the door open and stood at attention. Two men—one in safari jacket and Tilley® hat—walked out, followed by the driver pulling their luggage. He took them around to the tailgate and helped them into the back. With handshakes exchanged with the man in the sunglasses, they settled in for the ride.

"Safari Shelly's Safari Camp," Jack muttered to himself, reading the words on the side of the Land Cruiser. Rather redundant. He pulled out his phone and called. "This is Chastain. Call Samuel. I'll meet him out back." He listened as the message was relayed.

He dropped a thousand shilling banknote on the table, downed the last of the Guinness, and left the bar.

Watching the zebra-striped vehicle turn onto the road, Jack stepped through the door, hung a right, and quickly walked to the back.

A Land Cruiser sat idling in the alley.

Jack slipped into the passenger side.

Samuel took hold of the gear shift. "Which way?"

"Right. Safari Shelley's."

Samuel dropped his hand. "That is easy." A tired smile came over him. "Let us think this through. Take our time. It is just beyond the end of the fence, on the west side of the park. Small, luxury safari camp. You can identify the man?"

"The ones who hired him, yes, without a doubt. The poacher, maybe."

"That gives us a start."

Jack noticed the lines on his face. His dazed, exhausted eyes. "Samuel, you need rest. Maybe we should call for help."

"Yes, we should, but we will not," Samuel said, slapping the Land Cruiser in gear. "We are not waiting. We are not letting this son of a bitch get away."

Outside the city, Samuel pulled off the road, killed the engine, and appeared to organize his thoughts. He checked his gear—a flashlight, multiple sets of flexi cuffs, and rifle. Exchanging the magazine for another, he decided to take two more, slipping them into a cargo pocket. Then, he took a deep breath, let it out, and turned. "I will try not to get you killed, my friend, but I need you to identify these men."

"Understood."

"You identify them, then leave."

"No." Jack reached behind the seat and pulled a handful of Springfield shells from the case of the thirty-aught-six. "Won't let you go it alone." He put the shells in his pocket. "Shouldn't be dangerous."

"It can be. Before I can act I need proof they are poachers. That means, they may be armed."

"Understood."

"When I am ready to engage, if I do, you promise to leave?"

"Fair enough."

Samuel checked the sky. "It will be dark when we get there."

"That good or bad?"

"Depends. On how soon they head into the bush. And, who has the jump on whom." He started the vehicle and pulled onto the road.

CHAPTER
15

Samuel stopped and turned off the headlights. He sat, possibly letting his eyes adjust to the night.

Jack squinted, trying to make out more than flickering lights through the trees.

After a moment, Samuel eased his foot onto the gas pedal and inched the Land Cruiser forward. He turned onto the approach road. Two hundred meters in, he pulled into the brush and killed the engine. "We walk from here."

He grabbed his rifle and slipped out, closing the door with no sound. Jack did the same.

Samuel stepped off the road, moving quickly through the brush, Jack behind him. Approaching the main lodge structure, Samuel slowed, glanced around, then crept forward.

On the back side, lights, activity, laughter, conversation. Staying in the shadows, Samuel moved along the rail surrounding the deck. He peeked into the great room. He waved Jack forward.

Jack slipped alongside.

"Are they here?" Samuel whispered.

Jack raised himself high enough to see over the rail. Half a dozen tables. Four occupied. Women at each. None of the men looked familiar.

They stepped back.

Jack shook his head, confused. "They're not there," he whispered. "Did . . . did we lose 'em?"

Samuel pointed right.

Lantern lights. Half a dozen tents on the edge, overlooking savannah. Canvas wall tents, pitched over wooden platforms.

Samuel ducked and moved toward them, staying off-trail, out of the light.

They approached the first tent. A lantern illuminated a table and two empty chairs.

They moved toward the next tent. A waiter in white bush jacket approached, scurrying up the trail, head down, carrying a tray laden with covered plates. Samuel pulled Jack by the arm, into the shadows. The waiter, not seeing them, entered the third tent on the row. In a matter of moments, he was back on the trail, heading to the lodge.

They stepped out of the shadows, on to the next tent.

The second, same configuration. Under the lantern sat a man and woman, eating dinner.

On to the third tent.

Two couples.

The next tent, empty.

The fifth tent, empty.

The last tent. It sat at a distance, off to itself.

The waiter approached, marching head down, carrying a tray, this one with bottles.

Samuel pointed Jack into the brush. They crept back, out of the reach of the lights.

Jameson Irish Whiskey. Bombay Gin. Bucket of ice. The waiter vanished behind the tent, reappearing as a shadow against the back wall. He set the tray on a stand, bowed and backed away. "Very good, gentlemen," he said. He returned to the trail, and hurried toward the lodge.

They waited, listening to the waiter's footsteps. Then, quiet. Too quiet. Too far from the noise. Jack noticed his own breathing. If not careful, they'll hear us.

"Must be the one," Samuel whispered. "That, or we lost them.

Wait here." Taking the rifle in both hands, he crept forward, stopping at a corner of the tent. He crouched behind an acacia.

Jack watched. Shadows lined the back wall of the tent—the wooden tent frame, ropes, a pair of headboards—but no outlines of people. Just low mutterings from the other side of the tent.

Samuel waved him forward.

Jack snuck to the tent, head down, holding the thirty-aught-six. He stopped at the acacia and peeked around the corner.

Three men in camp chairs, around a campfire. The backs of two heads. The third man obscured by the others. Faces. Let's see your faces.

". . . took two shots to bring him down," said one man. He laughed. "Never been so damned scared in my life. Couldn't believe a wild pig could turn on ya like that."

Another man threw back his head and laughed. "You dumb shit." He reached for the gin on the tray two feet away.

"That's a fret. You gents need some real high adventure," said a third voice.

Irish brogue? Jack leaned in to listen.

"That ain't danger," the man continued. "I'll give you danger. None of that piddly-ass hog shit."

The other two exchanged glances. "Come on," one said, sounding insulted. "Hogs can kill you. They're not child's play." He leaned over his knees.

Jack saw the third man's face. The man in the felt hat.

The Irishman smiled and took a sip of his drink. "Then, why are you two here in Africa?"

"What are you saying?"

The Irishman shook his glass, rattling ice. "Hit me."

The man nearest the table reached for the whiskey. He poured.

The Irishman took a sip. "You've run out of tales. You're down to boring stories about pigs. You're here for trophy. You're here for excitement. You're here to prove you're a man. To have a story or two to share at the pub. A trophy to show your friends. One they'll never forget, or be able to beat."

"Hell, I don't care what other people think."

"Hell, you don't."

Jack stepped back. "It's them," he mouthed to Samuel.

Samuel nodded. "I want to listen," he mouthed.

The pourer refreshed his own drink, then sat. He turned to the Irishman. "Is it time to go?"

"No. Soon, but not yet. Never hurts to let the right people settle in for the night." He smiled, and gave his glass an appreciative look. "Patience. Relax. Enjoy your whiskey." He turned his eyes to the fire. "I'll let you know when it's time."

"Is this how you make your livin'?" asked the man in the safari jacket.

The Irishman looked up. "You ask a lot of questions." He tilted the glass back. He stood, stepped over to the tray table, scooped up some ice, and poured whiskey to the brim. "There. That's more like it." He sipped as he made his way to his chair. He looked into eyes of the man with the question. "Consider me a businessman."

"What kind of businessman?"

"What do you think?"

"This kind of business?"

He broke into a laugh. "Okay, you got me." He took another sip. "I'm what you call a supplier. You need it, I get it. I know who needs supply. I know who to turn to for inventory. Or rather, I know where to find people willing to get me that inventory. I've got a network. I know people in the right places. When the wrong people start sniffing around, I have people in the right places to take care of that. People who owe me favors."

"You mean, you don't typically work with people like us?"

"I do and I don't."

The Americans gave each other confused looks.

"You saying, we approached the wrong guy?" asked the man from the bar. "You do know what you're doing out here, don't ya? In the bush, I mean."

"Quare, gentlemen, quare. Yes, you stumbled onto the right man. At the right time, because I'm gettin' out of the business. Takin' my profits." He cleared his throat. "A bit of advice. Next time you approach a man at an outfitter, take a little better care. You're liable to get yourself shot or arrested. You're lucky I saw you as packing shillings. No point lettin' someone else take your money."

"You drunk?"

The Irishman focused his eyes on the glass, his head bobbing. "You think I can't handle my whiskey?" He gave a hard stare, then laughed. "We're only on our third shoulder. No worries. I'm just being sociable. Who am I not to enjoy a man's company, and his whiskey?" He laughed and took another sip. "Where was I? Oh, yes." He cleared his throat. "Like all good businessmen, I typically let others take the risk getting product." He laughed. "But, when I see a consumer needing product, on deadline, and if they understand the value of the product, like you two fine gentlemen . . . then I don't mind helping 'em myself—if I can trust 'em. I can trust you gents, can't I?" He locked eyes on one. "Of course, I can, you drunken bastards."

"So you know what you're doing?"

The man shook his head in disbelief. "What did I just tell you?"

"It's just that . . ."

"Look, I've got product with your name on it," he said, slur starting to show in his speech. "Scouted it today. It's nearby unless someone chased it away. We simply need to go get it." He took a long gulp. "You're lucky. You stumbled onto the man. I can even get it delivered, straight to your door."

"So, you da man?"

He took a sip and flashed a smile. "Guarantee it. I guarantee everything. You gents will go home with souvenirs."

"I'm starting to think you're full of it," said the man in the safari jacket. "Not even a little uncertainty? I mean, this is hunting."

He glared. "Nope, none."

The men looked at each other. "Nothing's that certain," one said.

Samuel pulled Jack back from the tent. "It's time for you to leave."

"Heard all you need?"

"Not yet. I've heard everything, yet I fear I have heard nothing. If indeed he has people in high places protecting him . . . then . . ."

"I'll wait."

They slipped back to the tent.

Laughing, the Irishman reached into a nylon bag on the ground, and pulled out a binoculars-like piece of equipment, with a head strap. "Know what these are?"

One shrugged. The other shook his head.

"Night vision goggles. Not the latest model, but they get the job done."

"Where'd you get those?" said the man from the bar.

"An arrangement made with a man needing product."

He took another sip and pulled out a dark, six inch cylinder from the bag. "And this?"

"Silencer?"

"Hell no, I ain't one to carry something as criminal as a si-lencer." He threw back his head and laughed. "This, gents, I prefer to call a suppressor."

The man from the bar leaned forward, studying the cylinder. "Aren't those just different words for the same thing?"

"Silencer sounds so . . . criminal . . . so . . . Hollywood."

"Ever run into game wardens out here?"

"Rangers?" He waited for nods. "All the time."

"Ever been arrested?"

"I never let it get that far."

The man from the bar let out a sigh, appearing to relax.

The man in the safari jacket glanced at his friend, then back at the Irishman. "What does that mean?"

The Irishman laughed. "You're such a candy-ass."

"Why do you say that?"

"Because you are. Like a client a few weeks back. Another candy-ass from the States. Needed product. Worked for someone who wanted to impress some Saudi prince with a nephew in Ye-men. This man's boss heard the prince wanted to give his nephew a jambiya for his fourteenth birthday."

"What is a jambiya?"

"A knife. A saber. Carried by Yeminis and other assorted Arabs. Worn with a sash at the waist. The finest are made from the horn of the rhinoceros."

"I thought rhino horn went to China . . . or Viet Nam. Traditional medicine or some sorta shit."

The Irishman laughed. "Gents, I don't believe you two are from China . . . or Viet Nam."

"No, but. . . ."

The poacher staggered to the drink tray and poured another drink. He gave a long look at what was left in the bottle, tipped it back and drained the last of the whiskey. He tossed the empty into the savannah, beyond the light of the lanterns. He dropped into his seat. "You know the funny thing about it all." He looked up, then into his glass. "I got three horns that night. Two adults and a year old calf. My client got his horn. Put it in a box. Leather, gold trim. To be picked up at the airport, carried to the prince by some big shot from America. Very big, supposedly. Wouldn't do to have it delivered by an average Joe like you or me. Had to be someone important. And as far as I know, the prince got his horn." He laughed.

"What's funny about that?"

"Three horns." He took a sip. "One to help in a business venture. From someone in the United States. A country at war with terrorism." He laughed. "The other two horns? Well, let's just say, when horns go to that buyer, the proceeds end up in the coffers of the local franchise of al Qaeda."

"You sold to al Qaeda?" said the man from the bar.

The Irishman shook his head, letting out a laugh of disdain.

"What'd you mean, you never let things get that far?" asked the man in Safari jacket.

The Irishman raised his glass. "Damn, you're both candy-asses. Worse than my client a month ago. Or was it weeks? Doesn't matter. Two rangers, hangin' round near the rhino. Never saw it coming. That's the beauty of the suppressor. But the courier . . . a man who came all the way from the States . . . New Mexico . . . to receive and deliver the product to the big shot . . . he panicked. Wanted to leave. Woulda, had he not been expected to deliver the product to the airport. Hell, I coulda gotten it to the airport, but no, they wanted this guy. Took a whole bottle of Jim Beam to calm his nerves. Candy-ass American whiskey won't calm a man's nerves. But this, your choice of whiskey, it'd do. Not the best but I'm not complaining."

Jack leaned in to hear. New Mexico? That can't be right. He watched the man from the bar get to his feet.

The man glared, jaw trembling. "Bubba, let's go."

"Where to?"

"I don't know, but let's go." He turned to the Irishman. "Forget it. Forget we ever talked. We're not going through with this."

The poacher reached into the bag and pulled out a rifle.

Eyes grew wide. "That's not a hunting rifle," one said.

"No, it's not, and yet it is. This is an AK-74, advanced version of the AK-47. Effective range, six hundred meters. And no, it's not designed as a hunting rifle. Its purpose is more utilitarian." He smiled. "Dropping a rhino might require more rounds, but at seven hundred a minute, I'm prepared if I bump into someone who shouldn't be here." Smiling, he stood, and on steady legs knelt over the bag and pulled out the suppressor. With eyes on the man from the bar, he twisted the suppressor onto the barrel. "So, gents, let's get this straight. It's too late to back out. We've got a deal. You don't have to come, but you sure as hell are paying for the product. If you're gone when I return, I'll track you down. I'll find ya."

Samuel stepped back, pushing Jack into the shadows. "Leave," he whispered, then raised his rifle and moved into position. He peeked over the acacia.

From where he stood, Jack could see almost everything.

A hat hung from the back of a chair. Two men from Louisiana sat shocked and speechless, staring into the darkness.

The Irishman was gone.

"Watch those men," Samuel whispered.

"Samuel, he's a killer. The toys he has, you'll never see it coming. Get help."

"This is my fight. If I wait, he kills more rhinoceros." He pointed at the other two. "Do not let them leave. Shoot them if you have to. And not in the leg." He skirted around the tent without sound, and disappeared in the undergrowth.

Jack chambered a round, stepped forward, and listened. Nothing.

The men sat staring into the fire. After a moment, the man from the bar looked up at his friend, then away. The other man seethed, eyes not moving.

Jack backed away, pulling into the shadows. These guys are in over their heads, and they know it.

—·—

Samuel Leboo slowed, and eyed a shadow at a bend in the trail. Is that him? No. A tree. Or is it? He squinted, letting his eyes adjust. No movement.

Where is he?

If you lose him, you could end up walking into his sights. He'll have no hesitation.

But, he is drunk. His senses are dulled, but do not count on it.

Where is the trail? Not enough light. Where did it go? Samuel pulled out his flashlight, and pointed it downward, hand over the lens. He pulsed the switch, letting darts of light escape through his fingers. The trail lay four feet away. Slipping onto the path, he flicked it again. Boot tracks. Grass stems, broken.

He picked up his pace, eyes moving, every tree looking as if it might have someone behind it, pointing a rifle. The brush grew thick. He slowed, letting his eyes adjust, and pulled in several short, rapid breaths. Loud ones. Too loud. He took a long, slow breath and regulated his breathing. He moved on.

The trees began to open. Light filtered in from the stars. Suddenly, grassland. Ahead, a band of trees. More shadows.

Is he out there? Did he hear me? Samuel stepped behind a tree and scanned. Nothing crouching in the grass. Nothing in the trees. Not that I can see. If I am wrong, I will be dead before I know it.

Grasping the rifle in one hand, he ran, quietly, zigzagging across the opening, then ducking behind a tree. He listened, hearing nothing. He let his eyes adjust, and watched for movement. None.

He stepped forward.

— · —

Coming to the edge of the trees, the Irishman stopped and donned his night vision goggles. He peered through them, made an adjustment, and quickly scanned the area. Grassland. Scattered acacia. Fever trees in the distance.

"Are you out there?" he muttered to himself. "Anyone? Rangers? If you are, show yourself." He made a slow pass with the goggles, searching the landscape for anything of symmetry. Vehicles. Anything boxy. Men. Men looking out from behind trees. Rifle barrels, moving about. None. Not here.

He moved on.

Recognizing a fork in the trail, he stopped, and slipped behind a fever tree. "Okay, Mr. and Mrs. Payday, now for you." He made another sweep. Acacia. Only acacia, even in the distance. "You should be close."

He took the south fork, and crept through the brush, past another familiar spot. "Two hours ago, you were here, you cute little female, you. A face that only a mum could love, but that big lug of a male just can't stay away. So, where are you two lovebirds?"

— · —

Samuel cupped his hand over the flashlight and switched it on, letting a flicker of light escape through his fingers. He ran the light over the ground. Boot track. He switched it off and moved forward.

— · —

"There you are."

One rhino lay near the edge of the trees, head down, appearing to be sleeping.

The Irishman flipped up the goggle and sighted in the rifle, then relaxed. Not good enough. Bad angle. Might not hit anything vital.

He stepped left, staying in shadows.

He stopped. What was that?

He turned back, and listened. In the brush or the grass? He held his breath and listened. Nothing. Maybe imagination. Don't think so. Definitely something. On the move. He lowered the goggle and scanned.

— · —

Samuel slowed. Something made a sound. Something on the edge of the trees. He stopped and listened.

Footsteps. Someone stepping on twigs. A few feet away.

He held still, finger on the trigger.

— · —

The Irishman made an adjustment and scanned. Trees, downed limbs, bushes, grass. Nothing there. But something made that sound. No doubt about it.

He raised the AK-74, switched it to automatic and gave the suppressor a pat. He flipped down the goggle. Okay, you maggot, where are you? You can't hide. I'll find ya.

— · —

Samuel listened. Twigs breaking. Close.

The fever tree felt small. Too small. Too late to move.

He palmed the flashlight.

— · —

The Irishman picked up his foot, stepped a few inches forward, and stopped.

Feet locked to the ground, he raised the rifle, and turned, eyes scouring the scene.

Nothing to the right.

He rotated back the other way, moving his sights past the trunk of a fever tree.

Something there?

He locked his eyes and aligned the gun sights.

He took a step forward.

A sound.

He whipped around, releasing a pulse of bullets. Got you, you maggot.

Light. A beam. On the ground. A flashlight.

He tried turning back. He briefly saw movement—a man in a beret and flashes of light. The goggle went white, but it no longer mattered.

— · —

The men from Louisiana jumped to their feet, startled by gunfire.

The man from the bar circled the campfire in fits and starts, looking confused. The other stared into the night.

Jack stepped back, further into the shadows, ready to move, depending on which man emerged from the trees. The need would not come from these men. These two were going nowhere.

Minutes passed.

"Maybe we just got ourselves rhino heads," said the man from the bar. He attempted a smile.

"They're yours. I don't want 'em," said the other. "Wait a minute. Isn't he using the suppressor?"

They settled into their chairs, and waited, jumping at every little sound.

With each passing minute, Jack inched further into the shadows.

A snap of twigs. The men whipped around.

"Who are you?" one asked, his eyes wide.

The man emerging from the trees wore the uniform of Kenya Wildlife Service. He carried an AK-47. "Gentlemen," he said, his accent Kenyan, their ears likely picking up tinges of proper English. "I would like you to keep your hands where I can see them. You are under arrest."

— · —

After turning the body and detainees over to others, Samuel and Jack walked the road to the Land Cruiser. Late, on a moonless night, they drove the edge of Nairobi, toward the airport.

Samuel parked under the porte cochere of the Nairobi Skies Hotel and killed the engine. "When is your flight?"

Jack pulled out his phone and opened email. One from Molly. "Six. In the morning." The screen went black. "And now this thing's dead."

"The hotel desk will have an adaptor." Samuel glanced at his watch. "You will not get much sleep. Three hours, maybe four."

"You're the one who needs sleep."

Samuel nodded, staring into the night. "They were good men. Two good rangers."

Jack watched his face contort with whatever ran through his thoughts. "What's wrong?"

"I should feel pleased. Relieved. A poacher is dead, no longer preying on rangers and wildlife. What a waste of life he was. Worthless, yet he snuffed out the lives of two very good men, possibly more; who knows how many rhinoceros, elephant, and whatever people with money wanted. I should be pleased, but others will replace him. It is a never-ending battle. "

"But with him gone, maybe things will settle down."

"Maybe."

"I can cancel my flight. Continue Gabriel Kagunda's research."

"Under-Secretary Mwangi sent word to your director, told him you are coming home. The research is over. He will do everything he can to prevent restarting Kagunda's work."

"Why does Mwangi care?"

"I do not know. Maybe connections to someone with plans for land to the south, maybe politics, or maybe simply the desire to control." Samuel turned his eyes back to the night. "Here is the odd thing. Despite the politics, despite the corruption, despite the privilege and lack of justice, Gabriel Kagunda saw a way through it all." Samuel shook his head. "He was convinced his science would help. Even as migration corridors are choked off, he harbored no anger. Even for those corrupted by power here in Nairobi. He was sure that if only he could provide the data, the science, it would help."

Jack watched his face again contort. "What's wrong?"

"Nothing."

"Samuel, I can see it on your face."

"A conversation—one that continues to trouble me." He removed his beret, and ran a hand through his hair. "During our last conversation Gabriel explained again what to expect from his research . . . the limits, the qualifiers. I grew impatient and told him I did not need gibberish, I needed the truth. The truth without all the baggage." Samuel wrung his hands. "Gabriel's answer? 'Science does not give you truth, it gives you data, information to develop theories . . . an understanding. Even theories, when accepted as fact, are not truth. Facts are often used to mislead. Facts are used in lies,' he said." Samuel turned to Jack. "I became frustrated and angry. I asked if he was avoiding responsibility, being unwilling to commit himself to answers. I wondered how dedicated he really was, to anything other than doing his research."

"What did he do?"

"He remained calm. He promised his best effort, good data, information I could treat as fact, but, he said, he could not give me truth. Truth, he said, would have to come from me." Samuel sighed. "I grew angry. I demanded to know what he was suggesting." He turned to the window. "Gabriel said I could use his results honestly, or pick and choose, or try to mislead, or run and hide, but. . . ." He paused. "I accused him of saying I was afraid of what he might learn. Or worse, suggesting I planned to use it in a lie."

"What did he say?"

"He didn't. I threw him out of my office."

Jack studied him. "So that's why. That's why the burden. That's why you asked for two people, not one. You wanted someone to help assure truth would come from you. Truth, not rationalization."

Samuel nodded, and rubbed the scar on his chin.

"Samuel, our people are no more masters at that than you. You don't need us for that."

After a moment, Samuel extended a hand. "Thank you, my friend, for coming, for trying to help, even in a lost cause."

Jack ignored the hand. "It is not a lost cause. And you will speak the truth, Samuel. You are capable of dealing with the challenge. Gabriel's work will yield results. You will use those results with integrity and honesty, no matter how difficult. No matter how much you're beaten up."

"I may be in over my head."

"You're not. Go get the universities. Let them take care of

you." Jack now offered his hand. "I'm glad I came. I found a man who taught me lessons I'll carry with me all the rest of my days."

"Likewise, my friend. If I can ever invite you back, will you come?"

"In a heartbeat." Jack smiled. "Don't lose my thirty-aught-six."

"Such a foolish choice in weapons."

"No one ever said I was smart."

"I do. Except when it comes to rifles."

CHAPTER

17

The flight Molly arranged would route through Brussels to Atlanta. From there, he would catch another to D.C.

Jack woke early, emailed the coalition report to Kip Culberson and Karen Hatcher—finally—then showered and shaved, and caught the hotel shuttle to the airport, taking off from Nairobi at sunrise. He said his goodbyes to Kenya from a window seat, watching as the sun peeked over the horizon, sending shadows of fever trees reaching across the savannah.

He sat back and considered it all. Before nodding off, one particularly complicated topic kept clogging his mind.

Truth.

—·—

By early the next morning, after 23 hours of flying and sitting in airports, Jack Chastain was in Washington, D.C. He took the Metro blue line to Rosslyn, and inquired about checking in at the hotel.

No rooms till noon.

He grabbed a cup of coffee and loitered about the lobby. Promptly at eight, he called the Main Interior Building. The director's receptionist had no opening on his calendar until the next day. The briefing would have to be then.

He sat back, closed his eyes, and came close to dozing when his cell phone began to ring. Washington number. He answered.

"The director asked me to fit you in. Can you be here at nine?"

He took the Metro to Farragut West, emerging into the sun. Duffle in hand and pack on his back, he stopped for a coffee, then sipped as he took the direct route to Main Interior, skirting around to the south entrance, through security, and up the elevator to the Park Service wing.

The receptionist relieved him of his bags and escorted him into the director's office.

Shirt sleeves rolled up, his suit coat thrown over the arm of a chair, the director appeared deep into his day. He looked up from his reading. "Little casual, aren't you?"

"Depends on your definition of casual. Cargo pants are quite fancy in parts of the world."

"I see." The director gave only a hint of a smile. "Have a seat. You're home early."

"Out of my control. I was of the impression you'd been informed."

"I was, in a strange sort of way, yes."

"A Mr. Mwangi?"

"Whoever that is."

"He's an undersecretary in their ministry. Interesting guy. Made a strange comment about Americans and favors. Seemed to think I'd know what he meant."

"Did you?"

"No clue. Confused the hell out of me."

"I'll take that as good. So, how'd it go, and what'd you think? Should we be helping?"

"Ended unexpectedly. Went okay. Unfortunately, another ranger was shot, so priorities changed. A shame, but yes, I'd say we should help when we can. The person I worked with was capable. Quite capable. Has a long list of challenges. Poachers, a park that's too small, migration corridors cut off, too much to worry about inside the system."

"Politics?"

"I suppose."

The director narrowed his eyes. "I've got questions about that, but first . . ." He leaned over his hands. "Did you obey my order?"

"Which one?"

"The little thing about staying at headquarters?"

"I'd rather not answer that."

He rolled his eyes. "Did you have any problems?"

"I'd rather not answer that."

He ran fingers through messy hair. "Did this ... whatever ... that seems deserving of, but lacking in answers, cause anything that could come back to haunt me?"

"Don't think so."

"Good. I don't need an international incident." Lucas sat back in his chair. "You're alive, so ... tell me about politics. Hear anything of concern?"

"Only from that Mr. Mwangi. I'm not sure my observations are worth anything. Had a hard time understanding the game he was playing. One moment I think he's a good guy. The next I think I should run. He talked politics, but there's also so much I don't understand about tribal culture. Corruption? It's talked about ... higher echelons of government. But not the people I worked with." He paused. "Doing everything they can to preserve their heritage. Against tremendous odds."

"Would you go back?"

"In a heartbeat."

He nodded. "Things haven't blown over yet. I can't let you go back to Piedras Coloradas."

"Can't keep me away forever."

"Maybe not, but I can for now. I'll find you something here."

Jack squirmed in his seat. "What if I took personal leave?"

"Not to go to Piedras Coloradas. I will not let you be crucified."

"That's not what I'm proposing." He dropped his eyes. "I'm thinking Montana."

"That's hardly better."

"I know, but maybe I could sort some stuff out."

"What could you sort out? For you, Montana's water under the bridge."

"I'm not saying that. Stuff I saw in Kenya. I could use time to think about what I saw. Get it out of my system."

The director gave a quizzical stare, and drew in a long, slow breath. "I can give you a few tasks, things you can do for me. Go to Missoula, by way of Salt Lake. I'll pay for the flight. Get things out of the way, then take annual leave. Clear your mind. In another week, maybe two, you go home. Maybe."

Jack nodded. "Understood."

—·—

Within half an hour, he had flight reservations to Missoula. Leaving the building, he caught sight of the shuttle to Eye Street, the agency's auxiliary office building. The bus sat waiting to make its next run. He checked his watch. Plenty of time. He ducked in and took a seat.

At Eye Street, he hopped off, entered the building, and approached security. "Here to see Iggy in International Affairs."

"He expecting you?" the uniformed guard asked.

"Nope."

A call was made.

A few minutes later, Iggy—a man with a friendly smile and a shaved head—appeared in the corridor. He signed Jack in and led him to the bank of elevators. "After you," he said, as a door opened.

Iggy leaned against a wall as they rode to the ninth floor. "How was Kenya?"

"Beautiful."

"You're back early."

"Couldn't be helped. Change in priorities."

The elevator door slid open. Jack followed him out, waited for Iggy to cardkey his wing, then followed him to his office. Inside, he offered a chair. "You didn't need to report in. You could've just emailed your trip report."

"I know. I'll get you one. Give me a week or so." Jack paused. "I'm here because I wanted to ask you something. Is there a way to learn who from the U.S. flew into and out of Kenya in the last month?"

Iggy rubbed his chin. "Maybe from State Department. If that

doesn't work, I've got a friend at Kenya's Embassy. We could see if they'd release information on visas issued for that timeframe."

"Would you please make those requests?"

"Certainly. What's this about?"

"Rhino poaching."

"I'll start with State Department. What name you looking for?"

"No clue. Supposedly big. Very big." He stood and backed to the door. "Actually there's two people I'm looking for. A big name and a courier. May've misunderstood the guy who said it . . . too much accent and way too much whiskey. I think he said the courier was from New Mexico."

"Wow, your neck of the woods. It'd sure be easier if this guy would give you some names."

"The guy ain't talking."

— · —

Jack took the Metro to Reagan National Airport, found his gate and plopped down to wait. He fished out his phone and made a call. "Bad news," he said, when Kelly answered. "Can't come home. Not yet."

"Why?"

"Director doesn't think it's calmed down enough."

"What are you gonna do?"

"I'm on my way to Montana."

She gasped. "Jack, are you okay with that?"

"My idea."

"Are you all right?"

"Not sure. Thought it'd be better than D.C. Maybe I can sort out a few things. I'll explain when I understand it better myself."

Jack ended the call when the flight began to board. Standing in line, he decided to make one more quick call. He flipped through names in his phone. He tapped a number. It rang twice.

"What?" growled a voice on the other end.

"Pug Pendagraph?"

"Yeah. Who is this?"

"Jack Chastain."

Quiet, then, "Well, I never thought I'd hear that name again. Not in these parts."

"Pug, that fishing cabin down by the river. If it's not in use, could I impose? Stay a few days, pay you what it's worth."

"You think I need your money?"

Jack smiled to himself. "Well, you were a rich bastard, but who knows, the recession might've changed all that. Could be dirt poor for all I know."

Pug laughed. "The cabin's yours. I don't need your money, but you can earn your keep, with a rod and a fly."

"You can afford a better guide than me."

"Maybe, but you know a few things about reading a river. Things I ain't heard before or since. You might have more tricks up your sleeve. Why you coming here?"

"Things I need to sort out. Someone I should try to see."

"What makes you think anyone here wants to see you?"

"Good point, but I still have things to sort out. I've been through a few things of late."

"You mean, like facing down an armed militia?"

"You know about that?"

"Who doesn't? You're all over television. You have fans all over the country. Hell, you're popular."

"Let's not talk about that. Nothing to do with why I'm coming. Won't bore you with details."

"When do you get here?"

"End of the day. Flying into Missoula."

"I'll pick you up at the airport."

"I can rent a car. I need to drop something off at the Forest Service regional office."

"I'll be at the curb. Black Hummer."

"Still wasting gas. Guess the recession didn't hurt you any."

Pug laughed.

— · —

The flight landed in Salt Lake City, and Jack quickly made his way out of the airport. He caught a cab to the federal building housing the Bureau of Reclamation, Upper Colorado Region. He took the elevator to the regional director's floor and located the executive suite.

"I'm here to see the Regional Director," he said to the secretary.

The young blonde pored over her calendar. "He expecting you?"

"He's not. I have a package from the Director of the Park Service."

She inspected Jack's state of dress, finally shaking her head, accepting cargo pants and a sweat-stained shirt as acceptable. She stepped inside the door, whispered a few words, then turned, waving him forward. "He only has a few minutes."

"Me, too." Jack stepped past her, into the suite. "I'm Jack Chastain, Park Service." He offered a hand to the balding man in short-sleeved shirt and tie. "Got something for you." He passed him a blue envelope, marked for his attention only. "From our director."

"I'm surprised this is a priority to you people. This is gonna cause a fight."

"He seems to think you started it."

"You people . . ." He shook his head in mock frustration. "You need to understand some things."

"Understand? Hammer away." He let his fatigue show. "Take all the time you need."

"Uh . . . no." He scowled. "But your director will be getting a call from the commissioner."

"He's looking forward to it, and your commissioner will get a call from Interior." Jack cracked a smile and backed to the door. "Thank you," he said, walking past the secretary.

He reached the hall and glanced at his watch. Plenty of time to get back to the airport. Wonder what that was about? No, not really. But the director was right about the reaction.

Jack hailed a cab. With his bag checked through to Missoula, he jumped out at the airport curb, made his way to the gate, then onto a regional jet.

It arrived in Missoula on time. Four thirty. He made his way through the terminal, to baggage claim, and out to the curb. A black Hummer sat running. Jack slipped into the passenger side and extended a hand. "Good to see you, Pug."

The graying, wiry man shook the hand, nodded, and flashed a cocky grin. He gave the side mirror a glance and pulled into traffic.

"Kind of you to come all this way."

Pendagraph gave another nod. He turned toward the interstate highway.

Jack gave him a once over. No different than last time. Worn jeans and denim shirt. White, sweat-stained hat, floppy from years of use. Still looking like an old cowhand. Probably still describing his situation with a dismissive wave and a comment about the comfort of old family money. With his wife in another part of the country, and rarely coming to Montana, he could be any way he wanted to be.

Pug took a Missoula exit, and turned toward downtown.

"First stop, Forest Service office." He pulled into the old federal building and found a parking space. Pug kicked up a leg, rested a foot on the dashboard, and pulled his hat down over his eyes. "Take your time."

Jack dug out the second blue envelope and climbed out of the truck.

He entered the granite-faced building through a door under a limestone arch. He approached the reception desk, staffed by a woman in Forest Service uniform. "Jack Chastain, here to see the Regional Forester."

"End of the day." She picked up a phone and called, conversing only a few seconds. "He's expecting you. Do you know the way?"

"Yes, thanks," Jack said, heading up the narrow hall.

As he approached the end of the hallway, a door swung open and a man stepped out, boyish, blond, crossing his arms as he waited.

Jack slowed. "Shea Pinkley? You're regional forester?"

"I am, now." He led Jack past the unoccupied desk of his secretary, into his office. "Have a seat. They didn't say it was you they were sending. Are you here again to try taking our best lands?"

"Nothing to do with that. And you know as well as I do, that idea started with people who live here. People you and I both work for."

"It didn't seem to help any." Pinkley dropped into his chair and leaned over his desk. "You got pretty far in creating a park, but that only meant you crashed and burned all the harder. Why you here? Why you?"

"Read nothing into it. The director needed someone to deliver a message. If delivered by him, it'd need to go to his counterpart in Washington. He thought it best this message be informal."

"Informal? Why? What's in the envelope?"

"Observations from people in the field. Something to make you aware they're watching. Aware of what you've let happen. Informally, because our two agencies have such a long history of working together. We've valued that relationship, but things have happened under your watch."

"I've got a job to do, and it's not you or your director I have to satisfy."

"No, it's not, but the director wonders if there's a bit of arrogance at play in the Forest Service."

"Your director thinks the Chief Forester is arrogant?"

"No. I think he gets along quite well with the Chief Forester. I believe he thinks you're arrogant."

Pinkley laughed. "Get to your business."

"Every park in Montana. They're talking. What was a good working relationship has gone sour. Threats to every park. Activities starting on Forest Service land. It's not gone unnoticed."

"Why Jack Chastain, I thought we were friends."

"Shouldn't it be me saying that?"

"Whatever do you mean? Just because you left under a cloud doesn't make me a weather-maker."

"Didn't think so, but you were awfully cagey in the end. Helpful for so long, then you weren't."

"In the end, it wasn't exactly safe being seen with you. Don't hold it against a guy for recognizing danger, someone tainted."

"How? How was I tainted?"

He smiled. "Never mind. So, why are you really here, Jack?"

"As I said, passing on a message. Stop the games, do your job, or someone will call for an investigation. Don't force our director to put at risk his working relationship with your boss in Washington. Don't force him to choose between you and our director."

"I believe I'm safe. Our mission is not the same as yours."

"No, it's not." Jack dropped the blue envelope onto the desk. "But it's not our mission to spend all our time protecting parks from what's happening on the forest."

"Then relax. You can't stop progress," Shea said. He eyed the envelope.

Jack stood and moved to the door. "Beware. Inside that envelope is enough to keep an inspector general investigating for months."

"Good to see you too, Jack. Welcome back to Montana."

Jack slipped out and closed the door behind him. What an ass.

Intersecting a hallway, he turned, to get out of Forest Service offices as quickly as possible.

He continued down a hallway, walking past door after door. After a turn into another hallway, he encountered doors with gold lettering on glass panes. Congressional field offices. A door opened, and a man in a suit slipped into the hall. Jack started past, then stopped. "Senator Tisdale?"

He looked up and studied the face. "Hello, Jack." Tisdale tentatively offered a hand. "Thought you were in New Mexico."

"Yes." Jack sighed. "Senator, I never had a chance to . . . I'm sorry. Sorry things went the way they did. I'm sorry we failed your constituents. Sorry the things we briefed you on became so misunderstood, disputed, convoluted. Things I presented as fact . . . I should have anticipated how they might be misunderstood or misrepresented. I'm sorry. About everything. I failed you."

"Water under the bridge," Tisdale said. He attempted a smile, looked away, and locked eyes on the wall. "Those things happen. Gotta go. Good luck in New Mexico."

CHAPTER

18

"That didn't take long," Pug said, as Jack slipped into the vehicle. "Thought you'd be there for hours, hanging out with your government buddies."

"Hardly. Just delivering a message."

"So, now you're a mailman?" Pug started the Hummer, backed out, and turned onto the road. He drove without words.

Jack stared out the window, at mountains, meadows, and rivers, watching it all pass him by, letting his mind flip through pages past.

Why the hell are you in Montana? This place is like a lover, turned assassin. The danger's in getting too close. Being intrigued. Letting her get under your skin.

So, why the hell are you here?

Because, you're little different than Samuel Leboo, and there's something you have to do.

"Well, you're lousy company," Pug said, breaking the silence. He adjusted his hat.

"Sorry Pug, figured you wanted quiet." Jack sat up. "Where are we?"

"Half an hour from the ranch."

"I see," he said, recognizing a bend in the river. "Picking me up . . . that's beyond the call. And thanks for giving me a place to stay."

"You can use this rig while you're here."

"What'll you drive, and can I buy you dinner in town?"

"Goin' out of state day after tomorrow, so I won't need this." Pug cracked a smile. "Sure you wanna be seen in town?"

Not really. Jack held his tongue.

"Thought so. We'll eat at my place. Buster's cooking steak for tonight."

"Buster, your hired hand? He cooks?"

"Convinced me to send him to chef school. Only has to fuss over me when I'm here, and I'm gone most the time."

"Cow hand and chef?"

"Don't be surprised. Cow hands have a way of working magic with a Dutch oven."

"But chef school?"

"Way I see it, it's an investment."

"What if he leaves for some fancy restaurant in town?"

Pug shook his head. "Won't happen. Buster can't handle people."

"How's he handle you?"

"Good question. Might have something to do with the paycheck."

— · —

"Dinner's ready!" Buster hollered, his words echoing off the rock and timber of the great room.

Jack took a sip of his beer. The sunset's orange glow lay over the meadows and meandering river below. He spun around to see Buster setting plated steaks at one end of a massive timber table. Wiping his hands on something of an apron, he turned back to an archway tucked behind the massive stone fireplace and disappeared into an alcove.

Jack fought back a smile. Buster. Well-waxed handlebar mustache, black hair greased back. Boots. Starched Wranglers. Not a common look for a chef, except maybe in Montana.

Buster returned with stemmed glasses and a bottle of wine.

"Would you happen to like red? This is a blend Mister Pendagraph likes with his steak."

Mister? "Love a good red."

Pug appeared at the top of the timber staircase. "Smells great, Buster. What're we having?" He started down the split-log steps.

Buster twisted the cork from the bottle. "Lobster bisque. Steamed asparagus. Sautéed mushrooms. Steak, of course. I'll surprise you on dessert."

"Sounds great." Pug reached bottom and moved to the head of the table. "Jack, have a seat."

Jack slipped around the table. "I get the sunset?"

"Aim to please," Buster said. "Noticed you at the window." He tipped the bottle and filled Pug's glass.

Pug took a sip. "Good choice. How we doing on wine?"

"Fine for now. We'll need to restock. I'll plan a trip to Sonoma."

"Good. There'll be time in the fall when I'm away." He set down his glass, and picked up a steak knife. "Tear your eyes away and eat up, Jack. Good to be back in Montana?"

"Still beautiful," Jack said. "I forgot how much."

Buster retreated to the kitchen.

"Easy to forget, especially in winter." Pug sliced off a piece of meat. "Wishin' you were still here?"

"No. Too much happened here. Wouldn't want to go through that again. New Mexico's my home now. They treat me well."

"Real well. Appreciation parties with assault weapons." He smiled. "I saw it on TV. Trouble seems to follow wherever ya go."

"Might seem like it, but those things happen."

"Not to most people." Pug picked up his glass. "So, why ya here?"

"Hard to explain. Someone I need to check on. Something I need to confront."

"Hell, Jack, don't look back."

"Had all sorts of people tell me that. But something continues to trouble me. Can't quite put my finger on it." He speared a piece of steak and took a bite.

"Then, forget it."

"Can't," Jack said, still chewing. He swallowed. "I've been through some things lately . . . in Africa. Won't bore you with details . . . but events, that awoke a voice in my head. It seems to be saying, look closer, don't you see it? It's right under your nose."

Pug's eyes narrowed. He leaned closer. "What do ya see?"

"Couldn't tell you. It's there but it won't come into focus."

Pug laughed. "Hell, Jack, go to a shrink, get liquored up, do something, but get on with your life."

"I have. Life's good, really. I love it in New Mexico. Good people in my life. Public treats me well—other than a few armed lunatics. The job's good."

"Then why ya here?"

"I owe something to people here, I just don't know what."

Pug cut into a sprig of asparagus. "They've moved on." He took a bite, then a sip of wine. "Hell, jobs are coming. They're lining up, making plans."

"Good for them. What kind of jobs?"

"Mine jobs."

"Mine? What mine?"

"You don't want to know."

"Tell me. What mine?"

"Oh, it's south of here. Thereabouts."

"In the park study area?"

"Thereabouts."

Jack set down his fork. "Where people wanted a national park?"

"Don't give it any thought. Your life's good."

"People up in arms?"

"It's progress. It's jobs.

"That's how they feel?"

"Not everybody."

"But most?"

"Couldn't tell ya. Whatcha gonna do? They've moved on. So should you. There's no reason for ya to be here."

Jack sighed. "Maybe not, but there's someone I want to see."

"Do they want to see you?"

Jack shrugged and said nothing.

"Go home. Back to New Mexico."

"Can't," Jack said, his mind going different directions. "That welcoming party. The one with assault weapons. That hasn't blown over yet."

"You're getting nowhere working for the government. Quit. Come work for me."

"Doing what?"

"Run one of my ranches."

"Pug, I live in New Mexico now. Got a life there."

"Doesn't sound like it, but hey, I've got a place in New Mexico. Haven't spent much time there yet, but you could run it. I can always use a good man."

Jack held his tongue.

"Think about it."

"I'm not sure that's who I am."

"Just think about it." Pug took a bite, chewed it well, and swallowed. "Now, if we're gonna spend time fishing, has to be tomorrow. I'll bang on the door at first light. You'll find all the gear you need in the mud room."

— · —

Jack climbed into the Hummer. Keys hung from the ignition.

The road down the mountain was longer than he remembered, but after a straight stretch the beams of the headlights fell across logs and stone. The old fishing cabin, overlooking the river. He pulled up outside, dropped his bag at the door, and walked to the river in the light of the moon. The river, its current steady. He dipped a hand. Cold. It'll be here tomorrow. Pug will be here early.

He trudged upslope, found the cabin door unlocked, and flipped on the light. He looked inside. Rustic and elegant. Little different than last time. The easy chair sat at a different angle, near a bookcase not there before, filled with fishing guides and novels—many by Hemingway. Old bamboo fly rods hung above the mantle. The wood box beside the stone fireplace sat filled with split pine. The old bent-rod bed on other side of the room had pillows piled on a hand-stitched quilt. He crossed the floor, and peeked in the back room. The monster of a gas stove, still there. He opened the door on a cupboard. Well stocked. Jack stepped past the toilet, into the mudroom. Waders, boots, vests. Several sizes and options. Something oughta fit. He inspected the collection of fly rods and reels. Nothing low end. He flipped on the outside light and slipped outside. Flagstone, rock fire ring, and rustic chairs and benches. And something new, at the far reach of the porch light. A stock tank. Galvanized steel. Jack stepped closer, and caught sight of a propane burner. A hot tub. Ranch version. He laughed. That might get some use.

Tomorrow.

Been a long day, for a body still recovering from being on the other side of the world. He stepped back inside. No army cot tonight.

— · —

The bang on the door came later than expected, but not by much. Into his third cup of coffee, Jack swung open the heavy timber door.

Pug stood in waders, wading boots, and fishing vest. He pulled off his old sweat-stained hat. "Everything to your liking?"

"Quite elegant. Well stocked," Jack said. "Just finished eggs and coffee."

"Good. Grab some gear."

— · —

Jack slowed, steadied himself, and watched as Pug waded upriver, into the current, approaching mid-stream. He stopped, pulled a length of line from his reel, flipped the rod back and cast, laying the fly alongside a boulder a few feet from shore. In the soft light of an impending day, Jack watched Pug's fly drift into still water, sheltered by the boulder. Two seconds ticked by, the fly sank, the line grew tight, and Pug jerked his rod back, setting the hook. The trout tried to run, flashing left to right. The rod bent double. Pug reeled. When he had the brown at arm's reach, he raised the rod high, took hold of his net, and dipped it under the fish.

"Sixteen inches," Pug shouted. "Not a bad start."

"Not bad at all," Jack shouted back. Scanning the far side of the river, he made a few casts, then laid the wooly bugger alongside a log. He let it drift. Strike. His rod tip dipped, he jerked the rod back, and he found himself in the midst of a fight. Holding the reel steady, rod up, line tight, he let the trout run. Watching for flashes, he gave it a moment, then started to reel. Slow, steady spins, bringing the brown in, careful not to pull too hard. He tucked the rod under an arm, took the fish in both hands, and flipped the hook lose. He held it facing into the current, let go, and watched it make a slow move, then dart away.

"Nice one?" Pug hollered.

"About eighteen inches."

"Likely story."

Jack inspected the fly and prepared to make his next cast.

— · —

Pug handed Jack a stainless steel cup, and poured coffee from a Thermos.

Jack sat on a boulder and took a sip.

"You better tell me that's good coffee, or Buster might poison our dinner. There's pastry of some sort in the pack."

Jack reached in, dug out a wax-paper sack, and pulled out a bear claw. "Very good coffee."

Pug poured himself a cup. "How long you think you'll be here?"

"About a week, if you don't mind."

"It's good someone's getting use of the cabin."

"I noticed something new out back."

"Oh, you saw my tub. Like it?"

"Haven't tried it, but looks inviting."

"A little elegance here in the wilderness. Asked a guy in town to design it."

"Pretty fancy . . . for a stock tank. This is such a nice stretch of river, Pug."

"Anything I should do different?"

"You mean, like, taking care of the river?"

"I sure as hell wouldn't wanna screw this place up. I was thinkin' about finding a hotshot fisheries biologist, have 'em make sure I know what I'm doing."

"Is there something you're concerned about?"

Pug tossed a pebble. "How does one know if there's reason for concern?"

"It's a system, Pug."

"What's that mean?"

"A system. Keep it whole. It's not just about water in the river. A healthy river is just part of a larger, more complex system. The channel margin, the floodplain, organic inputs, the shading on the river's edge, the connections to upland areas, even the larger forest, even the critters on the land. They're all factors in how healthy an aquatic system is."

"How the hell can the critters on land be a factor?"

"Elk can browse away the willow on the riverbank. Without controls on their population, they tend to devour it all. River margins become sunny. A river can become wide, shallow and warm. If wolves are part of the system, elk are always watching, always wary, an eye open, under cover, unwilling to spend too much time in the open. Willows and other plants have a chance to survive. The channel margins stay shady, and with the right inputs of organic material and nutrients, and with cool waters, the aquatic system stays healthy."

"Elk. Wildest thing I ever heard."

"The thing to remember is, preserve the foundations of the system. The best trout streams seem to be alkaline. Alkaline waters, with nutrients, contain more carbon dioxide. That supports algae. Algae supports insects. Algae and insects support everything else, including the big browns."

"How the hell do I protect alkalinity?"

"Shouldn't have to. If there was some sort of runoff to worry

about, something acidic, or maybe an excess of dust, maybe you'd
. . ." He paused. "That new mine you told me about. It is opera-
tional?"

"Yeah, but that's on the other side of the mountain. Too far
away."

"Hope you're right." Jack shrugged. "Hard to know. If you
hear it's kicking up dust, you might hire someone to see if it's having an effect."

"I'll do that. I'd sure hate to see this place get hammered."

"I'm sure you're fine. Elsewhere, who knows. What kind of
mine?"

"Some kind of metal."

"Any talk of impacts?"

"You hear everything, from nothing, to the world's gonna
end."

"Enviros?"

"Mostly? Saying it'll kill the river. So do some government
folks, but they've gone quiet."

Jack sighed, and gave a rub to the knot forming at the back
of his neck.

"Other government folks, and the mine people, they say there's
nothing to worry about."

Jack looked away. Would they let something happen?

"Come work for me, Jack. Take care of this river." Pug set
down his cup. "Live in New Mexico. Spend a little time here, a little
time there, running my place. Best of both worlds." He looked Jack
in the eye. "We can make it work."

"I'm not sure that's who I am, Pug."

"You like abuse? Look at what happened when you were here.
Downstream. All that work, for nothing. All you got was abuse. At
the end of the day, they didn't hear a word you said."

"It wasn't that simple, Pug."

"Maybe not to you but it's obvious to me." He picked up a stone
and gave it a toss, skipping it twice on the river. "The government
doesn't deserve ya. They give ya the runaround. You work too hard
not to be appreciated."

"I don't seek appreciation, and it wasn't the agency giving the runaround. Well . . . to some extent." He picked up a stone, and let it roll through his fingers. "What happened downriver was more than government machinations. There were games people played. Lots of games."

"Hell, Jack, there are unscrupulous people in this world. People out for themselves. There's nothing you can do about that. Just respond in kind. Be in it for yourself. Enjoy the good life. Work for a man who enjoys the blessings of a little family money."

Jack laughed. "Pug, I appreciate the offer, but you don't need to look out for me. I'm just a guy you met at a fly shop. A fishing buddy. You don't owe me anything."

"Hell, I'm not worried about you. I'm a selfish bastard. I like getting my way. If I can hire a guy to take care of this river, hell, I'll do it. I wanna make sure it stays my little piece of heaven. Monster browns, rising with the hatch. Think about it?" He offered the Thermos. "More coffee?"

Jack stared out at the river. "Had enough, and I will."

CHAPTER 19

Early afternoon, Pug prepared to depart to pack and get ready for travel. "Stay as long as ya like," he said, climbing into his pickup. He rolled down the window. "Come work for me, Jack. Look out for yourself. Run my place in New Mexico."

— · —

Jack turned the knob and watched the water stream into the stock tank. He turned on the propane and hit the striker. The burner burst into flame. He stepped back and watched the blue glow lap at the metal from its notch in the flagstone beneath the tub.

When full, he left to let it finish heating. He hung the boots and waders on pegs in the mudroom and stripped down, grabbed a beer, and sauntered out. He waited at the edge of the flagstone, looking out over the river. What a good gig this would be. Big browns, no worries, and calling it work. He tested the water and turned off the burner, then settled in and lay back against the tub's wooden backrest. The chill from the river soaked away. He took a sip looking past meadows rimmed by mountains. Solitude. Perfect.

— · —

The following morning, Jack woke, spent an hour on the river, kept one catch for dinner, and released the others.

Over a pot of coffee, he planned his day. Nothing complicated. Today, town.

— · —

Jack drove up the mountain and stopped at Pug's timber gate. A pickup sat nearby, surrounded by horses, Buster in the bed rolling out salt and mineral block. A big black stud, ears back, kept others at bay, ready to nip as he worked over a block.

Jack lowered the window.

"Mornin'," Buster shouted. He stood and wiped sweat from his brow. "I hear Mr. Pendagraph made you an offer."

"He did, yes."

"Ya gonna do it?"

"Don't know. What's he like to work for?"

"You'll hardly see him. He pays well. All he requires is loyalty."

"Tell me about his place in New Mexico."

"Hell, I never been there. He's only had it a few years." Buster picked up a mineral block and gave it a toss. "But, I promised I'd remind you to think about it."

"I am. It's a good offer, but I've got a job. A good one."

"Yeah, right. I know all about that good job. Cable news. Things they say don't exactly sound like the man I know, but hey, gotta admit, they made me wonder." He gave his mustache a twist. "You might be needin' a change, Mr. Fed. Consider Mr. Pendagraph's offer. It wouldn't do you no harm."

Jack gave him a wave. "I'll be back. Going to town."

On the other side of the mountain, he checked his phone for signal. Two bars. He called Kelly's number, got her voicemail, and left a message. Who else, while I have signal? He pulled over and checked email. One from Karen Hatcher, saying the coalition report looked good and that she and Kip were making contacts. He scanned for one from International Affairs. Nothing. He pulled up Iggy's number. It rang once and Iggy answered.

"Heard anything from State Department?"

Iggy laughed. "Not a thing. Give 'em time. Try back in a few days."

— · —

Jack steered the Hummer around a bend and onto the straightaway into town. The valley opened and he noticed something new. Rails. A spur line for a railroad. New cross ties, new ballast, new signage, rusty but probably new rails. Below the reach of the ballast, new disturbance. Fresh dirt. Old, one lane roads still ambled through the foothills toward the mountains, but the signage along the track made them now seem intrusive.

He passed a gas station. The edge of town. The rail seemed dominant. You belong to me now. Jack slowed, passing lodges, cafes, and fly shops. All seemed different—almost bewildered by the change. He glanced at a metal-sided structure standing over the tracks. Arms and elevators to load what's being mined. High above the river, he made out the first sign of mining—tailings, perched over the town. He slowed and stared. The pile sat catlike. Would it toy with the river, or kill it quickly?

Jack pulled into a general store. He climbed out, head down, not ready to be recognized. He approached a dark-haired girl at the cash register and asked for a phone book.

"Sure." She pulled it out from under the counter. "Who you looking for?"

He avoided her eyes. "Can't remember the first name. Not certain about the last."

She handed it over.

Jack ran his finger down the names. LeBlanc. Where is LeBlanc? Could his parents be unlisted?

"Find who you're looking for?" the girl asked.

"No."

"Remember the name yet?"

"LeBlanc."

"They moved. Had to."

"Had to? Why? Where'd they go?"

"No clue. All I know is, people ran 'em out. Especially the new people, people down river. Last I saw Toby, he said he wanted a fresh start."

"Just Toby, or his parents, too?"

"Both, I guess. I haven't seen 'em in . . . oh . . . two, maybe three years."

— · —

Jack drove through town, did a U-turn, and started back for Pendagraph Ranch.

Would they really run Kid and his parents out of town?

When Jack arrived at the fishing cabin, he climbed out of the Hummer, ambled down slope, and stopped a few feet from the river. He watched the current make its way past boulders and an old pine bole jutting from the bank.

Cool water, a beautiful mountain river, and miles from here, a valley, the same river, the same cool waters. What'll come of it there? A place loved by so many, a place where so many found life and wonder, connections to nature and all its stirrings. What will change and what will the change bring? And when will it happen?

He took a step, then another, pulled by the direction of flow, drawn by memories of people and passion, of inspirational people whose dreams drove him. People, who lived in that valley.

Pug mentioned the mine brought jobs, maybe high paying jobs, maybe something they need.

He plopped down and let his eye wander, staring at nothing in particular.

So, what happened to Kid?

— · —

Jack headed upslope, cutting a beeline for the cabin, uncertain how much time had lapsed. He pushed back a huckleberry branch, noticed a faint trace of trail, and followed, under stately pines. At a break in the trees, he spotted the cabin, and behind the Hummer, another vehicle. A pickup.

Who the hell's that? He snuck downhill of the pickup. Forest Service emblem. No one inside. No one milling about. He crept toward the cabin door and swung it open. No one. No one in the easy chair. He stepped inside. No one in the kitchen. Or in the bathroom. He went through the mud room and turned the knob on the outside door, swinging it open. Chairs, empty. A sound. The tub burner, roaring. A hat jutted over the rim of the tank. He eased out and stepped over clothes scattered on the flagstone. He stopped.

A woman lay stretched the length of the tub, the hat shading her face. In the crystal clear water, shimmers of light flashed the length of a lean, shapely body.

He tapped the tub with his boot and cleared his throat. "Are you supposed to be here?"

The woman stirred. She raised the brim of the hat, squinting as sun hit her face. "Hi, handsome. Or, should I say . . . stranger."

He let his jaw go slack. "What are you doing here?"

"Didn't you recognize me? You should know this body a mile away."

"Why are you here, Courtney?"

"I'm soaking." She flung the hat toward her clothes, and pushed a strand of reddish blonde hair from her eyes. She laughed. "That hadn't been the plan, but I got tired of waiting, when I saw this nifty little tub, and realized it might get your mind on other things before . . ." She paused.

"Before what?"

"Before you started asking questions. I hate it when you ask questions. Especially when the questions are hard, and the answers are nothing I want to talk about." She wrinkled her nose.

"That won't work."

"It did before. Wanna join me? There's plenty of room." She sat up and drew in her legs.

"Why are you here?"

"Finished my patrol for the day. Little bird told me you were here, so I took a detour."

"Hell of a detour. Who said I was here?"

The smile melted into a look of uncertainty. "I was at a trail-head half a mile from here. I just came off the trail, okay? I wanted to see you."

"Who? Buster?"

"No. Pug told me."

What the hell? Jack scowled.

"He said there was someone you needed to see. He assumed it was me."

He let out a breath, and dropped his arms.

She reached, grabbing the tail of his shirt. Water splashed at his feet.

He pushed her hands away.

"What's wrong, baby?"

"You made your choices. You could've come to New Mexico." He glanced at the clothes at his feet. Forest Service uniform. "You've changed agencies."

"Everything went to hell. Everyone was gone. I was the only one left to shut down the office. After that, there weren't any Park Service jobs in this part of Montana. Shea Pinkley offered me one."

"You sure it was after?"

"Before, after, what does it matter?"

"You stayed."

"I was tired of moving, Jack. I needed a place to call home."

"So this is your home?"

"Felt good for awhile. Not so sure anymore. Maybe I'm ready to move on." She frowned. "Turn that thing off before I cook like a lobster."

He stepped back and turned the knob on the gas. The flame died away. The burner went quiet. Only the sound of wind in the pines.

She sank back into the tub. "Thank you." She attempted a pout. "Get in with me, Jack baby. There's plenty of room. For old times."

He crossed his arms.

"It wasn't me you wanted to see, was it?" She twisted a lock of her hair.

"No."

She dropped her eyes. "Who'd you come to see? A woman?"

"Toby LeBlanc."

"Kid?"

"Yes, The Kid."

She broke into a laugh. "The kid whose life you screwed up?" Laughter overcame her, then she fell silent. "That or he screwed up yours." She smiled, and let it slip away. "Why? Why do you need to see him?"

"To check on him? See if he's okay."

"After all this time? You sure haven't checked on me. And after all the hell that kid caused, and that stupid ass effort you made to defend him."

"What happened to him?"

She shook her head, looking bewildered. "You took a hometown hero and destroyed his reputation. People here loved that kid. They were state champions in football because of him, never before, never since. Everyone saw him as their son. When The Kid came back from college, everyone had high hopes, and somehow, you found a way to screw that up, make 'em hate him. That or he did it to himself and you weren't smart enough to stop it."

"It was complicated."

"What's so complicated about a little science project?"

"That's a stupid comment."

"Sorry, I'm not a scientist. All I know is, people were scared, believed his work would give 'em answers, something to fight the fracking coming into the foothills. Then, the report came out and it did the opposite, justified it. Didn't matter what side you were on, you felt betrayed. You both were bad guys."

Jack glared. "His work would not've proven either point. That's not what he was trying to do. He could not've claimed his results pointed at or away from fracking."

"Why not?"

"Because it wasn't designed to isolate those kinds of variables."

"Jargon." She scowled. "What's that mean anyway?"

"It means to identify influences you have to isolate variables.

He wasn't trying to do that. But something he found got someone worried, and talk started. You saw what happened. He wasn't being an advocate, for either perspective. He was trying to be a good scientist."

"Good scientist," she said, sarcastically. "Well, I guess he wasn't."

"He was."

"Don't try convincing me, Jack. I saw how hard you fell on your ass. If the attacks had been against you, you would've handled it, professionally, but you went stupid. You should'a let him crash and burn, but no, you tried to save his silly ass. You looked stupid. Wishy-washy, like now."

"Maybe I could've done better, but that was my job."

"You should'a let him fail. Instead, politicos got involved. They went after you."

"I was responsible."

"He screwed up. You paid the price."

"He didn't screw up. He found something. What he found scared someone. In the end, Kid's data were changed. Our conclusions were changed. Not by him, not by me. I know who directed the final changes, but I don't know where the pressure came from or why. Maybe someone protecting themselves from the family of that little girl—the one who died of cancer, whose well water was toxic. Or maybe it wasn't, I don't know. All I know is, he didn't design his work to isolate those kinds of variables, or attribute those kinds of effects. For some reason people thought he did."

"Maybe because that's what they wanted to know." She crossed her arms. "I'm feeling unattractive. Here I lay, without a stitch on, and you want to talk about *variables*."

He ignored her. "The Kid needed my support."

"Hell of a lot of good it did. Last I heard, he'd moved away, never went back to grad school, turned his back on everything. Left in shame, a target to everyone who used to love him."

Jack sighed. "Where is he?"

"Hell if I know. No one seems to know. Why worry now? It's been three years."

"Hard to explain. I have to find him."

"Forget The Kid. Think about me. Take me away from here, Jack."

"You made your choice, Courtney. When I needed you, you chose to stay."

"It's not the same here now. With the mine here, new people are moving in. People here only for jobs. They don't care about this place. Old timers were worried about being invaded by huge resorts. They never thought it'd be a mine, right on top of 'em. Now they're either being forced out, or they're leaving, heartbroken, knowing what's going to happen."

"What is gonna happen? What did happen?"

"You're asking me? You were the one at the center of things."

"I know, but maybe I was too close. Maybe I couldn't see it. What happened? What did I miss?"

"I don't know, Jack," she said. She dropped her face into her hands. "Why are you asking me? You were so idealistic. Wore it like a point of pride, like it was beneath you to be drawn into it."

"Into what?"

"The power players, the games they thought you should play. The pandering they expected . . . that you refused to do."

"That's what came back to bite me?"

"No," she whispered. "You really don't know, do you?"

"No."

"Jack, it was the money.

"The money?"

"Tons of it. Pouring in. To everyone. Turning 'em stupid."

"What are you talking about?"

"Money. With conditions. That's why politicians were showing up. Right and left, like flies to honey. Don't you get it? That congressional hearing didn't just happen. Someone wanted the politicians here. They were willing to put out the money. Politicians came."

"But . . ."

She glared. "Damn it, Jack, quit being so damned naive. It was the money."

CHAPTER
20

"Turn on the heater."

"Huh? What?" Jack said, his mind elsewhere.

"The heater. Light it. I'm cold."

He shook his head. "Time to get out. You're starting to prune."

"Nice of you to notice." She stood, and flashed a flirtatious eye.

"Towels in the mud room."

She stepped out of the tub and waited.

He pointed at the side door.

"Are you being mean to me?" Pouting, she stomped off, dripping across the flagstone. "And don't be looking at my butt!"

"How can I not?"

She slowed, strutted to the door, and reached in for a towel. She walked back drying the ends of her hair. "There's someone in your life, isn't there?"

"There is."

"Is she good to you? You deserve someone good to you."

"She is. Very good."

Courtney wrapped the towel around herself. "I'm glad." Tears formed in the corners of her eyes. "I'm sorry, Jack. For everything."

"Let's not talk about that. But I've got a request."

"For what?"

"That you keep your ears open. Ask a few questions. Find out where Kid is."

"I doubt I'll hear a thing. People could care less."

"Just try, please."

She gave him a bit of a smile. "Gonna give me your phone number? In case I learn something?"

"No, but you know how to find me."

— · —

Jack watched the Forest Service pickup make a three point turn, and head up the mountain.

He sat listening until he could no longer hear its tires fighting for bite on the rocky road.

She's gone.

Once again, her departure leaves me feeling lonely. Only this time, not for her.

He waited a few minutes more, then climbed in the Hummer and drove toward town, checking his phone for reception.

On the outskirts, he stopped. Four bars. He called Kelly's cell.

She answered on the first ring. "Hi stranger."

"Why do people keep calling me that?" He sighed. "Never mind. I wanted to hear your voice."

"Ooh," she swooned. "Good. Come home."

"Can't. Not yet."

"You're needed here. You've been hard to get hold of."

"I know. No cell phone reception. The owner likes it that way."

"I don't blame him, but Father needs you to call him."

"About?"

"Dinner with Senator Baca. He said you need to be there."

"Coalition Report?"

"Partly. There's a rumor about a bill working its way through the House."

"To do what?"

"It has something to do with Moony Manson. It's all very secretive, with favors being called in, and supporters lined up. The senator fears it might let Manson do anything he wants, anywhere he wants."

"It's public land. Who's bill?"

"No one will say, but Father thinks it could be trouble for the coalition."

"Why?"

"I don't know, Jack. Father didn't tell me everything. He knows how I feel about politics. But he's worried, and he thinks Senator Baca needs to hear from you, so he has what he needs to combat this."

"Tell Kip to call the superintendent. Joe Morgan's better with politicians."

"He knew you'd say that."

"Did he call Joe?"

"Joe's not available. Another commitment. Too short a notice."

"Did he tell Joe how important this is?"

"I don't know, Jack. All I know is, he thinks you should be there. The senator wants assurances the agencies support the report, that they won't throw a wrench in the works if timing's a factor. The best way to show that is you being there."

Jack sighed, eyeing the tracks stretching into town. He turned away, and gazed out over the river. A riffle slipped between rocks into still water. A perfect place to put a fly. Unless nothing's there, as in gone . . . dead.

This fight's decided. New Mexico's not. This time, you've got to do more. Fight more. "Probably get me in trouble, but . . . I'll be there. When?"

"Tomorrow night."

So much for finding The Kid.

He ended the call and tucked the phone in his pocket. Fight more? Than here? How?

And what have you just done?

— · —

Jack found Buster in one of the pastures, moving tarp up a ditch to get water onto a different piece of ground. Jack killed the engine and climbed out.

Buster leaned on his shovel. "Here to help?"

"I'm a lousy irrigator."

"Who isn't?" Buster gave his mustache a twist. "Ya have to make water flow uphill. It's harder than it sounds."

Jack eyed the water pooled behind the tarp, beginning to tickle through the grass. "I'm heading home, Buster. Give my thanks to Pug. For everything."

"You're not takin' the job?"

"I'm thinking about it. Tell him that. If I get fired, I'll need it."

"Fired? What'd you do?"

"Nothing, but the act of going home might be seen as insubordination."

"Hell, they can't fire you guys. You've got a job for life."

"Misconception. Any suggestion on how I can get to the airport?"

"I'd take ya', but I've got a guy showing up to work on the backhoe. Take the Hummer. Toss the keys under the seat and lock the door. I'll use the other set, get it this weekend. Treat my lady friend to a day on the town."

"Sounds like I'm an imposition."

"Nope," he said, with a shake of his head. "Why the hell you heading home if it's only gonna get you in trouble? Stay. Fish, drink beer, and fish some more."

Jack laughed. "Something's come up."

— · —

Jack tossed the keys under the seat, hit the lock button, and closed the door on the big, black Hummer. With his pack and his duffle, he made his way into the airport.

He changed reservations and an hour later climbed onto a plane to Salt Lake City, where he caught the next flight to Albuquerque, by way of Los Angeles.

—·—

Kelly stood outside security, in jeans, white silk shirt and boots, her hair pulled back. When she saw him, her eyes lit up.

Jack let his bag slip from his shoulder, onto the floor. He took her in his arms.

"You seem even taller," she said, her face against his chest. "You okay?"

"Am now, why?"

"Kenya. Montana."

"Quite a journey. In more ways than distance."

"We can talk about it." She ran a hand across the stubble on his cheeks. "I've missed that face. Those blue eyes, the gray showing amidst the brown on your temples. How about a drink in the lounge?"

"Let's head home. We can talk in the car. I could use some carne asada at Elena's. Maybe a margarita."

"Won't make it before she closes the restaurant. You'll have to wait till tomorrow, at dinner with Senator Baca."

—·—

Heading north out of Albuquerque, Kelly turned off the radio. "Get done what you hoped to in Montana?"

Staring, enjoying the sight of her, Jack sighed. "I'd hoped to find someone. A college kid I'd hired. No luck."

"Why was that important?"

"Got to admit, I'm not entirely sure. Felt like I needed to check on him. See how he was doing. See how the mess in Montana affected him. See if I needed to fix something."

"Was this because of something you did?" Kelly asked, eyes locked on the highway.

"No, what others did. Things he got caught up in. Things he didn't deserve." Jack took his eyes off the road. "Couldn't protect him. He kinda disappeared, unexpectedly. Failed to show at a hearing. When politics were overrunning us. Things going to hell."

"Why's it important, now?"

"Parallels. With something that happened in Kenya."

"Explain."

"I was there because a young scientist was killed. One working on important issues. It wasn't till the last day that I learned why Samuel Leboo carried such a burden. Angry words he said to the young man, last time he saw him."

"Poor Samuel." She shook her head, and brushed dark strands of hair from her face. "But why is that like Montana?"

"I failed to protect the kid." He sighed. "But it's really not like Kenya. Samuel . . . he's fighting the odds. Complex issues. Politics. Risks to his own future."

"Well, this sounds familiar."

"Yes and no," he said, studying her beautiful brown eyes. "For me it was humbling."

She glanced his way. "Why?"

"Because of the circumstances. Samuel and his rangers . . . and rangers all over Africa . . . they face death every day. The creatures they dedicate themselves to preserving . . . they face extinction. It may happen, on their watch. My life's easy compared to that."

"Easy?" Kelly said, a furrow forming across her brow. "How can you say that?"

"This is America. We're a nation of laws. Societal norms. Nothing like Africa."

She slowed. "Jack, before you left, men were pointing automatic weapons at you."

"Semi-automatic." He shrugged. "They were bluffing. They wouldn't've done anything."

"Are you crazy? You looked down the barrel of a gun. Did you think they were bluffing then?"

"No, but in hindsight . . . "

"But in hindsight, you've chosen to wear rose colored glasses."

"No, it's just that . . ." Words escaped him.

"I appreciate that there are differences. I'm making a big deal of it because I don't want you doing something stupid, thinking you have it easy. I don't want you stepping in front of a gun, just because you're in America, just because most of us abide by laws and societal norms. More people die from guns in America than about any place that isn't a war zone. Promise me you won't do something stupid."

"I promise, but it is different there. Samuel has a very difficult job." He paused. "Change of subject. I want to help him, if I can."

"You're going back?"

"That's not what I'm saying. The young scientist who died . . . his murder had a strange circuitous connection to someone here in the States, probably New Mexico."

She sped up. "Who?"

"Don't know. Got clues but not many. International Affairs is trying to get me contacts."

"You're doing that, plus trying to find a college kid in Montana?"

"Hoping someone will help me on that, too." He sighed. "An old girlfriend."

"The one in the staff photos on your office wall?"

"The same."

"She's beautiful. How much did you see of her?"

"Talked only a few minutes." He caught Kelly's eye. "But, I saw more than I wanted to."

— · —

Moonlight on the distant plateau, shadows ominously lurking in the canyon, lights from the hamlet of Las Piedras flickering on the plain below. He reacquainted himself as they drove toward Piedras Coloradas. It had not been that long, but it felt somehow like years. Without words, Kelly steered through town and onto the road to the canyon.

She had told him what little she knew of the issues her father was working to untangle. None of the thoughts of those things now competed with the first sights of home.

She turned down the road to his cabin. "Can I come in?"

— · —

Jack rose early. Kelly was gone.

He slipped on jeans and a T-shirt, intent on being the first person to see the Park Superintendent, and intending to be gone before anyone else arrived. In the early morning light, he walked the trail to headquarters, and stood waiting in the hall when Joe Morgan unlocked the front door to the building.

"Morning, Joe."

Joe paused, then without words unlocked his office, stepped in, and dropped his briefcase on his big timber desk. "Come in," he said, without turning back. He took off his Stetson and laid in it on the credenza. Uniform and graying hair perfect, as always, Joe sat and waved Jack to a seat. "The director told me he ordered you to say away."

"He did."

"He said he sent you to Montana, which surprised me, by the way."

"This may surprise you even more. It was my idea."

"Then, why back so soon? Why risk the ire of the director? Why cause me work?"

"Because it's home, and because Kip Culberson set up something with Senator Baca. You weren't available."

"True, but I'm not sure that constitutes a reason to come back from Montana."

"There's rumor of a bill in the House. Something to do with Moony Manson. Has Kip worried."

"Legislative Affairs heard it, too, and told me not to worry about it. There's no talk of a bill in the Senate, and if there was, it doesn't appear to have the votes to give it any life. The House, yes, but not in the Senate."

"What if they did have a senate bill?"

"It'll suffer a painful emasculation in markup."

"Kip also wants to begin talks with the senator about the co-alition report. Hopes to strategize the legislation needed to move recommendations forward. To that end, the senator wants to know that the agencies support what's been done."

Joe picked up a pen and gave it several clicks. "Maybe it's

good you'll be there, but other than that, you've got to stay invisible. Discreet."

"Things haven't died down?"

"They've peaked, yes, but we're still getting congressional inquiries. All partisan."

"What'd BLM do about Manson?"

"Nothing. They're still considering options, and so is the Justice Department. Things could be really ugly by the time they take action."

"Anyone talking about me?"

Joe smiled. "Cable news. Every other day or so, your mug makes an appearance. Edited, of course, to serve one purpose or another." He paused. "Do you understand why the director doesn't want you here?"

Jack nodded.

"I expect you to lay low. You're still on annual leave. I don't want to end up on some phone call, explaining why you were seen in New Mexico when the director thinks you're in Montana."

"What about this dinner tonight with Senator Baca?"

"That's not exactly lying low. Explain things to Kip. Tell him I want things under the radar. I want things discreet."

"I'm always discreet."

"Yes, you are, but it doesn't always play that way." He picked up the pen and gave it more clicks. "In fact, it hardly ever does."

CHAPTER
21

Jack slinked home to lay low until time for the meeting.

He called Kip and passed on Joe's expectation that the meeting stay under the radar. "The director thinks I'm still in Montana."

"Understood," Kip said. "The senator and I go way back. He'll understand the sensitivity. But, it's important you're there, to make the pitch for legislation."

"Kip, I can't lobby. You can, I can't."

"What're you saying?"

"You and Karen need to make the pitch. In fact, I'm here to show agency involvement and support, maybe answer questions, but it'd be best if I said nothing."

"Why do you say that?"

"Because Baca's a politician. I'm not good around politics, or politicians."

"Son, you're talking to someone who spent a good part of his life in politics. I've never seen you as incapable."

"It's different. You're not in office."

Kip laughed. "Once in, one rarely gets away from politics entirely. It keeps drawing you back."

"Maybe you're different."

"Maybe you're thinking too hard."

"Kip, let me put it another way. We should play to our strengths. You like working with people like the senator. So does Karen Hatcher. I don't."

"Hogwash."

"I don't schmooze."

"Good. Don't even try. Your credibility's what's important. Kelly's joining to cover those bases."

"Kelly?"

"Simply to be her charming self. Baca's always been more charmed by my wife than he ever was by me. So, I invited Kelly, who can be as charming as her mother." He laughed. "But she doesn't see it that way. She's trying to get out of it. All sorts of excuses." Kip paused. "Here's the plan. Reservations at Elena's, seven o'clock. Table near the kiva fireplace. Dinner party as follows: Senator Baca, senior senator from New Mexico. One of his aides. Karen Hatcher, you, me, and finally, Kelly, the junior charmer from Las Piedras."

"Very funny."

"Not to Kelly."

— · —

"Knock, knock."

Kelly stood at the door, dressed to the nines, in long skirt and sleeveless blouse. A bit of a business look about her. Different but not out of the ordinary.

Jack set down his book and went to the door. "It's the junior charmer from Las Piedras."

"That's not funny. I shouldn't be doing this."

"You'll be great."

"I will not. At least you've got something to contribute. Me? I'm just there to smile and laugh at his jokes." She looked at Jack's jeans, then his T-shirt. "You think you're wearing that?"

"Give me a moment." He went into the bedroom, pulled off his T-shirt, changed to a white shirt with a button-down collar, slipped on a black sports coat, and returned. "How's this?"

"Better. Guess the jeans are okay." She scowled. "No, hold it."

Her face went blank, then grew a smarmy smile. "You look perfect, Mr. Chastain. Just perfect."

— · —

They crossed through the bar. Jack approached the hostess. "Joining the Culberson party."

The hostess led them down the pine-plank hallway, into the dining room, its walls bright with whitewashed adobe, its ceilings crossed by vigas and latillas. A small fire burned in the kiva fireplace on the furthest wall. She walked them past windows overlooking the courtyard, where rows of plants in Elena's garden—herbs, peppers, tomatoes—stood in bounty, in the warm glow of the evening sun.

They approached the table and the hostess departed. Kip and Karen Hatcher—Kip in a western-cut sport coat, no tie, and Karen in a navy blazer—sat hunkered over notes. They looked up.

"Sweetheart, you look great," Kip said to Kelly.

"Don't talk to me," she said, forcing a frown.

He laughed and turned to Jack. "Karen and I know what we want to say. You fill in the gaps. Glad you're back. They can't hide you forever." His eye flashed to the door. "The senator's here."

"Kip," Baca shouted from across the room, his suit the same hue as his shock of gray hair, his build stout and compact. He stepped past the hostess.

Kip took two steps toward him. "Bob, thank you for coming." He shook the senator's hand, and made introductions.

"Good to see you again, Ms. Hatcher," Baca said. He continued around, stopping at Jack. He gave him an eye. "We've met, I believe. I'm good with names, but in your case, your face is more familiar."

"We've never met." Jack turned to Kip. "This might not be a good idea."

"Jack's been in the news of late," Kip said. "Couple of weeks ago." He paused. "This mess concerning our friend Moony Manson." Kip seemed to watch the senator process the information. "That's not why Jack's here. He's the one who convinced us to look for common ground. That pulled us together, reminded us we're community."

Baca nodded. "Glad you're here. If you're worried about partisan politics, you needn't worry about mine. Kip's party's raising the ruckus." He flashed a teasing smile. "Have him make some calls."

"Not that they're listening to me," Kip said. He pulled out a chair. "Everyone have a seat. Bob, I thought you were bringing an aide."

"Last minute issue with a constituent." He set his eyes on Kelly. "It's a pleasure to meet you, my dear. You look like your mother."

"She would've enjoyed seeing you, Senator."

"Always a pleasure seeing her."

The server arrived and passed out the menus. "Drinks?" She went around the table, scribbling orders.

Water. Margarita. Margarita. Water. Whiskey neat.

Kip raised a weathered hand. "Change mine. Another whiskey."

She scurried off, returned with drinks, then took their orders.

"This bill we're hearing about . . . rumors in the House. Anything to worry about?" Kip asked.

Baca took a sip of his whiskey. "Not sure. There's a push by someone to make Moony Manson a symbol. To do what, I don't yet know. Before leaving D.C. I got a call from leadership. There's even talk now of a bill in the Senate, and favors being swapped to get it out of committee."

Hatcher placed her hands on the table. "We do not need that distraction. We need people focused on recommendations of the coalition. They mean too much to too many people." She glanced at Kip, then Jack. "Manson acts like the lands he grazes are his, but they're public lands. If we fight over who has a right to be here or not, the battle never ends. If we work together, we achieve living together, all benefitting from public lands." She paused. "We've had ups and downs, but all parts of our community—and society—are here, involved. Local, regional and national influences, all involved, working with the Park Service and BLM. We don't need a bill that could tear us apart."

"I understand. I'll do what I can. This might blow over, but . . ."

"But what?"

"I learned the House bill's sponsor is Congressman Brent Hoff, conservative favorite for the White House. He's riding sentiment pushed by those wanting to change who controls public lands."

"Those people are playing politics," Karen said, now angry, the dimple in her chin all the more prominent. "They want decisions made locally, where they're influenced by money. Senator, these are public lands. They belong to all of us."

Baca glanced at Kip.

"Don't forget," Kip muttered, "the senator and I both started in the state legislature. I for one—and I'm guessing the senator—don't exactly lack faith in state and local government."

"I know, but . . ."

"I don't lack faith," Baca said, "but the depth of ideology varies state to state, especially in the west. In some places, I'd be afraid to see what might happen on nationally significant lands."

Kip nodded.

"What do you think, Kip?" Baca continued, eyeing his whiskey. "What would happen in New Mexico? Think these lands would be managed better or worse by state or local government?"

"If we're honest, it wouldn't change much. If left as range," Kip said. He sat back, and unbuttoned his sport coat. "Range management practices don't vary. Parks and monuments? The national label is much more a draw. The risk might be, funding strangled off at the state or local levels by people pushing an agenda."

Baca turned to the others around the table. "If Manson paid his fees he'd be paying a buck sixty nine per animal unit month to BLM. That's a third of what he'd pay if he grazed on state land. The state's required by law to maximize the value of its lands. It makes four dollars, eighty cents per animal unit month. If renting private land, he'd pay quite a bit more. Those details are never mentioned," Baca added, exchanging looks around the table. "But the battle cry's out there, some singing it loudly, trying to get the nation to sing along."

"How do we stop it?" Karen asked. "The rhetoric . . ."

"I know . . . rhetoric," Baca said. "It's always out there. I'll stay involved, do what I can, underscore the history of collaboration here. That'll count for something. I'll underscore the public support for the monument. I'll also touch base with the House members in our delegation, suggest changes to make during mark up."

"That's what we were hoping for," Kip said.

"Things aren't quite that simple," Baca said. "Something else is trying to raise its head. Another bill in the Senate to force concessions for wild horses, or turn the monument into a horse sanctuary."

"You can't be serious," Kip said, sitting upright. "Who's bill?"

Baca smiled. "Haven't seen it yet."

Jack's back stiffened. He scooted closer. "Not someone from New Mexico?"

"Definitely not someone from New Mexico."

"Why would another member of Congress care what's happening here?" Kelly asked. She sheepishly glanced around the table. "If it's not their state?"

"It happens." Baca shrugged. "A constituent takes interest, maybe one that's a major donor. The member sees political hay to be made."

"Doesn't seem smart to get involved," Karen said. "Counter to preservation. Counter to science."

"There are powerful people passionate about mustangs."

"Can't we turn 'em around?

"You could try, if you knew who they were."

"So far, no bill for horses in the House, right?" Kip countered.

"There's a rumor," Baca said, running fingers through his gray shock of hair, "that there's work on a House bill, but it's not clear they're working together. In fact, it might only be a procedural ploy."

"Why?" Karen asked, gripping the lapels of her blazer, glaring through blonde strands of hair falling over her eyes.

"To create bills that make it out of committee, and go to the floors for a vote. Then, in conference committee, they could get stripped or reworked."

"Maybe that's good," Kip said.

"Depends on what angle they're working."

Silence settled over the table.

Kip cleared his voice. "What we need is the bill authorizing the coalition's recommendations."

"Your timing's not good," Baca said, shaking his head. "It's about to be election season. Election politics."

Kip stared back.

"Do something now, you risk having something you need turned into something you don't."

"If we don't move now," Kip said, "we risk losing support."

"Then get me something quick," Baca said. "But, we'll be taking a chance, considering everything else we've discussed."

"I talked to someone in D.C. about the wild horse lobby . . . ," Karen interjected.

"Hold it," Baca said. "Is this someone in the wild horse lobby?"

"Not sure that's a good idea."

"You won't learn much about Baptists talking to Presbyterians." Baca smiled. "Even less about Catholics." He picked up his whiskey and let laughter die away. "You're only gonna learn what he thinks he knows, or what he wants you to believe."

"Senator, they don't have a reputation for rational . . ."

"If you save your seeds, all you've got is seeds."

"Meaning?"

"If you don't share your ideas with people thinking differently than you—even the wild horse lobby—then you're just talking to yourself."

"But the horse lobby, they worry me. They operate only on passion. They have their own take on science. They ignore anything inconvenient to their cause."

"You've got to find time to work on understanding. See if they've got ideas to help your cause."

"I wish they'd just go away. Take their seeds and go home."

The senator laughed.

The server arrived with a tray and circled the table, putting down plates.

"Isn't the most productive pasture . . ." Kelly said, ". . . planted in different seed, different ideas, for different seasons." She glanced around the table. Sheepishly she dropped her head. "Sorry."

Kip rested a hand on her shoulder. "If you're gonna make it in politics, you'll have to work on your folksy analogies."

"Well, I'm not, so I'll shut up."

"Are you saying, consider all perspectives?" Baca asked. He picked up his fork. "Not make it winners and losers?"

"Yes, sir."

"Then, well said, my dear." Baca smiled and raised his glass, then turned to Kip, then Karen Hatcher. "For now, I'll work on getting these bills killed. I'll watch for something from you."

"Understood," Kip said. "Is there anything more we can do? Talk to anyone? Ask for support?"

"I'll let you know."

They ate as the sun set. The room grew dim. Candles and the fire held back the darkness.

When dishes were pulled, the senator sat back and made himself comfortable. He ordered another drink. "Kelly, how's your mother? I'd ask Kip, but it's much more pleasant hearing your voice."

"She's doing well. It's strange, but she's much more inclined than Father to divide time between Santa Fe and home." Her brown eyes caught her father's. "Suits her. She thrives in both worlds."

Baca nodded. "Almost as if she were the one who should've been mixing it up in the legislature." He shot Kip a look. "Your father was a fine legislator, but he's a bit of an introvert. Sometimes it's hard for him to dive into the crush of people."

"I'd rather spend my days with my cows."

"And your land." Baca took a sip of his whiskey. "Kip, I've got something to share, and it needs to stay at this table." He sighed. "This will be my last term in office."

"That's a well-kept secret."

"Keep it that way." He winked. "I'm tired, ready to come home."

"I understand."

"You may understand, but look at yourself. Maybe you should make a run for my seat."

"Bob, retirement's good, and you'd have a hard time saying that in public. I'm the wrong party."

"Change parties."

Kip laughed. "That's not gonna happen. Too conservative."

"Hell, I've got a conservative streak, along with my other colors. We all have a little bit of everything in us, but I'm less concerned about party affiliation than I am with finding someone good to represent the state." He sighed, and took another sip. "I realize, that's a losing perspective these days. The game is so different now."

"Very different."

"These days it's hard to work with, much less vote with, people across the aisle. Maybe it's a phase. Maybe things will get better."

"I don't see a reason to think it will, and I'm not cut out for today's politics."

The server delivered another drink to the senator. He whispered a request for his check. "Kip, I think you are. The state could use you."

"I'm retired."

"You're not. You're as active as ever. Think about it. I'd rather see a good man running against us than a bad one. It'd make us work twice as hard to put up a good candidate." He gave a sheepish smile. "Sorry how that sounded, Kip. If you ran, I'd find a way to support you."

"That'd be hard to do."

"Yes, but I would."

"I'll make it easy. I'm not interested."

"Had to try."

The server returned with the checks. With everything taken care of, Baca tipped back his whiskey and stood. Kip and Karen dropped their cash on the table and walked him to his car.

"Think he's interested?" Jack asked, standing to leave.

"You mean Father? The senate seat?"

"Yeah."

"Not a chance. He's wise, isn't he?"

"Baca or your father?"

"Huh? . . . Oh, . . . both."

CHAPTER
22

Kelly took Jack's hand. In the hall on the way to the bar, she pulled him out a side door, into the courtyard. A breeze pushed her hair, more black than the night, back from her face.

Light from the dining room fell across rows of plants. The lilt of music drifted from the bar.

Jack leaned against a wall in the shadow between windows.

Kelly rested against him, taking his arms, wrapping them around her. "Glad that's over." She laughed. "We were silly, weren't we?"

"Why do you say that?"

"Neither one of us wanted to be here. Both of us, worried, yet everything turned out okay."

"We'll see." He nestled his face in her hair, taking in the scent.

"Didn't you think it went well?"

"With the senator, yes. Doesn't mean it'll turn out okay."

"Someone that wise? How could they not listen to him?"

"Hope you're right. I, for one, won't get my hopes up."

"You're troubled. Why?"

"Because it involves politics. Baca will have to deal with his counterparts. Politicians."

"I'm sure they'll listen."

"You really think they will?"

"Father and Karen Hatcher seem to think so."

"If there's anyone who understands how this works, it's those two. I have more faith in them than I do in politicians. Me? I fear being pulled into politics. Dealing with egos. Their games."

"What are you not telling me?"

"Nothing."

"You're the most idealistic person I know. I've never heard you so cynical."

"Sorry."

"Answer me. What are you not telling me? Is it something that happened in Montana?" She turned to face him. "What is your secret?"

"I don't have a secret."

"I think you do. I think there's a reason you act like that. Who could blame you, by the way, for not trusting politicians, but . . . you trust everyone. You give everyone the benefit of the doubt. What are you not telling me?"

He sighed. "Nothing."

"I don't believe it." She took his hand and pulled him through the door, her skirt flapping with each hard-placed step. "I want a margarita."

He tried to slow her. "Kelly, I need to lay low. The restaurant is one thing. The bar quite another."

"Don't be silly. You can't just hide." Holding his arm, she walked him around the corner, past the hostess, into the bar.

"Boss," came a voice, from a table against the wall.

Jack turned.

Johnny Reger. Others around him. Two men and a woman. Young people. Fire crew. Wearing a T-shirt that accented his state of conditioning, Johnny flashed his easy smile and waved them over. "Didn't know you were home."

"I'm not."

Johnny looked confused. "What's that mean?"

"Don't tell anyone you saw me."

"He's being silly," Kelly said.

A dark-haired, bearded man at a nearby table stood and headed for the door.

Johnny watched him leave. "That guy here to see you?"

Jack turned and caught a glimpse of the man. "What are you talking about?"

"Me? What are you talking about?"

"I promised Joe I'd stay under the radar. Who was that guy?"

"Says he's investigating something. Figured he's here to talk to you or the superintendent. Started to mention you're gone, but figured that'd be presumptuous. And nosy." He threw his head back and laughed. "Well, I did get nosy. He didn't bite. Didn't seem to mind that we spilled beer on him." He paused. "Well, the waitress spilled the beer. I just didn't know she was behind me. Talking with my hands." He gave a demonstrative wave. Something caught his eye. He hollered, "Hey, turn that up, would you?"

The bartender picked up a remote control.

Jack glanced back, catching sight of a television on the wall. "Where'd that come from?"

"They're trying it out. For sports mainly, but tourists keep wanting news, so it gets changed."

The bartender un-muted the sound.

"*. . . just how would you sum things up, Congressman?*"

The anchorman dissolved away to Congressman Brent Hoff, his black suit coat buttoned, a microphone extended toward him. Seemingly cornered in marbled halls, Hoff furrowed his brow.

"*Manson's a patriot. I encourage him to fight. Bureaucrats can't be allowed to make stuff up.*"

From the host, came:

"*If you are elected president . . .*

Smiling, Hoff cut him off.

"*Hold it, hold it. It's too early to speculate about the race for president. I want to determine who's accountable for this mess in New Mexico. Why did the federal bureaucracy think they could swoop in and take a man's land and his livelihood?*"

"Heard enough," Johnny shouted. "Turn it off."

The volume muted.

"How's that for a welcome home?" Johnny smiled. "Things are the same as when you left, and what'd you mean you're not here?"

"Never mind." Jack ran a hand across his brow, staring at the door. "That man. Who was he?"

Johnny glanced at the others.

Shoulder shrugs.

"What's happening with Manson? With everything?"

Johnny stood. "Can we do this tomorrow? Fitness time comes early. Story might get long, and we gotta get outta here. Got just enough time to hear about Africa."

Jack attempted a smile. "Same. Too much to tell."

"We'll talk over beer. Sounds like you're buyin." Johnny waved the others to follow. He headed for the door.

Jack looked at Kelly.

She shrugged.

"Hello stranger."

Why do people keep . . . ? Jack turned to the voice.

Lizzy McClaren sat at a table covered with overturned cocktail glasses, her green eyes glassy, subdued amidst her red, swarming hair. She smiled. "Need a place to sit?" She gestured at the now near-empty bar. "Seating's tight this time a night."

"Didn't see you, Lizzy. You must've been hiding behind all those glasses."

She wrinkled her nose and giggled.

"Lizzy, this is Kelly Culberson." He turned to Kelly. "Lizzy's a guide on the river."

Lizzy offered a hand. "Same Kelly Culberson on the paintings in the gallery?"

She nodded.

"Cool. Those ain't cheap. Leaving or having a drink?"

They looked at each other. "Guess we're having a drink." Jack pulled a chair out for Kelly. "Drinking a little heavy, aren't we Lizzy?"

"Quite the lush, huh?" She laughed. "Most of those aren't mine. I had dinner and drinks with clients, retirees from California. They kept buying me drinks, one after another. Wonderful people.

They're heading out tomorrow, so they said their goodbyes and went to bed." She let out a giggle. "So, here I sit, me and the last grasshopper. Alone." A realization settled over her. She smirked. "Till now."

"How're you getting home?"

"Walkin'." She giggled.

"Lived here long? Your face is new to me," Kelly said.

"Been here awhile. I don't come here often. I get along fine with my own cooking, and I don't drink much." She smiled self-consciously, and turned to Jack. "Can you tell? Did one of the Parkies say you were in Africa?"

"Kenya."

She glanced down. "Hey, my new dress. Like the colors? Should get me through the summer." She turned to Kelly. "Do not let him near me with scissors." She giggled. "Oh . . . were you on safari?"

Kelly appeared confused.

Jack started to explain, and decided not to bother. "Work."

"Nice. I'd love to go to Kenya. It's on my list. A trip like that would take a lotta tips, wouldn't it? Big tips. How long were you there?"

"Maybe a week."

"Nice. That's long enough."

"Except I left with unfinished business. Unfinished science."

"You and your science. You get around, Jack Chastain."

"Feels that way. How are river levels?"

"Oh, . . ." She raised her eyes to the ceiling, considering the question. "Holding up. We may get a few more weeks in. That's more than we thought at the beginning of the season." She took a sip of the grasshopper. "We're lucky Colorado got snow. A few more weeks and us guides might stay in the black over the winter."

"Any rain?"

"Not since that flash flood." Lizzy's eyes grew wide. She turned to Kelly. "Did he tell you about some woman running around half naked?" She giggled. "That was me."

Kelly gave Jack an eye. "Somehow he forgot to mention it."

"Whoa. What a wall of water. Monster. Lucky we're alive." She shook, reliving the experience, then grew still. "Why was I telling that story?"

"You were running around naked."

"Oh, yeah." She giggled. "All he noticed . . . no life vest." She took a sip and set down the glass. "Guess he sees that sort of thing all the time."

"Yeah, all the time," Kelly said, still eyeing him.

"She had clothes on," Jack said. "Just ripped to shreds."

"We were on the river," Lizzy said. "That sort of thing almost goes without saying."

"You don't say."

Jack gave Kelly a nudge. "I saw more of you when we met. A lot more."

Kelly's eyes sprung wide. She covered her mouth.

Lizzy's eyes lit up.

They laughed.

"Do not tell her about that."

"I just did."

They laughed.

"Did he hit on you?" Lizzy asked, turning serious.

"No." Kelly shook her head, equally serious. She broke into a laugh. "I hit on him. He wasn't wearing anything, either."

Lizzy's mouth flew open. "Gonna tell me about it, girlfriend?"

"No."

They laughed.

Jack shook his head. Women.

Kelly waved down the bartender. "I'll have what she's drinking. Anything for you, Jack?"

"I'm driving."

The bartender delivered her drink, then another.

When Lizzy finished hers, she turned over the glass and set it on the table, upside down. "Did I tell you I owe Jack a favor?"

Kelly's eyes narrowed, her face stern. "What kind of favor?" She burst into laughter.

Lizzy giggled. "Not that kind of favor. He saved my client. He saved me. That night at camp, we told stories like it was the best day we'd ever had. All of us. In our lives. It could have been very different. I owe him."

"You don't," Jack said. "I told you that. I do not keep scores. I do not collect favors."

"You don't, but the rest of the world does," she said, sounding sober. "I know when I'm indebted."

Change the subject. "Notice the dark-haired guy sitting by himself?"

"The one with the beard, who left when you came in?"

"Yes, that one."

"Yeah, nice guy. Parkies spilled beer on him. Acted like it was no big deal, but he also seemed to listen to everything they said. I could tell, especially when the loud Parkie was talking."

"Johnny? Did you talk to this guy?"

"Me? No. He talked to my clients. Asked if they were local."

"And?"

"They said they weren't. He turned back to his beer."

"Happen to mention his name?"

"Yeah." She contorted her face. "Alex, something. Alex Tras . . . Trax . . . oh, I can't remember. I'm bad with names."

"Never mind. Lizzy, we're driving you home."

——·——

Jack drove past the edge of town, toward the river, and onto the property of Enchanted Rivers Rafting.

Its sheet-metal building, trimmed in timber, sat amidst a graveled lot, looking buttoned up for the night.

"Go past the boat barn," Lizzy said, pointing to a road that ran alongside the building.

Jack slowed and steered past the barn.

"There," she said, pointing into cottonwoods, at a cluster of single-wide trailers. "Third one. That's my mansion."

Jack braked to a stop.

At the door to the trailer sat a single rusted-metal lawn chair, a wood and cement block contrivance of a table, and a pink flamingo, standing on one leg at the edge of the small lawn.

"I'd invite you in, but I don't have any alcohol. Good thing, huh?"

"We're fine," Jack said.

"Good night," Kelly shouted, as Lizzy climbed out.

Lizzy staggered into the beam of the headlights, turned, waved, then swerved her way along the path to the door. She unlocked it, stepped inside, waved again, and slammed it closed.

Jack put the vehicle in reverse and backed toward the road.

Kelly broke into a laugh. "I like her."

CHAPTER
23

THE NEXT MORNING.

"Marge," Jack said, when the superintendent's secretary answered the phone. "Can I get on Joe's calendar?"

The line fell quiet, then, "He'll talk to you now."

"I'm here," Joe said, coming on the line.

"I'm reporting in on the meeting with the senator."

"What happened?"

"Culberson and Hatcher asked him to fight off the bill about Manson. It's Congressman Hoff's. Baca said he'll do what he can, but that could be difficult. Hoff's influential at present. Baca shared a rumor about a possible Senate version, as well as another to elevate wild horses to primacy in the purpose of the monument."

"You're kidding."

"That was our reaction. Apparently there's also a House version of that bill in the works, but it's uncertain whether it's honestly intended to help or to hurt the cause."

"Interesting. I'll call Legislative Affairs, see if they've heard anything new." Joe cleared his throat. "Now, . . . will anything get back to the director?"

"I don't think so."

"Let's hope you're right. For now, lay low. Be invisible."

"Joe, I'll take leave. I'll stay away from the office. I'll do everything in my power to keep from drawing attention. But, if the coalition needs my help, I'll help. And, I will not hide."

"If things come up, we'll take care of it. You're on leave. You . . . go get a hobby."

Jack laughed.

Joe did not.

— · —

Jack made a pot of coffee, read a newspaper online, then started a murder mystery. A chapter in, he grew restless.

He checked his watch. A little before nine. He ambled into the kitchen and pulled his service radio out of its charger. He turned it on. Promptly at nine, the dispatcher started her daily report, beginning with the day and date, then the weather. No change. Sunny with little chance of precipitation. Molly covered the large groups the rangers could expect in the campgrounds, and the nature walks and interpretive programs the naturalists would give over the course of the day. Molly signed off, and Jack reached for the radio, then stopped. Hell, it's company. Leave it on.

Knocking around his storage room, he cleaned an old pack, shook the sand from several pairs of boots, and checked out an old kayak, now that the pieces of the new one lay scattered along the river. This one will suffice, if needed.

With nothing more to clean or organize, he went back to the living room and turned on his laptop. He opened email, then stopped.

Joe said to get a hobby.

Should've taken up drawing. Or poetry.

Would tracking down poachers count? Until Iggy calls, who else might be helpful? Fish and Wildlife Service.

He made quick call to a colleague in the Biological Resource Division for the Park Service's Washington office, asking who in

Fish and Wildlife he should call. She gave him the number for their Chief of Wildlife Trade and Conservation.

At that office, a secretary answered, transferring Jack to a man, first name Barnes.

Jack introduced himself and gave the reason for his call.

"Let me get this straight," the man said. "You heard a poacher talking, but got no names. What more you got?"

"It's sketchy." Jack stood and began to pace, the phone at his ear. "Supposedly a big name picked up the rhino horn. A courier came from New Mexico, simply to get the rhino horn to the airport in Nairobi."

Silence, then, "When was this?"

"Within the last month." He stopped and stared out a window.

"That's not much to go on."

Jack watched as sunlight sifted through the weary branches of a hackberry tree. So different, so unlike the fever trees in Kenya. He sighed. "Thought it worth checking. Maybe you've got an agent tracking someone fitting that description."

"It's not much of a description, but give me your email and number. Someone will call if we do."

Jack thanked him and ended the call.

Two minutes later, his phone rang. He answered.

"Jack, this is Iggy. I heard from State Department. The desk officer covering Kenya."

"Can they help?"

"They can, and they have. They called the embassy, let 'em know they'd be receiving an inquiry directly from you."

Jack rubbed his eyes. "So, I just need to call?"

"I'm sending a name and contact information. Try email first. They're sometimes fast, sometimes slow, but they love working with Park Service so I suspect they'll be in touch in a reasonable time frame. If it doesn't pan out, let me know. I have a few more ideas."

Ending the call, he checked email. Iggy's sat waiting. In it, a name, phone number and email address. A woman named Akingi at the Kenya Embassy.

He set about crafting an email, keeping it simple, asking if they might converse by phone. He typed in his home and cell phone numbers, and pushed send.

In the kitchen, the radio popped. *"Dispatch, this is three ten."* Jack turned to listen.

"Go ahead, Luiz."

"Traffic stop, New Mexico license plate . . ."

Jack closed his mind to the numbers and turned his attention to his lap top.

A few minutes passed and Luiz's voice came back over the radio. *"I'm clear, Molly."*

"Copy."

The phone rang. Jack picked it up. "Yep."

"Mr. Chastain?" The voice carried a familiar tinge of British accent.

"Yes."

"Mr. Chastain, my name is Akingi. I'm with the Republic of Kenya's embassy in Washington. You wish to talk?"

He told her of his recent trip to Kenya.

"Yes, your email reminded me, I saw your paperwork prior to your visit. Rather hasty."

"Yes, it was. Is it possible to get a list of Americans receiving visas for travel to Kenya? From, say, three to six weeks ago. I'm looking for a connection to a poaching incident."

"This is highly unusual, Mr. Chastain. Ordinarily, such a request would come from Kenya Wildlife Service."

"I understand, and maybe you will. Maybe you should. From Samuel Leboo, or someone else in law enforcement. But I overheard the words of a poacher. Been thinking about those words. Cryptic words. Words that might mean something, and possibly something obvious."

"Are there specific names you are looking for?"

"No. It would be a big name. Someone very big."

"Mr. Chastain, a large proportion of Americans getting visas are wealthy. In the eyes of those in their circles of influence, I presume many would be considered big, even very big."

Didn't think of that. "I understand, but there's the possibility that the name might jump off the page. It also involved a courier from New Mexico, my home state. I'm looking for information to share with Samuel. You could even copy him on anything you provide."

"That won't be necessary. I'll send you what I can. Possibly today, more likely tomorrow. I hope it helps."

"Thank you, Ms. . . ."

"You may call me Akingi, and thank you, Mr. Chastain. I can tell you wish to help. These are difficult issues." She ended the call.

And then there was nothing to do but wait.

— · —

By mid-afternoon, he'd had enough. He pulled out his cell phone and made a call.

Kelly answered.

"I could use a hike."

— · —

Her dark hair pulled back, Kelly worked her way across the boulder, then sat, and scooted under the waterfall. Her place. Sitting cross-legged, head back, she seemed to slip into a world all her own as water streamed the length of her body.

Jack watched, enjoying the sight of her. For brief moments, his eye would drift to the ledge where Caveras Creek poured in from above. Or, to the travertine pools, or higher, to the canyon walls parting to let sunlight flood in from the west. Then, he would pull back to the sight of her, naked, oblivious, absorbed in her moment.

Minutes passed before she leaned forward and sheltered her eyes, looking for his.

Jack stood.

She smiled.

He dove for the deepest part of the pool, and waited as she worked her way down the rock. She dove. They met, oblivious to anything but each other.

— · —

On a rock that tilted toward the early evening sun, they lay and soaked in the warmth.

Kelly rolled over and put her head on his shoulder. "Tell me about your project."

"Not much to tell, yet, but I'll find him." He nuzzled damp, dark locks of her hair.

"You sound confident."

"Determined." He ran a finger over the lines of her ribs.

"Don't tickle me." She gave him a poke.

"Joe told me to find a hobby."

Kelly slid her leg over his. "Do I count?" She touched his face. "Stay at the ranch tonight. Keep me company. I did a lot of thinking while you were away. Maybe too much."

"Something wrong?"

"Everything's perfect, but that didn't keep me from thinking."

"About?"

"Nothing in particular. Life. Changes."

"Changes?"

"I'm not getting any younger."

He put a finger under her chin, and looked into her brown eyes. "What are you saying?"

She laughed. "I don't know. I wasn't thinking that before, but you were away. I couldn't help it. I sat here, waiting, wondering if you'd ever come back, wondering if my life might waste away." She laughed self-consciously. "Sometimes it felt like worry. Other times, premonition."

"What kind of premonition?"

"About changes. Things I couldn't do if you never came back. Things I should do if you did. Feeling it was time for a new phase of life."

"Ticking clocks?"

"No, nothing like that. It was like, it's time for a change. Not, I better have a baby now or forever lose my opportunity. I thought about lots of things, but there were times when I thought, *why wait?*" She looked into his eyes. "Know what I mean?"

"I suppose."

She scowled. "I need a drink." She stood, and reached out a hand. "Get up."

He took her hand. "What's wrong?"

"Nothing. Get up. We're going to Elena's."

He stood. "What about the ranch?"

"If I took you there, you'd think I was setting a trap." She let go of his hand and dove.

Jack watched her emerge. She waded to shore, dried herself off, and started to dress. He dove in toward her.

— · —

"Table for two, please," Kelly said to the hostess.

The young woman led them down the hall, into the dining room.

She stopped at a table and pulled out a chair. Kelly slipped in, as a blonde-haired waitress approached carrying water. "Hi Kel," she said. "Can I get you something to drink?"

"Margarita for me. How's your little man?"

"He's discovered mud." She laughed. "He's his father's son now."

"How cute. I'd love to see pictures."

Eyeing a nearby table, Jack said, "Same for me. Margarita. Rocks. Salt."

"I'll be back with your drinks."

Two tables away, a man sat staring at his phone, reading, scrolling with one hand, stroking his beard with the other. Middle aged, maybe younger. Slender, dark hair.

Something about him . . . "Is that the guy from the bar last night?" Jack whispered.

"I didn't see him."

The man reached for a mug of beer, took a sip, then returned to scrolling.

"Quit staring," Kelly whispered.

"I'll be back." Jack ambled over, stopping at the table.

The man's eyes remained locked on his reading.

"I'm Jack Chastain, Park Service."

"I know." The man gave a flip to the screen, then looked up, studied Jack a moment, and ran a finger along the dark lines of his beard framing his chin. "You look different in person."

"And you are?"

"And taller than you look on television." He smiled. "I'm Alex Trasker."

"Did I see you in the bar last night?"

"Might of."

"I'm told you're an investigator of sorts. You might be here to see me or Joe Morgan."

"Whoever told you that must've assumed it from something I said. I'm investigating something but I'm not what you'd call an investigator. And no, I'm not here to speak to you, or the superintendent."

"Then, I should mind my own business." Jack turned back to his table.

"You are curious, however."

He stopped. "Not if it's none of my business."

"Oh, it very much relates to what you might call, *your business.*"

Jack spun around. "Okay, what?"

He smiled. "I'm not at liberty to say."

CHAPTER

24

The sun broke over the canyon rim. Rays of light pierced the bedroom window. Well before eight, Jack picked up his phone and dialed. The phone rang once.

"Find a hobby?" Joe Morgan asked.

"I did, but that's not why I'm calling."

"Tell me you're staying out of trouble."

"I am, but last night at Elena's I met a guy digging for information. Wouldn't say what, but he admits it's related to us in some way."

"And?"

"That's all he'd say."

"Troubling. I confirmed the rumors you heard from Senator Baca. There's talk of a bill in the Senate, unless our friends can talk 'em out of it. There's one senator on the fence. Both sides think it'll decide the outcome if he's on their side."

"Who?"

"Senior senator from Montana."

Jack sighed.

"Do you know him?"

"I do. The only member of Congress I ever felt I could trust."

"Still feel that way?"

"I do, but I'm not sure he feels that way about me."

"Somehow I doubt that, but we'll keep our fingers crossed. By the way, the regional office is sending Erika Jones to squire around that committee staffer working on the horse bill. They hope Jones can convince her that serving the public interest is bigger than giving priority to horses."

"Not sure Erika Jones is the one to convince Prescott of that. Not sure I would be either."

"You're not available. You are to have no contact with Prescott. I don't need word getting back to the director that you're not in Montana. I don't need him hearing from Jones that you were at the bar."

"Erika wasn't there."

"Nevertheless, keep your head down."

"Joe, I've got a life."

"You did."

— · —

An email had arrived in the early hours. In it, Jack found an attachment. A spreadsheet. An endless stream of names and addresses. He paged to the end of the list. Over ten thousand names.

Well, Joe, here's to having a good hobby.

He sat down with a pad of paper. What first? Limit the search. How? Eliminate international flights to Mombasa. Look only at travelers into Nairobi. He scanned the list. That won't help much. The largest portion fly into Jomo Kenyatta International Airport, Nairobi.

After that, what? Search for one or two day trips, looking for the big name, and New Mexico home addresses, looking for the courier.

He dove in.

First, New Mexico home addresses.

The list filled the screen. Two hundred names. Less intimidating than ten thousand, but . . . still intimidating. He scanned. Fairly common names. How do you recognize the name of a working class stiff?

After an hour, poring over names and recognizing none, he

closed the New Mexico sort. Focus on the big shot. Forget the courier. He turned back to the full list.

He sorted for one and two day trips, cutting the list down substantially, but still thousands of names. Scanning, no name caught his attention. Most appeared to be business travelers. Sales reps, repair technicians, maybe couriers, and none of these names appeared on the New Mexico list. He went slowly through the sort. When a name touched a nerve—typically, for no obvious reason—he did a quick internet search and dismissed it out of hand.

He returned to the original list. What's another way to cull these damned names? What do most people do, that the rich and powerful don't? He rubbed his eyes. What's the answer? Tours. The rich and famous don't take organized tours. What big name is gonna ride around Africa on a bus, sharing a tour guide with a few dozen others? He sorted to eliminate names connected to organized tours.

Still, a long list.

In the kitchen, the radio popped. "*Dispatch, this is three ten.*"

"*Go ahead, Luiz.*"

"*Traffic stop, . . .*"

Jack tuned out the voices, and turned back to the names. He scanned.

None appeared recognizable.

At noon, overwhelmed, Jack switched from coffee to beer, then spent the next hour scrolling the list, hoping a name would jump off the page. Someone famous. Someone obvious. He took a break, eyes tired, back hurting, mind numb.

He turned on the television, flipped through cable news and caught Congressman Brent Hoff talking about Moony Manson. Rehash. Nothing new, just fresh fuel to the fire. Two other channels carried variations, some with opposing views, but Hoff's comments were the newsmaker. Fellow patriots continued to stream into New Mexico to help their brother-in-arms fight against the mighty bureaucracy. Jack took hold of the remote and shut off the television.

Another hour of poring over spreadsheets, and Jack stepped outside, into the hot afternoon air, focusing on distant canyon rims to rest his eyes. Names. How else can these names be reduced to find a needle in a haystack?

He pulled his phone from his pocket and called Iggy. "You said you had other ideas for attacking this list?"

"No luck so far?"

"Ten thousand names, none jumping off the page. Mind-numbing."

"Two possibilities," Iggy said, "Kenya's Ministry of Foreign Affairs, to see if they're involved in anything with someone influential. Requires protocol, so I'll make the call."

"Thanks."

"Certainly. Second, I'll give you a name. Fritz Carlson. Good guy. Executive Director of an NGO called the Greater East Africa Anti-Trafficking Network. They raise money for field ranger training in East African nations. They bring in retired rangers from US agencies, mostly law enforcement. Also Australian military. They've got an undercover investigative arm building a list of people above the law."

"What do I ask this Fritz guy?"

"Ask if they have names you should look for. I'm sending his email and phone number, now." The line fell quiet, then, "Okay, you should have it. I'd suggest email. He's a busy guy."

Jack emailed Carlson, gave a brief explanation, and asked if they could talk. Carlson—in New York City for meetings—responded politely, suggesting Jack contact another fellow in their organization.

". . . *Call Angus Donaldson. Put your question to him. He's in charge of our investigative arm. He came to us from Australian military, Joint Operations Command. No Crocodile Dundee jokes. He has no sense of humor.*"

Jack located Donaldson's contact information at the bottom of the email.

What time is it in South Africa? Doesn't matter. Leave him a message. He called and let it ring.

Donaldson answered, a gruff, "Who is this?"

Jack gave his name and agency. "Sorry to call when you're off duty."

"I'm never off duty," Donaldson groused, nothing light-hearted about him. "What's this about?"

"Poaching in Kenya. Nairobi National Park."

"Get on with it."

"The long and short is . . . I'm following up on words I heard from a poacher, about an American given a rhino horn at the airport in Nairobi."

"Ongoing interrogation?"

"The poacher's dead, Mr. Donaldson."

"Gotcha, go on."

"I managed to secure a list of Americans with visas from the timeframe in question. The list is long."

"You're chasing your tail, Mr. Chastain. Unless you've got something more to go on."

"Supposedly a big name. A very big name."

Donaldson growled into the phone.

"I was told you had a list of people you're watching. That you could give me names of Americans on your list."

"There's no way in hell I'm gonna share m' list. No offense, but I don't know who the hell you are. Why aren't I getting this call from Kenya Wildlife Service?"

"I suppose you should, but I'm just trying to help. They seemed overwhelmed."

Donaldson let out a snarl. "Do this. Send me your list. I'll have my people go through it. If any of our names are on your list, I'll let you and Kenya Wildlife Service know. That's all I can do for you."

"Fair enough. Can I give you my point of contact in Kenya?"

"That would help."

"Samuel Leboo."

"Your credibility suddenly increased tenfold."

"I understand."

Jack forwarded the list to Donaldson.

— · —

After trying several new approaches with the spreadsheet—yielding nothing new—Jack set it aside and called Kelly. "I need another break."

"Good. Come to the ranch. Father wants to talk."

Jack threw a few things in a pack, locked the door behind him, and climbed in his Jeep. He drove out of the park and up onto the plateau, turning at the sign into Culberson Ranch. He followed the winding road around the hill to where it crossed the meadow to Culberson's adobe casita. At a rock bridge over a small, spring-fed creek, he slowed and took in the view off the plateau toward the distant hamlet of Las Piedras, past vertical walls and canyons.

Kip Culberson's slice of heaven.

He stopped in the shade of a cottonwood. Kelly stepped out the side door, in shorts and white cotton blouse. Barefooted, she met him at the edge of the courtyard, gave him a quick hug and took his hand, pulling him inside.

"Father's in his office. Go on back. I'll bring you a beer. When you're done I'll show you a painting I started while you were gone."

Jack made his way through the great room, to a part of the house he'd set foot in only a few times—Kip's inner sanctum, at first glance small, tucked into a corner behind the staircase. He stopped at the door. Light streamed through windows on two sides of the room. An outside door stood open. Kip sat reading, sprawled in a big leather chair, his glasses perched on his nose.

Jack knocked.

"Come in," Kip said, without looking up. "You need to read this. It's garbage."

Jack moved to a wall where paintings hung. One, a masterpiece, Kip's favorite by Kelly. Expansive. Reaching canyons. Layered plateaus. Below it, in just as ornate a frame, another. Pines and canyon walls. Same artist, when very young. Both paintings appeared equally cherished.

On the other windowless wall hung mementoes from a career of service, intermingled with photos, many of a younger Culberson, a man with fire in his eyes, a young woman beside him—Juanita, his wife. Jack glanced at a closet door, behind which he knew sat a stack of framed photos Kelly had shown him when alone in the house. Once revered—photos of Kip Culberson in handshakes with the rich and powerful, including two presidents, a handful of governors, and an impressive list of prominent individuals. They now sat in the closet, clutter remedied by a man who knew now what made him most proud. Accomplishments.

"Read this," Kip said, handing him a page. "An article. Yesterday's paper."

Jack scanned. *Washington Post.* An account on the still simmering conflict between Moony Manson and BLM. He read, seeing inflammatory rhetoric tossed around by all sides. Missing were words from BLM. He handed the page back to Kip.

"Just a damned deadbeat. It'd cost him more to rent pasture, but he won't pay his fees. That's lost in the story. Talk to anyone knowing Manson, they'll tell you he's shady, deserving of whatever he gets. But to everyone else, this is a debate over government overreach versus role of government."

Jack laughed. "It's not?"

"Hell no," Kip said. "There are legitimate reasons to debate those matters, early and often, to keep the pendulum from swinging too far either way, but it's not healthy doing so under these circumstances. It's contrived. No basis in fact."

"Is that what you wanted to talk about?"

"Hell, no. Sorry." He chuckled to himself, and laid the page on his desk. "I've gotten calls about this fella hangin' around town. It's hard to tell what he's up to, but he's asking lots of questions, mostly about the monument. Apparently, your name comes up, but it doesn't seem to be expressly about you."

"Good."

"Yeah, but it's hard to tell what he's gettin' at, and who he works for, what his game is. People tell him to call me."

"Has he?"

"Hell, no. Apparently, he's got no interest in talking to me or anyone involved in the coalition."

"Told Morgan about him this morning. He said he'd talked to our Legislative Affairs office. They're now hearing the same rumors Bob Baca told us the other night."

"Baca called this morning. Asked me to arrange a briefing for his staff and others regarding the coalition report. He wants to move fast, and he wants you there in D.C."

"Can't have me, and you don't need me."

"Of course we do."

"Better without me. You know best how to give the senator what he needs."

"Hogwash. You know very well how to give him what he needs. Information. An agency perspective. Is there something you're not saying?"

"I'm not good around politicians."

"I don't believe that." His brow furrowed. "What's the name of this guy hangin' around town?"

"Alex something. Escapes me."

"When you remember, let me know. I'll track down who he works for, and, if you see him again, talk to him. Convince him to open up."

"Kip, you keep forgetting, I'm supposed to be hiding."

"Ridiculous. Well, hell, . . . convince him to talk to me." Kip turned to his desk. "Speaking of talk, I tried calling members of Congress about these bills. It's hard as hell to get someone to talk if you're not a major donor. Things have changed. I've got connections, and it's even hard for me. Imagine what it's like if you don't have contacts or dollars."

"Don't want to. Don't want anything to do with those guys."

"Do you want to see all your work go down in flames?"

"No, I don't, but when politicians are involved . . . never mind. You have more faith than I do."

"I do have faith. It can be messy, but politics are what I know." He smiled. "I have a deep-seated belief in the person chosen to represent his fellow citizen. It doesn't work at times, but still, if you're gonna have faith in anything, it's should be that person."

"If you say so."

"I know, it can be ugly." He shrugged. "And more than I have in the past, I have faith in people like you, but some of you make it easy to paint the rest of you as heartless bureaucrats, out of touch, not accountable to the public. That brings things back to people like me, or like I used to be. Elected by the people, to serve the interests of the people."

"But do they?" Jack swept brown strands of hair from his eyes and smiled. "Sorry."

Footsteps echoed from the hall. Kelly rounded the corner, carrying a tray. Beer, chips and salsa. "Whatcha talking about?" She set the tray on a table.

"Nothing that'd interest you much," Kip said. "Politics." He eyed the tray. "Might be a bit early for me on the beer."

"I'll come back." She handed a beer to Jack, and backed to the door.

"We're done." Kip turned to Jack. "Make plans for D.C., and talk to this guy in town."

"You're trying to get me fired."

Kip laughed. "Hell, I wouldn't do that. A guy like you, who hasn't worked a real job in his life? That'd put you on welfare. How could I live with myself after that?"

Jack shook his head. "Might not have to. I have a job offer. Private sector."

"Don't lie to us. Don't blow your credibility."

Kelly stepped closer. "What's the job offer?"

"Managing a ranch for a guy I know from Montana. More likely a fishing property, somewhere here in New Mexico."

She picked up the other beer. She took a sip. "Where?"

"Don't really know. He made me promise to think about it."

"Are you?"

"Forgot about it till now. Couldn't just tell him no. He gave me a place to stay. Seems to think I need a fallback of some kind." He paused. "I won't take it. I like what I do, most of the time."

"Finish your beer," Kelly said. "I need a hike."

CHAPTER

25

Kelly tapped the brakes as they approached the county road. She flipped on the turn signal. "Caveras Creek? Hike and a swim?"

"How about someplace different?" Jack asked. "A place I've never been. Somewhere with a little discovery, to keep my mind off what your father talked about."

She turned right, up the Terrace Road.

Climbing, they topped the plateau and drove along the rim. At a spot near the boundary between national park and national monument, Jack said, "Slow, a minute." He stared out the window, searching sagebrush flats and broken terrain.

"Looking for something?"

"Horses."

Kelly pulled off the road.

He took in the expanse. The west desert.

They sat a minute before he pointed. "There."

A distant knoll, to the northwest. One horse, somewhat gray, standing upslope of others picking at earthen-colored ground. Mares, maybe one colt. Only one? The drought.

"Too bad we're not closer," Kelly said. "Horses are so beautiful."

"Those aren't beauties. They're starving. Johnny told me they're testing the boundary fence. If it wasn't uphill in that stretch of the boundary, they might've jumped it by now."

"Hey, I've got a place to show you." She killed the engine

and opened her door. "A place we'd go watch antelope when I was young."

They took their packs, Jack following, Kelly in hiking shorts, leading him along the rim.

"It's in here somewhere," she said.

"What are we looking for?"

"A cairn . . . that marks an old miner's trail. Not much of a trail, but it's safe, with switchbacks in the rock for pack mules."

"Who knows about this trail?"

"Maybe a few old ranchers. Father showed it to me. He's known about it all his life." She stopped and pointed. "There."

A cairn. Stacked sandstone, no more than two feet tall.

Kelly walked quickly toward it, then veered onto what hardly seemed a trail, breaking right, hugging the rim until slipping below it, descending through dirt and broken rock. At a sandstone wall, the path turned back and descended. A switchback. Downslope lay visible tread, cut from the rock.

He stepped down, over the side. More switchbacks, and trail disappearing beyond vertical rock. "Never seen this trail."

"Father could show you lots of places like this. After you. Even rangers can't get lost."

He laughed, and started down.

Another switchback, then another, then a long stretch curving through talus, then a point in the rock. They rounded the bend.

Jack stopped, and adjusted his sunglasses.

Two people approached, head down, trudging uphill, carrying packs. Women, pacing themselves. The first stopped, took hold of her pack straps, and sucked in a breath. She looked up, then glared. "What . . . are you . . . doing . . . here?" she said, forcing words between breaths.

Claire Prescott.

Erika Jones stepped past, eyes wide, putting several paces between her and Prescott.

"You are not supposed to be here," Erika whispered. "You're in Montana."

"I was." He exchanged glances with Kelly.

Erika turned back to Claire. "Kelly Culberson. Claire Prescott. Kelly, talk to her." She walked Jack up the trail, out of earshot. "You're making me look like a fool. Like I don't know what the hell I'm talking about."

"Because I'm here? Tell her I'm home to feed my dog."

"You don't have a dog."

"Been thinking about it."

"Very funny. How did you find us?"

"We're not trying to find you. We're taking a hike."

"On the same trail?" she said, exasperated. "Right. Claire expressly said she has no interest in talking with you, or anyone from the park. She doesn't want the company line. Thinks she can better understand what's happening on her own. We're lucky she's letting me tag along."

"So, tag. Ignore us."

"Here in the middle of nowhere?"

"We'll be on our way, which will allow you to tell her the truth. We're taking a hike."

"But you're in Montana," she muttered. She turned and stomped back to the others.

Prescott stood, pensive, sweat streaming from her brow, her white tank top soaked.

"Jack, Claire is a Senate committee staffer," Kelly said, oblivious to the tensions.

"We know each other." Jack forced a smile. "Quite a coincidence. I came home to see Kelly, and this is the hike she wanted to do."

Prescott eyed him, then turned to Erika. "So, you and Kelly are old friends. Quiet trail, huh? Nobody knows about it, huh?"

"Hardly anybody. Kelly showed it to me, years ago."

"I see." Prescott looked from person to person. "What are you people up to?"

Kelly glanced between faces, clueless.

"Obviously, you don't believe us," Jack said, "but this was not planned. Just happenstance, but we need to talk."

"Save it."

"But, . . . we . . ."

"Save it."

"All the work people here have done, trying to make things work. You can't ignore that. Why are all of you here, and why won't you talk to the people who've given their time to find common ground?"

"What are you talking about?"

"Guy in town, doing some kind of investigation. Talking to people about the national monument but avoiding anyone involved with the coalition."

"I know nothing about a guy doing an investigation. It has nothing to do with me, the Senate resource committee, or the bill we're considering." She paused. "Who is this guy? What's his name?"

"Alex, something or other. Uncommon name. Starts with a T."

"Alex Trasker?"

"That's it."

Prescott's face hardened. "It's true."

"What's true?" Erika asked.

"Hoff's introducing bills. Rumored to be similar to ours, with key differences."

"That good or bad?" Kelly asked.

"Bad. They want a conference committee exercise, where they're confident they can make it their own. If that doesn't work, they'll mess with it till no one supports it. It dies. An old trick of Trasker's. Low risk for them. High frustration for everyone else."

"I, uh, . . . I don't understand," Kelly said.

"Trasker works for Congressman Brent Hoff. Behind the scenes guy. Not many people know his name, but he's influential." Prescott sighed. "He's good. Very good, not in a good way. Ideologue, like most of Hoff's people. Previously worked for a congressman in Ohio—not nearly as competent or as smart—where he had a bad experience, which means he's loyal to Hoff. Keeps him from doing stupid things."

"Why is that bad?" Kelly asked.

"His politics." She turned to Erika, then Jack. "He's not your friend. Not like we are."

"You're our friend?" Jack said.

"Of course we are. Even when you guys are screwing up, we're still your friend. It's our party you can count on."

"This horse thing isn't exactly being our friend."

"When we're done, you'll see. When the truth comes out, when the dust settles, you'll see, our party's the one you can count on." She frowned. "But I'm not getting into this. Not now. I have work to do." She turned to Erika. "Let's go." Prescott started up the trail.

"Bye," Erika said, following after. She stopped at the bend, and hollered, "Have fun in Montana."

— · —

Jack rounded the last switchback, waited for Kelly, then navigated a crooked path through talus, stopping at an expanse of rock, broken by what would have been grassy plain, except the grasses were gone. Bare ground. Swells of sand, shaped by wind. Jack stared out over land stretching to the breaks of the river and beyond. More dirt and sand. More dust than plant life. Wasteland.

"This is not good," Jack said.

A sound came on the breeze. Hooves on rock.

Two horses emerged from behind a house-sized boulder, coming fast, carrying riders. The one in the lead carried a holstered pistol, the other, in camo, a rifle slung over his shoulder.

They reined the horses to a stop, kicking up dust.

The man with the rifle—an AR-15—slipped it off his shoulder. He leveled the barrel.

Moony Manson, in a dusty, sweat-stained hat, leaned over his saddle. "You!" he growled, fire in his eyes. He pointed up the trail. "Get off this range!"

— · —

Jack stopped when he reached the top, letting Kelly go on ahead. He turned, took in a few deep breaths, and searched the landscape for Manson and his protector. Both gone.

He spun back to the road in time to see a van accelerating away. Its markings, *Inn of the Canyons*. The shuttle, carrying Clair Prescott and Erika Jones back to town.

"Well," Kelly said. "This is a busy little place."

— · —

Alex Trasker unlocked the door to his hotel room and stepped inside. He settled into an easy chair near the kiva fireplace and picked up his phone. He pulled up the direct line to the Congressman's desk.

It rang once. "Alex, what are you finding?"

"About what I expected. It's not quite as interesting as I'd like."

"Well, we'll make it interesting. Plans are in motion."

"What plans?"

"We'll talk when you get back but the immediate plans, a Congressional investigation, an inquiry into agency activities near Las Piedras, New Mexico. The major news sources have details, with instructions not to release the story till Monday. All under the pretense that they're being given time to put reporters onto the story. It's been sent to newspapers in Albuquerque and Santa Fe, and also a rag called the *Las Piedras Gazette*. Only the *Gazette* thinks they can run the story tomorrow."

"Why the *Gazette*?" Trasker asked, confused. He stood.

"To start local conversation."

"Brent, you've got to move cautiously. I've spoken with this Moony Manson. He's a wild card. We don't really know what he'll say at any given moment."

"He's a symbol, not a mouthpiece. We've got someone else to crank up the rancor."

Trasker walked to a window, stroking his beard. "Who? And, to say what?"

"Don't worry. It's taken care of. Along with something to keep the horse people busy."

"Brent, this could get complicated, depending on the Senate. We've got to be careful."

"Alex, someone in the Senate owes someone favors. Those favors are being called in by a horse lover. As I always say, it's better to be owed than to owe, and some spineless senator sits in his office right this moment, wishing that weren't true."

"Understood, but we've got to deal with it."

"We are. Ironically, by calling in favors."

"Boss, you never cease to amaze me, but . . . hear me out." He sighed. "I haven't found anyone willing to admit to being one of the Wild Horse and Burro Babes. I haven't figured them out. You're taking a chance till I do. There's nothing to go on. I haven't figured out why they're even here."

"They're there, because the mustangs are there." Hoff cleared his throat. "Alex, I have to take a few risks if I hope to turn this nation around. That is my cause . . . our cause . . . to make this nation strong again. Just remember, . . ."

"I know," Trasker said, cutting him off. "You're Godiva, I'm Godiva's horse."

Hoff laughed. "Oh, yeah. Thanks for reminding me."

"Sorry, what were you going to say?"

"Doesn't matter."

— · —

In the late afternoon, the *Las Piedras Gazette* changed its lead story for the next morning's paper. Setting aside an article about the economic impacts of the drought—choosing to run it another day—they went instead with a hastily written story borrowing heavily from a press release issued by the Office of Congressman Brent Hoff, in his role as Chair of the House Resources Committee and Member of the House Science Committee.

After deleting one headline, the editor mocked up a second. This one would stand.

AGENCIES BEING INVESTIGATED
Support for local rancher in the works

The reporter assigned to the story miraculously found a congressional aide still in the office of Congressman Hoff. They, in turn, confirmed the source of the email and details of the Congressman's intent. The investigation would ascertain whether federal agencies sought to erode the rights of individual ranchers, and whether they overstepped their authority in the management of public lands, in essence usurping the role of the U.S. Congress. The targets of the investigation would include agency representatives. The staffer confirmed the Congressman was drafting a bill, but its final version would be shaped by the investigation. "Who knows what the future will hold?"

The reporter also learned of a forthcoming Science Committee subpoena, covering documents and communications, to be delivered to agencies in the days to come. The staffer would not speak to the types of communications sought, but stated agencies would have two weeks to comply. The reporter ended the call, with twenty minutes remaining before deadline.

With five minutes to go, an email arrived from Hoff's staffer. The reporter quickly added a sidebar and posted the story. The sidebar would read,

The investigation requires BLM and NPS to:

1. *Preserve all e-mail, electronic documents, and data ("electronic records") created in the last three years, that can be reasonably anticipated to be subject to a request for production by the Committee.*

2. *Exercise reasonable efforts to identify and notify current employees, former employees, contractors, and third party groups who may have access to such electronic records that they are to be preserved.*

A few states away, another narrative was being written and polished. The plan: to post it as a letter to the editor, shortly after release of the online edition of the *Gazette* and its story about the investigation. A letter to the editor posted online would avoid the editorial requirements—including name and town of residence—required for publication in the hard copy edition. This would put it where those who read such letters could quickly find it and react.

Shortly after the posting of the online letter to the editor, an old friend of the *Gazette*—of the anonymous kind, who calls himself, *All Is Not Ducky*—added his own thoughts. An I-told-you-so, speculating that Congress knew exactly what they would find. Piles of evidence suggesting government conspiracy. Within hours, others with their own theories joined the fray.

CHAPTER
26

Jack woke with sun hitting the western wall of the canyon. He made coffee.

Too early to call the superintendent, he opened email instead. One sat waiting from Angus Donaldson, Greater East Africa Anti-Trafficking Network. Jack clicked on the message.

"We looked at your list, mate. Nothing to offer. Sorry."

Jack took out his phone and called International Affairs. Iggy promptly answered.

"East African Network had nothing," Jack said.

"Same for the Foreign Ministry. I thought at first they were being tight lipped, but it might simply be tensions, between us and them."

"You and the ministry?"

"No, higher. Presidential levels."

"Got it. Any other ideas?"

"Just one, but it's not likely to yield much. Still, might be worth a try. In the House, there's a group called the House International Conservation Caucus headed by a conservative member of Congress interested in conservation. It's a bipartisan group with connections to the dark side, but for all the right reasons—to educate members and their constituents."

"Why would they know anything?"

"They probably won't, but they're involved in an effort called the rhino and tiger conservation fund, which reports to Congress. The staffer coordinating the caucus might know of intelligence of value. Someone to point to. Some way to narrow your list."

"Let's try it."

Jack ended the call and dialed the number of a staffer, a Mr. Skip Cassin. Jack introduced himself.

"Park Service? Don't talk to you guys much," Cassin said. "So you were in Kenya. I'd love to know more about it."

"I'm sure our International Affairs Office would share my trip report. That is, when it's finished."

Cassin laughed. "Being busy's our problem, too. Most members are interested. Plight of the rhino. Elephant. Tiger. The list goes on. Some are too busy to walk the talk, but we're working on 'em. Even had a member scheduled to visit Kenya recently, but he cancelled. Too busy, something came up, and that's unfortunate." He sighed. "Glad to hear someone's showing some American leadership and concern."

"Just worked on some science, that's all."

"I'm sure it helped. What can I do for you?"

"Not sure. I was told you might have ideas, maybe intelligence. About poaching rings. I'm looking for a big name, an American."

"Let's see. I could connect you to a guy I work with in Fish and Wildlife."

"Talked to 'em already. They're working on it."

"Good. The contacts I have with intergovernmental sources of intelligence, well, they're usually working to persuade us to do things to help stem the tide. They share intelligence as needed to make their point. Usually for more legislation. I could see if those contacts are willing to share."

"Think they will?"

"They want CITES to work—the Convention on International Trade in Endangered Species of Wild Fauna and Flora. They might have ideas, watch lists, other things to pass along."

"Could be helpful."

"Don't get your hopes up."

After ending the call, Jack stared out the window. Helpful guy. No games.

He checked the clock. After seven. He called the superintendent.

"Bad news," Joe said, when he answered.

"Director knows I'm here?"

"Not yet, but you'll find this hardly better. Read today's paper. The House Resource Committee's starting an inquiry. We're being subpoenaed."

"What's on the subpoena?"

"I haven't seen it, and neither has Legislative Affairs. All we know is what's in the *Gazette*. It appears to have been leaked, just to them."

"Why the *Gazette*?"

"Go online. I think you'll find the answer to that. Has to do with Moony Manson."

He sighed. "Ran into Manson yesterday. On a trail. Also Erika Jones."

"Together?"

"No. Jones was with Claire Prescott, middle of nowhere. Manson nearby, with one of his wannabe militia. Told us to leave. His goon leveled his weapon."

"You didn't call me?"

"Wasn't carrying a radio. By the time I was near a phone, I had no idea where he was. Figured we'd be talking now."

"I'll pass it on to the Chief Ranger. Barb might want to put a few rangers out to keep him from scaring visitors."

"And, we don't need him trespassing his cattle."

"He was in the park?"

"No, the monument, but there's no grass left. His cattle need feed. They've left their part of the range. They'll soon be testing the fence . . . along with the mustangs."

"I'll talk to BLM. Odds are increasing that the director will learn you're here. Keep your head down, but go read the article in the *Gazette*. It's causing reactions."

— · —

Jack went on line. Two letters stood out. One from a well-recognized pseudonym among readers of the *Gazette*, '*All Is Not Ducky*.' The other, anonymous. The brush fires started by Ducky typically burned out in hours. The one likely stared by the anonymous letter—the one igniting Ducky's rants—might burn for days. Something about it stood out.

Dear Editor,

Why are government bureaucrats allowed to run amuck, trampling the rights of heroic Americans like Moony Manson? Why are they allowed to trample the constitution, in ways our forefathers intended to protect against? Why are they allowed to lock away lands, when jobs and the bounty from those lands would enrich us all, providing support to proud American families whose only desire is to live in peace and pay their own way? Answer: Because the voices supporting the nanny state are being listened to, and drowning out the voices belonging to the rest of us.

So, a Congressional inquiry is being announced. Finally. I have no doubt what they'll find. Lies, fabrications, and manipulations. Evidence of a campaign to rip away Manson's rights and steal his land, for no other reason than because he fought the tyranny of the mighty federal government.

Signed, Anonymous

Jack read the letter twice more. He went outside, fuming, and paced under a hackberry tree until he could take it no longer. He stormed down the trail to headquarters. At the office of the Chief Ranger, he knocked on the door and entered without invitation.

Barb Sharp, wearing dress uniform, her weapon on her belt,

spun away from her desk facing the wall. "I thought you were in Montana."

"Luiz working today?"

"He's on patrol. I can have Molly call him."

"Do that. Did anything come of the investigation into the guy who burned that old pickup out on the desert? Last year."

She pulled a graying stand of otherwise black hair behind an ear. "Yes and no."

"Which is it?"

Sharp picked up the phone and punched in three numbers. "Molly, would you get Luiz on the radio, please? See if he's close." She listened. "Ask him to come to my office. Thank you." She hung up. "He'll be right here. When did you get back?"

"Few days ago. Did Joe tell you about my encounter with Moony Manson?"

"I've been in a meeting in town."

Jack recounted the episode, describing the man in camo, his actions with the AR-15, and the demand to leave from Moony Manson. Barb made notes, and checked on the availability of rangers to cover the backcountry.

Luiz Archuleta appeared at the side door to Sharp's office, his dark hair a wind-blown mess, his wiry frame inflated by the bulk of a bulletproof vest. "Hey, guy," he said, seeing Jack. "When did you get home?"

Sharp waved him in.

Jack ignored his question. "Luiz, what came of your investigation into Harper Teague?"

"Why do I know that name?"

"Teague. The guy we think burned that pickup out on the desert, creating all that buzz a year ago. The guy Thomas and others at the pueblo accused of being behind the letters to the editor. The ones inventing all those conspiracies theories."

"That guy." Luiz's smile disappeared. "He dropped off the earth. The deputy I worked with in Montana lost his trail, thinks that wasn't his real name. Why you asking?"

Jack turned to Barb. "Pull up the *Gazette*."

She turned to her computer, went online, and pulled up the newspaper.

Standing over her shoulder, Jack read the letter aloud. When finished, he said, "Sound familiar?"

— · —

Walking home, Jack made a call to Kip Culberson.

"Karen Hatcher's contacts think the story was leaked to the Gazette," Kip said. "So do mine."

Approaching the house, Jack heard the phone ring inside. "I'll call you back." He went in and answered.

"Barb told me you were in the office," Joe said. "Stay away."

"You'll have to let me come in from the cold when you see the subpoena."

"I do not. We will handle it. You go back to your hobby."

— · —

"I'm in trouble. I need a drink."

"I'll pick you up," Kelly said, and ended the call.

An hour later, wearing jeans, sandals, and a sleeveless blouse, she took Jack's hand as they walked up the steps at Elena's.

Jack glanced into the bar. No Johnny Reger. No merry band of firefighters.

In the middle of the room, Lizzy McClaren sat with a middle-aged couple. Clients.

They worked their way through the tables. "How many grass-hoppers?" Kelly asked.

Lizzy smiled, and tugged on a strap on her sun dress. "It doesn't matter, I'm walking."

"She always says that," Kelly muttered, leaning into the ear of the man. She slipped into a chair at the next table.

"I've got three days off and I'm sure I can find my way home."

Kelly laughed as Jack spun off to the bar. He returned with two margaritas, and noticed Alex Trasker sitting alone at a table against the wall.

His beer half empty, Trasker worked his phone, seemingly oblivious to the goings-on in the bar, then, without looking up, he said, "You're wondering what I'm working on."

Jack took a sip. "I'm wondering why you're here."

Trasker eased his head around, then back. "Doing work. Something you wouldn't understand."

"Funny, but work's something we understand very well. We put a lot of time into it."

"Good for you. I'd love to chat, but people in Washington anxiously await my thoughts."

"That's interesting, but I'd rather hear what brings you to Las Piedras. I suspect it has much to do with this Congressional inquiry I read about today."

"You connect dots pretty well," Trasker said, his eyes down, "but that wasn't my doing."

"But it was your boss'. I'd like to know what your boss hopes to accomplish, and how it'll affect the work of people who've come together to find solutions."

"All you need to know is, I'm here to make sure everyone has a voice."

"I respect that, but who's voice?"

"I'm not at liberty to say."

"Moony Manson's?"

"Yes."

"Moony Manson is not exactly a man without a voice. His voice is louder than anyone's. I suggest you talk to Kip Culberson."

Trasker reached for his beer. "Sorry, but I'm not sure he has anything helpful to offer."

"If not him, Karen Hatcher. If not her, Senator Baca."

"Same."

"Why are you here?" Jack said, growing frustrated. "What are you really trying to do? What kind of bill are you working on?"

"Who said I was working on a bill?"

"Little bird."

He smiled. "Smart bird, but it's a little too early to say what we'll do." His eyes moved.

Jack turned.

Clair Prescott. She moved toward them, stopping at Jack's table. She folded her arms and glared at Trasker. "You're gonna play games with our bill. That's why you're here, isn't it?"

Trasker seemed to search for words. "I'm in conversation here, Claire."

"Yeah, right."

"No, he is," Jack said. "He's in conversation. In fact, Alex was about to join our table."

"I was?"

"Pull up a seat. I'm buying."

"No thanks."

"You, too, Claire, join us."

She dropped her arms, glanced at Jack, then turned back to watching Trasker.

Trasker stood. In slow steps, he switched tables. Prescott took the seat beside him.

"I'm not at liberty to talk," Trasker said, "but I don't mind another beer."

"Good. You can't talk today, and Claire couldn't talk yesterday," Jack muttered. "I find that interesting, since I really don't want to talk to either of you, but I do wish you'd talk to people I know who could help you do your jobs."

"Our jobs are different than yours," Trasker said. "I don't care to explain."

"I know what your plan is," Prescott said, eyeing Trasker. "But not the details. You and your boss hope to hijack our bill in conference rather than let it die for lack of a House bill."

"Don't conference committees focus on differences?" Jack asked.

"Theoretically, yes. A conference should focus on a scope of differences. But, . . ." She smiled. "Alex here has tricks up his sleeve. His boss will propose to work on a compromise, based on our language or theirs, doesn't matter, then introduce a new concept not found in either bill. Although a point of order is all it'd take to keep it from going to either floor for a vote, it doesn't. Momentum's so strong that Rules Committee waivers are easy to get. When it comes back to the Senate, some lucky senator finds something attached to his bill. They'll have to filibuster what started as their bill, just to keep it from coming up for a vote, or accept whatever Hoff wants as legislation. Very, very smooth, and slimy."

Trasker stared into his beer. "Jack, it could conceivably work that way," he muttered. "But to pull that off would take skill and luck. What she described is not our intent at present. All you need to know is, we intend to give voice to those without a voice. Let them be heard. If your work stands up to scrutiny, good. If it doesn't, we'll do something about it."

"What does that mean? And why does it involve me? Manson grazes on BLM land."

"I'm not saying anything more."

"Fine. Don't talk to me. Talk to Kip or Karen. Things would be better for me if you did." He turned to Prescott. "And, why make wild horses more important than anything else?"

"Save it. I'm not showing my cards. Not in front of Trasker."

Trasker smiled. "Seen any good movies lately?" He glanced at his watch. "Look at the time."

Jack clenched a fist. "How can you two be effective if . . ."

Arms draped over the backs of Trasker's and Prescott's chairs.

Trasker raised his empty mug.

"I'm not your waitress."

Jack looked up, following Trasker's eyes. Lizzy McClaren, now alone.

"Hey Jack, how's it going?"

"Sorry Lizzy, we're kinda busy here."

"Thought I'd see if you and your friends wanted to join me on the river tomorrow. I need to work out some bugs on new equipment. It'd be safer with someone along."

"Excuse me?" Jack said.

"River trip. Two or three days. No cost. It's on the company." She looked down at Trasker, teasing him with green eyes. "Ever been on the river? Running the rapids? Deep canyons? People running around half naked?"

"Uh . . ." Alex glanced around the table. "I, uh, . . . no. I always . . . thought I wanted to. The river, wow. I'm busy, but . . ."

"There's always Monday. Weekend's coming. Start a day early."

"But I don't have gear. Got the wrong shoes . . . and . . . I have phone calls tomorrow."

"We can loan you some gear." Lizzy put on a stern face. "But phones? Nope, I collect 'em at put-in." She winked. "But, there's a place or two where I might let you have 'em. Only a few minutes. I'll be timing ya." She looked down at Claire. "How 'bout you?"

"Uh . . ." Claire exchanged looks with Trasker. "The river? Seriously?"

"Seriously," Lizzy said. "Show up with things you don't mind getting wet. River shorts, swim suit. If you don't have 'em, we can supply from what we have in the boat barn. Bring your own beer, wine, or whiskey, whatever you drink."

"But . . . I'd need to check my calendar."

"Do it now."

Claire pulled out her phone, then, resigned, set it on the table. "The river."

Trasker sat speechless.

Lizzy turned to Kelly. "Do you cook? I could use some help with the meals."

Kelly smiled. "I'm a lousy cook."

"Perfect. Me, too." She flashed a wink at Jack, then a smile. "Bring your kayak. We'll be tight in the boat."

Jack ran his fingers through his hair, fighting frustration.

Lizzy glanced at her watch, then down at the two below her. "See you at the boat barn at six. We're located on the other side of the bridge, edge of town. That's six in morning."

"Uh, . . . okay." Trasker stood. "Better go. I'm still on Washington time."

Prescott got to her feet.

Lizzy stepped out of their way. "See you in the morning."

They watched as the two congressional staffers reached the door and parted ways.

"Kelly, we need to go buy food," Lizzy said.

Jack scowled. "Lizzy, there were things I needed to discuss with them. Important things."

"My suggestion would be, let it wait till day two. Tomorrow night at the earliest."

"What the hell are you talking about?"

Lizzy smiled. "The rhythm of the river. Trust me."

"What just happened here?"

"Call it a favor. Remember, I owe you."

CHAPTER 27

"Lizzy left for the put-in," a man shouted, emerging from the main bay of the boat barn, hobbling on a cane. "Said to tell ya she'll meet you there. I'm drivin' ya."

"You must be Zach Danner."

"What's left of him." The man, slender and graying, extended a hand. "And you're Jack Chastain. I've seen you around."

"Heard a lot about you. You and your legendary trips on the world's toughest rivers."

"All lies I started."

Jack laughed, and pulled a fleece sweater on over his T-shirt and river shorts.

"Where're the others?" Danner gave a tap on the ground with his cane.

"Give 'em time. There'll be three more."

"I'm guessing two. Kelly Culberson showed up early to help Lizzy pack."

They watched as a car pulled into the lot. Blue sedan, likely a rental, its tires crunching through gravel as it pulled into a space. A door swung open. Alex Trasker stood and stretched, holding a paper coffee cup. He reached into the car and pulled out a day pack. Sipping, he watched another sedan enter the lot. It parked. Clair Prescott climbed out with her pack. Trasker started for the bay, Prescott not far behind.

"Morning," Trasker muttered. "I thought about this all night, Chastain. Don't know what you're up to, but I'm still not at liberty to talk."

"Tell it to Lizzy. Her idea."

"You being straight?"

Jack nodded.

Prescott joined them, and dropped her pack.

"I shouldn't be doing this," Trasker muttered. "Too many things going on."

Prescott nodded agreement.

"Then, don't go," Jack said.

Trasker gave a shrug. "But, it's the river."

Jack turned to Prescott. "You?"

"Don't talk to me. I haven't had my coffee."

"The first rapid that soaks your shorts . . . hell, you won't need coffee," Danner said. "Follow me." He led them inside, to a row of benches. "Got a few things to give ya. Have a seat."

Gear lay on the cement floor. He picked up river bags and tossed them to Trasker and Prescott. "Clothes and gear go in those." He held out a pair of life vests. "Try these on. Don't want 'em too big or too small."

They slipped on and buckled the vests, then tightened the waist straps.

Danner inspected the fits, giving each vest a tug. He pointed to a van marked *Enchanted Rivers*. "After you pack your bags, toss 'em in the van." He turned to Jack. "Let's load your stuff."

— · —

The put-in sat outside the national park, below the depths of the main canyon, in bottoms where the river known as la Fuente de los Fuegos—*Fountain of the Fires*—came together to form a confluence with a somewhat lesser known river, typically referred to as the West Fork but not by the those whose area ties spanned generations, and not by those who raft the river. Their name: Rio Savaje. Savage River. Its source, north, in Colorado. Its end, the Rio Grande. Its path, a swath through the national monument, its upper reaches managed by Park Service, its lower reaches managed by BLM.

Danner turned the van off the highway, onto a gravel road. After minutes of driving the dusty road, the put-in came into view. Only a dirt track lay beyond. One pickup sat parked, an empty trailer behind it. This early, only one raft sat in the water, tethered to a cottonwood, *Enchanted Rivers* emblazoned on its tube. The river, wide and slow, pushed lazily at the boat, bumping its bow against the shore. Jack watched as Lizzy and Kelly sat inside, heads down, going about their work.

Three night's worth of provisions. One boat. It'll have to be packed tight.

Danner pulled the van alongside the pickup. He limped to the passenger side, without his cane, and slid the side door open. He offered Prescott a hand. "Enjoy yourself," he said, as she climbed out. "If you can't come back in one piece, don't let us find your carcass."

She laughed.

Danner stepped out of Trasker's way. "Have a good time."

Jack slipped out, and pulled his kayak off the roof rack.

Danner opened the rear door and tossed out the river bags. He shuffled his way to river's edge. "You sure about this?" he shouted, getting Lizzy's attention. "Oar locks? I've used pins and clips on this river for over thirty years."

"I just wanna try 'em. See what they do for me." Lizzy stood and wiped her hands on her dress. "Listen up," she said to the others. "Safety talk, then we hit the river."

—— · ——

Jack squirmed into his paddling jacket, pulled on his helmet, and dragged the kayak to river's edge. He settled inside and paddled into still water to wait.

"You two, sit there," she said, pointing Prescott and Trasker to the front of the boat. "And one last thing. Cell phones and cameras. Hand 'em over."

"I'm not giving you my phone," Trasker said.

"We hit big water right away."

"I need it."

"Suit yourself." She collected a phone from Prescott and stashed it in an ammo can tethered to the boat frame. She gave Trasker one last chance, then took her place at the oars. She slipped her vest on over her sun dress. "I'll let you get the line," she said to Kelly. "Then, sit behind me, here on the tube. That's where I like to keep my slaves." She winked.

Kelly, in river shorts and red swimsuit top, slipped into her life vest and jumped off the tube. She untied the line and gathered it in, tossing it at the feet of Trasker and Prescott.

"Push us off."

Kelly shoved, and the raft began to drift. She waded in, pulled herself over the tube, and worked her way back.

Watching her get settled, Jack set the kayak adrift.

Lizzy took hold of the oars, swung them out to the side, and skimmed the water with the blades. Rolling her wrists, she feathered the blades, then leaned in, arms forward, and set the oars. She pulled, sending the raft into the current. Using one oar, she spun the raft and pointed its bow downstream.

Jack dipped an end of his paddle, and steadied the kayak as her wake rolled past.

Lizzy pulled back on the oars, dipped the blades, and pushed. "The journey begins."

Jack glided alongside, beyond the reach of her oars. He watched Trasker and Prescott study first the river, then the low canyon rim.

Flatwater.

Ahead, a bend in the river.

Lizzy sculled, in slow, easy moves.

The raft floated through the bend. Ahead, glassy-still water, this side of boulders.

Jack watched Trasker and Prescott. Clues unfolded, none yet appeared to register.

The raft settled onto the glass.

A sound, a rumble, a hint. Neither Trasker or Prescott seemed to notice.

They approached the twin boulders. The pinch point. The rumble grew, echoing off canyon walls.

"What's that sound?" Prescott asked, looking upstream, not down.

"Fun," Lizzy shouted.

"What kind of fun?"

"The kind that starts here. Hold on. Be ready to bail."

Trasker's head whipped around. "Bail?"

Giving one oar a push, Lizzy turned the bow toward shore and let the raft drift, an oar pointed downstream. "Go first," she shouted at Jack. "Collect the bodies." She gave him a wink.

He paddled past, between the boulders and into the tongue. Smooth water melted away. He dropped into the boil, paddling left, around one hole, and through another, then broke through a wall of splash, finding himself at the bottom. Flat-water. He spun around to watch.

The raft entered the rapid. Lizzy set the oars and spun the bow forward, plowing into a wave. Water washed over the tube. The raft rolled into one wave and over the next, then into another, a wall of water bathing Trasker and Prescott. The raft settled onto flat water.

Trasker and Prescott stared, eyes wide, both gasping for air.

"Did we survive?" Lizzy shouted.

"I'm awake," Prescott said, staring into nowhere.

"Bail," Lizzy ordered.

Trasker found a plastic bucket and began to dip, pouring it over the side.

"And look at me," Lizzy shouted, and waited for heads to turn. "Dry." She laughed, flapping the folds of her dress. "How's your phone, by the way?"

Trasker dropped the bucket. Digging his phone from his shorts pocket, he pulled it out in a slosh of water. He tapped on the face. His jaw went slack. "It's dead."

"Better let me have it. You don't have signal here anyway."

"No signal?" he said, still trying to poke it back to life. "I have calls to make. And receive."

"You won't be making 'em here," Lizzy said. "I'll put it in the ammo can. Might be okay. This isn't salt water."

Trasker fussed a moment more, then handed it over.

Lizzy popped open the ammo can and set it inside. She locked it down. "Got a place or two you can make calls. If your phone's ruined, I'm sure you can borrow Claire's."

"She doesn't need to know who I'm calling."

"Then borrow Jack's." Lizzy spun around. "Have your phone?"

Jack nodded.

"There you go. Everything will be fine." Lizzy let her eyes drift downstream. She set the oars and gave them a push.

The next rapid—more a riffle—gave a quick, wild ride, eliciting smiles from Prescott, and none from Trasker. He bailed the boat.

Jack came alongside. "Liking oar locks?"

"Might find I prefer 'em." Lizzy feathered the blades. "I'm hoping for a little finesse on rapids like Black Hole."

"What's Black Hole?" Trasker asked.

"The big rapid. The monster."

"Oar locks?" Prescott said. "What's that about?"

She slid her hand down an oar, to the U-shaped device pivoting on the frame. "This. Zach Danner prefers pins and clips."

"Oar locks new or something?"

Lizzy gave the oars a push. "Nope. Old as time. Pins and clips are newer. They have advantages, especially in rough water. Found these among the cobwebs in the back of the boat barn. I want to try 'em." She wiped sweat from her brow.

"At eleven o'clock, will we be someplace with signal?" Trasker asked.

"If you want to make a call at eleven, I'll get you where you can." Lizzy chuckled to herself. "But, relax, enjoy yourself."

"Gotta job. I don't have the luxury of ignoring it." He sighed, stroking his beard. "Maybe this was a mistake. Maybe I shouldn't have come . . . but it's something I always wanted to do."

Lizzy nodded.

Kelly lay on the tube, facing the sun, eyes closed.

"This woman knows how to relax," Lizzy said.

"What does she do, by the way?" Trasker asked. "Have a real job?"

"I'm not defined by what I do," Kelly muttered, her eyes still closed.

"She's an artist." Lizzy gave the oars a hard push. "If you can afford one of her paintings, you ain't workin' for tips."

"Artist," Prescott mused. "That'd be nice. No worries about people with hidden agendas. People wanting or promising favors. Just canvas, paint, and whatever happens at the end of a brush." She sighed.

"Try it a week. You'll be going out of your mind," Trasker said.

"Maybe. I know you're right. I need a real job, too, but it sure sounds nice."

"Hey," Kelly shouted, not looking up. "Artists are business people. We have to make someone want our work."

"Okay," Trasker said. "Fair enough. What're you working on now?"

"Uh . . . I'm kinda between pieces. Looking for inspiration."

"What's that tell ya?" Trasker muttered.

Lizzy let the boat drift. She raised a hand and pointed. "See that beach, river right?"

All heads turned.

"If you need to make a call, that's a good place. Climb part way up, you'll get signal. Wanna stop?"

"Please," Trasker said.

Lizzy steered the raft toward the beach. It bumped the shore. "Someone get the line."

Alex jumped the tube, line in hand.

She pointed. "Tie off on the boulder. A wrap will do."

Jack beached and rolled out of the kayak.

Trasker returned to the boat. "Phone?"

Lizzy popped open the ammo can and handed him his phone.

He tapped the face. "Dead."

"At lunch, we'll leave it out in the sun," Lizzy said. "Jack, can he borrow yours?"

Jack pulled a dry bag from the cockpit, dug out the phone, and handed it over.

"Be right back," Trasker said. He crossed the sand, and climbed onto rock, ascending to a perch overlooking the river.

He fiddled with the phone, tapping its face. He put it to his ear. "This is Alex," he said, his voice carrying down to the river. "Something's come up. Can we reschedule for Monday, late afternoon?" He stood staring at the bluff across the way. "Yes. Yes, I knew you'd understand. Thanks. Talk to you then." He held up the phone, touched the screen, studied it a moment, then tapped again on the face. "Hi Virginia, this is Alex. Is the Congressman available?" He stood waiting. "Good morning, Brent. Just confirming you got my email. . . . yes, last night. Yes. . . . those are my suggestions . . . yes . . . I'll call when I can, bye." He started down.

He reached the sand and handed the phone back to Jack. "Thanks. You've got voice mails. Two, to be exact."

Jack glanced at Lizzy.

"Go ahead."

Jack climbed to Trasker's perch on the ridge. First message, from Fish and Wildlife Service. The second, Joe Morgan. He pulled up the number at the Washington office of Fish and Wildlife and pushed call. "Jack Chastain, returning your call."

"Got an agent who wants to look at your list. He's watching people in New Mexico."

"Likely the big name or courier?"

"Doesn't want to share names at present, but he's watching several. He'd like to see if he can connect some dots."

Jack promised to send it Monday.

He ended the call and phoned Joe Morgan. "You rang?"

"Talked to the director this morning."

"He knows I'm here?"

"No, he's gotten wind of congressional staffers in town, asking questions. He called to tell us to be careful, especially with a guy named Alex Trasker."

"Did you tell him I'd had contact?"

"I told him contact had been made, but I didn't say it was you. Where are you now?"

"On the river."

"Good. You can't get in much trouble there."

"Oh, how wrong you are, Joe."

Joe laughed, likely thinking about whitewater.

— · —

"Lunch," Lizzy said, steering the raft toward shore. Beyond the bank stood an alcove, carved by the high flows of spring. She and Kelly set up a table and brought out chopped veggies and makings for sandwiches. The others explored. Cool and dry, protected from the heat of the day, the alcove offered little except reason for amazement. They grabbed their food and plopped down amidst depressions in the sand left by previous visitors. Trasker retrieved his small bag and went off, just him and his papers.

"It won't last," Lizzy whispered.

— · —

Back on the river, Trasker appeared nervous, repeatedly checking at his watch. At a little before two, he asked where he might use a phone."

"There, up ahead," Lizzy said. "River right."

"Where from?"

"From the bank."

"There's nothing but sand with a wall behind it. Is there someplace with privacy?"

Lizzy laughed. "You're among friends, man." She beached the raft.

Jack paddled to shore and pulled out his phone.

Trasker jumped the tube and wrapped the line around a beached log. He came for the phone, tapped in a phone number, then waited. "Vern, it's Alex. . . . yes. . . . Sorry, but I can't talk about that. . . . Anything but that. . . . No, not now. . . . Let's talk Monday. . . . Why? . . . Because, I'm standing here looking at him." He flashed a smile. "Plus, I'm on his phone."

Trasker ended the call and handed the phone back to Jack. "Sorry," he said, striding back to the raft, "can't talk about it."

CHAPTER 28

Flat water, river wide, current slow.

Lizzy let go of the oars and wiped the sweat from her brow. "Who needs a hike?"

Prescott turned. "In this heat?" she asked, her pale delicate skin now pink.

"Short one. To a waterfall." She waved Jack to shore and beached the raft.

She led them into a side-canyon, stopping a few yards in. A thirty foot wall. Hands on her hips, she stared up at smooth, serpentine cuts above a dry sandstone lip.

"Where's the waterfall?" Trasker asked.

"Gone. Wasn't much last time, but it was here."

"What happened?"

"The drought. Means cooling off in the river."

Back at the boat, they waded in, then climbed aboard for more flatwater in the heat of the day.

The long stretch ended at a riffle. Lizzy avoided the tongue, bumping into a boulder to hoots and hollers. The raft settled into still water. She rolled her neck and stretched. "Might be time to look for camp. What'd'ya you think, Jack?"

He checked the angle of the sun. Two hours of light. "Got a preference?"

"There's a good camp straight ahead. Anyone bring sleeping bags?" She let the thought settle in, then shouted, "Just kidding."

Open sand came into view, river left.

Lizzy steered left, gave one oar a nudge, and turned the bow toward shore, letting it drift. It bumped the bank. "Line," she shouted.

Trasker slipped over the tube and walked the rope out, tying it off on a boulder.

"Everyone line up," Lizzy shouted. "Let's unload." She pointed to the edge of the sand. "Kitchen over there. Pile the bags off to the side." She unlashed the load and started handing bags over the side.

Jack joined in as they passed gear from person to person, climbing in to help Lizzy jockey the heavy items—ice chest and kitchen box—over the tube.

Kelly pulled off her vest, adjusted her red swim suit top, and went about setting up camp tables and laying food out for a meal.

"Go pick a good place to sleep," Lizzy said, to Trasker and Prescott. She pointed at gear. "Sleeping bags. Lightweight but enough. The little bags, tents. Help yourself."

"How'd you get all this stuff to fit in the raft?" Trasker asked.

"Very slowly." Lizzy peeled off to help with the meal.

Trasker and Prescott headed in opposite directions.

Jack dragged his kayak upslope, stashed it, and pulled his gear from inside the cockpit.

"You travel light," Lizzy shouted, standing at the kitchen box, chopping celery. "I threw in an extra tent."

"Won't need it. I like the stars."

"Set me up, would ya?" Kelly asked Jack, as she fussed with the stove.

He found a place upslope, on a spit of sand between willows. He laid out a tarp, then his sleeping bag. He sauntered back to the pile of river bags. "Which bag?" he asked Kelly.

"Number nine."

Jack sorted through and found it.

Trasker ambled in, carrying papers under his arm. He pulled a collapsible chair from the pile and popped it open. Papers fell and blew across the sand, pushed by an up-canyon breeze. He gathered them in.

"One more," Jack said, picking up a newspaper page, blown under the chair.

"Thanks. You're welcome to read it," Trasker said. "Got other stuff to read first."

"Maybe later."

"Economic news. Not exactly liberal media, but . . ."

"Wouldn't call myself liberal."

"Really." His eyes lit, as he gave his beard a stroke. "You a conservative?"

"Wouldn't call myself conservative."

"What are you?"

"Human."

"What do you believe in?"

"Data."

"No, I mean, you have to believe in something."

"I do," Jack muttered. "Data. Analysis. Testing the options. Learning what works."

Trasker laughed. "Which party do you send money to?"

"I don't give money to political parties."

Claire joined them. "Where'd you get the chair? You two talking politics?"

"There's another chair in the pile." Alex pointed. "I'm trying to figure out if Mr. Ranger here is one of mine, or one of yours."

"This'll be fun." She picked up the chair and popped it open. "What'd you learn?"

"Nothing. He's being coy."

"I'm not."

"He's likely a *big government* guy. One of yours."

Prescott rolled her eyes.

Jack cringed. "Has anyone ever said they believe in big government?"

"They wouldn't, but you're part of the machinery. I'm sure it's your camp. Your point?"

"It's rhetoric. I hate rhetoric."

"You're not saying make government small. I do."

"Small, like in Reagan days," Prescott groused. "Big talk, big deficits. Contempt. All the while, growing government and debt."

"You're misconstruing the facts."

"Am I?"

"You and I, we'll fight later. I wanna hear what our ranger friend has to say."

"What do you believe in?" Claire asked.

"Tried that already. All I got was mumbo, jumbo. Data, analysis, testing options."

"Progressive or conservative?" Prescott asked.

"That's ideology," Jack said. "No ideology has answers for everything."

"You've got to stand for something," Alex said. "You're either with me and against Claire, or with Claire and against me."

"Why?"

"Because it's war out there. You either stand for American values and conservatism, or societal erosion and liberalism."

Claire laughed. "Wait a minute. He can be on the side of American values and progress, or the side protecting the wealthy, letting 'em buy society, telling everyone else go to hell. That's the choice."

"You both try to make yourself right," Kelly said, "and the other side wrong."

Trasker turned his eye to Kelly. "Okay, so what do you stand for?"

"Getting people together. Give and take. Accepting responsibility for ourselves, but being willing to look at the needs of society. I don't think it's bad if someone thinks differently than me."

"Now that's something I can believe in," Lizzy said, looking up from the stove. "In fact, if I had a little money burning a hole in my pocket, I'd throw some at that way of thinking."

"If you had it," Trasker muttered.

"Yeah, if I had it."

"Well, you don't, and you can't solve anything being politically correct."

"Alex, your guy is scum," Claire said. "There, I just needed to say that."

"The Congressman's a great man. What this country needs," Trasker said, now agitated. "Why are we here, Jack? What did you want to discuss? I'm ready to change the subject."

"Whatever you want to talk about." Jack fought back a smile. "The weather?"

"Dinner's ready," Lizzy hollered.

— · —

Darkness settled in.

"No moon tonight?" Claire asked.

"Later," Lizzy said. "It'll poke over the rim about there." She pointed at a canyon wall lying in shadow. "Didn't bring a lantern. Trying to save space, but I do have flashlights."

"I'm fine," Claire said.

Jack tried reading Claire's face in the depth of the darkness.

"Jack . . . we on BLM or Park Service?" Lizzy asked. "I've wondered where the line is."

"BLM. We crossed the boundary about half a mile back."

"Good," she said. "Anyone for a campfire? Don't tell the ranger, but if he wasn't here, I'd a gathered wood and had it burning already."

Jack laughed.

"So, he has no jurisdiction?" Trasker asked.

"Different regs," Lizzy said, "but I'm not exactly sure how that works."

"BLM allows campfires on most lands," Jack said. "We don't."

"Heavy handed?"

"No, it's a matter of pressures. Demand. Parks get more visitation, more impact. BLM confronts the impact where they need to."

Lizzy picked herself up off the ground. "I'll get wood."

"I'll go with you, master," Kelly said, getting to her feet, dusting sand off her shorts.

Lizzy giggled.

"So, Trasker, your boss," Prescott said. "He's an ass. Why would we want him for president?"

"I'm sure you wouldn't, but he's not an ass. He's what the country needs. I believe in him."

"We know what you believe in."

"I'm not sure you do."

"I know enough, and your boss scares me. Like he's trying to be some conservative populist."

"Is that bad?" Trasker asked.

"He gets people fired up in ways that make 'em do things not in their best interest."

"In your opinion."

"Yes, in my opinion. Why does he go to such lengths to turn the opposition into bad guys?"

"He's making a point." Trasker sighed. "I admit, some fights seem unnecessary, but at least he's moving the ball. That's more than can be said for most members of Congress, my former boss included, congressman from Ohio. All talk, no action. Didn't matter what people back home hoped to see. He was smooth talk and glad hand. People thought he was in Washington dealing with their issues, but no, just talk. Hoff, on the other hand, pushes fights and causes. I protect him when I can." Trasker turned in his seat. "Why aren't you talking, Mister Ranger? I can call you that, can't I?"

"I'm not actually a ranger, I'm more a . . . a . . ." He paused. "Never mind, ranger's fine . . . and I'm enjoying not being part of this conversation."

"Wear you down?"

"Nope. It's a conversation that doesn't interest me."

Alex laughed. "So, Claire, you've changed jobs. What's your story?"

Jack noticed her glance toward him.

"I don't want to talk about that," she muttered. "So, why protect Hoff?"

"Don't worry about it."

"I'm not worried. I hope he crashes and burns."

"If I can keep him from doing that, I will, for the sake of the country. I'll say this. There are causes he takes on that I wish he wouldn't. Risks he doesn't need to take."

"Risk, hell," Prescott said, "he's grandstanding."

"He's trying to save the country. More than your guy in the White House. At every turn, he violates the constitution, eroding the values this country's built on."

"Are you people idiots? You know that's not true. You only say that to rile up your base, but you know it's not true. It was your guy before him who shredded the constitution."

Lizzy and Kelly returned with armloads of wood.

"Who here believes any of that?" Trasker said, waving his arms in frustration.

"I missed it," Lizzy said, dropping the wood in a pile. She knelt to make a fire. "Start over."

"Don't," Jack said. "You didn't miss anything."

"Sure she did. I just scored a point," Trasker said. "An important one."

"You're not on high ground," Jack said. "Both parties portray the other as running rough shod over the constitution. The difference is which parts they try to defend. Your party's particularly bad at acting like they're the only defender, but they're not."

"So, you're a liberal!"

"I'd rather hear from experts in constitutional law, than self-proclaimed defenders stoked up by party rhetoric. I don't believe the constitution's so prescriptive that we can't find solutions for today's problems. I don't care which camp the idea comes from."

"Easy to say," Claire interjected, reaching as if to button a non-existent suit coat. "But if talking conservation, solutions don't come from those guys. Conservative does not equate to conservation."

Lizzy struck a match and lit the kindling. Flame lapped at the driftwood.

"I can't think like that. It'd be a mistake for me to forget champions of conservation have come from both parties," Jack said. "I think it's a mistake for you, too. Generalizations push people away, make them do stupid things, on principle, when they might've been supporters."

"Thank you," Alex said. "But do you really believe that, or are you just buttering me up?"

"Alex, right now, if you were among your kind, you might sound pretty smart," Jack said. "But you're not. Chill." He turned to Prescott. "Why are you attacking him?"

Fire lit the glow on her face. "Because I know what he's gonna do when he gets back to Washington."

"You're sunburned, and maybe he won't. What if you two found ways to work together?" Jack glanced at Trasker, catching a smirk.

"Wishy washy. That kind of crap bit your ass in Montana."

Jack searched for works. "Uh . . . I'm not sure what you mean."

"You had everyone convinced you had research to take on the concerns of the public. Then, you said you didn't. You stiffed us."

"Hold it," Jack said. "What're you talking about?"

"Fracking. All that fracking research you were doing."

"We were not doing fracking research. We were gathering baseline on water, wetlands, plant communities, everything."

"Word on the street, you were. That you found something. People wanted answers. People were scared. Afraid they were getting nothing but distortion from the industry. But, . . . "

"What?"

"Never mind. I won't let you do that again."

"Do what again?"

"Nothing."

"Woo-hoo," Trasker shouted. "Bang, you just took a shot to the choppers, Mr. Ranger. For a second there I thought I'd been set up."

"Why?" Prescott asked, fiddling again with her non-existent button.

"You two know each other. You worked together when you were on Senator Tisdale's staff."

She shook her head. "Not really. I was in D.C. Jack worked more with staff in Montana."

"But this is not the first time you've met," Alex said, more a question than a statement.

"No, it's not. I sat in on briefings in D.C."

Trasker laughed. "You two have history. More than you've let on. If I connect the dots, I know the answer to my earlier question."

"What question?"

"His leaning," Trasker said. "Our apolitical ranger. Bullshit."

"Since we're talking old times," Jack said, "Tell me why your boss came to Montana. Why get involved in a hearing that had nothing to do with him? Why was he interested in our little project?"

"Who said he was in Montana?"

"I did."

"Don't know what you're talking about."

"He was there. Appeared at a field hearing organized by the House, but one he'd not been scheduled to attend. Beforehand, I had a request to give him an hour of my time, but I was booked. Had been for months. The person I talked to was pissed. Said I wasn't being smart."

"Probably weren't, but I can't speak to it." Trasker leaned forward, his eyes piercing, and gave a stroke to his beard. "You say you saw him?"

"Yes. First, at the Forest Service regional office, then the next day at the hearing."

Trasker shook it off. "I don't know. He wasn't involved in anything important there, as far as I know." He sat back. "Now, changing the subject. I thought for sure you'd be peppering me with questions about why I'm in New Mexico."

"Why?"

"You're not the only one he wants to talk to, you ass," Prescott muttered.

"Guess not, but . . . there are things you wanted to know. I thought that's why we were here." Trasker glanced at the faces around the fire. "No?" He smiled. "Are you getting us way the hell out in the middle of nowhere to try to knock us off?"

"I'm not. Lizzy, you intending to knock 'em off?"

"Not yet. Should we?"

Jack watched as Lizzy took a break from repacking the raft. Oblivious and distracted, she settled in at the oars and stared out over the river in the minutes before sunrise. A look came over her, almost affectionate, blissful, happy. Jack looked away, not wanting to intrude on her moment.

"Pancakes and sausage, coffee and orange juice," Alex muttered, bracing against the breeze blowing from upriver. "Last night, steak and sautéed vegetables." He took a sip of his coffee. "You always eat this well on the river? Or, just buttering us up?"

Lizzy turned. "Buttering you up, of course. With clients, I toss cans of beans in the sand and watch 'em duke it out." She pointed at the ice chest. "Couple of ya, help me, would ya?"

Kelly, in a purple swim top, took hold of the handle. Jack helped walk it over.

Lizzy hefted it into position and shoved it under the frame. She stood. "These are common meals on the river, and why not? The raft can handle the weight. Gives us stability, and when in such a great location, why not make a meal an experience?"

"Wouldn't want to think you're trying to influence us," Claire said.

"Me, throwing money around? I'm sure nobody ever throws money at you congressional types." She laughed. "Kelly bought the groceries. She insisted on it."

"Let's split the cost," Claire said, sheepishly.

"Don't worry, wasn't much," Kelly said.

—·—

A rumbling echoed off canyon walls. From upstream, the river appeared to head directly into the rock.

Lizzy gave her left oar a push and steered the raft to shore. "Line!"

"What's wrong?" Claire asked.

"We're scouting the rapid."

The raft bumped the bank.

Trasker took hold of the line and jumped the tube, pulling it tight.

"You can hold it there," Lizzy said, "or join me."

Alex tied it off and followed her along a narrow trail of broken rock. They stopped at a perch above the river. Jack joined. Lizzy gathered folds of her dress and squatted, studying, squinting, her green eyes moving from top of the rapid to flatwater below.

"You do this rapid all the time, right?" Alex asked, stroking his beard.

"Yes," she whispered.

"Then, what are we doing?"

"River levels change. Rapids change. Flat water one trip might be big hole the next." She paused. "What're you thinking, Jack?"

"I think I'll start down the middle, move left, and avoid the boulder."

"I would, in a kayak. Think I'll have trouble going right?"

"Only if you get sucked in the hole early, kicked into the boulders against the wall."

"Okay, oar locks, make momma proud."

"Is this . . . the . . . ?" Alex stuttered.

"This is Carousel," Lizzy said, anticipating the question.

"What do you mean early? What if . . ."

"Then we all die," she said, eyes on the rapid. "Except Jack here. He'll collect the bodies."

"You're full of it."

Lizzy gave him a wink.

They started back.

Claire, aglow with sunburn, and Kelly, lay waiting in the raft.

"Guess we're all gonna die," Alex said, untying the line as Lizzy climbed in.

Jack pulled on his helmet and forced his tall frame back into the kayak.

Lizzy reminded the others to put on their vests, then put on her own. She took hold of the oars. "Push us off."

Alex nudged the boat off the sand and dove over the tube.

Lizzy pulled and the raft spun around. "I'll go first," she shouted. "Let 'em watch from below as you make your run."

Jack paddled into still water, sheltered by rubble. He readied himself to watch.

Lizzy rowed into the current, midstream, and pointed the raft toward shore. Drifting, she feathered the oars, her eyes on the rapid. The raft floated into the tongue. At the point of no return, she dropped the left oar and pushed, spinning the bow forward, just as it plunged into the boil. She drove the oars down, and shoved, moving the raft right. The bow dipped. A wave rolled over the tube. The bow rose, and Lizzy shoved one oar, holding the other steady. Pushed by the current, the raft swept toward a boulder, riding the stream between it and the hole. Lizzy stood, holding the left oar deep, pushing hard on the right, keeping it moving. The raft spun, caught in the water swirling on the rim. Overcorrecting, the back of the raft slipped into the hole, water flowing over the back, washing Kelly forward. Lizzy pushed hard on the right, dropped to her seat, and shoved on both. Again. And again. The raft pulled away, bumped the boulder and spun, floating stern first. The rush of water kicked it away from the wall and Lizzy glanced back, keeping the oars moving, sending the raft crashing through another wave.

It settled onto flat water.

Claire panted, her chest rising and falling.

"What a ride!" Trasker shouted, eyes wide.

Lizzy stood and pulled wet fabric away from her skin.

"Was that good or bad?" Trasker asked, picking up the bucket to bail.

"Anytime we're sucked between the rock and the wall without flipping, I call a success." She turned and signaled to Jack, and watched him paddle into the current.

The kayak entered the tongue and slipped over the edge, picking up speed. Smooth water turned turbulent. Paddling hard, he pushed the kayak left, skirting the swirl of the hole. The kayak disappeared into a wash of white, only his head, shoulders and flashes of paddle visible as he pushed left, avoiding the rocks.

He glided onto still water.

"Woo-hoo," Trasker hollered. "Nice run."

Jack floated alongside, catching his breath.

"Why didn't we go where he went?"

Lizzy flashed a crooked smile. "You didn't like cheating death?"

"Well, . . . uh, I . . . are you serious?"

"My clients pay for the ride, and I try to make it worth it. Plus, those are the tip makers for guides."

"Serious?"

"Sure. I'm honest about it. If people are afraid, we put 'em on a separate boat, try not to scare 'em. Since you're riding the bus for free, I chose. I wanted to try out the oar locks." She turned to Jack. "Oar locks. I like 'em. Pins and clips would've been handy getting out of the hole, but I think I got further into the move before anything happened."

"You mean, you knew that would happen?" Trasker asked.

"Planned to take us around the Carousel a few more times. Didn't work out." She gave him a wink.

"You're so full of it."

"Let's find a place for lunch." She turned to Kelly. "Take the oars. I need to dry out."

— · —

Lunch finished, Kelly popped the lids onto containers of chopped veggies and chicken salad and carried them back to the raft. Lizzy collapsed the table.

Trasker joined Prescott, dropping into the sand in the shade of a cottonwood. "What a ride this morning! As scary as being stuck in a room full of liberals planning their next raid on free stuff."

"Very funny." Prescott let sand slip through her fingers "Take you an hour to come up with that?"

"Just came to me. Easy, really. I don't have the intellectual handicap."

Prescott tossed sand in his face.

"Hey." Trasker stood and moved out of range, shaking sand from his hair. "Get a sense of humor."

Cheeks flashing from pink to red, she shouted, "I've got one, you ass. You get one."

Lizzy jumped down from the tube, stepping between them. "I'm taking the ladies swimming."

"A swim?" Trasker said. "Good idea."

"You're not invited. We're going skinny dipping."

"We are?" Prescott said.

"We are. It'll be good to split up for a while. We'll go upstream. Guys, downstream."

"Actually," Jack said, "I've got something else I could do. Any chance we'll camp tonight near Enos Trace?"

"We can make that our camp, if it makes any difference." Lizzy gave Prescott a push in the upstream direction. "Unless it's taken. Why?"

"I'd like to check on a watering hole. See if it's holding up in the drought. If there's water, it'll be getting lots of use. I've got a camera I could leave and pick up in the morning."

"Sounds like lots of walking," Prescott said.

"The river goes around a thumb and cuts back on itself." Jack pointed south. "You'd hit river in less than a mile if you walk that direction. It'll be easy getting back to the camera in the morning."

"How long will you be?" Lizzy asked.

"Hour, hour and a half," Jack said. "Alex, you go with me. Fill your water bottle."

— · —

Lizzy led to an eddy cut off from the channel. Twenty feet away, the river's current ran strong. In the eddy, still water. Deposits of sand sat above and below the opening to the channel. Willow and tamarisk lined the shore, none too large, having been stripped by spring runoff. The red sandy bottom, easily seen through clear water, held bits of detritus, mostly leaves and twigs. Water striders skimmed the surface. Top minnows darted in the sun.

Lizzy started undressing.

"I'd feel better having a swimsuit," Prescott said, eyeing the depths of the eddy.

"I'm not unpacking the boat." She tossed her dress over a limb. "Don't worry about paparazzi. There's no one here from the *Post* or the *Times*."

Kelly stepped out of her shorts and pulled off her top. She dove in.

"It's just . . ." Prescott wrapped her arms around herself. "If another raft comes, or Alex . . . ."

Lizzy laughed. "We'll try not to scare 'em." She dove in, surfacing near Kelly.

Kelly gave a kick, floating on her back.

"Why here?" Claire shouted. "Look at all the crud in the water!"

"Woody debris. Nothing to worry about." Lizzy ran her hands across her face, shedding water, then pulled back her red hair. "We're here because it's warm."

"It is?"

"See those little fish. The tiniest ones. Look close. There, at the back of the eddy. They're here because it's warm. This is a nursery for little guys."

"Do they bite?"

Lizzy laughed. She pointed toward the river. "See those sand deposits?"

"What about 'em?"

"Hydrologists call those separation deposits and reattachment bars. Sediment drops out of the water when it slows at the mouth of eddy. Because of those types of deposits, there's only so much water exchange. Sun warms the water. It stays in the eddy."

"You're a hydrologist?"

"Hell, no."

"How do you know this stuff?"

"Yeah, how?" Kelly said. "I'm impressed."

"I read. I study. I'm on the river all the time. It's a beautiful thing. I learn what I can."

Claire glanced downstream, then up, before stripping off her clothes, exposing skin still delicately pale. She worked her way toward water's edge. "If I get eaten by fish, I'm killing someone."

— · —

"There," Jack said, pointing at a break in the rock. "We'll climb out through there." Slipping the camera into a cargo pocket, he stepped out of the creek bed and worked his way up layers of cross-bedded sandstone. Climbing, Trasker behind him, he approached a vertical section of wall. With nubbins and cracks, he hefted himself up and over the rim, turned back, and offered a hand. "We could've found an easier way, but this'll save us some time."

Trasker felt along the wall. "Let me see if I can do what you did."

"Careful."

Trasker ran his hand over the wall. "What'd you do here?"

"Wedge your hand in the crack."

Trasker pushed his hand in and pulled. Raising a few inches, he reached with his left, catching hold of the rim. He pulled his hand from the crack, tried grabbing the rim with the right and missed, tried again and caught it. He pedaled at the wall with his feet, managing to get an elbow over the rim, then his upper body. Jack took hold of an arm and pulled.

Alex lay on his back, gasping for air. He rolled over and looked around. "Where . . . the hell . . . are we?"

"If you drove the road through the BLM part of the monument, you would've been up there." He pointed toward at a rim above the expanse of desert.

"That . . . doesn't . . . look familiar."

"Looks different from up there."

"Where I went looked like a hell hole."

"It is a dry year. Drought."

"Even if it was wet, it woulda been a hell hole." Trasker laughed. "Guess I shouldn't say where I've been. Might make you curious about what I've been doing."

"Less curious than you think." Jack turned and started walking.

"I thought you wanted me to talk, to get me to tell you everything."

"Not exactly. I want you to talk, but to people who have faith in the likes of you and your boss."

"You're saying you don't?"

"I'd prefer to avoid politicians. I know the cost of getting 'em involved. But, I owe it to people who put their trust in me, to do what I can to advance the recommendations of the coalition. There are some in the coalition who feel differently. You should talk to them. Not to me. Them."

Trasker stopped, and stroked his beard. "Hold it . . . what cost?"

Jack turned back. "The games. The abuse. The politics."

"What are you talking about?"

"Tell me there's nothing behind Congressman Hoff's leak to the press that he's starting an investigation, issuing a subpoena for communications related to the national monument."

"That's Congressional oversight. It's their job."

Jack started up the hill. "I have no qualms about oversight. It's a travesty it's done by politicians."

"What are you saying?"

"It's ironic. Like a pimp giving sermons on chastity." Jack picked up his pace.

"Very funny." Trasker took quick steps to catch up. "You're saying you avoid working with Congress. I thought you worked with Claire's former boss, Senator Tisdale."

Jack forged on.

"Did you hear what I said?"

"I did." Jack stopped. "He was the only member of Congress I ever really trusted, and yet . . ." He paused. "Never mind. Your boss played his games. Didn't help. Everything went to hell."

"In Montana?"

"Yes."

"What are you not telling me? Why did you stop mid-sentence?"

"I don't want to talk about it." Jack started walking.

"Then, I'll do the talking. I don't know what happened in Montana. End of story. But, I know very well what'll happen here. Congressional Field Hearing. You better be ready."

"Field Hearing? To do what?"

"What do you think? You've got Moony Manson bullied by a federal agency. You've got overreach. Then there's the monument, and a coalition Manson was never a part of. What better place to look into who is and isn't accountable?"

"None of that's true and you know it. If you were Moony Manson—not paying your grazing fees—would you sit around with neighbors who have, and are trying to preserve a way of life, sorting through conflicts with people who value the land as much as you do?"

"That's not how he tells it."

"Of course it's not, but don't talk to me about it. Talk to BLM. Talk to other ranchers."

"It can all come out at the hearing."

"As if the Congressman's hearings are for fact finding and inquiry. It'll be scripted, to achieve whatever it is the Congressman wants to achieve." Jack stopped and turned back. "So, what does the Congressman hope to achieve?"

He smiled. "He wants to give voice to those without a voice."

"Good line, but I'm not buying it."

They topped the rise.

"Well, I'm glad we talked," Alex said, more than a hint of sarcasm. He stepped past, then stopped. "Where we going?"

Slickrock extended hundreds of yards.

"Stop," Jack whispered, putting up a hand. He pointed the other way.

Two hikers—women, carrying backpacks—walked along a ridge.

"They think they're miles from anyone. Let 'em think that."

"Why? We're here."

"And undoubtedly others, too, but quiet and solitude are part of the beauty of this place."

They watched the women start uphill, disappearing beyond an outcropping.

"That's where we're going." Jack pointed. "There, at the base of the butte. A catchment, engineered by nature, fed by a spring."

They crossed the slickrock and approached, stopping at water's edge. Dirty. Inches deep.

"It's used," Jack said, eyeing a spit of sand. "Hard to read track in sand, this time of day. But, this is good. Critters have water. While it lasts." He let his eyes follow the clues. Trailing. Tracks. Scattered shreds of hair. "Predators picking off meals." He pulled out the camera. "Let's see who uses this."

Where to put it. He felt along a crevice at the base of the butte. Here. He dusted the lens with his T-shirt, turned on the camera, set it for motion activation and night vision illumination, and jammed it into the crevice. Taking out his smart phone, he tapped into the app and checked the image. Water. Approaches from all directions. Perfect.

"That thing got a flash?" Trasker asked.

"Infrared."

"Nice toy."

"I prefer to call it a tool."

"Right. Can we watch on your phone?"

"When we're close enough that the devices can talk, but I need to save battery. We'll do a download tomorrow, see what we find. Let's head back."

They skirted outside the camera angle.

"So, what's left of your assignment?" Jack asked, as they started back downslope.

"I've told you all I can."

"C'mon."

"I'm afraid you're associated with a symbol."

"What symbol?"

"Figure it out."

"What does the symbol have to do with Moony Manson?"

"You've got a guy here considered a patriot by many, pushing back in ways that many want to. To them, he's the most important player here."

"You need to get to know this guy. He's not who you think he is."

"In some ways that doesn't matter. He's started a fight that others want to see won."

Jack stopped. "You're willing to create losers to turn a deadbeat into a hero?"

"Why do you call him a deadbeat? Makes him sound like he's not paying child support."

"What's the difference? His cattle don't get much care. He won't pay his fees. Acts like he's mistreated. Blames the system, but what he really doesn't want is to pay his way and live by the rules."

"It's a little more complicated than that," Trasker said, raising a hand to his beard.

"Is it?"

"You're a little too close to see the big picture."

"That is the big picture."

"Sounds like we're done talking."

— · —

The river came into view, then the Enchanted Rivers raft.

In the shade of the cottonwood, the ladies waited, two in camp chairs, Lizzy in the sand, her head resting on a rock.

"Safe to approach? Got your clothes on?" Alex shouted. "I could use some excitement after twenty questions from Mr. Ranger."

"You should've been with the guys on the other raft," Lizzy muttered, fighting a smile, her eyes closed. "Claire's gonna be page three girl for the *Washington Post*."

Claire turned from pink to red.

"If she'd just gotten in the water, but no, she had to be all prissy, afraid to get in." Lizzy sat up, giggling. "There she stood, worried about getting eaten by fish, this big." She held a finger an inch from her thumb. "Then, a raft pops around the bend, full of guys." Throwing her head back, she laughed. "Love it. They hollered. She walked into the water so fast she didn't see a turtle in the shallows. When she did, she came screaming out of the water, jumping up and down like a school girl." Lizzy fought for air as she laughed. "The rafters broke out their cameras. Must've fired off a dozen shots."

"Thank goodness we'll never see them again."

"Oh, we might. There's a chance we'll share camp somewhere downriver."

"Oh, good," Alex said. "Leverage."

"Can we talk about something else?" Claire said. "Even politics with Trasker. Anything."

"I'm talked out," he said. "After Mr. Ranger here, I have nothing left to say."

"What'd you two talk about?" Kelly asked.

Jack frowned. "Congressional Field Hearing, here. Concerning Moony Manson."

"Wild horses?" Claire asked.

"Not on purpose, but they'll come up," Trasker said. "It's my understanding, bleeding heart horse lovers pushed BLM into taking action on Manson."

"So?"

"BLM moved against Manson, because . . . the optics of not doing so if they wanted to remove horses."

"Probably an accurate assessment," Jack said.

"You're siding with him?"

"No, but that last point is accurate. BLM put off taking action for years. They should've taken Manson off the range years ago. Too many cattle. Not paying his fees. Exhausted his legal avenues. But he's a scary guy. BLM wasn't sure how to take him on."

"That's your story," Alex said. "Others consider him a patriot."

"That's a bunch of crap," Claire said. "He's a domestic terrorist."

"Name calling doesn't help."

"Neither does calling him a patriot. It gives patriots a bad name."

Alex attempted a smile. "Don't be ridiculous. BLM overplayed their hand, all because they're afraid of a bunch of elitist horse lovers."

"Why not protect the horse, symbol of the American West? Make the monument a sanctuary."

"If I had a little money burning a hole in my pocket," Lizzy said, chiming in. "I can't say I'd give it to either of you. Your people, your parties, whatever."

"I need a swim," Alex said. He took a step, then stopped. He looked at Lizzy. "Most people making political contributions have a little sophistication. They think they know where society should be going. Some, unfortunately, are wrong, but at least they have a little sophistication."

"In whose judgment? Yours?" Lizzy countered. "I count, too. I'm a citizen."

"Lizzy, out in the world, far from here . . ." He gave a sweep with his hand. "There's real work going on. Work you wouldn't understand." He started upriver. "I'm going swimming."

CHAPTER 30

"Enos Trace, straight ahead," Lizzy hollered. "Campsite, river right."

Downriver, they saw remnants of an old weathered road, visible above the floodplain on both sides of the river. In the flood plain—prone to spring flows and flash floods—no evidence of wagon trail.

"Anyone using the camp?" Jack shouted, straining to see past the willow and tamarisk at river's edge.

Claire craned her neck. "Any sign of those guys in the raft?"

Lizzy laughed. "I'm not seeing anyone." She gave a shove to the oars, and let the raft carry. She stood. "Nope. All ours." She gave a push to the left oar and turned the raft toward shore. "Ready with the line?"

Alex readied himself. The boat bumped and he hopped off, tugging rope toward a shattered trunk of a tree, jutting above ground.

"Line-up," Lizzy said.

Jack beached and stashed the kayak. He took the back of the line.

Kelly peeled off from the others and started assembling the camp table. "Stove goes here."

—·—

Jack dove into helping Kelly with dinner, slicing green peppers and onions, watching others set up their tents.

Finished, Trasker ambled over. "Planning testimony?"

"Do what?"

"Testimony, that Park Service will have to give. Probably your director."

"Why would you think I'd have anything to do with that?"

Trasker flashed a cocky smile. "An assumption. I know how things work."

"Where's your reading material?"

"Couldn't bring myself to open the bag." Trasker pulled a chair from the pile. "Thought I'd just watch the river." He dropped into the chair. "Everything will be there when I get back."

The rhythm of the river. Even the jerks.

Claire wandered out of the brush. "Where's Lizzy?"

"Setting up the latrine," Kelly said, wiping her hands on her shorts.

Claire popped open the other camp chair. "Alex, leave Jack alone. I heard you taunting him, teasing him about the hearing."

"Our ranger friend can take care of himself."

"Of course, but you don't have to be an ass."

"What day is this?"

"Saturday."

"Oh, yeah." Trasker laughed. "Week and half, maybe two, Las Piedras. A good place for a hearing."

Jack set down his knife. "Why the rush?"

"It's a good time for answers."

"Lots of people have answers. Ask."

"They'll have their chance, on the record."

"Or, rather," Claire growled, "splattered over the butcher room floor."

"You're being dramatic."

"Am I? Why here? You'd get more attention in Washington. All the reporters on the D.C. beat. CSPAN would pick it up."

"You think we're wanting attention?"

"Of course you are."

Trasker flashed his smile.

Claire's eyes grew wide. "Alex, what are you orchestrating?"

"Only what the Congressman asked me to do."

Lizzy appeared in the fringe of willow along the upstream bank. "Potty's available."

"Alex first," Claire responded. "He's full of it."

"Poor Alex," Lizzy said. "Are you being picked on?"

—·—

Jack finished a second helping of chicken piccata, and set his plate on the camp table. He stepped over to Kelly, sitting in sand, and leaned over her ear. "Good meal. I'll do dishes when I get back."

"Where you going?"

"To find some quiet."

Kelly nodded. "I'll clean up. Be careful."

"It'll soon be too dark to go far."

He headed downstream. Following a path through the willow, he stopped before reaching the trace—going far enough to hear only the river, except the occasional laugh.

He leaned against a boulder and closed his eyes. He took several breaths, then reopened them. Venus, in a sea of dark blue. Minutes later, Jupiter. He turned and waited for Saturn and Mars. They appeared.

Blue gave way to dark. The Milky Way emerged, then burst through the black, spreading across the sky, deep and bright. He found Orion's belt, then the Big Dipper, fixing his place in the universe.

"Oh, Ranger?"

Jack jumped, startled. "Over here."

"Being antisocial?" Trasker—a dark silhouette—asked. "Ouch. What is that plant?"

"Tamarisk," Jack said. "I'm just getting some quiet. Enjoying the stars."

"Don't you get enough of that sort of thing?"

Jack laughed. "Suggesting I should be tired of this?"

"No, it's just that . . . forget it."

"I never tire of the stars. They satisfy a need. Something primal. A connection."

Alex's shadowy outline plopped down in the sand. "Connection to what?"

"The universe. To those who came before us. Who stared at these same stars, awed by the depths of these same heavens." He paused. "Don't you ever wonder about people long ago? The thinking they did, the uncertainties they faced, the stars that might've affected their thinking, opened their minds, shaped the options they considered."

"It's hard enough figuring out why modern man does what he does."

"These stars, these heavens, they might've helped shape what we've evolved into. Not just us. Our cultures."

"I don't know if I believe in evolution."

"Didn't say evolution. I said *evolved*, and what do you mean, you don't know?"

"I don't. Some constituents are adamant. They don't believe in evolution. Expect us not to. I'm not at that place. It makes sense. Who's to say God would not've done it that way? Who's to say seven days weren't figurative? It's a topic I avoid. Not as safe as talking politics."

Jack laughed. "Politics safer than religion. That's funny."

"How do you suppose politics evolved?"

"That's not something I've ever given a moment's thought to."

"Those people way back when, those simple humans, looking at the stars . . . how far back do you think they started evolving into different political camps, different approaches to life?"

"You mean like conservative and liberal?"

"Yeah."

"Get a life . . . and that sounds like a trick question."

"Nope."

Jack sighed. "I think people sitting under the stars way back when were instinctively wary, trying to provide for themselves and their families, competing but dependent, connected to others by necessity. Instinctively, they looked out for themselves, but learned they couldn't survive on their own. They faced predators, other tribes, the difficulties of hunting and bringing in a harvest. They had to band together, to survive. They probably learned to deal with dominant humans, even bullies, by banding together."

"I'm not sure you answered my question."

"I'm building to make a point, but I'll answer. Probably always. Our populations, our behaviors have probably always been variable. Those inclined to stay rooted in established ways, approaches that worked in the past. Those inclined to try new things, find new approaches. Those who were independent, those inclined to connect. Those who sought to achieve. Those who sought to nurture."

"You're saying there was no point of departure?"

"Somehow I doubt it."

"But, as we evolved, which do you think shaped us more, willingness to take care of one's self, or a tendency to rely on others?"

"That a trick question? I don't think you'll like my answer."

"You think the latter?"

"Didn't say that." Jack paused. "I suspect we're successful as a species because we drew from both. We drew from all. I suspect our societies evolved the way they did because those tendencies were there to be drawn from."

"Maybe, when we were afraid of being eaten by lions, but not today. We must've evolved too much, because now one perspective is dragging society down, and it's not mine."

Jack laughed. "Alex, I believe we're still stronger because of our differences. I think it unfortunate some people don't see it that way."

"How can we?"

"I'll give you an example, and not one going back to the caveman. The colonies, having gained their independence. The effort to create a charter to govern those states united together. The men who wrote it. They had disagreements. They came into the constitutional convention seeking to do different things. Adams,

Hamilton, Washington, all of them, different agendas—and no, Jefferson wasn't there, he was in France—yet, they created something. Despite their differences."

"Why Mr. Ranger, you do know a little something about politics."

"I know history. I don't claim to know politics."

"What's the difference?"

"You tell me."

— · —

Fire light flickered through brush. Jack wove toward it, Alex following.

". . . and he flipped out of the boat," Lizzy bellowed, arms waving. "Raft rolled right over him. We get to the bottom of the rapid, we're looking and we can't find him. Suddenly, his head pops up. First thing he does is scream, 'Hot damn, let's do it again.'" She threw her head back and laughed.

Claire chuckled to herself. "And that's where we'll be tomorrow? The Black Hole?"

"After lunch."

"Why do you call it the Black Hole?" Alex asked, dropping into the empty chair. "Dark water or something?"

Claire rolled her eyes. "You idiot. Don't you remember astronomy class, or physics?"

"Never took astronomy. Sounded like something for people with no idea what to do with their lives. Physics, little different. My focus, economics. Any electives I needed, I took political science."

"That's your problem, Alex. Limited perspective."

"Okay, smart ass, what'd you study?"

"Law, at Berkeley."

"Oh, that's better. Gives you a hell of a perspective."

"It does. Taught me how to dive into any issue."

"Hell it does. All they teach in law school is how to argue. Lawyers argue about everything."

She laughed. "Who taught you to argue? Or maybe they didn't, 'cause you're not very good at it."

"Hold it!" Kelly shouted. "Why do you two keep beating up on each other?"

"Because he's an ass."

"I'm trying to bring her back from the dark side."

"Can't you two find a reason to be civil?"

"I don't need a lecture," Claire said.

"Apparently, I do," Alex said, "but still . . . not interested."

"I'm angry . . . I know when he gets back to Washington, he's gonna pull something. He's gonna make something happen, and I'm not gonna like it."

"Sometimes success is measured not in what you make happen," Trasker muttered, "but by what you keep from happening."

Prescott bored her eyes into him. "Is that your plan?"

"Was that Hoff's plan in Montana?" Jack asked.

Trasker looked away from Prescott. "I don't know what you're talking about."

"The things people wanted to protect. The park they fought to get. Denying them that?"

Trasker shook his head. "Again, I don't know what you're talking about."

Claire glanced from one to the other, looking confused. She opened her mouth to speak, but seemed to stop herself.

"What?" Jack asked, eyeing her.

"I'm not sure. I need to think about this."

"Like thinking about wild horses," Trasker said. "That's a loser."

"It may go nowhere, but people want to see more done for the mustang."

"Good for them. Tell 'em to go buy some land and get busy."

"If I had a little money burning a hole in my pocket," Lizzy said, "I sure wouldn't . . ."

"Enough, Lizzy," Trasker said, cutting her off. He laughed. "I don't want to hear that old saw again."

"Why?"

He slowly exhaled. "Because . . ." He shook his head and chuckled, as if to himself. "There's a world out there, where things get done, where people take risks, live on the edge, where money is not easy, where families fight to make a living, where things are not simple, where you have to live in the world of grey simply to make ends meet, or to advance the world in the right direction. Sometimes you have to fight to win, and you have to get your victories when and where you can. You, dear Lizzy, would never understand that."

Lizzy looked shaken.

"I'm afraid he's right," Claire muttered. "There's serious work to be done. A fight to be fought." She glanced at Trasker. "I can't believe I'm agreeing with him. . . . but . . . this life is like living under a shell."

Silence. Awkward glances.

"I'm calling it a night," Alex said, pulling himself out of the chair.

"No," Lizzy growled.

Jack looked up from the flame.

"My turn," Lizzy said, fire in her eyes. "You think it's easy making ends meet on tips and a river guide's wages?"

"No, I don't," Alex said. "But you've made a choice. You're here on the river, enjoying life. Having fun. If it's tough making ends meet, it's because of choices you made."

Lizzy turned to Prescott. "You agree with that?"

"Kinda, yeah."

"You assume a lot. Afraid to do anything but play . . . hell, you don't know my story. You don't know my life."

"I'm sorry, Lizzy, but that's how it appears," Alex said.

"I'm here on the river, because the river is real. Every day, I wake up and experience what it has to offer, and I can trust it. I have to be ready for danger, but even danger is real. The risks are real. The river is real."

"Lizzy, this life isn't real. Kind of you to invite us along, but you don't understand what we're talking about because you have no sense of what society, or business, or life are really about. You know life chasing fun. Forgive me for putting it that way, but . . . it seems like you're avoiding responsibility."

Lizzy threw back her head and laughed. The sound carried, echoing off walls. Her laughter died away and even the river seemed to fall silent. Lizzy dropped her head. Firelight flickered off red tresses hiding her face. She raised her eyes, glared, and began to speak. "For fifteen years, I was an investment banker. Wall Street. Working my way up from trader, to researcher, to manager." She smiled. "For more years than I'll admit, I made more in a year that most people make in a lifetime. I answered to stockholders, boards of directors, pension fund managers." She paused, boring her eyes into both.

Claire scooted back in her chair.

Alex's eyes grew wide.

"Nothing to say, do you? Didn't think so." Lizzy let out a humorless laugh. "I know the good and the bad. I know the risks people take, and I know the responsibility of people depending on me to take risks on their behalf. For security, dreams, retirement. I know people with a cause. I had investors from the biggest non-profits and pension plans in the country. I know what they expected of me. I know the responsibility of investing someone else's money. I took that responsibility seriously."

She gave them each a momentary glare. "But, you know what? Not everyone does. Some people think they're entitled to play whatever games they want to play, even when the money isn't theirs. My firm hired a couple of smart ass risk takers. Financial innovators, they called them. 'Derivatives are the way to go,' these guys said. Off-the-balance-sheet financing, leveraging, cushioning our capital, taking advantage of the shadow banking system, all that. The firm moved more and more into mortgage-backed securities, and derivatives not worth their salt. We short sold against ourselves and our clients." She sighed. "I told the managing partner I would not play those games. I would not buy into derivatives, and I didn't. Even after Warren Buffet called them weapons of economic mass destruction, our other managers couldn't buy them fast enough. Know what happened? Gone, all of it. The shadow banking system, derivatives, nothing but ways around the regulations, built on shifting sand. Brought the whole company down. People's investments, dreams, gone."

Alex stuttered, "Y-y-you . . ."

"I'm not finished. You don't get to lecture me until you've been the one who's lived by the rules, working day to day, only to have the Securities and Exchange Commission freeze your assets and investigate every financial move you've ever made, leaving you without even a dime to use." One side of her mouth twitched. "You don't get to make judgments. Not about why I'm here. It is none of your business. All you need to know is this place gives me a sense of what's real and what's not." She glared. "Now, tell me you know more than I do about risks. Tell me you know more than me about responsibility."

Claire opened her mouth to speak. No sound emerged.

Alex Trasker slumped in his chair.

"I didn't think so."

Trasker stared into the fire, then cleared his throat. "I'm sorry, Lizzy."

She glared.

"I was a jerk. I insulted you." He lifted his eyes. "I owe you an apology."

"I don't want an apology."

"Then, an explanation." He lowered his head. "Every time you said that old yarn about money burning a hole in your pocket . . . it grated on my nerves." He sighed. "Because . . . never, when I started working for people in public office did I think money would become such a constant focus." He ran a hand across a now tired face. "That's why I reacted. Unfair. I'm sorry."

"I'm going to bed." Lizzy stood, turned, and snaked into the shadows.

All eyes watched her disappear.

"Such an ass, I am," Alex mumbled, to himself.

Silence.

Alex hunkered over his knees.

"Money . . . I agree," Claire said. She dropped her head. "Takes every legislator's attention."

"Lizzy and Wall Street," Trasker muttered, still sounding shaken. He looked up at Prescott. "I'm sorry, you were saying?"

"I was agreeing. We convince voters we have their interests at heart . . ."

He flashed a sad smile. "When we're really taking care of big money donors, some of whom do things we don't admit. Sending jobs overseas, for example, and although I don't think we should regulate where jobs are created, I sure as hell want to believe we're helping businesses thrive and create jobs here, and I'm not sure we are."

"Constituents contact us with ideas, suggestions, needs," Claire said. "At most, they tell it to an aide, if that, because legislators are too busy drumming up support for the next election campaign."

"Constituents. Average Joes. They want to be heard, but party elites, activists, and lobbyists, they get the ear. They have the time, money, and public relations skills. They make up no more than three or four percent of party membership, but they run the party."

Prescott sighed. "Same for us."

"Travesty, isn't it? The masses, they don't have a way to affect public policy."

"Not with party organizations dominated by activists."

"It's unfortunate," Trasker added.

"You're kidding," Kelly said.

"What?" he asked, giving a stroke to his beard.

"Now, you see eye to eye?" Kelly asked.

"Yeah, her words could've been mine," Trasker said. He dropped a hand, and ran his fingers through the sand. "I came to this job because I wanted to make a difference, help make government work the way the constituents back home want it to work. It was the people at home who mattered. To be perfectly honest, conservatives don't consistently oppose social programs or government regulation of the economy. They simply want a government not holding them back."

"And liberals and progressives support expanding government programs only when it's justified," Prescott said. She toed the sand. "Alex, looking back, what'd you expect to find that you didn't when you came to Washington?"

He sat back and stared at the sky. "The first congressman I worked for . . . I thought he'd work closely with constituents, having the difficult discussions. He didn't." Trasker sighed. "I tried. On one issue, I'd brought sides together, and thought we'd found a solution after many hours of work. Then came the primaries—our party—and then the general—the opposing party—and every opposing candidate played politics with what we'd worked out. The Congressman distanced himself, disavowing any attachment to what we'd done." Trasker clenched a fist. "I jumped ship as fast as I could. Congressman Hoff? He's not inclined to work across the aisle, but at least he's willing to fight for the things he has me working on. And maybe I was naïve. The reality is, there's a game to be played, polls to be understood, talking points to script. I thought we'd educate people on issues, admit when we needed to educate ourselves. I thought we'd have political will to bring constituents together to find solutions, willing to tell 'em when they're behaving like kids, or need to be tolerant of their neighbor. But that's political suicide. Still, I wish it were seen as the sign of a wise politician." He laughed. "If I ever saw someone able to do those things and willing to do them, I'd quit and go begging for a job."

"Sad," Jack said.

"Politics. The rules of the game are set."

"Afraid so," Claire agreed.

"Are you sure?" Kelly asked, skeptical.

Alex sighed. "There are so many people working at cross purposes. Lobbyists. Donors. Over five hundred congressional districts, plus a hundred senators, it all becomes a battle of differences. I came to the job dedicated to a defined set of values. It wasn't long before I saw lots of gray. It's hard dealing with gray in the midst of all-out battles to win."

"Well, Alex Trasker, you are human," Prescott said.

He let out a chuckle. "What's your excuse?"

She kicked sand at his feet.

Jack watched eyes settle onto the fire. Minutes passed.

"So," Kelly said, breaking the silence. "Why can't you two find a reason to work together?"

"Different agendas. Philosophically, politically, lots of ways," Prescott muttered.

"I'm not letting you off that easy."

Prescott shook her head.

Trasker held his eyes on the fire.

Kelly turned toward him. "Why do you want this job?"

"I think we've covered that. Might be hard to understand . . ."

"Hell, it is." She stood and crossed her arms. "I'm a politician's brat. Kip Culberson's daughter. I hate politics, but I know what drives a good person to feel they need to serve."

Trasker rubbed his eyes. "Uh, okay, why do I want this job?" He paused. "Might sound hollow after everything Lizzy said, but I want to make a difference. I believe in the American dream. I took this job to help assure everyone has freedom to make of himself or herself what they can. That he or she has opportunity. That government doesn't get in the way. That government is not holding them back."

Kelly spun around to Prescott. "Agree with that?"

"The problem is," Claire said, looking at Alex, "your guys only fight for their rich friends. Help them get richer. Nobody else. Tax breaks, anything they . . ."

Kelly threw up a hand. "Stop. Do you agree with what he said?"

"Yes, but what they're . . ."

"Stop. Answer the question. Do you believe in that?"

"Yes. May I speak?"

"Only if you're telling me why you took this job."

She sighed. "Okay. I want this country to succeed. I want to help everyone have a fair shot, to make sure everyone gets that shot at being all they can be, achieve all they have the potential to be, that everyone plays by the same rules, everyone has a chance."

"But what you really want is government intervention," Trasker said.

"Stop," Kelly said, raising a hand to him. "Would you disagree with those words?"

"No, but . . ."

"Stop. No buts. Agree or disagree?"

"Agree."

"Fair enough. You're fools if you can't find a way to work together."

CHAPTER
31

Jack rose early and headed for the trace, pulling on a fleece sweater to fight the nip in the air. Above the floodplain, he stopped. Cattle track, in long-dried mud. Hooves, having slid in the rush to the river. Urine pools, dry, stench faint. Ground, devoid of grass. He glanced back at the river. Willow, stripped of leaves and stems.

No reason for cattle to be here, other than water. No feed. Surely nothing recent. Months ago, maybe. Or, was it after the rain that caused the flashflood?

He followed the trace beyond the breaks of the river, turned north, leaving the trail and hiking cross-country through barren lands, only nubbins of vegetation. Keeping an eye on a distinctive erosional remnant—sandstone, spire-like, standing over the desert—he found the catchment and retrieved the camera. Then, he turned and ran back, arriving at camp with Kelly working on breakfast, her hair tousled, her dark eyes not quite awake.

"Coffee's ready," she muttered.

"Be right there." Jack retrieved his phone from his dry bag and turned it on. He tapped the app for the wildlife camera, fidgeting to start the download as he sauntered back to the camp table. Kelly held out a cup of coffee. He set down the camera and phone and he took it. "How can I help?"

"I've got it," she said, standing over the griddle, soaking up warmth, flipping buttered toast. "Lizzy's on a walk up the river. She didn't sleep very well."

"I'm sure. What else we having?"

"Eggs."

"I'll do 'em. How'd you protect the eggs?"

"Modern miracle."

Claire crawled out of her tent, wearing dark-framed glasses, and made her way to the camp table. "Someone say coffee?"

"Morning," Kelly pointed at the pot on the stove. "Glasses?"

"No way I could put in my contacts. Not yet." Prescott pulled a plastic mug from the box, filled it with coffee, and turned to the river, grasping the mug in both hands.

Jack set a skillet on the camp stove and palmed a handful of eggs.

A moan rose from inside a tent. The zipper slid up the front. Alex Trasker skulked out pulling on a gray sweater, stood, and stretched. "Clouds. We might get some rain."

"Doubt it," Lizzy shouted, coming from upriver, holding up the hem of her dress. "They're teasing us. They always tease us." She pulled a cup from the box. "Today's the big day. The Black Hole. I'll need a little extra time packing, to make everything secure."

Trasker stumbled toward the table, stopping at the sight of the camera. "You got it already?"

Jack nodded. "Hope everyone likes 'em scrambled."

"Get anything?"

"Don't know. It's downloading."

"May I?" Alex picked up the phone and tapped the screen. "Wow. Says seventy eight images."

"That's a lot," Jack said. "For one night's work."

"This one's interesting," Alex said, raising the phone to his eyes.

"What?"

"Coyote. Here's another. Then a cat of some kind. Short tail."

"Bobcat. Camera's mostly catching predators."

"Nope, here's a horse. Several horses."

"Can I see that?" Jack reached for the phone, held a hand up to block the sun, and let his eyes adjust to the image. A form took shape. A horse. The big stud, ears back, head down, bearing its teeth. But at what? He held the phone closer. Behind the stud, three mares, watering, the stud not focused on them but on something standing back. Something small. He zoomed in on the image. Pronghorn. He swiped the screen. Next photo. More pronghorn. Several waiting to approach. The next photo, chased away. The next, cattle. The next, more cattle, the big stud keeping them at bay. The next image, nothing but cattle.

"Jack," Kelly said, "Don't let the eggs burn."

He scowled and sucked in a breath. He handed the phone to Trasker. "Tell me what you see."

He eyed the screen. "Cows. So?"

"Move," Kelly said, pushing Jack aside. "I'll do this." She took the spatula.

"Cows aren't supposed to be there. The only cattle on the range belong to one man. This isn't his allotment. Even in a drought? Give it to Claire."

Alex handed her the phone. She stared into the face. "What am I looking for?"

"Go back a few images."

She swiped the screen several times. "Oh, horses. Cool."

Jack shook his head. "Not cool. Are you looking at an image with antelope?"

She pulled off her glasses and held the screen closer. "Yes. What are they doing?"

"Waiting, trying to get to water. Are you as concerned about them as you are the horses?"

"Well, sure. Why?"

"You should be more so. Pronghorn don't need much water. They get most of what they need from what they eat. If they're at water, they need it. They belong here. Horses don't."

"I don't buy that."

"Whatever the consequences?"

"The antelope can find other water."

"They're good at it. They migrate long distances, but if drought covers all their range . . . then . . ."

"And the horses are chasing Manson's cows," Alex added.

"C'mon Alex," Prescott pled. She put on her glasses. "Those cattle need to go. According to policy people with the Babes, this land could sustain large populations of horses if his cows were gone, with virtually no impact. Even during drought."

Jack shook his head. "I don't buy that." He crossed his arms. "Who are these people? Who's looked at their work? Why aren't they talking to scientists? Why aren't you talking to scientists?"

"The horses don't belong here," Trasker said. "Not on Manson's range."

"This is not Manson's range. These are public lands," Jack said. "They belong to everyone."

Prescott scowled. "Jack, you're such a bureaucrat."

"Quiet, everyone," Kelly said. "Eat your breakfast and shut up."

"Then get packed," Lizzy added.

— · —

Rumbling echoed off canyon walls. Lizzy lifted the oars and let the raft drift. "Black Hole, straight ahead."

All eyes turned down-river. Sound grew in the distance.

"It's caused by a debris flow from the side-canyon on the right," Jack said, pointing his paddle.

The river narrowed, pinched between a canyon wall on the left and rubble on the right. A dry creek bed entered from river right. As they approached, the view opened. A vast sandy beach lay above the shore, the creek bed cutting across it, emerging from a slice in the canyon wall, fifty yards back.

"The slot canyon is called Devil's Gate," Jack shouted, "but the creek above has a friendlier name. Big Sandy. Nice hike if you follow it up. Eventually ends at the road."

"*The Trail of Chickens,* some people call it," Lizzy said. "Anyone?"

Claire laughed.

"Too much build up. Can't leave now," Alex said.

"Let's have lunch and scout the rapid." Lizzy turned the raft toward shore. "Ready with the line."

The boat bumped shore and Alex jumped, landing in sand. He tied off the raft.

Lizzy and Kelly turned to lunch preparations.

"Let's check out the Gate," Jack said, waving Alex and Claire to follow.

They approached the slice through the rock and paused. Devil's Gate. Two people wide. Stone, sliced vertically, dozens of feet high. Jack stepped in and stopped. Beyond the entry, undulating walls. Darts of light reflected in from above, sending bursts of red and orange over the rock. No water in the creek, but cool air settled in the shadows.

"How far is it like this?" Claire asked.

"Quarter mile," Jack said. "Climbs up and out, into a valley." He stopped and turned back. "Go ahead if you want. I need to scout the rapid."

"Probably more of the same," Trasker said, following Jack into the sun.

Prescott fell in behind.

They climbed onto rubble—a high spot over-looking the river—finding themselves staring down into the rapid. In its midst, a depression, water swirling, collapsing into the hole.

"The rapid is a product of this debris field. Rocks we can't see are piled up above the hole, and directs the flow in a way that gives the rapid its name. All it'd take would be another big flood and the rapid's personality would change completely. Supposedly, it's only been called the Black Hole for about eight years. The last big flood."

"What happens if we get sucked into the hole?" Alex asked, staring.

"Someone might be washed overboard. Might flip the raft."

"What do we do if it flips?" He gave a stroke to his beard.

"Flip it back. Won't be easy with gear lashed to the raft."

Alex shook his head. "How often you down here?"

"Once or twice a year, monitoring resource conditions, mostly up-river." Jack stood. "Let's go eat some lunch. I've seen all I need."

Lunch was cold-cut sandwiches and chopped veggies.

When done, Lizzy went to scout the rapid. Kelly stayed to put away the food.

Alex dropped into the sand, to wait in the shade of a cottonwood. "How's your testimony coming?" he asked Jack. He waived Claire to join them.

"It's not," Jack said.

"So, the hard questions, from you, Mr. Ranger. When are they coming?"

"Told you before, I don't have questions." Jack turned to face him. "Suggestions, yes. Talk to someone who understands the situation, and our needs. Senator Baca, Kip Culberson, Karen Hatcher. They understand politics. They know how you people operate. I don't."

"I have a hard time believing that." Trasker's smile twisted. "I don't believe you're that naïve."

Jack scratched the brown stubble on his chin. "Believe what you wish, but talk to them."

"You're saying it doesn't matter to you what we do?" He shot a look at Prescott.

"Didn't say that. It matters a lot." Jack sighed. "I know how your boss operates. There's nothing someone like me can do, and I don't want things turning out like they did in Montana."

"What are you saying, or, more precisely, what are you not saying?"

Jack looked way.

"Tell me. The hearing you mention in Montana. Why such a burr in your side?"

"Your boss acted like he was gathering information, but he knew things only few others knew, including me. He acted sincere, then turned on us, lying his ass off, spreading misinformation. It confused and divided the public."

Trasker stroked his beard. "I don't know anything about that."

"But you know what he plans to do here."

"Of course."

"Whatever it is, it's politics. Politics make no sense to me. Confuse me. Makes no sense he'd protect a deadbeat rancher, when he could help people trying to make it work. Public lands, to benefit all. Preserving ways of life, things people value, including ranching."

Alex laughed. "You're talking legislation to authorize the coalition's recommendations."

"Yes."

"Dead on arrival. The Congressman will never let it out of committee."

Jack gritted his teeth.

"Let's step back," Trasker said. "You're a well-intentioned guy, but what about the next bunch of bureaucrats filling your shoes? What if they won't work with these people? What will the cost be then?"

"What cost? Economic benefits of the monument more than cover the cost. The recommendations are improvements."

"It's still government overreach. It's a symbol."

"It preserves a shared natural and cultural heritage."

"It limits individual freedom."

"If you give us the authority to do some things, that argument goes away."

"Not really. Only through the lens of today. You have no idea what economic opportunities might be prevented in the future."

"Alex, where do you come up with that crap?" Claire asked.

Jack turned toward her. "What if Senator Baca presented a bill prepared by the New Mexico delegation? What if he had bipartisan support? Would that pressure the House to act?"

"It'd never happen. The bill would go nowhere," she said. "Like in the House, it won't get out of committee, not this close to the election, not without changes."

"Changes? You haven't even seen it yet."

"It'd need to accommodate the mustang."

Jack clenched his fist, and got to his feet. He noticed Kelly watching, reading him. Holding her eye, he took in a long, slow breath.

Kelly jumped down from the boat. She edged closer. She stopped a few feet from Prescott. "You people, why are you even in your jobs?"

"I remember your little lesson from last night, but there's still a battle going on," Trasker said.

"No, there's not. Not here."

"There is. A battle of ideas. It has to be won."

"If you win, we're screwed," Prescott said.

"You're both talking winners and losers," Kelly said.

"Yes, we are," Trasker said. "The future's at stake and there's a presidential election coming to determine that future. If Congressman Hoff is elected, the right ideas will win."

"Lose. He'd take us backwards." Prescott shook her head. "How did we get into this? We were talking cattle versus horses."

"No, you were talking horses. I was talking something bigger."

"Winners and losers," Kelly said. She put her hands on her hips. "If either of you prevail, our piece of the world will lose. That doesn't bother you?"

"As the Congressman says, that's the price if we hope to become great again as a nation."

"You don't have a clue. Neither of you. Talk to Senator Baca. Both of you. I demand it."

"Won't do it," Alex muttered.

"Neither will I," Claire said.

"Then leave us alone. Leave New Mexico alone. Work with Baca, or butt out."

"I'm afraid you're part of the big picture. This is a constitutional matter. A skirmish that has to be won. The gentleman from New Mexico is irrelevant to that fight."

"He's not irrelevant. He's our senator," Kelly said. "Claire, you talk to Baca."

"Nope. Baca's not involved. There's no reason to get him involved until we have a bill."

Kelly threw up her hands. "Why are you here, either of you? Why are you in your jobs?" She leveled her eyes, and growled, "What are you hiding?"

"Nothing," Trasker said. "Can't speak for her, but what you see is what you get."

"Bull. You're hiding something. That, or your boss is, and you're drinking the Kool-Aid. What you're doing here doesn't make sense." She turned to Prescott. "Same for you."

"Don't be insulting," Prescott said.

"You forget, both of you, I'm a New Mexican. Our history is full of people coming here to enrich themselves. I know it when I see it. People using the political machinery for power or money. They want government out of the way, until they know how to use it to get what they want. Or to protect the power they have—when even ordinary people push back. They manipulate the law, feeling entitled to do so, protecting wealth and power and people they're beholden to." She glared. "So what are you hiding? Who are you beholden to?"

"Nothing, and no one," Alex said.

"No, I can feel it. Someone wants your boss to manipulate the system. Robber barons."

"What are you talking about?" Alex looked aghast.

"Our history is full of robber barons. Colonel Catron and the Santa Fe Ring, to modern times, robber barons, who made the system work for themselves, even as everyone else struggled to survive. That's how this feels. People here have worked through difficulties. Now, you show up to manipulate the system, to make it work for someone you're beholden to."

"Members of Congress are not robber barons." Trasker glared. "That's absurd."

"Not Congress. Not you or your boss. You're enablers. Congress is often the enabler for the rich and the powerful, turning their backs on the very people who need them. You said so yourself, last night. Who are the robber barons? Who's manipulating? Who's calling in favors?"

Trasker laughed, shaking his head. "Congressman Hoff does not owe people favors. He's a master at being owed without owing."

"Doesn't smell like it. He's beholden to someone. Or pandering. No other explanation."

"You'd be funny if you weren't so insulting."

"I know it when I see it, so stop." She took two steps toward him, and raised her hand. "Hard work has been done here, getting people to find common ground. Don't blow that up. Don't pander to the robber baron. Don't undo what ordinary people have fought to achieve."

"I'm not the bad guy here. Neither is the Congressman," Trasker said. "We're trying to help ordinary people. Make sure opportunity is here to be found."

"I'll tell you a story," Kelly responded. "Billy the Kid, our famous gunfighter. Seen by many as a murderer, by others as Robin Hood with a six gun." She smiled. "William Bonney, later known as Billy the Kid, was avenging the deaths of men killed by robber barons to protect their monopoly. The Lincoln County War was not good versus bad. In many ways it was bad versus bad, but what's amazing is that ordinary people—even exploited, cheated and lied to, manipulated and robbed—they held on. Despite the robber barons, despite the Lincoln County war, they endured."

"What does that have to do with anything?" Trasker said.

"Why do you think I told that story?"

"You're comparing the Congressman to a murderer?"

"Are you being purposefully dense?" Kelly said, sounding exasperated. "Your boss is not trying to help people."

"Not true."

"Then work with Senator Baca. Learn what people actually need. We don't need your boss grandstanding for a deadbeat connected at most to an oblique interpretation of constitutional rights." She turned to Prescott. "And your cause ain't passing the smell test either."

Prescott glared.

"Hey!" Trasker shouted. "My turn. The battle here is about restoring freedom. Keeping government from trampling individual rights. Nothing more or less."

"The rights of the individual are key," Kelly muttered, "but no individual can be allowed to run roughshod over the rest of us. The community has the right to protect itself, and that's where government comes in. But in the words of my father, the community cannot forget it's made up of individuals with individual rights." She held up a finger. "Now, my words. When I hear someone screaming their rights are being trampled, I look for evidence. If I don't see it, I have to wonder if they're trying to make us forget that they or someone they're pandering to has a history of running roughshod over the rest of us."

From the direction of the rubble pile, Lizzy approached. "We're all gonna die," she said, her voice sing-song, a smile on her face. Seeing the others, the smile melted away. She slowed.

"Let me talk," Trasker said, stepping back from Kelly. "I need to explain some things."

"What do I not understand?" Kelly growled. "I watched my father struggle over what was in the public good, or not. Necessary or not. In the public interest, or of personal interest, or the latter dressed up as the former. I saw him struggle over how and where government should be involved and where they should not. I saw him struggle over what's good for our community and our state, and how to work with others who interpreted things differently. I saw him torn to shreds during campaign season. I saw him criticized by political enemies, and I saw those same political enemies praise him for being a worthy collaborator." She paused. "So, there's a lot I do understand. Your boss is beholden to someone, and it ain't the people who put him in office."

"That's insulting."

"If it isn't true. Members of Congress should bring people together, not pick winners and losers. Work with Baca, or butt out."

"I don't have to take this." Trasker turned. "Jack, I enjoyed watching the stars and talking about whatever that was, and Lizzy, thanks for the good time. Sorry to miss the big attraction, but I'm blowing this popsicle stand. How far to the road?"

"Four miles."

"That's easy. I'll flag down a ride."

"Not out here you won't. Not in the middle of nowhere."

"The Inn of the Canyons has a shuttle," Prescott said. "I stayed there. They'll pick us up, take us back to the Inn."

"You coming?"

"Yes," she said, sending glares at the others. "If you're gone, I'll be next. The target of unfounded accusations. I can handle your insults. I know how to ignore you."

"How kind," Alex said. "Lizzy, we need our stuff."

"I'll have to unpack the boat."

CHAPTER 32

"Be safe," Jack said.

Trasker nodded and slung his pack over his shoulder. He turned and started for Devil's Gate.

Prescott followed, offering no goodbyes.

"I'm sorry, but not really," Kelly whispered. "They were jerks to you and Lizzy." She took hold of Jack's hand. "Will this get you in trouble?"

"Not sure it'll be any worse."

"Any worse?" Lizzy repeated.

"I was told to stay away from those two," Jack said, without thinking.

"But at the bar . . ." A look of horror came over Lizzy. "You mean . . . when I invited them . . . I . . . ?"

"Don't worry about it."

Lizzy dropped her head into her hands.

— · —

Trasker trudged up the slot canyon, his foot strikes echoing off rock. He took his eyes off the ground only to keep track of the undulations in the walls.

"You in a hurry?" Claire asked, breathing hard.

"Angry."

"I understand, but you're marching my ass into the ground."

He slowed. "Sorry. I'm pissed. So pissed, I can't talk. Enjoy it while you can."

"Well, yeah, but you're missing a very interesting canyon. This is beautiful."

He stopped and looked around, catching sight of waves in the sandstone, lit from above. He dismissed it. "Not in the mood." He took a few steps and stretched out his arms. A few feet short of the distance between walls. "This *is* unusual, but I don't exactly feel like communing with nature. How far did Chastain say it'd be before we're out of here?"

"Not long. Then we come to a drainage called Big Sandy. We watch for a trail on the left, and climb out of the canyon. From there, we follow the trail till we come to the road."

Trasker surged, stepping up layers of cross-bedded sandstone, pounding his way up the drainage. He slowed, glanced back at Prescott, then up. Sky's not getting any closer. "We should be close to the end, but . . . think anyone ever gets caught in here?"

"Like in a rain?" Prescott looked up. "I'm sure it happens."

— · —

"It's gonna take me awhile to repack," Lizzy said. Avoiding eyes, she backed toward the raft.

"Relax, Lizzy. We're in no hurry."

"I know but, I need to keep busy."

"What if they blow off some steam and come back? You'd have to start over." He studied her eyes. Regret. Then Kelly's. Something different. Hard to read. "Chill. Both of you."

"I'm so sorry, Jack," Lizzy said.

"I'm not," Kelly said, her brown eyes glaring. "They were jerks."

— · —

Hand over hand, they climbed a jam of boulders and battered tree limbs. Prescott stopped. "Give me a second." She sucked in a few breaths, then moved on.

The rock floor grew level. The walls began to open. A widening valley came into view. They walked into the sun and Trasker slowed, taking it in.

A sandy river bottom stretched hundreds of yards up valley, disappearing beyond a bend. River bed, straight, no meanders. Sand, boulders, scattered logs. Above the bank, on both sides of the canyon—woody debris from past floods.

"Let's make some time." Trasker took off. "My mind is racing. They are so gonna pay for that."

"What are you thinking?"

"Don't know." He glanced at the sand giving way at his feet. "This is gonna be a slog."

"We're in no hurry," Prescott said, struggling to keep up.

"They want us working on *their* legislation, yet . . . not smart. Bad politics. They have no idea how hard we can make things." He settled into a pace. Wind tore at his face, gusts from up canyon. "How closely did you work with Chastain in Montana?"

"Not as closely as field staff in Missoula. Plus, he got along a little too well with the senator. I had to start being careful."

"Why?"

"Let's just say, in the end, the senator and I were not seeing eye to eye. Chastain may have had one message, I another. It all came to an end, differently than I would've expected."

Alex locked eyes on a distant butte, high above the valley, its face in shadow, the bend in the creek bed winding past its base. "I see no trail on the left. Must be beyond the bend." He glanced back. "I suspect you have an idea or two on dealing with Chastain going forward."

She nodded. "I won't let him do what he did in Montana."

"Which was?"

"Hide behind the science."

—·—

"Any chance they'll get lost?" Kelly asked.

"They'll be fine." Jack smiled. "Don't second guess yourself."

She glanced at Lizzy.

Lizzy shrugged, looked away, and twisted a strand of red hair around her finger.

— · —

"Hell of a note, isn't it?" Alex said. He adjusted his pack.

"That she could insult us both?"

"Yeah."

They exchanged glances.

"I shouldn't say this, but the hearing may be more than just Moony Manson. The Congressman's willing to take on the national monument. Do away with it altogether."

"I somehow feel I could care less."

"I was close to disclosing that on several occasions, but . . ." He paused, his attention pulled away. "The wind's coming from there now?" he said, looking left. "Am I imagining things? I thought it was coming from there." He pointed up-canyon, heard a sound and a gentle echo. "That thunder?"

"Not that I heard."

He glanced at the sky. Clear. He shook it off.

They reached the bend and followed it around. More sand. More distance to cover.

Claire pointed, fighting to catch her breath. "There."

A hundred yards away, the beginnings of a trail, left bank, cutting a diagonal path upslope, disappearing from sight at a saddle between buttes.

"Good eyes."

They moved left, climbing out of the creek bed. On firm ground, Alex picked up his pace, bounding with each step, swinging his arms, taking the hill like on one of his runs through the hills of Arlington. Nearly to the top, he stopped and turned back. "Hear that?"

Head down, Claire said, "Hear what?"

He looked at the sky. Blue. "Must be the wind." He took two steps, then stopped. The wind. Now from the opposite direction. He spun around and the wind died away. From gusty to still, just like that. Then he heard it.

A rumble, low and continuous.

He turned an ear to the sound. Thunder? But continuous? As if it's coming from . . . the creek. Can't be.

He jogged to the top, and stopped in the saddle. The scene opened up. He spun around. In the distance, dark, anvil-shaped clouds, lightning pounding the ground. A veil of rain obscured the plateau.

Claire slogged up the last of the hill.

Alex pointed at the light show.

"Damned good storm. Strange thunder."

"It is. Almost sounds like it's coming from . . . there." He pointed into the canyon, upstream.

They saw it.

Movement, gelatinous and dark. Dirt, debris and rock, inching forward. Mass, a meter or more deep, gobbling up terrain, like an army of ants advancing on food, wave upon wave, pouring over the next.

"What is that?" Alex muttered, in absolute awe.

"Debris flow?"

"You're kidding. Looks destructive." Wind bit his face. He could smell the mud. "We've got to let them know."

"There's no way."

"Look how slow it is. There is a way. Dangerous, but I can stay in front of it."

"Don't be foolish. They've probably left by now."

"Not till they repack, and Lizzy takes her time. We've been gone maybe fifteen minutes. At most."

"Feels like an hour. You can't take the chance, Alex. Listen to that. They'll hear it too. They'll get out of the way."

"We don't know that. There's no time to think about it. I either go now, or I don't go at all. I can outrun it." Backing down the trail, he dropped his pack. "You get to where you can make a call. Let 'em know we have people in danger."

He noticed the disapproval in her eyes as he turned and broke into a run.

— · —

Claire watched Alex Trasker reach the stream bed fifty yards ahead of the debris flow. His pace slowed when he hit the sand. He spun around, running backwards, watching debris move toward him. He appeared to be gauging its speed. He turned and ran.

"Alex, this is not the smartest thing you've ever done," she muttered to herself. "You may've just gotten yourself killed."

She watched his choppy steps as he fought to keep ahead of the flow.

A raindrop. She looked up. Clouds, fast approaching.

Losing sight of Trasker, she grabbed a strap on his pack and began to jog.

— · —

Jack turned, and set his eyes on Devil's Gate. "Guess they're not coming back. They should be beyond Big Sandy by now."

"I'll pack," Lizzy said, climbing into the raft.

"I can help," Kelly said.

"No, just relax. I've got it." She stepped over the gear in the bow. "If in flat water, we'd repack downstream, but not here. Not at the Black Hole."

Jack caught sight of clouds, moving across the sky. Cumulus. "We could get some rain."

"Don't get your hopes up," Lizzy said. "They're teasing. They're always teasing."

— · —

Damned sand. Alex veered past a log. His foot hit cobble. He stumbled, plunging head first. Catching himself, he regained his footing. Slow down. No, don't. Keep up the pace. He looked over his shoulder. Flow churned, enveloping a log, picking it up and forcing it into the march downstream. Alex shook his head in frustration. It's faster than it looks.

— · —

Kelly felt something on her face. "I think I felt a raindrop."
Jack held out his palm.
"Wishful thinking," Lizzy shouted, without looking.

— · —

Rain falling, Claire ducked under an overhang, dropped Alex's pack and slipped out of her own. She dug out her phone and turned it on. Waiting for it to power up, she tapped her foot, then checked for signal. Bars. Good. She pulled up a number she'd been given by Erika Jones. She pushed *call*.
"Park Service, can you hold please?"
"No, I can't. This is an emergency."

— · —

The dispatcher rolled her chair back from the radio, phone to her ear. She turned toward her desk. "What is your emergency?" Molly asked, pulling a pencil from her uniform pocket.
"People are in danger. There's a flood in Big Sandy Creek. I think it's what's called a debris flow."
"The people in danger . . . are they from your party? And what is your name?"
"My name is Claire Prescott. Our party includes a ranger from the park. Jack Chastain. Also Kelly Culberson and Lizzy McClaren. They're on the river."
"And you're not?"

"No. I'm on the trail above Big Sandy."

"You're saying Jack is unaware? You're sure he's in immediate danger?"

"They don't know it's coming. They're on the river, at the raft."

"Jack would know to get to high ground."

"Okay," the woman said, "but Alex Trasker's ahead of the flow, trying to warn them. He thinks he can outrun it."

Molly sucked in a breath. "That is not good."

—·—

Alex approached the narrows. Without slowing he dashed into the slot.

Firm ground. Good footing. Gentle slope.

The walls closed around him.

Maybe that'll slow it down. He charged forward.

Quiet. No wind. Only a deep, distant rumble behind him.

He slowed to a jog, fighting to catch his breath.

The rumble changed, sounding unmistakably like a freight train barreling down upon him.

—·—

Jack thought he heard something. He sat up. Holding his breath, he listened. A rumble, low and distant. Thunder? Echoing off canyon walls? He checked the sky. Clouds, but nothing serious.

Did the ground shake?

—·—

Ahead, the rock and log dam. No time to climb down. Alex glanced back. A dark, muddy wall bore down, logs and limbs jutting from the mass.

He reached the shattered log and jumped.

—·—

Leaves rustled.

Jack turned to the sound.

Wind burst from the side canyon. The dirty smell of mud.

"Lizzy."

Head down, she didn't hear him.

"Lizzy!" He pointed Kelly uphill.

Stepping over the oars, Lizzy reached for something in the bow.

The rumbling—like a freight train—grew deep. Then, a dark spew erupted high above the rock. Then, another. And, another.

"Lizzy!" Jack shouted, eyes not on her, but on the eruption.

A person shot from the slot, arms flailing. "Run," he screamed.

Lizzy looked up. She jumped the tube and tugged at the knot. Alex's knot.

"Run," Alex screamed again, stumbling forward, fighting to stay on his feet.

Jack took hold of the kayak, following Kelly.

Lizzy gave up and dashed after them.

Dark water burst from the slot, hurling logs. Water spread over sand, a swell quickly rising.

Trasker reached the raft, and turned. His eyes grew wide, rising to the height of the flood. He looked for a route to escape. Water surrounding him, he dove over the tube.

The flood ripped the raft from its mooring.

CHAPTER
33

The first surge lifted the bow, bucking the raft, throwing Trasker onto the floor. Muddy water washed over the tube. The second stood the raft on end, pounding its underbelly, pushing it dancing on its tail into the current. It fell in a nearly inaudible splat, and floated toward the tongue, quickly slipping into the rapid. Holding onto a rope, Trasker bounced off the boat frame as current sent the raft stern-first into the Hole, holding it there. The third surge hit.

—·—

Kelly and Lizzy scrambled upslope.

Dragging the kayak, Jack stopped and watched—stunned—as the raft disappeared into the rapid. The surge grew, rolling over the rapid, a wall of water pushed by the mass behind it. It grew in steady pulses, the swell consuming the rapid, flattening what had been the Black Hole. The raft popped to the surface, bobbing on the water like a cork. The surge swept it downstream.

Jack strained to see, trying to find Trasker in the floating mass of debris. Is he under the raft?

Jack started toward the river, then heard it. A deep, grating rumble, growing from the slot canyon. More than water and limbs, boulder against boulder. A mound grew, reaching out from the slot, moving toward the river. The mound bulged, collapsed, then bulged and collapsed again, spreading, reaching for the river, crossing it, forcing a battle of two flows, the flow from the slot canyon overwhelming the river.

In awe, he watched, shuffling upstream, dragging the kayak. What do I do?

"Jack!" Kelly screamed.

He glanced around. She sat high above the river, on talus at the base of the cliff. She's okay. Concerned, but okay. He turned back to the river.

Rubble reached the opposite shore. Water began to pool. The flow from the slot kept coming. Piling rock. Spewing water.

The raft, gone. Alex Trasker? No idea if he's alive or dead.

— · —

Molly hit a number on speed dial, the Chief Ranger, Barb Sharp, standing behind her.

When answered, she blurted, "This is Dispatch, Piedras Coloradas. Is your helicopter available?" She listened, then cut off the explanation. "No time for that. I've got a report of a flash flood or debris flow on BLM. Involves one of our rangers and someone trying to outrun the flood."

She listened, then said, "Not sure. We need your ship. Either a rescue or body recovery."

— · —

Jack watched the river impound behind the growing pile of rock. Slack water stretched upstream.

The debris flow, still adding height to the dam.

"Stay high," he shouted to Kelly and Lizzy, over the rumble of boulders. "I'm gonna cross here, portage, get around the dam from the other side. Try to find a place to get downstream. Try to find Alex Trasker."

"Don't do it, Jack," Kelly said. "It's too dangerous."

He gave a glance across the river. "Yeah, but if Trasker's alive, he could be in need." Seeing the conflict in Kelly's eyes, he flashed a smile. "I'll be okay." He pointed at an upstream break in the canyon wall. "Try to climb out if you can. Go for help."

Kelly nodded, then exchanged looks with Lizzy. Lizzy gave him a thumbs up.

Jack moved upstream, pulling on his helmet and splash skirt. He chose a spot to slide the kayak into the water, climbed in, and wasted no time paddling across. Beaching, he rolled out of the cockpit and climbed onto shore, dragging the kayak. He worked his way to high ground, traversing around the rock dam.

Downstream, he looked back. Dirty water poured through boulders near the slot. On the opposite shore, water cascaded through rubble, running almost clear. Below the dam, in what had been rapid, a flat-water course ran well below the height of the boulders. He stared, assessing the risk. The dam—unstable, riddled with logs and debris. It will not last.

The river, two different streams—one dirty, one clear—flowing side by side. Dirty brown, river-right. Clear, pushed to river-left.

Working his way around a bend, he ledged out, unable to go further. Looking downriver, he saw it. The raft, in flat water, capsized, near shore. Too far away to be certain of anyone on or near it. Straining to see, he thought he saw something in the water, floating alongside, but no, too hard to tell. How far to the next rapid? Probably not far enough.

Jack scanned for a route to the river. Below him, a twenty foot drop, onto rock and scree. The kayak wouldn't make it. Wouldn't do a man much good either. He looked up river. Toward the dam, the river lay closer. An overhang stood over an eddy. A twenty foot drop, into water running mostly clear. He dragged the kayak upstream and tried to assess the depth. Ten feet? Maybe. He climbed in, secured the splash skirt, and hopped the kayak onto the lip. Teetering on the edge, he took hold of the paddle, gave one last look at the drop, then shifted his weight, sending the kayak over, nose first.

It hit, knifing into the eddy, plunging to the bottom, then

shooting to the surface. He paddled, cutting a line out of the eddy, into the current. He kept left, avoiding debris.

After some distance, it didn't matter. He avoided logs, the best he could.

Ahead, the raft rounded another bend in the river.

Paddling hard, he worked to close the distance. He took the bend, and spotted the raft.

Where's Trasker? Jack scanned the area around the raft. Limbs and brush in a sea of red. Jack pushed, paddling faster, harder, fighting to close on the raft.

He squinted. He saw it.

A head, bobbing alongside the raft. Shoulders rising and falling, a T-shirt red with mud. Reaches. Slips. Attempt after attempt to climb onto the tube. No life vest. Trasker won't last.

Jack plunged the paddle. The current. Is it changing? Is the flood level dropping, or . . . what? He glanced upstream. Hard to tell.

He located Trasker, still trying to pull himself onto the raft.

Closing, he checked the shore. Lines of detritus, clean sand below. Water's dropping.

"Get away from the raft," Jack shouted. "You could be pinned by the tube."

Trasker's head spun around, tracks of red on his face.

"Get away." Arms growing tired, Jack forced another pull on the paddle.

Trasker kicked back, into dirty stream.

Jack checked the shore. Still dropping. Fast. Not sure if that's good or bad.

He gave a tired pull on the paddle.

Behind him, a rumble. He looked upstream.

At the bend, it appeared. A wall of water. The dam had collapsed.

In alternating strokes, he glided toward Trasker. Feet away, he ripped off the splash skirt, fumbled for the throw bag and found it, cranking his arm back to throw. "Grab hold, and kick. As soon as you can, run. Hard." He threw the bag. Rope fed out.

Flailing, Trasker reached, managing to grab the line. "Need . . . to rest."

Jack saw the fatal look in Trasker's eyes. "Rest later." He plunged the paddle and shot the kayak forward, then hit Alex's dead weight. "Kick."

The burst of wind rolled him over. A thrust on the paddle and the kayak kept rolling, up righting, still moving to shore. Sound of wind grew deafening. He bumped the bank, rolled out, and yanked the rope, pulling Trasker in. "On your feet." In quick moves, Jack scrambled up the embankment. He glanced back. Water, fifteen feet high. Wall to wall. God. He shoved Alex uplope. "Run. High ground. There." He pointed at a crevice.

They reached it. He pushed Trasker up and in, jamming a hand into a fissure, holding on, his back to the flood.

Water hit, shoving him, in, out, ripping at his body.

Chest high, water swept past. Jack fought to hang on.

Trasker held on to him.

Rock bit into Jack's wrists. Water jerked at his joints.

Power and force. Shoving. Pulling.

Forever. When will it stop?

Jack glanced back, over a shoulder. Mid-stream, trees floated by. Sticks and detritus, in swells. Water, dark as chocolate. The raft, gone.

And then it began to subside.

When it dipped below his feet, Jack relaxed his hands.

Quiet settled over the canyon.

"Did it get Claire?" Jack asked, finally, not quite able to look into Trasker's eyes.

"No."

Jack let out a sigh. "Good." He stepped out of the crevice, onto a boulder covered in mud.

Trasker climbed down. He found a boulder for himself and sat. He took several deep breaths. "We were out of the creek when we saw it coming. She went to make a call."

"You saw that and came back?"

"Looked slow. A slow moving mass of mud and sticks. Wasn't sure you'd know it was coming. Seemed like a good idea at the time. Right now it feels pretty stupid."

"It was stupid, but it was brave. Might have given us seconds. Might have saved lives."

Alex gave a nod at the river. "Looks like we're even." He sighed. "This sort of thing happen often?"

"It can. From a number of factors."

"Like?"

"You can figure it out."

Alex sighed. "Overgrazing?"

"That can do it, but floods happen."

"Kelly and Lizzy okay?"

"They're climbing out. Finding a way to the road." Jack attempted a smile. "Alex, you may be last person to ever run The Black Hole."

"It's gone?"

"Different. Harder, easier, who knows, but it will be different."

"I'm sure there's a war story to be had, but for now, everything's a blur." Alex lay back on the rock. "I'm tired. Wasted." He closed his eyes. "Tell Kelly I'll meet with Senator Baca, with Congressman Hoff, one way or another. I promise."

"Maybe you should tell her yourself."

He laughed. "Might be safer for you. She can be feisty." Alex lay in silence a moment, then said, "I think I can get Claire to meet with him, too."

Minutes passed.

The river continued to recede.

A helicopter appeared, a quick pass down river, gone just as quickly.

A Bell 407. The BLM ship. Jack turned, listening until he could no longer hear it. Must not have seen us. "Let's get closer to the river. A place they can't miss us."

Trasker forced himself to his feet, ignoring the mud on his shorts.

They made their way to water's edge and picked their way downstream, past boulders and debris-draped willow and tamarisk. They reached an alluvial fan below a cleft in the canyon wall. The beginnings of a creek, but not much of one. They waited, kicking about in open sand, ready to make themselves visible.

Evaporation clouds hung along low canyon walls.

Smells of fresh rain wafted through the stench of dirt.

Twenty minutes passed before they heard the muted beat of rotor blades coming from down canyon. The sound grew. Loud, then thunderous. They raised their arms. The helicopter appeared, fifty feet off the water, moving upstream, negotiating the river with what appeared to be conscious intent.

Probably think they're looking for bodies. Jack waved.

Trasker joined in.

The helicopter slowed, hovered, and spun around toward them. Rotor wash sent waves across the water. The pilot appeared to be studying the situation.

Canyon bottom. Sand. Not something he'd want sucked into the engine. Jack pointed. The bluff behind them. On top.

The helicopter rose, tilted forward, and flew over the rim, setting down beyond it.

Jack and Alex climbed up the cleft, scrambling, up and out, onto flat terrain.

The helicopter sat, rotors turning, skids resting on an expanse of rock.

A man in green flight suit and white helmet climbed down from the passenger side. He opened the rear door and pulled out two bags. Head down, he walked out from under the rotors and approached, tossing one bag to Jack. Over the noise, he shouted, "You know the drill."

Jack nodded.

He handed the other to Alex. "Flight suit, helmet, and gloves. Just your size." He cracked a smile. "Bigger than you need, but let's make it work."

Alex unzipped the bag and pulled out a flight suit.

The helitack foreman turned to Jack. "Man, it's sure good to see you alive."

—·—

Looking out the side window, Jack searched the ground. He keyed the intercom and heard the hum in his helmet's earpiece. "Seen any women down there?"

"On the prowl?" the pilot asked.

"Very funny."

"We saw three, actually. Two and one. All making their way to the road. Park Service dispatch has a vehicle en route to pick them up."

— · —

The pilot landed the helicopter near the Enchanted Rivers boat barn. The helitack foreman climbed out and opened the door opposite the rear rotor, holding it as Jack and Alex disembarked. Ducking their heads, they walked out from under the blades and stopped to remove the flight gear. The helitack foreman bagged it, shot Jack an easy salute, and returned to the ship.

They watched it take off to return to base, then headed for the parking area to wait at the Jeep. In time, a Park Service vehicle arrived and unloaded three passengers.

Standing in a circle in the graveled lot, they expressed relief and began trading stories.

Zach Danner emerged from the barn and handed out car keys. "That's why I collect 'em," he said. He turned to Lizzy.

She dropped her eyes.

"Those things happen, Lizzy. Don't think about it. Not now. Consider yourself lucky." Danner excused himself and returned to the barn.

"I oughta get back to D.C.," Trasker muttered, sounding tired at the thought.

"Me, too," Prescott said. "Maybe tonight if there's a flight out of Albuquerque."

Alex nodded. He turned to Lizzy. "Thanks for the experience, Lizzy. I will never forget it. For days, I didn't give my phone a moment's thought. It's been years." He turned to Kelly. "I'll call Baca tomorrow and set up a meeting. I'll find an angle to get the Congressman there." He broke into a laugh. "Claire, I promised Jack I'd bring you along."

"That's the second most stupid thing you've done today, but okay, I'm in."

With the exchange of handshakes and hugs and goodbyes, vehicles departed in different directions.

— · —

Jack jumped in with Kelly, joining her for the drive to the ranch, his clothes still damp. Sitting back he closed his eyes.

"You okay?"

"Better than I should be, but tired."

"Why better than you should be?"

"Should be dead. I'm not. Should be in trouble for interacting with Trasker and Prescott. Maybe I won't be. Who knows . . . something good might come of it."

"Of course it will."

He yawned. "Yeah, maybe for the monument. Things could work out. Who knows about me and the director."

"Why would he care?"

"He gave me orders." Jack sighed. "But, I have options."

"The job offer?"

"Yeah, but I'd rather not think about that." He paused, eyes still closed. "What about you? What about the things on your mind?"

"Life? Changes?"

"Yeah."

She drummed her fingers on the steering wheel. "The future? Does it include changes? Who knows?"

He nodded. "What about children?"

"I don't know, Jack. My life is full. My life is good. I want to have kids, someday, but it doesn't have to be now. But it could be. I need time to think. While you were gone, what I didn't have was you, and that had me thinking. Silly thoughts. You're back now, and . . ."

"Feeling differently?"

"Not exactly. The thought of change keeps filling my head, but nothing specific. Mostly, what do I want to do with the rest of my life? It'll pass. You're back."

He ran a hand down a shin, probing a sore. "What if I have to take another job?"

"I'll go with you." She watched his hand. "What'd you do to yourself?"

"Bruise, who knows how." He flinched. "You'd leave the ranch? All the things you love?"

"It's close, right? You said the job's somewhere here in New Mexico."

"I've been afraid to ask where. Afraid it'd encourage Pug but . . ."

"But?"

"I might need the job." He closed his eyes and leaned against the door. "Let's not talk about that now."

"What'll you tell Senator Baca?"

He cocked one eye open. "Not me. Your father, Karen Hatcher, whoever."

"They'll want you involved."

"If they trust him, they can deal with him. Me? I wanna avoid 'em. All of 'em."

She slapped his arm. "Quit saying that. You know you can't."

"What happened on the river doesn't change the fact that we're talking politics . . . with politicians. They come in and pull us into their games. If your father and Karen Hatcher think they can keep that from happening, more power to 'em."

"I don't believe you think that. You're very good at working with people."

"Normal people. Not politicians."

"Look how the river trip turned out."

Jack opened his eyes and looked out at sage-covered terrain. "Alex and Claire are staffers."

"What are you not telling me?"

"Nothing."

She slapped at his arm again. "No, there's something."

"Nothing. I know we can't avoid politicians, not if we need legislation, but I'd rather just work with people to find common ground, work together, preserve the things they value."

"I got all that. I understand that. But there's something you're not telling me. Something about Montana. This senator you trusted. What was his role at this hearing Hoff was at?"

"Nothing. It was a hearing for the House, not the Senate. He was there only to listen."

"And?"

Jack turned away. "Nothing. That's it. He was just there."

She took her eyes off the road. "I don't believe that. There's more to it than that. Tell me."

"He wouldn't look at me, okay," Jack said, now angry. "Not afterward. I failed him." He turned to the side window. "I failed him and his constituents. I failed at defending The Kid. The senator surely felt I'd mislead him. I could see the disappointment in his eyes. For himself. For his constituents. For people who worked so hard, gave so much to get us where we were. Passionate people, who drew their strength from that place. Who wanted to see it protected, preserved. Their dreams? I'm sure the senator saw their dreams slip away, and it was my fault."

"It couldn't have been just your fault. I know you too well."

He jolted around. "Everything I assured Tisdale to be fact was picked at, turned into something it wasn't. He probably felt cut off at the knees. Hoff knew almost as much as I did, and I don't know how." Jack sighed. "Hoff knew the facts and he used them to distort."

"Hold it. How could he use facts to distort?"

"Distortions are often filled with facts. The public was confused. Support for the park began to wane. Not support, actually. Confidence. It went away."

"Because of what Hoff said?"

"Questions he asked. Facts he brought up. Information he got from somewhere. He paired fact with fiction. Repeatedly asked me to confirm facts without allowing me to refute the fiction. Then, he used it all to make assumptions about motives. Assumptions he presented as fact."

"How could he make such a leap?"

Jack clenched a fist. "Because he's a pro. He knows what he's doing. Made us look like we were pulling findings out of our ass, all for the purpose of locking up as much land as possible. Big federal land grab, he said, when in reality, it was all public land, and our efforts started at the request of people who lived there. I became a liability. Senator Tisdale heard it all."

"I'm sure he knew it was all Hoff."

"I told you, he wouldn't look at me. He didn't move forward.

We wouldn't cross paths again until the other day in Missoula. Saw him in the Federal Building. In the hall. He was friendly enough, but subdued. I suppose time heals. A little."

"What'd you do?"

"Apologized. I wanted to promise that . . ." He looked away.

Kelly slowed the vehicle and pulled off the road. She turned to face him. "I know what you're hiding. I know your secret."

"I don't have a secret."

"You do. It's not that you don't understand politicians. Or even how or what they think. You're secret is, you don't trust yourself. You fear you'll fail another politician. Another community. Another special place. You're afraid your actions will set someone up for failure, like Senator Baca."

He held his tongue.

"Thought so." She laid a hand on his arm. "You're not going to repeat what happened in Montana. It's totally different circumstances."

"How?"

"For one, Senator Baca is from . . ." She scowled. "But Congressman Hoff isn't from . . ."

"Check and check. What else?"

"Alex. You have Alex Trasker on your side."

He sighed. "Maybe."

"You do. Have faith. You will not fail Senator Baca, and Baca can't do his job without input."

"I will not allow myself to set him up."

"You won't." She let out a sigh of relief. "It's gonna work out. Senator Baca will meet with Alex and Claire, then Congressman Hoff. Things will work out." She flashed him a confident smile.

The sign into the ranch appeared on the right. She turned and followed the road around the hill, dropping onto the meadow overlooking the Culberson casita. With dusk settling over the canyons, the lights of Las Piedras flickered in the distance. They parked under the cottonwoods, and crossed the flagstone to the house.

"Father!" Kelly shouted, as she slipped inside.

A faint voice responded, "In my office."

She led Jack down the hall.

Kip met them at the door, hugged his daughter, then turned to Jack, looking relieved.

"You heard?" Kelly asked.

He nodded. "Park Service called. Said you were safe. Thank God!" He motioned them into the office, then took a seat in a old leather chair. "Tell me what happened?"

"We will, but . . . first." Kelly glanced at Jack. "Alex Trasker promised to meet with Senator Baca, and to bring Claire Prescott, the senate staffer." She smiled. "Good, huh?"

Kip stared back, unfazed.

She cocked her head. "This is good, Father. Baca will convince Hoff to back off. Then, he can introduce the coalition's legislation. Everything." She paused. "Call Senator Baca."

Kip ran his hands across his face, and let his head fall back on the big leather chair.

"What's wrong? This is good, Father."

"Would be. Except, . . ." He picked a newspaper off the desk. "Friday afternoon, the Congressman announced a hearing, in three days."

"But, . . ." She frowned. "Alex Trasker's gonna talk to him. Maybe that'll change."

"Won't happen."

"Alex is close to Hoff. Very close. All you need to do is call Senator Baca."

"That won't happen either." Kip dropped his eyes. After a long moment, he looked up, appearing overcome. "Kelly, Senator Baca is dead."

"No!"

"This weekend. Heart attack. After a long day with constituents. He died in his sleep."

CHAPTER 35

"Joe, it's me," Jack said, into the phone. "I'm off the river."

"I heard," the superintendent said. "Glad you're safe. You home?"

"Yes. Kelly just dropped me off."

"When we spoke the other day, I'm guessing Alex Trasker and Claire Prescott were with you, maybe even listening?"

"Yes."

"I guess I can't hold that against you." Joe let out a sad little laugh. "I was dense about your clues." He paused. "Just glad I won't need to call and tell someone Trasker was killed."

"He did some stupid things today. So did I." Jack dropped into a chair. "Thought I had good news. He's willing to talk to Hoff about sitting down with Senator Baca. But, then, I heard about Baca."

"Unfortunate. Good man."

"Yes. I'm not sure now what to do about Trasker."

"Leave him to me," Joe said. "The director wants distance between you and anything that involves Congressman Hoff."

Jack rubbed his eyes. "He knows I'm back?"

"He knows. He's pissed. Wants you nowhere near our response to that subpoena."

"How can he keep me away? Most of the correspondence was mine."

"You copied me. On most things, anyway."

"Some things, maybe not."

"What I've got should be enough to get started. Hoff's trying to move up the deadline, hoping to get things before a hearing in three days, but the director's promised no more than a partial record . . . not with that kind of turnaround. He's sticking to his guns, wants you nowhere near that response. Seems to think you've had dealings with Hoff in the past."

"I doubt Hoff remembers me."

"Don't be so sure, and even so, doesn't matter. You're a symbol. The hearing's gonna be all about symbols."

Jack went to the window, and stared out. "Not much I can do about that."

"And not much the director can do either, but he can try to protect you. I have explicit orders not to let you anywhere near that hearing. Hoff is powerful. He wants to be president. He's got friends. He's in rut and the director wants you nowhere around."

"In rut," Jack repeated. He laughed. "That's funny."

"Nothing's funny about this, Jack."

"Does the director know about the river trip?"

"He does. I told him. This afternoon, when I heard about you, Trasker, and the flood."

"Must've been a nice call."

"Especially on a Sunday."

Jack walked into the kitchen. "You in trouble, too?" He pulled a beer from the fridge.

"That's what I'm here for. That's why it's gonna be me talking to Trasker from this point forward. Got his number?"

"I don't really know it. Plus, he lost his phone on the river. So did I, by the way."

"I'll ask Legislative Affairs to track it down."

He popped the beer open. "He's been through a lot. Catch him while he's affected by events and I'm sure he'll help. What's the latest on this hearing?" He took a sip.

"In three days, unless Trasker pulls a rabbit out of his hat. I haven't seen who's testifying but I've been drafting testimony all weekend, working with legislative affairs. Department's being coy, watering things down."

"What's that mean?"

"Avoiding controversy. Won't work. Manson's misbehaving. His cattle are testing the fence, and not the monument's, the park's. If they break through, we'll have to act fast."

"What can I do to help?"

"Nothing. You're going back to your hobby."

— · —

Jack woke early and made coffee.

He remembered his promise to Fish and Wildlife Service, and forwarded the spreadsheet from the Kenyan Embassy, on an email from his personal account.

He did a quick scan of emails from the previous few days, and went to pour a fresh cup of coffee. Upon returning, he noticed a new one. A quick response from Fish and Wildlife Service.

He clicked on the message.

"Keep your fingers crossed. We might have something to give you."

Jack stared at the words. Finally, good news. A lead that may play out.

Fingers crossed? On all fronts.

— · —

The op-ed sat buried below the fold on the editorial page of the *Las Piedras Gazette*. Likely glossed over by many during their early morning reading—as something to get back to, or as having only marginal relevance. Chatter began slowly, but soon reached a fevered pitch.

In the park, the dispatcher saw it first. Molly always saw the newspaper first. She had her finger on the pulse of everything happening not only in the park but throughout the county. She checked the online edition of the *Gazette* and saw a growing number of comments about the op-ed. She carried the newspaper down the hall to the superintendent's office. Door closed, his secretary not yet in the office, Molly raised her hand to knock, then stopped. Joe's voice. Must be on the phone. This can wait.

Traipsing back to her office, she called Jack Chastain. "Coming in today?"

"I can."

"Do." She hung up.

Jack pulled on his shoes and jogged the shortest route to the office, opening the back door and taking the stairs three at a time. He slipped into dispatch and stopped at the counter dividing the room. Across it lay the *Gazette*, opened to the editorial page.

"This why you called?"

"Bottom of the page."

"About Baca?"

"No. That's page one."

"Joe see this?"

"He's on the phone. He'll see it soon enough. Figured he'd ask someone to call you, so . . . I called."

Jack began to read.

Activists push for control

—Peter Peck, The Poppy Seed Institute

A massive amount of federal ownership has resulted in land mismanagement, stifled opportunities for recreation and resource production, and poor environmental management. Rather than recognizing that federal control is the problem, certain members of Congress are being encouraged by activists to authorize even more control. Congress should reject such attempts.

The Piedras Coloradas National Monument Coalition's recommendations will create environmental degradation because the federal government is large and bureaucratic, slow to correct problems, and disengaged from

proper land management. States, local governments and
private interests are in the best position to maximize the
value of the land, both economically and environmentally.

State, local and private interests have a clear incentive
to not only take care of these lands but to use them pro-
ductively, and certainly would not be ejecting ranchers like
Moony Manson from lands he's successfully managed for
decades. By devolving responsibility to local and private interests, the result will be better land use and environmental
protection.

Furthermore, without the national monument, the
lands would generate revenues from economic activity.
History indicates federal bureaucrats over time will expand
its boundaries regardless of protests by locals. The use of
private property within monument boundaries will be
sharply limited, as it is in the park, and eventually taken
with little or no compensation, as is being shown in the
Moony Manson case. Traditional uses, such as timber har-
vesting, mining, hunting and grazing, will all be banned.

Permanently authorizing the recommendations made
by the Monument Coalition is a recipe for prolonging
mediocrity and poor control of America's land.

—Peter Peck *is Ralph Rasmussen Fellow in the Hermann Straight
Institute for Economic Policy Studies at The Poppy Seed Institute.
He is author of six books and has testified before congressional
committees investigating irregularities in the activities of federal
agencies.*

*The Poppy Seed Institute nurtures the small seeds that sprout big
ideas in preserving our freedom."*

Jack looked up from the page. He sighed. "Best get this to Joe."
"Be my guest."
"I'm not supposed to be here. If he wants me, I'll be here."
Minutes later, Molly returned with the superintendent behind

her. He waved Jack to follow. Without words, they marched down the hall, into Joe's office. Joe closed the door, and took his seat behind his pine timber desk. The newspaper lay spread across it.

Jack took the chair near the wall.

Joe picked up a pen and gave it several clicks. He eyed the op-ed. "The orchestrations begin."

"Poppy Seed Institute. Who are these people? Where are they? A university somewhere?"

"No, Jack. This is not a research institute. This is an ideology institute. No research went into those words. They'll dig up a few facts to spice up the rhetoric, but they don't hurt themselves doing original work."

"You know these people?"

"A little."

"Read that part again . . . about . . . disengaged from proper land management, and the part about private lands and expanding the park boundary . . . and with little or no compensation."

"I don't need to read it again," Joe said. "Neither do you."

"Generalizations. How can they say that? That Peck guy has to know we can't do those things without going through Congress . . . or . . . the president proclaiming . . ."

"Jack, you're not naive. You know what's going on."

"But they're . . ."

"Doesn't matter. Yes, it's misrepresentation. Doesn't have to be correct. Just has to be said. It's not important that it's true. What's important is what they want seen as true. They say it. They get the ball rolling. Happens from both sides. People espouse an ideology. They stick to the message."

"It said the guy testified . . ."

Joe cut him off. "Before Congress. Only means he was invited by a member wanting someone to say the things he says, but . . . looks good on the page, doesn't it?"

"Like he's an authority."

"And yet he doesn't know much." Joe sat back and ran a hand through his hair. "Go home. Go back to your hobby. I need to think about this."

—·—

In a slow walk across the meadow, Jack returned home, making glimpses and deliberate efforts to appreciate the canyon walls. The sights hardly registered.

He walked inside and called Kip Culberson.

"Yep, seen it," Kip said. "You're the fourth call this morning."

"Anyone from the coalition?"

"Of those, two."

"What'd they think?"

"They're getting calls from other ranchers. It boils down to this. It made sense to be involved in the coalition when ranchers thought they'd lose everything, but the sort of talk in the newspaper now scares 'em. It makes 'em think they misread the situation, that there's more to lose by being involved than not."

"I suppose that's what Peck wants 'em to think."

"They know that. But fear and uncertainty are powerful feelings."

CHAPTER
36

Alex Trasker jumped off the Metro at Capital South and rode the escalator into the sunlight. Stepping out on the road, he slowed and let the crowd thin. Dozens of suits stormed past. Young congressional staffers, men and women, destined for the same stone clad structure. He watched them flood the door to the Cannon Office Building, U.S. House of Representatives.

He strolled toward the entry, taking in the scene. What's the rush? The trees along the lane. The buildings. He laughed, mostly at himself. It's good to be alive. And nice not to be worrying about things already demanding attention. No Blackberry, no worries. Yet.

He waited his turn to enter the building, worked his way through security, then headed down the hall. He nodded to a young lady in a navy blue suit. Who again does she work for? Doesn't matter. Just smile. He stopped at a door. *Congressman Brent Hoff.* He turned the knob.

"Morning, Alex," the graying receptionist said, looking up from her work. "How was your trip?"

"Amazing. I'll tell you about it." He walked past. "Let me check email first." He stopped. "I need a new phone. Same number. Everything. Lost mine on a river."

She arched an eyebrow and scratched out a note. "The congressman wants to see you. Right away."

"He's in?"

She glanced at lights on her desk set. "On the phone, but yes, for a while."

Trasker turned down the hall to the congressman's office. The door stood open.

Hoff, phone to his ear, waved him in, then returned to effusive, chummy conversation.

Tuning out the words, Alex took a seat and stared out the window. The Capitol building. One end jutting toward them. The dome, high above it all. You're home, Alex. Home.

Hoff ended his call and cradled the phone. "I've been calling you for two days."

"Sorry. I ruined my phone. Then I lost it."

"If you'd called, I would've told you to stay."

"I've been out of the office too long. Had things I needed to do."

Hoff leaned over his desk. "What more did you learn in New Mexico?"

"The most important thing . . . don't try outrunning debris flows. You could get yourself killed." He smiled. "Learned a lot about our man, Manson, too."

"Was that a joke?"

"Very much not a joke. Dead serious, almost." He laughed. "Now that was a joke. Get me started, it'll take all morning. I'll tell you about Manson, and run something by you."

Hoff appeared to pour over words on a page. "The hearing's in two days."

Alex let his mouth drop open. "Impossible. We have preparations. Testimony to request."

"Done."

"We need to secure a location."

"Done. The place you recommended." He glanced back at the page. "Inn of the Canyons. I need you there making preparations, pronto."

"I just got back, and boss, this issue's more complicated than we thought. For one, this Manson character's shady as hell. The word locals use is deadbeat. And, we also have horse people. They're a wild card. Do you really want to get tangled up with people we know nothing about, except that they're passionate about their cause? Another thing. I promised a local woman I'd find a way to get you talking with Senator Baca."

"Baca? That's . . ."

Alex cut him off. "Before you say no, hear me out, please."

Hoff's eyes narrowed. He leaned forward. "Something I need to tell you. But first, Alex, I appreciate you taking care of me. Trying to save me from tangential battles with wild horse advocates, but I have risks I have to take, to get the focus on what's good for the country. Regarding Manson? Trust me on this one. Whatever he is, his fight is one millions of Americans want to see won. Deadbeat? Hell, no. He's a working man trying to get by. Crusty? Cantankerous? Who wouldn't be? Outside the line? Probably. The government's keeping him from making a living."

"Congressman," Alex said, respectfully, "Manson's not exactly that kind of personality."

"Regardless, that's the message, and we control the message." He stood. "Gotta end this for now. I need to make an appearance at Ways and Means."

"Can we talk later? About this."

"Of course. You know I value everything you say." Hoff slipped on a gray suit coat, swept his blond hair into place, and started for the door. "Can it can wait for our trip to New Mexico? Get us on the same flight."

Alex followed him into the hall. "Brent, . . . are you good with me finding us time on Senator Baca's calendar?"

Hoff stopped. He turned. A grimace formed on his face. He stared a moment, then turned to the receptionist. "Suzie, tell Alex about Baca." He turned and departed. Before the door swung closed, he added, "Be easy on him."

— · —

Jack reread the email from Fish and Wildlife.

"Getting back to you sooner than I expected. Struck out on the obvious. None of the real names my investigator is watching showed up on your list, including some we've been trying to connect to an alias used by a man in New Mexico. Connections to money. Does this list include travelers on corporate aircraft?"

He clicked on reply, and typed, "I'll have to ask." He pushed send, and began preparing an email to Akingi.

The radio popped, from the kitchen. A static-covered voice began to speak. *"Dispatch, this is Luiz."*

"Go ahead, Luiz."

"I'm gonna need that assistance I discussed with you earlier."

"Copy."

"Have him prepared with options."

"Copy."

Jack eyed the radio. Options? What's that about?

—·—

Trasker tapped a finger on his desk.

Maybe it's best.

Makes things easy. What could've come from meeting with Senator Baca? The Congressman works on a different plain than Baca did. Would it have made any difference?

But it was a promise.

Frustrated, he gave his head a shake. Why does it matter? Because you promised. Close the loop. Call her. But you don't have her number.

But it was a promise.

He dialed directory assistance, waited for an operator, then said, "New Mexico, Las Piedras. Listing for Kelly Culberson."

"I have no listing for a Kelly Culberson."

"Try Jack Chastain."

"I'll connect you," she said. The call went through.

"Hello," said a man's voice.

"Jack?" Alex said.

"Yes."

"Alex Trasker. Can't find a number for Kelly. Had to call you."

"I'm guessing you learned about Senator Baca."

"Even talked to the congressman. Told him my promise to Kelly." Alex sighed. "I'm not sure I can even keep the intent of that promise. It's not that I don't want to. Things are moving fast."

"Understood. You'll be getting a call from my superintendent."

"It'll be hard to catch me. I'm flying back your way tomorrow. Can we talk then?"

"By then, won't the hearing be a foregone conclusion?"

"Feels like that already."

"I'll ask Joe to call you. At this number."

Jack ended the call and started dialing Joe when voices broke over the radio.

"Three-ten, this is Dispatch."

"Go ahead, Molly."

"Johnny Reger's en route."

Jack hung up to listen.

"Copy," Luiz said. *"How are his preparations?"*

"He knows what you need."

"Tell him to . . . Hold it. I'll just call him. Johnny, this is Luiz."

"Go ahead Luiz."

"Park at the overlook on the edge of the BLM part of the monument. Drop down from the road and skirt to the northwest. You'll come to the break in the fence. Hang out while I get around these cows. I'm gonna try to push em back your way. Just make sure they go through the break in the fence."

"What about the horses?"

"Don't know where they went. If you see 'em, let me know."

"Before or after they're afflicted with lead poisoning?"

Jack picked up the phone and redialed Joe. When Joe answered, he said, "Alex Trasker is expecting your call. Here's his number."

— · —

The phone rang. Molly scooted back from the radio and picked it up. "Park Service. Can I help you?"

"I'm listening to your radio transmissions," a woman said. "If one of you so much as harms a hair on one of those beautiful animals, we'll drag your ass to court. I'm talking horses, not cows."

"Excuse me?" Molly said. "Who is this?"

"You heard me. Leave the horses alone."

"They don't belong in the park. They're feral."

"Hogwash. They belong here more than those damned cattle."

"That's hardly the issue."

— · —

"Knock, knock," a voice said, in loud, precise words.

Alex turned.

The receptionist stood at the door, smiling.

"What? Something wrong?"

She put a hand on her hip. "Knocked three times. Where is your mind today?" She smirked. "The congressman's back from committee. He asked that you come to his office."

Alex slipped into the hall and followed her toward Hoff's office. He rounded the corner and stopped at the door.

"Come in," Hoff said, already in shirt sleeves. "I need you to join me on a call."

"With?"

"Call him Doc. Doc gives me advice from time to time. Call it polling and related services." Hoff activated the speaker phone, and began punching numbers.

Alex chuckled to himself. "Memorized but not on speed dial."

"Correct." Hoff sat back in his leather chair, his eye on the phone. "Let's call this a personal relationship. Services provided by a supporter." The phone began to ring.

"Hello."

"Doc?"

"Good morning, congressman."

"Good Morning. Joining us is my chief of staff, Alex Trasker."

"Hi Alex, I'm surprised we haven't spoken before now."

Alex exchanged glances with the congressman. "Should we have?"

Doc laughed. *"Not necessarily. I work with several members of Congress, in a great many ways. Some directly. Some with their staffs. Different levels of discretion. Understand?"*

"I'm not sure I do. Where are you located and who with?"

"Midwest, when I'm not in D.C." He laughed. "Let's call who I work for a think tank."

"I'm sure you're busy, Doc," the congressman interjected. "Let's dive in."

"Very good. I've run a number of things through focus groups. Hot button phrases, issues, that sort of thing."

"National or New Mexico?" Hoff asked.

"Both. Very little difference, except for response to some key phrases."

"What are we talking about?" Trasker asked.

"The hearing," Hoff said.

"If we're asking for testimony, why concern ourselves with focus groups?"

"I'll explain later. Go ahead, Doc. My apologies."

"No, that's a good question, Alex. It's never a bad idea to have ready responses. In your hip pocket, especially if they give you predictable results."

"Predictable results?" Alex rubbed his head. "I'm sorry. I've spent the last few days on a river. I should be tracking with this, but somehow I've slipped into a level of naiveté. I'm finding myself asking, why don't we limit our preparations to a few well researched questions, and see if we get answers?"

Doc laughed.

Alex looked up from the phone. Hoff watched through vacant eyes.

"It all boils down to this. What do we hope to achieve?"

"Oversight," Alex said. "That best describes our responsibility. Oversight." He flashed the congressman a quizzical look. "Right?"

"It's more than that," Hoff said. "Listen to what Doc has to say."

"Before I go on, I'd like to hear any worries Alex might have about doing a hearing in this part of New Mexico. I understand you were there last week, getting a feel for the issues. So, big worries?"

"I worry about the support for the national monument. There's plenty, because people made an effort to work together. I worry about what people say about this Manson guy. He's no saint. But my biggest worry—gut level, but it won't go away—is the horse people. We can't discount their level of passion. To wander into something we don't know well, risking blowback from a group we don't exactly understand . . . that worries me. Scares me, actually."

"First," Doc said. *"This is not about horses. Listen closely. Our work with focus groups underscores one point. This has to be a hearing about one thing. Government overreach. Nothing more, nothing less. Government overreach. If it is, and if the right messages come out during testimony, things will fall into place. Quite nicely, in fact."*

"But it's not. Horse people think it's about their cause. The agencies are caught in the middle, Manson on one side, horse people on the other."

"No, Alex. This is our hearing. The issue is government overreach. Nothing more. No horses."

"What if they want to be heard?"

"The hearing is for our message, to create our army of supporters, not theirs."

Alex shook his head. "If you say so."

"Keep this tightly focused and here's how it plays out. The base. We have them automatically. They'll take up the cause simply because we tell them it's important. Plus, this is their song. Their rallying cry. It's the other voting blocs we're after. Our research suggests a high probability of pulling portions of other voter groups into alignment with the base, if we create the right amount of fear and uncertainty." He paused. *"So, how do we create that fear and uncertainty? Through testimony. First, let agency testimony go as it will. In fact, it's best that it sound ordinary. Normal. The things people expect to hear. But we want to make sure all other testimony paints a totally different picture. We only want that totally different picture. If they're not saying they're being beaten back by the big, bad bureaucracy, then we don't want to hear from them. Got that?"*

"Got it," the congressman said, nodding at the phone.

"But Brent, . . . I've just spent a week with these people," Alex said, laying his hands on the desk. "Agencies have involved people. I heard stories of rangers on horseback, riding the range with ranchers, trying to understand their issues. Environmentalists and ranchers breaking bread. To do what Doc's recommending, we need a place with bad things going on. It'll be easy to find, I assure you, but not there. We need a place where things aren't working. A place needing a wakeup call."

"No, this is our place," Doc said. *"Ready-made for our point. Ready-made to build an army. Ready-made for our announcement."*

"Announcement?" Alex said, eyeing the speaker. "Is there something I'm not aware of?"

"Go ahead, Doc. Let's talk about the second phase of this."

"Very well. Keep the hearing short, focused—on fear and uncertainty—then, shut it down. You know exactly who'll give testimony, correct? Notices went out on Friday?"

"Correct," Hoff said, nodding. "Includes the people you recommended."

"Good. And you'll see their testimony sometime today?"

"Correct."

"Let me take one last look when you get it. See if they're on the mark."

"Done. Anything more I should know?"

"I'll email the testing results for key phrases. Use 'em. And one key multiplier of effectiveness is painting someone as the example of the heartless bureaucrat, the face of government tyranny. Give that some thought." Doc paused. *"So, . . . Alex, the plan is to have the final speaker be a no show. Flight problems, supposedly. The congressman shares a few thoughts, as if killing time. Dwells on fear and uncertainty, learns the speaker isn't coming, then concludes the hearing. We need to keep this short to hold people's attention."*

"Sounds contrived," Alex said, "but okay. Short, then get out of town."

"Not exactly. That's when the real show begins."

Alex raised a brow.

Hoff smiled.

*"The good congressman, spur of the moment and totally sponta-
neous, proclaims his disgust and frustration. He can't sit by and watch
while a community is victimized. He has learned what he can, but
now must bring peace to the victims. Someone must do something.
He has no choice but to take responsibility, and willingly shoulder
the presidency,"* Doc said, sounding like a drama coach. "You can't
avoid it, congressman. Someone has to provide the leadership to get
this country on the right path, to return it to greatness."

"I don't like it," Alex said.

"Why not?" Hoff asked, toying with the corners of his mouth.

"Shouldn't we just schedule a normal announcement, like
everyone else?"

*"Because, then, he'll look like everyone else. I don't want the
congressman compared to anyone. I want them compared to him.
I've tested and retested this scenario. The effect it has on focus groups
suggests it'll give him a bump that'll carry him through the primaries,
into the general election, holding enough penetration into other blocs
that it gives him an easy win."*

Eyes wide, Trasker searched for words.

"He's taking it in," Hoff said, fighting a smile.

"Any questions, Alex?"

"Uh, . . . plenty." He dropped his eyes to the table and ran a
hand through his hair. "Uh, . . . what do I do? How many staff are
we taking? Do we need committee staff? We're doing this under
the auspices of the Resource Committee, right?"

"No other members, no other staff." Hoff smiled. "Called
in a few favors, but it's mostly because of timing. Too soon for
members to fit on their calendars. It's . . ." He fell quiet when Doc
began to speak.

*"It's you, the congressman, and a court reporter, to make it
official. Bare bones. This needs to look spare. The more people you
have, the more it looks like a production. We don't want a production. This is a hearing of the U.S. Congress. Focused on one issue.
Nothing more."*

"That's workable," Alex said. "Hearings, I know, but I have no
experience making announcements for presidential candidacies."

"*Good. And that's how it needs to appear, and that's what you need to be ready to say. When everything is over, get the congressman in the car and on the road. No questions from reporters. Not for him. Only you. Spontaneous. Answer as a working class congressional aide. Nothing with the sound of spin or campaign language. Got it.*"

"That's easy. But reporters? Are you sure we'll have any? This is New Mexico. I doubt even C-SPAN wants to go to New Mexico on short notice."

"*There will be reporters. Cameras rolling. Footage from several sources. Repeated for days. Especially on cable. Commentators and the 24-hour news cycle will build us an army. Remember, after the hearing, everything appears spontaneous.*"

"Sounds more a production than something spontaneous."

"*It takes preparation to look spontaneous.*" Doc laughed. "*Now, Alex, there's much riding on you to make this work. The man you see across the table is a powerful, influential man. You know that. He's about to become considerably more so. Important people are counting on that happening. From what I understand, his plans include a role for you. Make this work.*"

The congressman gave Trasker a twisted smile.

CHAPTER
37

Jack opened email. No response from Akingi.

He stared at the screen.

All this effort, and nothing to help Samuel. Wheel spinning, nothing more. No names. No clues. No help whatsoever.

Maybe it's time to start over.

What do I know? The poacher, an Irishman. What did he say?

Jack closed his eyes and remembered the scene. Nighttime. Three men, around a campfire, under the African sky. Samuel standing beside him, in the shadow of a wall tent, listening. Stories. Whiskey. Two Americans, in over their heads, only they didn't know it yet. The Irishman, enjoying someone else's whiskey, letting his guard down.

And the rhino horn? Rather than destined for China or Viet Nam, as suspected, it was for someone in the Middle East. A wealthy Saudi prince, with a nephew in Yemen, coming of age. Some sort of cultural tradition, but what does that matter? Unless there's a way to dig into it.

There isn't. So what does it matter?

Whoever paid for the horn was buying influence. From the prince, or someone. But clues? What clues can be derived from that? None, on the surface.

It all seemed so simple that night in Kenya. A big name, but the courier who carried it to the big name came from New Mexico, for that express purpose. But why from New Mexico?

Significant? But why bring in the courier? No one's that important.

Was the big name the one seeking influence, or was he just part of the play? A tool. Brought in to impress?

Jack slammed his fist onto the table. No way to know.

It had all seemed worth doing. Clues, that seemed substantial, now thin.

Jack opened the spreadsheet and stared at the names. Thousands, and no clues.

Why are you doing this? You're not an investigator. You're a biologist. Who are you kidding?

He clenched his fist.

There's nothing to do but wait. Get an answer from Akingi, then see if Fish and Wildlife can find anything.

"Johnny, that you? Did you take a shot?"

The radio. Jack stepped into the kitchen, and turned up the volume.

"Wasn't me." Excited breathing bled over the radio. *"I think someone just shot at me."*

"Where are you?"

"At the break in the fence, behind a big ponderosa, wondering if it's big enough."

"You safe?"

"Hell if I know! I have no clue where it came from."

"I'm on my way."

"Are you sure that's smart?"

Jack picked up his radio and left the house. Direction, headquarters.

———·———

Johnny Reger sucked in a breath, and fought back the adrenalin. Trying to steady his pulse, he listened. Wind in the trees? Or someone in the brush?

Rifle in hand, barrel upright, he pushed his back against the ponderosa, fighting the bulk of his pack. He dropped a shoulder and pushed off a strap, then the other. He let it drop to the ground, and pressed his back to the bark. He took another deep breath, and listened.

Damn it's hard to hear when your heart's beating like a drum.

— · —

"It was one of the horse people," Molly said, turned away from the radio but staying close. She pushed her glasses up on her nose.

"What'd he say?" the superintendent asked, from behind the counter dividing the room.

"It was a she. She said not to hurt the horses. She said if we did, they'd take us to court."

The superintendent turned to the chief ranger.

"Sorry if I asked this before," Barb said, strapping on her service belt. It settled onto her hips as she holstered her weapon. "But . . . no threat of violence?"

"No. Not per se. But I may have insulted her."

Barb pulled her black hair back, the gray streak falling behind one ear "How?" she asked, slipping on her Stetson.

"The caller made a distinction between the horses and cows."

"And you didn't."

"Correct."

"Call me if you remember anything more," Barb said. "Do it by phone."

The door swung open. Jack Chastain rushed in, radio in hand. "What are we gonna do?"

Barb Sharp exchanged glances with Morgan.

"Go home, Jack," Joe said.

"*Dispatch, this is Luiz.*"

Molly spun in her chair, and keyed the microphone. "Go ahead, Luiz."

"Now *we're both pinned down. I have no idea where the shooter is.*"

Barb slipped around the counter, and leaned over the microphone. "Heads down. Stay put. Don't give 'em a target." She dashed out the door.

"What's she gonna do?" Jack asked.

"Let's hope she doesn't get herself killed." Joe exchanged looks with Molly. "Let me know if she shares anything . . . and call the sheriff."

"Done. First call I made after Barb. Also called FBI."

"Good." He turned to Jack. "Go home. Go back to your hobby. There's nothing you or I can do."

— · —

The phone rang as Jack opened the door to his cabin. He slipped in and picked it up, laying the radio on the kitchen counter. "Hello."

"Jack, this is Alex."

"You know I'm not supposed to talk to you. You really should call Joe Morgan."

"I need to tell you something. The hearing. It's not gonna be what I thought. And I'm sorry, there's nothing I can do at this point. It's planned out, things are moving."

Jack leaned against the counter, shaking his head. "Tell that to Joe."

"Stay away. Don't be there."

"Wasn't planning on it. Call Joe. He's the one to talk to, but shots have been fired, rangers pinned down. He might not wanna talk till he knows they're safe."

"That sort of thing happen often?"

"Not often but it happens. Could be one of the horse people."

"Why would they do that? I mean . . . they're passionate, but . . . why?"

Jack drew in a long, slow breath. "To protect the horses. There's a break in the boundary fence. Horses and Manson's cattle are in the park."

"Anybody hurt?"

"Not yet."

—·—

"Congressman," Alex said, standing at his door.

Hoff looked up from his desk.

"New development. Reason to cancel the hearing."

"Too late for that, Alex."

"Shots have been fired in Piedras Coloradas."

"By who? Does it involve Manson?"

"I don't think so."

"What do you know?"

"Not much. Could be the horse people. No one knows for sure. Two rangers pinned down."

"Horse people," Hoff growled, more to himself than to Alex. "What are they trying to do?"

"We should cancel."

"We should call Doc." Hoff pointed Alex to a chair.

Alex watched as Hoff dialed, turned on the speaker phone, and waited. It rang twice, then,

"Yes, Congressman, how can I help you?"

"Tell him," Hoff said, to Alex.

"Shots fired in Piedras Coloradas. It could be the horse people."

"They're determined to make this their issue, aren't they? Well, they can't have it."

"I think we should cancel."

"No, we will not let this be about horses. We will turn this to our advantage. Give me time to think about this."

—·—

"Three-ten, this is three hundred."

Jack went to the kitchen to listen.

"Go ahead, Barb."

"Things still quiet, Luiz?"

"Yes."

"I'm at the road watching for movement. Don't see a thing. I've had time to think about this. If you two are safe, sit tight. Stay where you are. We'll bring you in after dark."

"Copy."

"Johnny, you copy?"

"I copy." A strange pop echoed behind his words.

Quiet, then, *"They're listening."*

Jack gathered equipment and left the house. In his pack, a spotting scope and binoculars, a map, his radio and spare battery, apples, a bag of veggies, and two quarts of water. He threw the pack in the Jeep and climbed in. No stopping at headquarters. This, Joe doesn't need to know. Got a new hobby.

— · —

Driving past Barb's patrol vehicle—no sign of her—Jack continued up the road. From Luiz's description, he guessed both Luiz and Johnny to be overlooking a glade falling away to desert. The break in the fence sounded to be along that clearing, them sitting a little upslope.

Where would a shooter be? Taking his eyes off the road, Jack studied the map. The creek below. No. Too low for a visual. Out on the desert? Maybe. He looked west on the map. Part of the plateau, or the headwaters for the creek, to the north. Where the rim of the plateau turns west, a peninsula, jutting south. On the other side of the creek, knolls, several heights.

He drove, one hand on the map, holding his place, considering possibilities. He glanced between topographic features. The peninsula. That's where I'd go. Has a view back toward the fence from high ground. The knolls? Possibly, but that might be too low.

At the next pullout he stopped. He'd been here before, with Kelly, on their hike a week ago. He folded the map—a tight square—and stuffed it in the pack with his gear. He took off, working his way along the edge of the plateau, in the opposite direction from the trailhead, closer to the glade and the likely positions of Luiz and Johnny. The peninsula came into view, and Jack slipped back from the rim, looking for places to hide. He chose a cluster of juniper and oak brush. Ample shadows. Not exactly camo, but in tan cargo pants, brown T-shirt, and deep gray cap, who would see him lying in shadows? He dropped to the ground and crawled forward, downslope, stopping under the largest juniper. He dug out the binoculars and gave the rim of the plateau a cursory look. Nothing. He dug out the spotting scope. Keeping the lens out of the sun, avoiding reflection, he set the scope on its tripod and sighted it in.

Starting with the peninsular part of the plateau, he searched—first with the binoculars, then with the scope, zeroing in on details—looking for surroundings similar to his own. Shadows among the pinyon and juniper. The brush at the lowest extent of the ponderosa. Nothing. The knolls below, in scattered pinyon and desert scrub. Shadows, but fewer of them. The shooter would have no place to hide. What about the rock heaps? Nothing. Escarpments. Nothing.

He pulled out his radio and checked the volume. On. Nobody's talking. He laid it against a pinyon and returned to scanning the scene, checking for movement and irregular shapes. Every branch looked like it might be a rifle barrel, every rock a man in prone, shooting position.

So, where are you, shooter?

— · —

Trasker dialed the number for Piedras Coloradas National Park. "The superintendent, please," he said, when answered.

"One moment." A short pause, then, "This is Joe Morgan."

"Mr. Morgan, this is Alex Trasker, Congressman Brent Hoff's office."

"How can I help you?"

"Jack Chastain asked that I call you. Did you find the shooter? Your rangers okay?"

"No and yes, so far. Pinned down, but so far no harm."

"Good. Know who it is?"

"We've got ideas. Nothing concrete. Are you sure you want to hold this hearing tomorrow?"

"I don't, but the decision wasn't mine."

"Mine neither. What happens if I choose not to testify?"

Alex sat back in his chair. "You risk contempt of Congress."

"I might just do that. I might have more important things to do. This feels like grandstanding."

"Are you referring to the congressman?"

"I'm sorry, but I'm in no mood for diplomacy. Yes, your boss. He's playing games."

Alex felt hackles go up his spine. "Congress has an important oversight responsibility, Mr. Morgan. The congressman is simply doing . . ." He paused. Said those words so many times they just flow off the tongue. "Uh, . . . he's doing his job, Mr. Morgan."

"Are you saying that with a straight face?"

"Congressman Hoff has a keen sense for issues that are bigger than they appear."

"Well, he's screwed this one up. He's playing politics."

Alex sat up and leaned over the phone. "Excuse me?"

"Politics."

He sighed. "I guess we're done."

"I suppose we are."

— · —

The sun hung overhead. Waves of heat rose off the desert. Everything seemed to move. Trees. Brush. Even canyon walls seemed to shimmer.

Eyes tired, Jack turned away from the spotting scope and took up the binoculars, scanning quickly. On two passes, he saw nothing. He laid them down.

A golden eagle soared overhead, riding the thermals. Circling, it seemed to study the ground.

He rubbed his eyes and picked up the glasses, giving the ground another quick scan. Then, along the plateau, the lowest trees, the pinyon-juniper, then higher, the ponderosa and gambel oak. Then back the other way, down off the edge toward the buttes. Hold it. In the rock. Did something move? Can't be. Maybe just heat waves. But it looked like a gun barrel. Or a dead branch. He scanned the other direction. Where was that? Where did it go? Pulling the glasses from his eyes, he checked where on the wall he was looking. Near bottom. That doesn't make sense. He resumed his search along the buttes. Nothing.

He set down the binoculars and sighted in the scope, targeting a spot on the cliff face. Nothing. He scanned right. Then left. Nothing but sandstone. Weathered red rock. Crags. Cracks. Long, smooth surfaces, covered with desert varnish. More cracks, in shadow. More smooth surface, bright from the sun. Which break in the rock was it? He scanned across and back. Hold it. Movement.

He settled in on the spot. A crevice, in shadow. Too much light on the rock to adjust to the shadow. He locked down the tripod and turned the scopes's knob for as much zoom as possible, zeroing in on the crevice.

He closed his eyes, resting them a moment, then opened his left, set it against the eyepiece, and let his eye adjust to the shadows. The crack—cave-like—five or more feet deep, shadows dark, growing lighter. On the floor of the cave, on what might be sand, lay a man in prone position, staring into a rifle scope, pointing the rifle across the canyon. He wore shooting glasses, desert camo, and a bandana over his head. Beside him lay gear—a canteen, binoculars and a radio. And something else. Lenses with head straps twisted on the ground.

Jack locked eyes on the man's head, waiting for him to turn his face. Finally, the man took his eyes off the scope, and rubbed his eyes. He took a swig of water and wet his bandana. Beard, a week or more of growth. Cropped brown hair. Somehow familiar, even with the distortion of the lens. Was he there that day at the BLM holding pens? Or was this the guy riding with Manson?

Jack pulled back from the scope and stared out over the canyon, studying the location of the crevice, memorizing its location. When he was certain he could spot it again from any location, he packed up and backed out from the shadows, staying low as he made his way back to the Jeep.

——·——

Johnny Reger rolled his neck, twisted his back, and stretched, trying to find relief. The bark on the ponderosa bit into his skin. With his pack and rifle on the ground and his radio clutched in one hand, he used the other to knead the knots at the small of his back.

He chuckled, imagining the sight of himself hiding behind a tree.

Without thinking, he gave both arms a good stretch.

He felt pain and caught sight of the radio exploding a split second before hearing the shot.

CHAPTER
38

"Luiz?" came Barb Sharp's voice.

"Here."

"Johnny?"

No reply.

"Johnny?"

No reply.

Jack punched the gas and sped down the hill in the direction of Barb's vehicle.

"Johnny," Luiz said, joining in, sounding near-frantic.

Nothing.

"I'll go to his location."

"No, Luiz, stay put. I'll get to him. Shooter doesn't know where I am."

Rounding a bend, Jack raised his radio. Hold her up, or let her go? Gotta stop her. "Barb, wait. I know something you need to know."

"Jack?"

"Yeah."

"Where are you?"

"Nearing your location."

"Copy."

Jack entered the pullout at full speed, then braked, skidding to a stop.

Barb came running out of the trees, no hat, her black, gray-streaked hair tied back.

Jack grabbed his pack and pulled it across the seat. He bolted toward her. "He's in a crevice at the base of the wall. Almost a cave. He's got a view of the hillside."

"Show me." Barb lead downslope through ponderosa and gambel oak. The vegetation began to thin. She slowed. Seeing the view open to the west, Jack dropped to the ground and crawled quickly into a thicket of oak brush. He stopped in the shadows.

Barb crept up beside him.

Desert lay in an expanse to the southwest. The plateau, north and northwest. The peninsular arm off the plateau, straight ahead, beyond the dry creek bed. Everything as expected, nothing the same. The angle, different.

Hunkering, Jack studied the wall.

"Where?" Barb asked, anxiously.

"Give me a second." He pulled out the scope and set it up, pointing it at the wall across the way. Shadows. More peninsula visible from this angle. He scanned, tracing a line down the wall to the bottom of the formation, just above talus. Now, left. There it is. A crevice in shadow.

He put his eye to the eyepiece, reset the zoom, and let his eye adjust to the scene. He panned to the crevice. A man lay inside, a rifle pointed in their direction. Jack locked down the tripod and rolled away from the eyepiece. "He's there. In camo. One of Manson's militia."

Barb scooted forward and ran an eye down the spotting scope's line of sight. She studied the wall a moment, then closed an eye and peered into the scope. "Son of a bitch." She scooted back. "Okay, I'll work my way down to Johnny, trying not to let the shooter draw a line on me."

"Are you sure that's smart?"

"Hell no, it's stupid, but I can't sit here. I need to get to Johnny."

"Know where he's at?"

"I'm guessing." She backed out of the brush. "Keep an eye on that shooter."

Jack watched her begin moving laterally. "He has night vision goggles."

"I won't be gone that long."

—·—

Joe Morgan stepped into dispatch. "Any word on Johnny?"

"Nothing more."

"I don't like this."

Molly sighed. "Sheriff has two deputies en route."

"Good."

"Jack's up there."

Morgan scowled. "Doing what?"

"All I got was, he knows something."

"Get him back here. He's not trained for that sort of thing."

"Are you sure I should call him on the radio? The shooter's listening."

—·—

Barb pulled back an oak branch, spotted the crevice across the way and moved right. Below, she made out the boundary fence. No Johnny.

Now where is that break in the wire?

—·—

"Chastain, this is dispatch."

Jack rolled onto his side and pulled the radio from the top pocket of his pack. "Go ahead, Molly."

"The superintendent orders you back to headquarters."

"He's busy," Barb responded, her breathing bleeding over the air.

"Standby." Quiet, then, "Joe said, Jack is not to get involved or become a liability."

"Copy," Jack said, his eye on the eyepiece, watching the rifle barrel pan the hillside, then stop.

A shot rang out. Echo bounced around the canyon.

"Luiz?" Barb said.

"I'm good."

"Jack?"

"I'm good."

"Me too. I'm guessing our shooter's trying to keep us nervous," Barb said.

"Hell, I'm not nervous," Jack said, keeping his eye on the gun barrel. "The shooter's a punk. A play solder, working for Manson. Why would we be nervous about that?"

"Now he knows we're on to him."

"Good."

— · —

Joe Morgan leaned over the counter. "I don't like this." He ran a hand through his gray, well-trimmed hair. "What's the latest on the FBI?"

"Agent en route."

"I want this turned over to them as soon as we can." Joe sighed. "And one more thing. Call the sheriff's office. Tell 'em this is likely one of the militia types hanging around Manson."

— · —

Forty feet away, through a curtain of rocks and trees she saw him. Barb crept forward, and knelt behind an outcropping. She studied the scene.

"Johnny," she said, her voice low and calm.

He looked up, holding one hand in the other, blood seeping through his fingers. "Really good to see you, Chief." He forced his usually easy smile. "Got any whiskey? I could really use some whiskey. There's no hope for my radio. It's a goner."

"Glad it's not you. How serious?"

"Not bad."

"Can you stay put a bit longer? Give me time to go get the bad guy?"

"You bet," he said, attempting to sound flippant. "So, you're saying no whiskey?"

— · —

Trasker knocked on the congressman's door.

Hoff looked up.

"Just got off the phone with the sheriff in Las Piedras. About your request."

"Willing to do it?"

"If no new charges have been filed by BLM or the Justice Department. Said he's willing to get Manson to and from the hearing in the hope it eases tensions, but . . ." Trasker dropped into the seat across the desk. "There's bad news. He got a call from the park while we were on the phone. The shooter may be connected to Manson. A militiaman protecting him and his cows."

Hoff scowled. "How would they know that? Are they dismissing the possibility that it's the horse babes, or whatever they're called?"

"A ranger got a look at the guy. The sheriff mentioned a name, Jack Chastain, the ranger I was with on the river."

"Chastain. The guy on cable news when the story first broke?"

"The same. Apparently, you've had dealings with him in Montana. A field hearing."

Hoff rubbed his chin. "I've met this guy?" He pushed a button, activating the speakerphone. He began pushing numbers. It rang once. "Stay," he said to Trasker.

"Yes, Congressman."

"Doc, I've got new information. It's not better. It's not the horse people. It's someone associated with Manson. The shooter was seen by that ranger we've had in the news lately."

The speaker remained quiet, except for a nearly imperceptible sound, like fingers drumming on wood. Then it stopped. "I'll get back to you."

— · —

Barb Sharp slipped through the trees, into the shadows, and crawled to Jack's location. "Johnny's shot in the hand. Destroyed his radio. In pain but should be okay till we get to him." She scooted alongside the spotting scope. "Our bad guy still there?"

"Yes. Splits his time between keeping track of Luiz with binoculars and Johnny through the rifle scope."

"Let me look."

Jack rolled out of the way.

She leaned into the eyepiece, took a long look, then muttered, "How do I get to you, you son of a bitch?" She stared a moment more, then pulled back. "Ever been in that canyon?"

"Close. Once. There's an old mine trail on the back side of the peninsular part of the plateau." Jack pulled his map from his pack and pointed at a set of swells in the contours. "It's not on the map, but the trail's about here." He tapped a mark. "Not hard to find. Look for a cairn." He offered the map.

"Give it to the deputies." She pulled her radio from its holster. "You're gonna love this." She keyed the mike. "Dispatch, this is three hundred."

"Go ahead, Barb."

"I can see Johnny. He's okay. Shooter got his radio. The guy likes destroying public property."

"Copy. What'll you do?"

"Sit here, talk to him. Babysit him till we get reinforcements."

"Copy."

She put her radio away. "If I had cell phone signal, I'd set the record straight, but I don't. I'm gonna go find that trail. When the deputies and FBI get here, see if anyone has signal, pass on the word about Johnny."

Jack nodded.

"Three hundred, this is dispatch."

"Go ahead, Molly."

"Message from Joe. If Johnny's okay, send Jack Chastain back to headquarters. He said he does not need someone out there who's not armed and not trained to defend himself."

Jack grabbed his radio. "I'm not in danger."

"Joe says this is not a debate. Return to headquarters."

"He's right," Barb muttered. "Go. I'll wait till the deputies arrive. Maybe the FBI. We'll organize and go after the guy. Tell Joe that Johnny's been shot."

"Are you sure? I can keep track of the shooter. He'll never be the wiser."

"Jack, this guy's possibly trained. Maybe a killer. Maybe former military, possibly a sniper. We just don't know. If you were able to spot him, given time, he could spot you."

"I'll risk it. I know this country better than he does. I can't sit at home, wondering if Johnny and Luiz are okay."

"I understand, but look, you've given us a chance to get this guy. We'll get Johnny and Luiz to safety, I promise, but Joe's right, you shouldn't be here."

— · —

The phone rang on the congressman's desk—the number given only to a select group of people. He picked it up, and with all pleasantries, said, "This is Congressman Brent Hoff."

"Hello, Congressman, this is Doc. Would you be so kind as to invite your chief of staff to join us on the phone?"

He put the call on hold, and keyed the intercom. "Ask Alex to join me, please. Tell him it's urgent."

"Yes, Congressman."

Hoff took the phone off hold. "I'm back. Alex will be here momentarily."

"I can wait."

Trasker came hurriedly around the corner.

"Thank you, Alex. This is probably important." Hoff pushed a button on his phone set. "Speakerphone's on."

"Good," Doc said. *"I did some checking. This shooting in Piedras Coloradas . . . it's a false flag operation."*

Alex scowled. "I'm not sure I believe that."

"I just finished talking to a professor in Georgia who tracks these sorts of things. He's been following what's happening in Piedras Coloradas. He's getting reports from people on the ground with evidence of a false flag."

"It just happened. There's no way."

Doc laughed. *"Alex, ye of little faith. Our professor friend has already posted the details on his blog. False flag. Park Service and horse lovers. In on it together. Planned it. Executed it. Pulled it off. All to smear our man Manson. We're lucky they're being watched."*

— · —

His gear packed away, Jack lingered, waiting for Barb to finish pulling equipment she needed from the back of her patrol vehicle. "Last chance," he said, standing at the open door of the Jeep.

"You're wired, tight as a fiddle. Relax. We've got this."

"Okay, but you wait for the deputies. Don't go down there alone."

"I won't."

Jack folded his tall frame into the seat and started the engine. Pulling onto the road, he tried taking a moderate speed but within minutes his pack slid onto the floor on a curve. His jaw tightened.

Manson is no little guy fighting tyranny. He's a bully. A self-righteous ass. A deadbeat.

Inciting guys who want to play army. Getting 'em hopped up on lies and anti-government rhetoric, pushing fantasies about pointing rifles at someone just doing their job.

He clenched a fist, and slammed it against the door.

— · —

Jack parked and ran in the back door of headquarters. He stuck his head into dispatch. "Johnny's been shot. In the hand."

Molly spun around from the radio. Her jaw dropped.

"Barb thinks he's okay." He headed to the superintendent's office, stepping past Joe's secretary.

"Joe's in a meeting," Marge said.

"This is important." Jack pushed the door open. "Excuse me, Joe, but I've got a message from Barb. She didn't want it on the radio. Johnny's been shot."

Joe's eyes grew wide. "Is it serious?"

"Hand. He's hurting but she thinks he'll be okay while she goes after the shooter."

"Jack, can we continue this in a few minutes? I'm in the middle of something."

Jack glanced at the chairs against the back wall. A middle aged man, retreating hairline, slacks, and multicolored polo shirt, scribbling on a notepad. "Sorry. Thought it was important."

"It is," the stranger said. "In fact, I'd like to know more about it. This is either very important, or you guys have a very elaborate script."

Jack flashed a questioning look, first at the man, then at Joe. "Excuse me?"

"Jack, this is Mr. Schell. Stringer with the wire service. Works northern New Mexico. Mr. Schell happened to be in Las Piedras getting background on tomorrow's congressional hearing. He got a call from his assignment editor. Interesting lead. About this. Breaking story."

"Breaking story? The shooter? They know about this?"

"Kinda," Schell muttered.

"Someone told 'em this whole thing is a false flag operation," Joe said.

"False flag operation?" Jack said, repeating the words slowly. "What the hell is a false flag operation?"

Joe exchanged looks with the reporter. "Want to explain or should I?"

"Are you serious? Is this a game?" Schell asked.

"Nope."

"Okay," Schell said. He paused, then sat up. "Okay, . . . a false flag is when a government carries out an action, orchestrated to make it look like someone else did it. Or in war, some other government. Typically done to sway public opinion or mislead."

"What are you saying?" Jack growled, his words precise.

"Just following up on a lead."

"What are you saying?"

"Not me. It's something we heard. That you planted this story about a shooter, because of the field hearing tomorrow night. To throw 'em off or try to get it cancelled."

"You're dignifying a lie. You're in here talking to us about some contrived thing we'd never do, when you ought to be knocking on Moony Manson's door, asking why his play-soldier shot a ranger."

"You're telling me you know who did the shooting?"

"Yes."

"Tell me his name, and don't give me crap about ongoing investigations. Prove to me you're not making this up. Tell me his name."

"I don't know his name. But I saw him with Manson a week ago, on horseback, in the National Monument, carrying an assault weapon."

"What'd he do?"

"Then? Nothing, but Manson did. He threatened us. The guy just sat there trying to look tough."

"Is that right," Schell said, writing as quickly as he could. "You're not giving me much. The lead I was given says the Park Service and some group of horse lovers planted this whole story, complete with contrived account of a shooter, all to pin it on Manson. So far, all you've done is paint a picture, then point your finger at Manson, just like they said you would."

Jack took an angry step toward the reporter.

"Hey," Schell said, raising his hands, "I'm not saying I don't believe you. I'm saying, give me something to work with. Give me a reason to ignore the lead. We get wild ass conspiracy theories all the time. Most, we dismiss as having no substance. My assignment editor expects this story to fall apart, but he needed it checked out. After all, there's a congressional hearing here tomorrow night. So, here I am. Show me something. Give me a reason to ignore the lead."

Jack drew in a long, hard breath, and slowly let it out. "Get in my Jeep. I'll drag your ass onto the plateau, march you downhill, let you interview a ranger sitting sheltered behind a ponderosa, his hand shot up, who knows how badly. His radio's destroyed, but I'll take you there to get the facts. You can hope the sniper recognizes you as a member of the press."

"I know you're angry but . . ."

Jack cut him off. "I'm pissed. Someone shot a man I've come to trust and rely on. A good public servant doing nothing but his job. Someone else plants some stupid fabrication—a false flag, whatever it's called—and you think you don't have a story unless you can follow it through. The story is this. There's a man breaking the law, not paying his way, thumbing his nose at society, robbing the rest of us, inciting a bunch of play-army thugs bringing semi-automatic weapons to this part of New Mexico. They're pointing guns at people who are not trying to control their lives but who are just trying to do their jobs, and one of 'em gets shot. A ranger. He and another ranger, pinned down, are waiting till it's safe to walk out. That's the story, not the one someone gave you, which is nothing but a contrivance of fact to make us look bad."

"I didn't mean it that way, and I didn't know about the ranger getting shot until now."

"And this is a drought. Everyone else pulled their cows off the range. He won't. Thumbs his nose, acting entitled to do whatever he wants to do. His cattle are ignored. They're sucking up water, taking every blade of grass, while wildlife have nowhere to go. Then, when we catch a wandering thunderstorm, there's nothing to help soak up the rain. We get a flash flood and people nearly killed."

"Jack, that's enough," Joe said. "Calm down. He's not the only one pursuing this story. Other reporters are calling, just in the last half hour. Someone's doing a good job of planting the seed. Mr. Schell has a job to do. Please let him do it."

Jack drew in another breath, rubbed his eyes, and slowly exhaled. "Sorry."

"May I use what you just said?" Shell asked, his pen hovering over his pad.

Jack glanced at Joe.

"You may," Joe said. "Couldn't've said it better myself."

—·—

"We've got a flight to catch," Hoff said, standing in the hall. "Are you packed?"

"Yeah, I went home at lunch." Alex pointed at the computer monitor. "See this?"

"About the shooter? Yes. It's breaking news. It's on all the news services."

"The latest is, a ranger's been shot. Injuries not life threatening, but shot. Possibly by someone associated with Manson."

"I saw that. Attribution made by a ranger named Jack Chastain. Bloggers say it's part of the script, the false flag operation planned by the Park Service."

"Not everyone's gonna believe that," Alex said, giving a stroke to his beard. "I think we should cancel."

"We need to move forward, do what we can to help ease tensions." Hoff dropped his bag and unbuttoned his suit coat. "People are gonna be interested in what I have to say, plus, the attention will have people tuning into the hearing. Remind me again . . . this Chastain fellow."

"Tall. Taller than he appears on television. Dark hair. Blue eyes."

"No. Mannerisms. Personality. You say I've met him?"

"Yes, in Montana. He's dedicated. Sincere. Good at listening. He could do quite well for himself, but he'd rather save the world."

"I don't remember him, but I called an old friend at Interior. About him."

"Why?"

"Nothing to worry about. A little something for the good of the people." Hoff smiled.

"I hope it's nothing to hurt him. He's a good guy."

"Have I ever hung you out to dry, like your old boss? No, I have always valued your work and your connections, so trust me. And by the way, you are very important to my future plans."

Alex studied him. "Brent, I've got a question. That trip, three or four years ago, to Montana."

"What's your question?"

"It had something to do with a new national park. Why were you there?"

Hoff held his eyes a moment, then smiled, and picked up his bag. "I don't remember much. This office takes me everywhere. It was a committee field hearing, called for by Montana's member at large. There was nothing in particular I wanted to see come from it."

"Thought so." Trasker pulled his bag from under his desk. "I'm ready."

—·—

Barb Sharp waved one deputy into position, and watched as the other, carrying an AR-15, skirted left to prevent escape. A solidly built man in out-of-place slacks, hardly better shoes, and a black bullet proof vest marked *FBI* followed behind her. Barb stepped past sagebrush. Keeping low, she peeked past a juniper, caught sight of the crevice, pointed without words, and un-holstered her Sig Sauer semi-automatic pistol.

"Nine mil?" the agent whispered. "Maybe I should take the lead. He won't get past this." He flashed his 45 caliber.

"If he gets past me, you're welcome to him." Sharp took two steps, waited as the farthest deputy slipped farther left, then nodded to the FBI agent. In a quiet rush upslope, they reached the wall, and slid along the rock toward the crevice. Giving one last nod to the deputy, she moved toward the opening. She leveled the pistol.

The crevice—empty.

In the shadows, no one. On the dry, dusty floor of the cave, only depressions. Not even footprints. No shell casings.

She spun around, crouched, and gave a quick check to the surroundings. Nothing.

She sighed, holstered her weapon, and keyed the microphone clipped to her vest. "Luiz, bad guy's gone. Go get Johnny. Get him to the hospital."

CHAPTER 39

Jack made a late visit to the community hospital, only to learn Johnny had been released. He stopped by Johnny's quarters and found him sleeping under the influence of painkillers, his hand thoroughly bandaged. A seasonal firefighter sat in his room reading, ready to get Johnny anything he needed. Jack slipped out to go home.

Sleep. Not a bad idea.

—·—

The phone rang early.

Jack rolled over and checked the caller before answering. Joe Morgan. "Morning."

"Go online. Look at the *Gazette*. When finished, come to my office."

"What for?"

"Conference call. The director."

—·—

The headline read:

RANGER PRESUMABLY SHOT

No shooter found. No proof of Manson connection.
False flag rumors burn up the internet.

Two articles ran down the left side of the page, the *Gazette's* account and another picked up from the wire service, the latter quoting a frustrated Park Service employee named Jack Chastain. Also on the front page, above the fold:

HEARING WILL GO ON

Congressman Hoff: "More important than ever."
Hopes to ease tensions.

Jack gave a quick look at the letters to the editor. One, anonymous, caught his attention.

"There is a global socialist agenda to seize rural private land and drive white farmers and ranchers into the cities. There, the government can keep a lid on their activities, seize their guns, and allow the UN to carry out its plans, called Agenda 21. We've been suckered by our government, which voted for the Agenda 21 resolution and is eagerly carrying it out."

What the hell is Agenda 21? He slammed his laptop shut. Conspiracy theories. Harper Teague. Gotta be. Same sorta thing he tried pushing last year.

Jack got dressed, picked up his radio, and started for headquarters.

— · —

"You don't need to be carrying that," Joe said, when he saw the radio. "You're on leave."

"Habit." Jack took a seat.

"Seen the headlines?"

Joe pushed the speakerphone toward the front of his desk. "Director's talking to you, Jack."

"I have. Local ones."

"You've got a special kind of talent, Mr. Chastain."

"Meaning?"

"Somehow everything yesterday turned into something about you and the agency."

"It's about Manson, not me."

"You'd think so, but it's not turning out that way. The reporter you talked to was kind, empathetic even. But when bloggers and talking heads got wind of his story, especially on cable news, hell, they went crazy. Suddenly, it's all about the Park Service. People saying they don't buy the government line."

"This is about Manson."

"I understand, Jack, but what am I to do? I have to contend with what comes at me, and as of this morning, I have a most interesting request, run through Interior. Congressman Hoff wants you to testify at tonight's hearing."

"Good. Got plenty to say."

"No," the director said, abruptly. *"I've denied the request."*

"Couldn't that get a contempt of Congress? I can take care of myself."

"You are not allowed at that hearing. I will not let you be cut open and splayed for sport. Wouldn't do you or the agency any good. Our testimony is prepared and vetted. Only to be given by you, Joe. Jack's not allowed to speak. Got that?"

"Yes." Joe gave Jack a stern eye. "And I agree. He's emotionally wrapped up in this."

"I'm pissed," Jack said. "Aren't you? Some ass shot Johnny Reger."

"I will not let this destroy you."

"I won't either," the director said. *"No appearance, no testimony. Stay away. I'm in trouble with Interior for not making you available—and I'm trying to figure the angle out on that one—but if you make a statement at Congressman Hoff's field hearing, the*

trouble I'm in will be nothing compared to the trouble you'll be in with me. Got it?"

Jack held his tongue.

"Answer me."

Jack sighed. "Got it."

"One more thing," Joe said, to Jack. "You may not've heard, but Manson's militia seized the BLM office in Las Piedras. Last night, late. They're occupying headquarters, saying they're beginning the process of returning land to its rightful owners."

"What about Paul Yazzi and the other BLMers?"

"I'm sure they're staying away, for their own safety."

"Be careful both of you," the director said. *"There will be people watching, prodding, provoking. Hoping you'll slip up and say something stupid they can use to rile people up."*

"Understood," Joe said.

"Keep me informed."

The phone call ended.

"Go home," Joe said.

——— · ———

Jack stepped out the back door of headquarters into the morning air. He checked his watch. Little after 7:30 a.m. Too early to check on Johnny. He took the long way home, walking fast, working off anger.

Back at his quarters, he called Kip Culberson. "Hear about Manson's militia? Taking over the BLM office?"

"I did, but I need to attend to something more important. You might want to join me. I'm riding out to Ginger Perrette's. She wants to talk."

"About?"

"The coalition. Meet me at the junction outside town. You can jump in with me."

——— · ———

Kip's pickup sat waiting at the Terrace Road junction. Jack parked and climbed in for the drive to Perrette Ranch, south of town.

They found Ginger in near-empty corrals behind the house, watering a few horses. A trickle from what appeared a dwindling supply. She walked toward Kip's pickup, head down. "Thanks for coming all this way," she said. "I'm getting pushback. Ranchers I'm working with."

"Me, too," Kip said. "What'd'ya hear?"

"Up to now, it's seemed wise to be part of the coalition. With everyone else wanting the monument, ranchers felt we'd lose out if we didn't have a role. Now, with battle drums beating, and rumors of Hoff wanting to do away with the monument, some think it's best to pull back."

Kip nodded. "Same thing I'm hearing."

Perrette dropped her eyes. "The more I talk to people with that way of thinking, the more I start wondering the same. We ranchers face enough uncertainty." She looked up. "Sorry, Jack."

— · —

"It's falling apart, Kip," Jack said, watching the highway.

Kip nodded. "Don't blame yourself."

"How can I not? My foot dragging slowed us down."

"Things take time." At a stop sign, Kip threw the pickup in park. He rested a boot on the center hump and looked Jack's way. "What did you want out of this, son? You've listened to all of us, made us listen to each other, but what did you want? What does your agency want?"

He sighed. "Hell, Kip, it's not about me. It's about our mission, the places we manage, the people we work for, the values people place on these lands." He looked out the side window at sagebrush. "Me? I want to hold people together long enough to make it work. Looks like that's not gonna happen."

— · —

Jack walked back into headquarters, and trudged up the stairs, then up the hall. Joe's office door stood closed. Jack approached.

Marge stopped him. "Not this time."

"I need to update Joe on something."

"It'll have to wait. Joe's on the phone with the director, making changes to testimony." She pointed. "Go see Barb. She's looking for you."

Jack ambled down the hall to her office.

"Follow me." Barb stepped into the adjoining office. A stocky man in a jacket marked FBI sat hunkered over a computer. "Agent Ward, this is Jack Chastain."

Ward stood and shook his hand. "I need your time. Have a seat." He pulled up a screen filled with photos. "Look at these. See if one's our shooter."

Jack hunkered close and examined the faces. Some bearded. Some bald. Some young. Some middle-aged. Some tattooed. Every one of them white.

After half an hour, he gave up. None appeared to be the shooter. He made his way to his office. Manson's gonna get away with it. He should be in prison, he and his thugs. Unlocking the door, he stepped inside and dropped into his chair. He glanced at a pile of phone messages, and noticed voice mail flashing. Might be dozens. Hundreds. Ignore it.

The phone rang.

He picked it up, stared a moment into the earpiece, then said, "This is Jack Chastain."

"Jack, this is Alex. Tried your home. I was afraid I wouldn't catch you."

"What do you need, Alex?"

"Stay away from the hearing. With what's happened in the last twenty four hours, you could . . ."

"Become a target?"

"Yes."

"Are you aware that Hoff asked that I testify?"

"I knew he did something. Are you?"

"Director won't allow it."

"Good. That's best. There'd be no way to come out looking good. It's planned out. The congressman knows the outcome he wants."

"I don't care. If this is about Manson, I have something to say. After yesterday, it needs to be said."

"How's the ranger?"

"He'll be okay but I haven't talked to him. He's on painkillers."

The line sat silent a moment. "I know it's hard to imagine anything good coming out of tonight, but it will. Although I wish he wouldn't take the approaches he does at times, what Brent does will be good for the country. The consequences here . . . they might be painful . . . but all in all, they'll set a course for change the country needs. You have to trust me on that."

"I don't, Alex. I think you're a competent, capable guy, and I guess I trust you. . . . I want to . . . but not on that. If someone comes here and attacks something good, because they think it's justified by some big picture of their own choosing, then that's just ideology." He gritted his teeth, fighting back anger. "It's ideology, Alex. No ideology has answers for everything. Give me data, give me analysis, but, god damn it, do not try to justify something on ideology and preconception."

"Jack, shut up. You look at the world through your own filter. Your own eyes. You don't understand the big world. The congressman understands how the big world works, and what it needs to reverse the problems in society."

"Alex, that is the problem in society. People on both sides defining the battle, blinding the rest of us with rhetoric about things that hardly affect our lives, ignoring us on things that do, and on things we value, because . . . they have their own agenda."

A sigh bled over the line. "I've got to go, Jack. Things to do before tonight. We'll have to agree to disagree."

"Are you aware Manson's thugs seized the BLM office in Las Piedras?"

"I am. I know why they did it. They feel if they push out the feds, they'll have control of their land and lives again."

"Again?"

"The way things were before the government took control."

"Alex, they don't have a clue. The good ol' days were never the good ol' days. It was always public land. Before the agencies, there were land barons, cattle companies, mining companies and water developers, pushing their way around, monopolizing anything of value. Some even killed homesteaders who got in their way. If the agencies were gone, do they really think they'd be the ones to benefit? Only if it's worthless. They'd be pushed out by modern day equivalents. BLM is their best friend. They just can't see that."

"Jack, my friend, you wear rose colored glasses. Please stay away from the hearing."

"No problem." Jack slammed down the phone and jumped to his feet. Stomping to the window, he glared, first outside, then at the walls, then at the door. He slipped over and closed it, stopping himself from slamming it. Clenching his fists, he shook one at the door, turned, and crossed back to the window.

The phone rang.

He snatched up the receiver. "What?"

Laughter. "Having a bad day?"

"Who is this?"

Laughter. "Your old buddy, Pug. Been hearing the latest Jack Chastain stories. People like talking about ya, Jack."

"I don't listen to that crap."

"Hard not to. Looks like you could use a change. Where the biggest frustration ya face in a day is what fly to use, and whether the big trout rise to your fly. Give my offer any thought?"

Jack sucked in a breath and dropped into his chair. "Sorry, Pug. Been a bit tough here lately."

"I noticed, and I still need a ranch manager."

"Tempting, Pug, but I don't know."

"What do you not know? What would make you stick around for that fun and games? Get away from that bullshit. I can be there in couple of days, show you around, get you started. All I need is a yes."

"Wow, Pug, it's . . . it's . . ."

"I'll pay you what you're making now, throw in a few thousand more, ask only that you take good care of the place. You'd answer only to me, not three hundred million knuckleheads. What's not to like?"

"Pug, it's just that . . . that . . ."

"I'll take that as a maybe. I'll call tomorrow. We'll make plans to meet."

The phone went dead. Jack cradled the handset. He rubbed his eyes, then dropped his hands into his lap. Maybe Pug was right. Maybe it was time.

Jack stood and turned to the window. He stared at towering canyon walls, bright and red in the glare of the sun. They'll be here with or without me. Pug, why me? Don't look a gift horse in the mouth, he told himself. *Go home, get out of here.*

He picked up his radio and gave the office a long look. Might be the last time the place had any real meaning. Any purpose. He slipped out, closed the door, and started down the hall.

Outside, he turned up the trail to the cluster of cabins at the base of the canyon wall. Eyes on the rim, he walked, taking it in. Blue skies and clouds. What did it all matter? Might be best. A new beginning. Let someone else take over.

"Chastain, this is dispatch."

He raised the radio. "Go head, Molly."

"Still in the building? A call rolled over to me on the switch-board."

"I left. Take a message."

"They say it's important. Information you're looking for. Said to tell you they found him."

He gasped. The big name, or the courier? Does it matter? "I'll be right there." Jack turned and jogged back to headquarters.

Inside, he dashed up the hall, shouting into dispatch, "Forward the call to my office."

He opened the door and plopped into his chair, catching his breath. The phone rang. He picked it up. "This is Jack Chastain."

"Hello, handsome."

He scowled. "Who is this?"

"You asked me to do you a favor."

That voice. "Courtney?"

"Yep. I found him. I found The Kid."

Jack sat a moment. "I'm sorry. You're not who I expected. Not today."

"Oh, Jack, baby," she said, sounding pouty, "show a little appreciation. I tracked down his number, supposedly in Idaho." She paused. "Want it or not?"

"Sure."

"Here it is." She read it out.

He scribbled it down, and wrote Kid above it. "Not sure what I'll do now, but thanks."

"Babe, you telling me I wasted my time?"

"Of course not. Learn anything?"

"Only that he might not talk. He's a shattered kid."

"How'd you track down his number?"

"Forest Service Regional Director. Shea Pinkley had it."

"Why did Shea have it?"

"He tracked The Kid down a couple a years ago . . . worried about him."

"That ass, worried about someone other than himself?"

"You're wrong about him, Jack. He's trying to survive. The tough exterior . . . he's doing his best to protect his forest supervisors and staff all over the region. He's not quite brave enough to do something stupid like you did, but he's trying, so cut him some slack."

"But his actions."

"Big money's pulling strings, Jack. Every time he tries to fix something, he's steamrolled. His perforated carcass is about the only thing left at the scene of the crime, so he gets blamed. He's lost control. He's trying to get it back. Politicians make it difficult."

Jack sighed. "Thanks. I'm not sure when I'll use it. Things are unsettled here."

"I know. You're all over the news. Started not to call, but I owed you." She let the words sit a moment. "I wish I could look into those blue eyes of yours." Silence. "Jack, baby, call me if anything changes. In your life, that is." She hung up without goodbye.

He sat staring at the number.

Sorry, Samuel. I'm not getting anywhere on your problem. This one's mine.

He set the number aside. What the hell. He picked up the phone and dialed. It rang twice.

"What?" Familiar voice, unfamiliar demeanor.

"I'm looking for The Kid," Jack said, finding his most cheerful tone.

"You have him."

"Kid, this is Jack Chastain."

Silence. Then, "I'm not sure I want to talk to you."

"I won't keep you long. Just give me a few minutes, please."

"What do you want?"

"To know how you're doing? I went to Montana looking, hoping you were okay, hoping the mess that enveloped us wasn't still hanging over you."

"Enveloped? Is that government talk for everything you worked for, gone? All the good things you were known for, forgotten? All the things you'll be known for in the future, lies?"

Jack sighed. "Feels that way sometimes."

"I don't like the feeling."

"Nobody does. I'm sorry you got wrapped up in that."

"Look, I don't know who to trust anymore. I'm not sure I want to talk to you, or anyone. Not now."

"Maybe I can help?" Jack said. Stupid comment.

The Kid let out a bitter laugh.

"What can I do?"

"Nothing. I left. Dropped out of college. I keep the paychecks coming. That's all I can hope for."

"That's not The Kid I remember."

"Screw you. What do you know? Plus, you're in as much shit there as you were in Montana."

Jack set his elbows on the desk. "Watching the news?"

"Not on purpose."

"Things aren't always as bad as they look."

"Yeah, right." He sighed. "I've gotta get some sleep. My shift starts sooner than I'd like. And, I need to keep my head on straight. I don't know if I even want to talk to you. Not now. Maybe in time I can talk without getting sick to my stomach. Today, the friendliest thing I can muster is: drop dead."

Jack searched for words. None came. He rolled a pen across the desk, remembering The Kid's hands, nails bitten down, the slight tremor of excitement whenever he talked about his research. His energy, bottled up, that came flowing out when he knew what he needed to do.

"Sorry," The Kid said, finally, breaking the silence. "I didn't feel that way then. I admired you. Trusted you. But you were in the middle of what happened. The center of everything. In the end, I couldn't . . ."

"What?"

"Nothing. I don't want to talk about it." A sniffle, then another. "All the people I ever knew . . . my friends. We'd achieved so much together. The things we did in high school. Forgotten. Taking state in football, together. Didn't matter. Forgotten. I was the guy they always said pulled us together. Then . . . word of my research and they treated me like scum . . . the enemy. I tried setting things straight but no one would listen. Called me an extremist. A job wrecker. They egged each other on."

"Those things blow over. Time heals," Jack said, not sure where the words came from.

"Shut up. You don't know. You weren't there."

"I've been through . . ."

The Kid cut him off. "It didn't blow over. It started bad and got worse. All after I got a call, invited to some kind of reception the morning of that big congressional hearing you wanted me at. Some kind of recognition, they said. Told me to bring my parents. Everyone from town would be there. We went. They took my parents into the seats. Pulled me up on stage. All my friends were there. They handed out jackets. Made 'em seem like something special, for all of us. Someone helped me put one on. I heard snickers. I didn't think anything of it. Then, . . ." The phone went quiet, then sobs.

"Kid?"

". . . they handed me this tray. Water bottles, like we'd used on the football field. I didn't think anything of it. They told me to spread 'em around and I figured it was because I was closest to the guy who brought 'em out. Passing out bottles, I turned my back to the audience. Everyone laughed. Some guy I'd never seen started talking. Calling out names, one by one, recognizing my friends for places they were working, jobs they were doing. I was happy for 'em. Then this guy . . . he says, 'Hey Kid, I understand you're taking care of the water?' Everybody laughed. I wondered if he was talking about my research. Then he says, all your friends have real jobs, and you're being a water boy. I was stunned. I looked at the audience. Everyone laughing. My dad walked up the aisle, mad. My mom's at the exit, tears in her eyes. Dad ripped off the jacket and threw it on the floor. That's when I saw it. On the back, it said, *waterboy*. Everyone's laughing. Dad pushed me out the door. We left town soon after. Haven't been back."

"That's why you weren't at the hearing?"

"Would you be?" He sobbed. "Everywhere I went that day . . . they . . . they were my friends. Look what we'd achieved. Together. They treated me like . . ." He didn't finish.

"Who were they? Who arranged the event?"

"Americans for Business, Business for America . . . something like that. I'd never heard of 'em. The worse part, days later, someone emailed a link to a website. Their newsletter. There it was. Photos. Words on the jacket. The taunting. Everything." He sobbed. "I just wanted to do science."

"Kid, I'm so sorry." Jack cringed, listening to the sobs.

"I gotta go."

"Wait."

"No, I gotta go."

"One thing, please. The day before the hearing, you called, wanting to talk. I was busy, asked if we could talk before the hearing. Do you remember what that was about?"

"Yes." He sobbed. "I found rhodamine dye in the water samples. The same sampling locations where we found methane."

"What does that mean?"

"It means we weren't the only ones looking. Someone was trying to figure something out."

"Who would . . . ?"

"I don't really care. I gotta go." The line went dead.

Jack hung up the phone, close to tears. *How did I let that happen? What do I do now? Leave him alone? Try not to screw up his life any more than it is already? He's damaged. Who wouldn't be?*

Jack stood. *Go home. There's nothing you can do. The Kid's a lost cause. Put your mind on something that isn't, like helping Samuel Leboo.*

He spun around and dropped back in his chair. He closed his eyes.

No.

Samuel, I can't help. I didn't help. I need to let you fight your own battles. I need to focus on my own. I've lost one battle already. And a kid whose only sin was to naively think he could help, I didn't protect. From lies and attacks. Probably too late, but I need to try to fix it.

You lost Gabriel Kagunda, while fighting to save a species against terrible odds. My problems are nothing compared to yours, but they're my problems. And in a way, The Kid died, too. An idealistic kid who wanted to save the world, and now that idealistic kid is gone.

Jack stood to go.

He stepped to the door, and looked back. In the middle of the desk lay The Kid's phone number. He could almost hear The Kid's sobbing.

Americans for Business, Business for Americans.

He slipped back to the desk, turned on the computer and opened the browser. He did a quick search. The search listing included events in different parts of the country, mostly the south and west. An organization, supposedly more business than political, but in the eyes of many, more political than business. He narrowed the search to Montana. The listing included publicity for an event, and a newsletter summarizing what happened, all of it three years back.

Jack clicked on the link for the newsletter. It appeared on screen, and described an event held the morning of June 12, 2014.

The day of the congressional hearing.

The event premise, to trumpet accomplishments and jobs available to young people. There, in black and white, Toby LeBlanc, The Kid, mentioned in less detail than his own words, but confirming everything he described. Even a photo of the back of the jacket, and a jab at *"a controversy of which he was a part."* Water research. Rumors of its intent to implicate fracking, despite claims to the contrary, *". . . probably because they had nothing to show."* *"Still,"* it said, *"a little gentle teasing was in order."*

Jack ran his fingers alongside the verbiage. The pain. The disappointment. Poor Kid.

He prepared to close the page, then noticed a passage near the bottom of the article. The keynote address. The speaker, one of several elected officials in attendance. Quotes from his speech leapt off the page, one passage in particular.

> *"They may say they found methane. They may say it's just science, but the danger is in how they use it. We must be careful about trusting them. I will not let them go after jobs, lock up the land, or change our way of life."*

Interesting diatribe, from a prominent member of Congress.

CHAPTER

40

He felt Kelly studying him, her dark eyes full of concern. "Stop it, I'm okay."

"You're not," she said. "I can tell."

Jack squirmed in his seat. "I'm thinking. You've been thinking. About change and all sorts of things. Maybe it's time for me to do the same. For you, for me."

She watched without speaking.

"Maybe I shouldn't fight it. It's falling apart, like Montana. There's gonna be no reason to hold onto this life. This job."

"I'm not sure that's what you really want."

"Hell, I'd get used to it. I have a good offer. Pug and I are talking tomorrow."

"You called him?"

"He called me, along with everyone else in the world. Alex, telling me to stay away from the hearing. The director, saying the same thing. Another call, giving me the number for the college student in Montana. The Kid told me stay away from him." He cracked a smile. "So, my calendar's clear."

She offered a sympathetic smile.

"Still open to a little change?"

"Whatever you want to do."

"You're just saying that. To comfort my weary soul."

"You're right, but if you left, I'd go with you."

Jack frowned. "Let's change the subject. Watch the news. Check out someone else's pain and suffering." He picked up the television remote and pressed *on*.

The television lit up. The face of Congressman Brent Hoff appeared.

"Different channel," Kelly said.

"No. Let's see what he has to say." Jack leaned closer. He turned up the volume.

"I understand you're in New Mexico," said an on-air personality.

"I am. For important congressional business. A field hearing, getting the facts related to federal actions against a rancher named Moony Manson."

"We've followed this story closely. I personally believe this is a federal land grab, an attempt to snuff out a way of life."

"I hope to have a better understanding after tonight."

"Will Manson testify?"

"Yes, I've given assurances he'll be safe to do so. I'm working with the county sheriff. There will be no harassment. Many see this man as a hero. A patriot in the purest sense. He'll have a voice at the hearing, and I personally hope he continues his fight."

Jack rapped his knuckles on the arm of the chair, then picked up the remote and turned off the television. It went black. "Let's go see Johnny."

— · —

"That went well," Alex Trasker said, as Congressman Brent Hoff re-entered the hotel suite. He handed Hoff a stack of papers. "Doc sent these. He's on the phone. Speaker's on."

"Thanks, Doc," Hoff said, voice raised, as he sorted through pages. "These numbers are better than last week's."

"Yes, Congressman, they are." Doc cleared his throat. The speakerphone crackled. *"My point all along. Your numbers are climbing. You can build on these numbers, not only with the base,*

but in other parts of the electorate. Create a sympathetic image for Manson, build the sense of fear and uncertainty—that this could happen to anyone—and you advance not just yourself but a cause that will seal the west."

Trasker nodded, and turned to the suite's window overlooking old town Las Piedras. To the left of the centuries-old bell tower he could just make out part of the plaza. He froze. Missed something. He turned back to the room. "That last point. What cause will seal the west?"

"The congressman, in a moment of utter disgust, will lay out the case for taking lands from irresponsible hands and turning them over to private interests."

"Little ambitious, isn't it? I think you're misreading the numbers. Support for public land is quite high, especially in the west. Tremendous support."

"Not after tonight. Not if we play this right."

"Why don't we just take things a step at a time? Go after the national monument. Do away with it as an example of federal overreach."

The congressman straightened his collar, giving Alex a twisted smile.

"Step at a time?" Doc laughed. *"We are, Alex. Things are progressing nicely, step at a time. Our efforts have been carefully orchestrated, waiting for a time like this to come along. Now it has, but . . ."* Doc paused. *"I have one worry. That Manson will go off on one of his tangents. Carry on about natural law, or the sovereign movement, or some subject that turns him into a wacko in the eyes of the masses. If he does, Alex, create a diversion. Give the congressman time to change the subject."*

"That won't be necessary." Hoff smiled. "I can handle Manson."

"Okay, then. That's better."

"I looked at the final list of witnesses," Alex said. "What happened to BLM?"

"Don't need 'em," Hoff said. "We took 'em off."

"Their testimony was laced with data and analysis. Discussions of range conditions, overgrazing, and monitoring data gathered

from Manson's part of the range. We don't need that on the record. It's irrelevant."

"Why is that irrelevant?" Alex asked, stroking his beard.

"In our view this is Manson's land. He should be able to use it as he pleases. Who are they to tell him he's overgrazing?"

"But this hearing is about government overreach. BLM manages the allotment."

"We have a Park Service witness. No one will know the difference."

"What about the seizure of BLM headquarters?" Alex asked. "Have you discussed what to say about that? And what about the horse people?"

"The congressman and I discussed the seizure at length," Doc said. *"Let's not go there. People who see it as good know everything about it. Everyone else? Might cause some to lose sympathy for Manson. We don't need that."*

"And the horse people?"

"None of the prepared testimony mentions horses. We've made sure of that. If horses come up, change the subject. Use procedural means, whatever. This is our hearing, not theirs." Doc paused. *"So, let's run through the script one last time. The message needs to appear spontaneous. That's key. Our message scores significantly higher in test groups that believe it is. So, . . . last person testifying runs late, you—with time on your hands—share heartfelt reaction to Manson's plight. Underscore the image of the Western individualist as a true American, and . . . most important . . . plant the seeds of fear. That this could happen to anyone. Then, Alex informs you that the final speaker won't make it—car trouble. You end the hearing, and in another spontaneous reaction, in anger, you conclude that someone has to accept responsibility. You are willing to be that person, to shoulder the responsibility of the presidency."*

Alex turned to the congressman. "You got all that?"

"Yes. Simple. Two phases. Reaction, then spontaneous announcement. After hearing this shocking testimony and being overcome with despair over the treatment of poor Brother Manson, I start with a bit of a ramble. I could say Congress needs to put legislation before the president to end such tyranny . . . to strip these lands from irresponsible hands. That any responsible president would have no choice but to sign it. From there, I'll bounce around, giving people various things to fear, including the prospect of jack-booted thugs showing up at their door."

"What if the people of New Mexico don't buy into that?" Alex said, turning to a mirror. He adjusted his red tie. "What if other parts of the country don't?"

"I've supplied talking points and phrasings. Phrases designed to get desired results. Then, afterward . . . tonight and tomorrow, a groundswell of voices will echo across the land. What the good congressman proposes would be good for the country. That people elsewhere should listen to what's being said by the quiet voices of the West. The country would be better served putting these lands into private hands or local control."

Alex turned back. "Whose hands?"

"Private hands."

"Robber barons," Alex muttered to himself, under his breath.

"What?" the congressman asked.

"Nothing. Sorry. My mind was wandering." Alex faced the speakerphone. "So, something's been orchestrated to amplify the message the congressman gives tonight."

"Exactly."

— · —

Johnny Reger took a sip of water, his eyes, half closed. "Any storms coming?"

"Big ones, unfortunately," Jack said.

"Oh, man," Johnny whined. He lowered his cup, and dropped his head. Blond hair dropped over his eyes. "Doctor said no fire shovels. No Pulaskis. Not till he says so."

"Thought you meant . . . " Jack studied his intoxicated eyes, then the wraps of gauze over his hand. "Never mind. Sorry, Johnny. There are no storms. No fires. Not for a while."

"Good. Cause I can't help. Might need surgery. For sure,

physical therapy. Would you believe the good doctor said I'd need his okay to even pick up a fire shovel?"

"Yes, you told us."

"I did?" He turned and appeared to try focusing his eyes.

"You don't need to worry. Your hand will heal. Everything will be fine." Glancing at Kelly against the wall, he noticed her cringe, her eyes on blood seeping through the gauze.

"Did we get the cows outta the park?"

"No."

"What about the horses?"

"No. We had more important things to do."

"Really?" Johnny said, sounding a woozy kind of surprised.

"Don't worry, we'll get 'em." Jack glanced at the pill bottle on the table beside him. Yellow sticker. *Narcotic.* "We should let you sleep."

Johnny laid his head back. "Don't go. Just let me rest a moment." He closed his eyes, and soon began to snore.

They sat ten minutes or so, then turned off the light and slipped quietly out the door, waving to his attendant as they left.

Outside, Joe Morgan approached on the trail, in dress uniform.

Jack stopped. "You look ready."

"How's Johnny?"

"Sleeping."

"Then I won't bother him." Morgan stopped beside them. "More bad news."

"Can't get any worse."

"It has. You're censured. No talking to anyone."

"The director?"

"Interior. If the director won't let you testify, then they won't let you talk. To anyone."

Jack rolled his eyes. "What if I don't care what they think?"

"I do," Joe barked. "I won't let you destroy yourself. Keep your mouth shut."

Jack drew in a long, deep breath.

"What's with you? I've never seen you like this."

"You know the answer to that, Joe. They shot Johnny. They had Luiz pinned down."

Joe stared back. "You're not the only one angry."

"I know."

"Then, cope. You have to learn to bite your tongue. Congressman Hoff is encouraging Manson to fight. It's little guy against the mighty bureaucracy. He's arranged for Manson to testify. Worked things out with the sheriff. He'll be allowed to appear without harassment."

"I heard. He should be arrested."

"There's no evidence to connect him to the shooter. Yet."

Jack shook his head in disgust. "Of course not." Clenching a fist, he turned away.

Joe turned to Kelly. "Keep him away from the hearing."

"I will."

"Maybe this will give you reason for optimism," Joe said. "Had a call from Legislative Affairs. There's a rumor that Senator Tisdale from Montana might be there tonight."

Jack turned an ear.

"The Wild Horse and Burro Babes asked him to intervene. He's on his way. Seems he wants a better understanding of the issue. They're hoping he'll throw Hoff off his game."

"How would that work?" Jack muttered. "The hearing's under the auspices of the House."

"No idea. The senator could have a trick up his sleeve."

"Championing the wild horse now?"

"I asked the same question. They didn't know. He may just have it in for Hoff."

"Hmm."

"Some kinda old vendetta, maybe. You told me you trust him, so have some faith."

Jack nodded.

"I'll call tomorrow." He turned to Kelly. "Good seeing you, my dear. Keep him away."

Jack waited for Joe to get beyond earshot, then whispered, "I'm going."

"You're not."

"I am, and it won't end well. Not for me. Pretty much the kiss of death, but I'm going."

"I won't let you say anything."

"We'll see. If I do, you'll know why I have to."

"People depend on you."

"They'll find someone to finish the job." He gave her hand a gentle squeeze.

— · —

Kip folded his napkin and tossed it on his plate. He raised his eyes to the window, taking a long look over Elena's garden. He mused about the moment. The times he'd thought about this possibility. He caught his own reflection. Gray mustache. Temples, the same gray. He nodded, mostly to himself, then turned to face the man in the brown suit, sitting across the table. "Tell the governor, I'm honored, but no. If I was a younger man, brought up in this kind of politics, maybe, but I'm not. Politics today . . . they're hard. Too hard. Plus, I'm in the wrong party."

"The governor would hope you'd go in as an independent."

"I'd have to caucus with someone."

The aide smiled. "You could always switch parties."

Kip laughed, and set his weathered hands on the table.

"In the conservative caucus you could counter what Hoff's doing in the House."

"Not if he's president."

"All the more important. Someone to blunt his power. Keep New Mexico from losing out. The governor has no doubt you'd be loyal to state interests. You're a respected man. That goes far around here, even in today's politics."

"Not far enough."

"Your name comes up more than anyone's. Even in conversations with Senator Baca before he died. He was convinced you were the most capable person to replace him."

Kip shook his head and scooted back in his chair, buttoning his suit coat.

"Hear me out. We need the right person in Washington, especially now. You'd have months to think about running for your own term, and the better part of a year to decide if you really want it. The governor promises his support."

"Frank, you and I both know how hard that promise is to keep. Party dynamics would make it impossible. I appreciate the compliment. The vote of confidence. But, I'm not cut out for today's brand of politics. Too callus, too many sticks and stones, too little listening. I'd be no good at that. I've been out of the game too long."

"The governor doesn't see it that way. He thinks you'd be perfect. More than anyone he can think of. Plus, you could champion this legislation you want written. You could move the work of the coalition forward."

"The latter point is tempting, but you'll have to tell him no."

"A year and a few months. In time, someone could emerge, able to shoulder the responsibility."

"Tell the governor, I'm honored, but no." Kip stood. "Now, I've got a hearing to get to."

The governor's aide stood and shook his hand. "Thanks for your time, Kip. May I join you? Might be quite a show."

CHAPTER
41

Jack checked his watch. Seven o'clock. Should be starting now.

Kelly turned into the Inn of the Canyons. Parking lot, full.

They found a space in a distant corner and jogged to the porte cochere. Jack pulled the hood of his sweatshirt over his head. "Hide enough of my face?"

"In a Unabomber sorta way, yes."

"We shouldn't sit together. People will know it's me." He tugged on the handle of the big timber door, swinging it open. He followed her in.

One desk clerk. No one loitering in the lobby. They turned down the hall to the Grande Meeting Hall. One door stood open, people stacked half a dozen deep at the back of the room.

"Standing room only," Jack muttered.

Kelly took a peek inside.

Cupping a hand over his face, Jack looked over the heads toward the front of the room. No one yet on the dais. "Running late," he whispered.

He slipped through the throng, Kelly several steps behind him. She stopped near the aisle. He settled into a corner behind three men clustered together, talking. Ranchers.

Throughout the room, a rumble of tense conversation.

Jack craned his neck to see. A room filled with chairs, divided by an aisle. Aisles along both walls. Chairs, all taken. At the front of the room, one table, floor level, with a microphone. One table on the dais, another microphone. At the head of the aisle, left side of the room, a small table with a woman seated at a computer. Probably a court reporter. Jack studied the backs of the heads at the front of the room. He recognized one man, in conversation. Western-cut suit. "Kip," he whispered to himself, then went back to looking. The environmental crowd. Where? To the right, clustered around Karen Hatcher. Ranchers? Scattered throughout the room, a large cluster to the left. Business people? Everywhere. Horse people? No clue. No clue who they are. How about Manson? A man in white Stetson sat three rows from the front, right side, near the aisle. Manson stared forward, conversing with no one. Around him, men in camo, not talking. Some scanned the room. Is one the shooter?

Jack took another quick look around. Claire Prescott stood against the right wall, in a tweed business suit and glasses, studying the crowd. No Park Service, other than Joe. No BLM. Lizzy McClaren, near the back, sitting with Zach Danner.

Behind the last row of chairs, television cameras on tripods.

Several in Kip's row in suits. Probably those giving testimony. Who are they?

"What are you doing here?" screeched a whisper from two feet away.

Jack turned.

Erika Jones stood hands on her hips, in a navy blue suit, her blonde hair pulled back. She scowled. "Why are you here?"

"I'm not," he whispered back.

"If the director learns . . ."

"I know."

"You look like the Unabomber."

"Know that too. Kelly said the same thing."

He glanced at Kelly. She stood eyeing them.

"Get him out of here," Erika mouthed without sound.

Kelly shrugged.

"Why are *you* here?" Jack asked.

"Region sent me. Support, if Joe needs it. Because," she said, dragging out the word, "you're not available."

"So you're me?"

"Not exactly. Also here to meet with Claire Prescott."

"She's against the wall." Jack gave a point with his chin.

"Do not say a thing. If you do, you're dead meat." Erika made her way across the back of the room, then along the sidewall, stopping alongside Prescott. They shook hands.

From a door on the left wall, Alex Trasker appeared. Black suit, white shirt, red tie. He approached the front, something in his hand. He stopped at the table on the dais, his back to the audience, and fussed at something. He stepped back. A placard now occupied the space in front of the microphone. *Congressman Brent Hoff.* Trasker spun around, appeared to give the room one last look, then gravitated left, hovering near the court reporter. He exchanged a few words, then disappeared through the door from which he came. As the door closed, the whispering rose.

Seconds later, the door reopened and Congressman Hoff emerged, suit coat buttoned, Trasker behind him. He proceeded to the table, said something to Trasker, then sat.

Trasker picked up a microphone. "Quiet please. We are about to begin."

Silence fell over the room, and Trasker stepped to the side, out of the way.

Hoff leaned into his microphone. "I call this meeting to order. This is a field hearing of the U.S. Congress, House of Representatives, Interior Committee," he said, his voice procedural. "I, Congressman Brent Hoff, committee chairman, presiding. No other members are able to attend. I will hear testimony from a number of individuals. Written testimony has been received and will be entered into the record. I may have questions. If so, we'll take time to ask those questions before dismissing the individual testifying. Those of you in attendance, I appreciate your being here, providing me the opportunity to bring accountable government to the people. I ask that you remain quiet for the benefit of those testifying.

"Many in the room undoubtedly come here with divergent opinions. The same is true of those of us in the Congress. For tonight, I ask that those opinions be set aside to allow us to focus on the facts in this important matter. The issue being, the treatment of a citizen at the hands of his government, and whether there is need for Congress, in its oversight role, to do something to reverse government infringement on the rights of its citizens. If the outcome of tonight's hearing so suggests, I'll introduce legislation to remedy the situation, whatever that remedy might entail. Let's proceed." He lifted a sheet of paper and began to read. "Our first witness is Joe Morgan of the National Park Service. Let me state for the record, I'm disappointed. I requested the testimony of a Mr. Jack Chastain, an example of the problem we face as a nation—bureaucrats who, through their actions, try to create their own public policy. He is not available, however. He is, in fact, censured. I don't know if that's protection or punishment, or if that's a sign his actions are called into question even within the bureaucracy. If the latter, I would have liked the opportunity to establish that fact, for the record, in a manner that explains the influence of his actions."

Jack's jaw tightened.

"That said, . . ." Hoff continued. He raised his eye to the witness table. "Mr. Morgan."

Joe, in well-pressed, dress uniform, stood and approached the table, every gray hair in its place.

"Mr. Morgan, because of the circumstances, I'd ask that you take an oath before testifying."

Joe raised his right hand.

"Do you swear to tell the truth, the whole truth and nothing but the truth, so help you God?"

"I do," Joe said, then sat.

"Proceed with your testimony."

Joe leaned into the microphone. "The National Park Service is not the principal agency acting upon the trespass by cattle owned by Rancher Manson, thus we are not in a position to give an accounting of why federal action was necessary. Those facts are best provided by the Bureau of Land Management. In their absence I will summarize. It is my understanding that Mr. Manson failed to pay his grazing fees, yet he continued to graze his cattle on an allotment administered by BLM, for over a decade. As sister agencies in the

Department of Interior, both act under the authorities of the laws of the land. I'm confident you will be provided with information and documentation, given their testimony is requested."

Joe glanced up, then continued. "With respect to recommendations from the Piedras Coloradas National Monument Coalition, concerning management of the national monument. They are not Mr. Chastain's, they are the public's. People from all parts of the community, working together to advise us on management practices and policies, to preserve the natural and cultural heritage valued by citizens. That concludes my testimony. I am available for questions."

"Pretty brief," the congressman said. "Why is Mr. Chastain not here to speak for himself?"

Jack leaned in to hear, tugging at the hood, keeping his face covered.

"At present, he is not available," Morgan said. "On orders from the director of the National Park Service, who did not want him undeservingly becoming the focus of criticism. I am his supervisor. I am superintendent of Piedras Coloradas National Park and of a portion of the adjoining National Monument. None of his actions representing the National Park Service or the federal government have been carried out without my knowledge or approval. If you have questions, you can address them to me."

"Somehow I doubt that, but I'm sure you'll try to protect him." Hoff consulted his page. "Let's see if I have more questions for this witness." He raised his eyes. "Maybe later, Mr. Morgan. Please remain available for questions following the testimony of others."

Joe stood and returned to his chair.

"Next witness, Moony Manson."

The rancher, in starched jeans, pressed white shirt and white cowboy hat, stood and worked his way to the aisle. A second man, in camo, followed. Manson turned and approached the table. The camo-clad militiaman, wearing sunglasses, faced the audience and folded his arms.

Hushed whispers filled the room.

"You may have a seat, Mister Manson."

"Gonna swear me in?"

"That won't be necessary."

Manson sat. He grabbed the microphone. "Thanks for allowing me to be here to defend myself, defend freedom, and defend a way of life that's being attacked. My family's been ranching here for generations, yet the government came with armed goons, ready to take my cows, intent on kicking me off land that's more mine than theirs. Land I've ranched all my life. Someone had to take a stand. Someone has to fight back." He paused and appeared to lock eyes on the congressman.

"Is that the end of your testimony?" Hoff asked.

"Hardly. I have much more to say."

"Were you afraid?"

"Of the feds?" he scoffed.

"Did they threaten you?"

"Waved papers under my nose an inch thick. If that's not a threat, I don't know what is."

Laughter.

The congressman smiled. "Understood. But physically, did they threaten you?"

"Jack-booted thugs, in uniform, storming over land you'd worked all your life, chasing your cows, not letting you or your family anywhere near them. You'd feel threatened."

"Your reaction?"

"I thought, bring 'em on. I'm ready for a fight."

Hoff appeared to resist a smile. "In the years your family's been on the land, have you ever witnessed anything like this?"

"It's been getting worse. For years. Harassment. Threatening letters. Dragging me to court. Threatening to take my cows. Sending bills that keep growing. But to this extreme? Not 'til last month."

"How'd you feel?"

"Attacked. Intruded on. Freedom violated. They got no authority yet they treat us like criminals."

A door at the back of the room swung open. Through it walked a tall, gray-templed man in a tailored black suit. Before him scurried a younger man, cheap-looking suit, clearing a path.

Kelly turned and mouthed, "Who's that?"

"Senator Tisdale, Montana. Intervention."

"Good, right?"

Jack shrugged, watching the aide step back as the senator approached the line of cameras.

Whispers rose up from the crowd. Video cameras swung in Tisdale's direction.

"Order," Hoff commanded.

"Congressman, forgive my breech of protocol," Tisdale said, his voice filling the room. "But . . . please ask Mr. Manson if he ever thought about just paying his grazing fees, like others here in the room." Tisdale folded his arms and looked out over the room. "Ask him."

Hoff stood. "Senator, how kind of you to join us. I do have questions. Several for Mr. Manson, but one for you as well." He smiled. "Why are you here?"

The room grew quiet.

"Wait," Hoff said, raising a hand before Tisdale could speak. "I know the answer."

"I'm here to suggest to the gentleman from Indiana that he seek input from others, including those with an interest in wild horses and their welfare."

"No, Senator, it's not quite that simple, is it?" Hoff crossed his arms. "You're the poor SOB who owes someone favors. So many, in fact, that you had to make a trip to New Mexico just to say that."

Heads turned.

"Of course not."

"Who owns the favors, Senator?"

"Don't be insulting."

"Join me on the dais. Ask your questions, but first, answer mine. Who owns the favors, Senator?"

Tisdale's aide stepped forward, cell phone to his ear. He offered the phone to the senator.

The senator took it, listened, then slipped into the throng, departing through the rear door.

Throughout the room, confused faces exchanged looks, then shrugs.

Hoff smiled.

Kelly turned to Jack and mouthed. "What just happened?"

Jack shook his head. Tisdale intervenes, then he doesn't. Is Hoff right, about someone pulling strings? Is that what happened in Montana?

Hoff cleared his throat and leaned into the microphone. "Where were we?" He looked around the room, making eye contact. "Oh, yes, I remember, but first . . . Can you believe the good senator left? Came all this way and left with unfinished business." He shrugged. "His decision." Hoff laughed. "I promise. I will not leave. As long as you good people are here, I will stay. I will turn out the lights."

Trasker stood. "Congressman, unfortunately, we have a schedule to stick to."

Hoff stared at his agenda. "Everything will be fine, Alex. Everything will be fine." He raised his eyes to Manson. "Where were we?"

"The senator asked about fees," Manson muttered. "We have more claim to the land than the feds do. They have no business being here. I'm willing to pay grazing fees, but not to the feds. Maybe the county, maybe the state, but not BLM. I don't recognize them as having authority. They made it up. Thank God, patriots came to my rescue, or they'd have my cattle. And then, what would I do? I'd be another government dependent, living on welfare, in subsidized housing, looking for handouts."

Chatter and laughter erupted.

"Order," Hoff said. He put on his reading glasses and peered over the top. "Continue."

"I stand before you a sovereign citizen. I answer to common law, to a natural law, and . . ."

"Mr. Manson, . . ." Hoff said, abruptly.

". . . I have not forfeited my rights, including those of prior appropriation. I have put those lands to use, and they are mine. The federal government has no authority, and . . ."

"I believe, Mr. Manson . . ."

". . . if anyone does have authority, it is the county, and I turn to the county sheriff and expect him to keep hippies, environmentalists and trespassers off my land."

"Excuse me, Mr. Manson." Hoff flashed a quizzical look. "How many cattle you got?"

"Five hundred cows."

"Thank you. I understand your anger. Who wouldn't? Your wife and sons threatened by armed federal agents. You, harassed. You're a hero, Mr. Manson. Fight on. Where others folded in the face of government overreach, you stood firm, a rallying point for like-minded people. Could've been Waco all over again. I'm glad it wasn't. Resistance from the righteous was too much for a bunch of bureaucrats. You were ready to fight and they wanted to be home by five."

Manson laughed.

"That'll do for now. I'll have more questions later."

Manson stood and started up the aisle. The militiaman stepped aside, let him pass, then followed him back to his chair.

Boos rose from a cluster of women.

A Manson militiamen, sitting in front of the women, turned, folded his arms, and stared.

The women quieted.

"Our next witness is . . ." Hoff studied the page. "Mr. Kip Culberson." He looked over his glasses. "Mr. Culberson, I've not been provided a copy of your testimony."

"It was provided, Congressman."

"I don't have it. It's customary to share those beforehand. I'm afraid it's necessary to move to the next witness." He looked down at his list.

Kip stood. "Congressman, I'll make it simple. How come Manson doesn't pay for his feed? The rest of us do. If I need more pasture, I rent it. His fight is solely for self-interest. He's good as subsidized."

"That's enough, Mr. Culberson."

"Your time would be better spent considering recommendations from the coalition, giving us authorities to do things that preserve what's important to us all, our way of life, our natural and cultural heritage, including ranching."

"Order," the congressman said, looking down at his paper. He waited, as if to defuse the moment. "Thank you, Mr. Culberson. You may be seated."

Kip sat.

"Next to testify, Max Barkley, Basin Legal Foundation."

A pudge of a man stood from the front row, scooted to the witness table, and gave his prepared statement, that in the legal opinion of his organization, land in public hands creates conflict not experienced with private or local government ownership. He returned to his seat.

A woman from a landowner's group detailed an unending list of victims and grievances.

Next, a man calling himself an economic policy analyst from the Poppy Seed Institute presented an analysis of improved land management and economic benefits under private, local, and state ownership. No outside sources were cited.

The congressman watched the man shuffle back his seat, then leaned into the microphone. "Our next witness is running late. His flight into Albuquerque was delayed, but the note I have suggests his impending arrival. While we wait, I'll make a few comments."

"First, Mr. Culberson mentioned a coalition. Very admirable that citizens would make the effort to hold their local public servants accountable, make them listen. However, it simply does not appear to be enough. I'm here not to help you make lemonade, but to rid you of lemons."

He checked his watch, stood, walked around the table, and sat on a corner, one leg draped over the edge. "Folks, I'm deeply troubled by what I've heard here tonight. To the point of despair. Look at what happened to a man just trying to make a living." He looked down, shaking his head. "Troubling."

He walked to the other end of the table. "This could happen to anyone. It could happen to you. They could come in, take what you own, declare you a criminal, and you, too, could find yourself facing this kind of tyranny." He gave his head another shake, eyes locked on the floor. "The fact that Moony Manson stood up to tyranny amazes me. Few would have." He looked up. "Keep fighting, Mr. Manson. But you can't do it alone. Someone needs to help. Someone needs to push for common sense amidst all the idiocy. Eliminating the national monument here in New Mexico may be a needed first step, if for no other reason than to push back on ever expanding government overreach." He walked to the other end of the table. "If I were president, and if Congress were to put legislation before me stopping such tyranny . . . stripping these lands from irresponsible hands, I'd have no choice but to sign it . . . considering what I've heard here tonight." Hoff stepped down from the dais, appearing to mull his next words.

Through the corner of his eye, Jack noticed Kelly move, pushing her way past others. She broke through the crowd and raised her hand.

The congressman looked away. "After tonight, I'm afraid. We all should be afraid."

"So," Kelly shouted. "That's what this is about. Your aspirations."

He glanced her way. "Excuse me. I'm not taking questions until after the hearing." He looked down. "As I was saying, I'm afraid. Afraid this could happen to many of you."

Kelly stepped through the line of cameras. She walked forward.

Hoff watched, appearing befuddled. "Madam, I can hold you in contempt."

She stopped halfway down the aisle. " Do it. I'm feeling contempt. Congressman, you're manipulating us. Stop it." She crossed her arms. "You're trying to make us afraid. You're a master with words, I know, but stop it."

Hoff glanced at Trasker, then Kelly. "I have something I'm trying to say here."

"This looks like campaign mode to me. Cameras rolling. American people listening. You, stoking the flames. If you're auditioning for a job, Congressman, let's turn this into an interview."

"Madam, there's . . . an ongoing battle, between very different ways of looking at the world. Dare we say, between right and wrong."

Kelly shook her head. "I could care less about ideology, Congressman. Don't go there. If you're running for president, let's hear your qualifications. Examples. You bringing people together, addressing their needs. How have you served society?"

"Madam, I do that every day. Please have a seat."

"We're waiting, Congressman. You have time. Until the next speaker arrives, remember. Give us examples."

"The job requires leadership. It requires holding people accountable. It requires . . ."

Kelly cut him off. "I'm sorry, Congressman, I suppose I wasn't explicit enough. Examples. Something you did, working with society without creating winners and losers."

He stared. "Madam, this is a hearing of the U.S. Congress."

"Careful. Remember, this is an interview. Cameras are on. This needs to be good."

"Madam, this country needs new direction. I'm willing to fight the battle, take the risks, advance the cause, even if it's unpopular."

"Not what I'm looking for. Maybe others are, but not me. I care about whether you can pull people together to make society work."

"Politically correct. That's the problem with this nation. Too many people being politically correct. To be great again, this country needs someone willing to say what needs to be said."

"I don't care what you say. I care what you do. Congressman, the problem is not people being politically correct. The problem is people like you being unwilling to tackle real problems, but stirring us up to hide the fact that you're not even trying, or that you're incapable of doing anything other than stir people up." She put her hands on her hips. "Let's start over. No charades. You're applying for a job. Show me you can find solutions. Bring us together. Fix the damage you've caused here. Now."

Hoff tried to smile. It did not quite form. He glanced at the cameras. "Madam, people are afraid."

"I know. You're dishing out fear." She turned back to the audience. "Who here's afraid?"

Hands shot up, scattered around the room.

"Fear is what this is about," Manson shouted. "Fear of tyranny. Time to eliminate tyranny, put power where it belongs."

"So you can manipulate someone else?"

"Those jack-booted thugs tried taking my cattle."

"Because you didn't pay your fees. No other reason. Everything this fiasco's about is of your making." She turned away and searched the crowd. "Who's afraid?"

"I'm talking," Manson growled.

Kelly appeared to ignore him. "Who here is *really* afraid?"

A man in a worn western shirt raised his hand. "I am. I'm afraid we'll lose our freedom."

"What freedom will you lose, Jose?"

"I afraid I'll be next. That they'll come take my cows."

Kelly walked up the aisle, and faced him. She sighed, and gave him a gentle smile. "Oh, Jose, no one's gonna take your cows. You're afraid because someone says you should be. They want you to worry, but no one's gonna take your cows. You're not a deadbeat. You're a good man. Don't worry. Don't be afraid." She smiled again and turned. "Who else?"

A militiaman raised a fist. "I'm not afraid, but I'm not buying what you're sellin'. I don't buy the government line. I will not let them take my rights, erode the constitution, take my country."

"I don't know your name," Kelly said. "But everyone in this room values their rights. Everyone here wants to preserve the constitution. You're not unique."

"Feds are trampling the constitution. Every day."

"Good thing for us you're no authority. Best for you, too. Founding fathers were not a bunch of likeminded people listening to each other talk. It took work to deal with their differences. Hard work. It takes work on our part, too."

"Ranchers," a man interjected, staying seated. "When they rape the land, it makes me afraid of . . ."

Kelly cut him off. "Most of them love this land as much as you do."

"Damned environmentalists." A woman stood and pointed.

"The things they do that I could never believe in," she said, staring the man down. "And the things I believe in that they don't."

"Both of you," Kelly said, glancing between them, "do you listen to each other, talk to each other, try to make things work?" She paused. "I want you two to try. It might not be easy but why does it have to be? Some things take work."

"We can't afford what they want."

"Can we afford what you want? Alice, making things work in community like ours takes give and take, but we do it, don't we?" Kelly's expression softened. "You afraid?"

She shook her head.

"Good." Kelly turned back to the congressman. She crossed her arms.

The congressman glanced right, searching. "Alex?"

Trasker stepped away from the wall.

"Escort this woman from the room. She's in contempt."

Alex Trasker moved toward her, then stopped. "Uh . . ." He eyed the ceiling.

"Remove her."

"I don't think so, Congressman." He sighed. "Isn't that what we're supposed to do? Engage. For years, I've thought if I ever saw someone willing to do what she just did, I'd quit and go begging for a job. . . . I don't want to be Godiva's horse. Not anymore. I . . . I resign."

Confused laughter rose around the room, then fell away to silence.

Hoff let out a weak little laugh. "Alex . . . you're my most trusted aide."

"And I thought you stood for something. That the cause was great. That the nation needed you. I'm no longer convinced."

"Alex, remove her."

"She has every right to be here. She's done things you won't. She's being the kind of person I hoped you were."

"Alex, we'll discuss this later."

"Did you hear her? Did you see her listen, then try to pull people together?"

"It takes more than listening. It takes vision, and more than that, influence."

Alex let out a chuckle. "Influence. Your favorite subject. The times I've listened to your favorite saying, . . . Influence and power come not from calling in favors, but from someone fearing you might." Trasker ran a hand across his face. "I'm tired of all that, Congressman. I'm tired of political games. I'm tired of that way of doing business."

The congressman turned, wide-eyed, and started for the door.

"Whoa!" someone shouted from the back of the room. "You said you wouldn't leave."

Hoff stopped. He eyed the cameras, and backtracked to his seat. "Folks, I . . . uh . . . I wish to return to our reason for being here." He set his eyes on Kelly. "This is my hearing, not yours."

She crossed her arms. "Then deal with the damage you've done. Bring us together."

The congressman's eyes worked the room. Attempts at a smile crossed his lips.

Jack scooted past others and stopped at the top of the aisle. He pulled off his hood.

Kelly caught sight of him. "No, Jack. Don't."

The room fell silent.

He walked toward her. "It's okay." He held her eyes until her look of concern slipped away.

He exchanged looks with Joe and approached the table.

Kelly backed down the aisle.

Jack sat and pulled the microphone toward him. "Congressman, I'm Jack Chastain. I'm gonna do you a favor. You're a little caught off guard by events, so I'll give you time to recover. I have things to say, and since I'm censured—told I can say nothing—my ass is yours." He smiled. "First, I want to tell a story."

The congressman glared.

"I was recently in Kenya. Rangers there are dying, trying to preserve their heritage, including rhino and elephant. My job's easy compared to theirs." He shrugged. "While there, a man told me something I'd never given thought to. About our country and his.

On the streets of Nairobi, he pointed at a traffic light. He asked, what do the colors mean? Red, green, yellow. I said red means stop. Not necessarily, he said. Not in Kenya. Red means maybe stop, maybe not. The difference in your country, he said, is you have rule of law. In your country, red means stop. If you don't stop, if you get caught, you face consequences. Most of you respect that."

Hoff remained quiet, glaring.

Jack leaned over the microphone. "Congressman, I have problems with Moony Manson, but my bigger problem is with you. The games you play. You fire people up complaining about us, crying things like government overreach. Hell, Congressman, you know better than I do . . . you write the laws, not me. My job is to carry them out. The job you and your colleagues give me. If you don't want me doing that job, simple, change the law. Instead, you play politics. You stir people up, for political purposes. Then, you encourage someone like Moony Manson to fight. In doing so, you put something very important at risk. Our rule of law. You risk taking us in the direction of lawlessness, making heroes of deadbeats. Putting our constitution more at risk than anything anyone else in this room's ever done." He paused.

The congressman seemed to search for words.

Manson jumped up. "This is my meeting. God brought these people together to hear God's truth, from me. Natural law. Prior appropriation." A militiaman stood.

Grumbling rose up in the room. "Sit," someone shouted. Others echoed. Manson sat.

Jack fought back a smile. "We are a nation of laws. Kenya is a nation wanting to be, and while they evolve to where we are today, you risk taking America the other direction."

Hoff said, "I don't need your lecture."

"Lecture's over," Jack said. "But I would like to clear something up."

"What?" he growled.

"Montana, three years ago. I've been thinking all this time you were there to lie your ass off, turn people against us, erode support for a national park that people there wanted. And, after watching your performance tonight, I'd say that's something you're capable of doing."

The congressman glared.

"But, I'm wondering now if you weren't just repeating something you'd heard. They were lies, but I'm thinking you might not've known that. Anything to say?"

"I don't remember what happened in Montana."

"I'll take that as confirmation."

"Whatever. Now's my turn," the congressman barked. He stood, transforming himself, letting confidence build. "I don't need a lecture on rule of law. Not from a low level bureaucrat. I sure as hell don't need schooled in the lessons of Kenya. Hell, I know Kenya. Been there many times, recently in fact. I know their problems. Their problems are irrelevant to what we're discussing here tonight. Furthermore . . ."

"Hold it," Jack said, raising a hand.

The congressman stopped, his words hanging on air, his eyes moving, his confidence fragile.

Jack turned, searching for Alex Trasker, finding him near the back of the room. "You said something a minute ago. Something I've heard before."

Trasker shrugged.

"What was it? . . . The saying . . . about favors," Jack said, more to himself, remembering Undersecretary Mwangi's words. Heard it from an American, only days before, he'd said. But Hoff wasn't on the list. He faced Hoff, resting his chin on a hand. "Go ahead, Congressman. Tell me about Kenya. Recent work. I want to hear this."

"I don't need to talk about Kenya.

"No, please."

Hoff appeared to try to reset. Confidence reappeared. "Because of my influence I had the opportunity to go to Kenya. Fact-finding trip. Plights of the rhino and elephant." He paused, his eyes working the room.

"And yet you didn't go. Not on the fact-finding part of the trip."

"Something came up."

He studied Hoff's eyes. "Did you know what was in the box, Congressman?"

Color flushed from his face. "I don't know what you're talking about."

"Leather box, gold trim. Do you know what was in it?"

The congressman's eyes grew angry. "Why would it matter what's in a damned box?"

"Because it held a rhino horn, Congressman. Three rhino and two Kenyan rangers were killed by a poacher hired to get you that horn. You picked it up in Nairobi. Carried it to Saudi Arabia. Someone else's bidding, I'm guessing. Someone with money. Someone willing to pay for your influence. Someone not afraid to call in a favor." Jack let the thought settle in. "One ranger . . . a scientist . . . had a wife and son. Believed his work could make a difference. In Kenya, to preserve its heritage."

"Mr. Chastain, Members of Congress don't . . ."

Jack cut him off. "I know you were only a glorified courier, chosen to impress. My question is, whose money gets you to do their bidding? Who are you beholden to, Congressman?"

"That is out of line."

"Maybe, but I'm in trouble already. What's it matter?" Jack smiled, then let the smile melt away. "For your information, proceeds from the other two horns went to coffers of the local affiliate of Al-Qaeda."

Hoff's lips moved, producing no sound. He stood, eyes flitting. Turning, he hurried off the dais, exiting the side door.

Whispers, then chatter.

Alex Trasker walked up the side aisle to the dais. He leaned over the microphone. "Guess it's not for me to say, but . . . this hearing is over."

CHAPTER

42

People moved toward the doors.

The superintendent met Jack in the aisle. "My office, eight o'clock." He frowned. "I'll try to protect ya. I'm not sure I can."

Jack nodded. "Thanks, Joe."

Joe turned and left.

Alex Trasker stepped down from the dais.

"What now?" Jack asked.

He shrugged. "Not sure. Maybe I'll hang around a few days. Take a few walks. Sit by the river. Get my head screwed on straight. What'll happen to you?"

"Sentencing in the morning. I deserve what I get, but I have options." He sighed. "Change is coming."

Claire Prescott joined them in the aisle. "Can you believe her?" She turned back, spotting Kelly at the back of the room. "I never would have expected what happened tonight."

Jack watched Kelly, reporters around her, a confused look on her face. Deer in the headlights. "We better go help." He starting up the aisle.

"She read his every move," Alex muttered, along-side. "Hoff never stood a chance. There's no way she knew what was supposed to happen, but somehow she saw right through it."

They approached the throng.

A black-suited man appeared in the hall.

Reporters peeled off from Kelly and converged on the man.

A cameraman backed through the door, video camera on his shoulder.

"What's this?" Alex asked.

"Unfinished business," Jack said, as the man turned and caught his eye.

Claire slipped behind Alex.

Stepping past the reporters, he entered the room, stopped, and smiled. He advanced toward Jack.

The cameraman stepped aside.

"Jack Chastain," he said, reaching out his hand.

"Senator Tisdale."

The reporters, photographers and cameramen formed a line.

Tisdale took hold of Jack's hand.

Flashes fired. Photographers and cameramen settled in.

"Good to see you," Tisdale said, his expression that of admiration. "I heard you were profoundly impressive tonight."

"Not profound. Just things I needed to say. Where'd you go?"

"Another crisis. One can only tackle so many crises in a day."

Jack gave a slow nod.

Tisdale faced the video cameras. "I've had the pleasure of working with Jack over the years. I value his word. I value his contributions. If you folks will excuse us, I would like to give him my regards, let him know how impressed I am."

"Question," a reporter said, extending a microphone. "What have you worked on with Senator Tisdale?"

Jack held his tongue.

"It's okay," Tisdale said.

"You sure, Senator?"

"Sure? Of course."

"I worked with the senator and his staff on a project in Montana. It never made it to Congress. Never made it to the president. Never had a chance. It all went to hell."

"Truly unfortunate." Tisdale shook his head.

"Especially for your constituents. Those who wanted the park."

Jack looked into one of the cameras. "I briefed Senator Tisdale on several occasions. The senator was one of the only politicians I ever thought I could trust." He glanced at Tisdale.

Tisdale smiled.

"We had a Congressional hearing, not unlike the one here tonight. Focused on our work to establish a park. Some of our science was called into question. I tried to explain, and the attacks started. Found myself defending the work of a young scientist. I made things worse."

"I'm sure it's painful, Jack. You don't need to go into those old details."

"I think it might help to talk about it."

The senator smiled.

"That wasn't the only thing I felt bad about. I felt bad about assurances I'd given the senator. About our findings, what we knew, what we didn't, what we could say with our results, what we couldn't. In the hearing, the facts were thrown in my face and the game of misrepresentation began. I worried from that day till today that the good senator thought I misled him. Painted too rosy a picture."

"Those things happen, Jack. Forget it. Don't worry about it."

"I'm not worried. Not after today."

"Good," Tisdale said, turning his smile on the camera, then glancing over. "Excuse me?"

"I'm not worried. Not anymore. I know now the young scientist and I were set up, maybe by accident, maybe intentionally."

"What are you talking about?"

"We were ripped to shreds, by none other than Congressman Hoff, using fragments of truth, and tons of lies, but I think he was repeating something he heard. The things that came out in that hearing included details few people knew. Boring details, but our reports hadn't been written. I assumed someone up the chain of command shared briefings with Hoff, but that wasn't it."

Tisdale turned his back to the cameras, his eyes wild. He whispered, "Maybe you and I should discuss this privately."

"I think this is a perfect place to discuss it." Jack turned to the reporters. "You're gonna want to hear this . . . and you may have questions for the senator. Should he leave, I'd be delighted to answer for him."

"What are you doing? What are you talking about?"

"Americans for Business, Business for Americans. Their event. You gave the keynote. Pandered your ass off. Instead of just giving facts, you couldn't help yourself. You avoided the truth and said what they wanted to hear. You told them you would not let us shut them down, inferring we knew something that could. Inferring we would shut them down, if not for you."

"I underscored the importance of jobs."

"You could have done that and kept to the facts. You could have told the truth. Instead, you made them need you, vote for you, continue to support you, because you were the only one who could protect them, or so you wanted them to believe. In other words, you told them what they wanted to hear."

Tisdale gave a warped smile, then turned his back on the cameras. "Jack, that's how politics works," he whispered. "Please stop this."

"What if it'd been a different bunch of people? What if it'd been the ones who wanted us going after fracking, even though we weren't? Would you've told them what *they* wanted to hear? Would you infer they were unsafe, or safe?"

Tisdale slid a foot, appearing ready to make an exit.

Jack grabbed his arm. "Stick around, senator. It's about to get interesting."

"Stop. You and I can talk privately. They threatened to support the other party, find a young conservative," he muttered in a whisper. "Run him against me, kill me with dark money ads. There's no way I could've fought that."

"At least you could've gone down honorably."

"There's no such thing. They ruin your reputation. Kill you with lies."

"Senator, I have no sympathy to give. Lies are what this is about. A young scientist and I gave you facts. You used those facts and wove them into a set of lies. Lies that spread like wildfire. All the way to the congressional hearing that night, where I was made to look like I avoided the truth. Government bureaucrat, looking like he was hiding something. The more I fell back on facts, the more I was made to look like a liar. The more I tried defending a young scientist, the more I looked like I'd pushed him toward preconceived notions, not science, which could not've been further from the truth. But the journey back to truth would've required going back to your speech, early that day, and I knew nothing of the speech until today. Why couldn't you just stick to the boring truth? That we picked up methane in our samples, and we couldn't explain why."

"There was all the talk about fracking," Tisdale said. "How it killed that poor little girl. People wanted fracking shut down. The industry was in a panic. People wanted answers. I gave them answers."

"Senator, I'm not a geologist. I know little about geologic structure and nothing about how fracking could've poisoned that little girl. Maybe, with a bad well casing, but . . ."

"That's all I was trying to say. But people that morning had political leanings. I had to speak their language."

"That's not what you said, Senator, and there can't be ideological litmus tests for truth. That only leads to more lies. More ignorance."

"It's not that simple, Jack," the senator whispered, now angry. "People don't want to learn. They believe things. You can't fight that. You have to appeal to their way of thinking, what's already there, be the one they choose. Take care of them once you're in office, bring them around. Suggesting ignorance would be political suicide."

"Senator, I'm ignorant on all sorts of things. Doesn't mean I want to stay ignorant. I realize, some people prefer us ignorant. Some people work to create ignorance. But should that be members of Congress? I don't get it. It should be a basic right that we hear the facts, the truth. Let us do with it as we will. What will we face as a society if people only hear justified lies?"

"All I did was tell those people I'd fight to save jobs."

"Worthy, but that's not what you said, Senator. And there's

something you didn't know, and neither did I. Another thing I learned today. In addition to methane, there was dye in our ground water samples. Rhodamine dye."

The senator gave him an uncertain look. "Meaning?"

"Someone else was studying springs and ground water movement. But, they had the scientific methodologies to figure it out."

"Figure what out?"

"Where the poison was going. Which means, they knew where the poison was coming from."

The senator swallowed hard.

"Who would be doing that, Senator?"

"I don't know."

"I wonder about that. I wonder if, like Hoff, you're beholden to someone. I don't know if it's that group you talked to, or someone else—maybe someone who wanted tonight's attempt at intervention—but I intend to find out."

Tisdale ripped his arm away, and barged past the reporters.

Jack ran a hand across his brow, watching the camera crews follow.

Claire stepped around Alex Trasker. "And that sorta thing is why I quit and moved to committee."

"You quit?" Jack said.

"You thought I was fired," she said. "Everyone does." She sighed. "I'm sorry, Jack."

"For what?"

"The hearing in Missoula." She stared toward the now empty hallway. "For thinking you hid behind the science, but wimped out on defending it."

43

At seven thirty a.m., Jack walked up the back steps of park head-quarters. Reaching the hall, he slowed, and took it all in, walking past Dispatch, his office, and the others on the way to Joe Morgan's.

He turned the corner and ran into Marge.

"You're here early," Jack said, surprised to see her before eight. She nodded.

"I've got a meeting with Joe."

"Not yet, you don't. I'll come get you. He's on the phone with the director."

"Talking about me?"

"Who isn't?"

He glanced at the door, then ambled out and down the hall.

Unlocking his office, he stepped in and tapped the switch on the computer. He sat down to wait. He checked his email. At the top of the listing, one from a Toby LeBlanc, the given name of The Kid. Jack clicked on the message. Not a missive, but more than he expected.

> Saw the news when I got off my shift. Video posted on a news site. Watched the part with Senator Tisdale, twice. Afterwards, for a few minutes, the knot in my gut went away. First time in years. I'm sorry. I do want to

talk. Give me a week, maybe two. Time to think. Time to
think about what the old me would say.

Toby

Jack clicked on reply, and let the words simply flow.

Don't know where I'll be. I don't even know what phone
number to give you, but I would like to talk. I'm told people are celebrating what happened last night, but in a
few minutes I'll likely be disciplined or fired. That's okay.
I did what I had to do, and I've got a job I can go to.

It's been a meaningful career, most of it satisfying, some
of it difficult. I remember you asking all sorts of questions
shortly after you started on the project in Montana. Typical
questions from a promising new hire. I saw you as someone with both the integrity and aptitude to do well.

I took you with me to the briefing for Senator Tisdale,
because I thought you'd benefit from the experience. That
was a mistake, but I guess there was no way I could have
known.

I recently made a trip to Kenya. Things there made me
think about what happened in Montana, to you, to me,
the circumstances we were caught up in. I've wondered
what I could've done differently. What I could've done to
protect you, help you get that start you deserved, help
you become that contributor to society you wanted to be.
Instead, things happened as they did. Did I fail you? Obviously. Senator Tisdale failed us both, but I failed you. I've
. . .

The phone rang, cutting into his thoughts. Jack tore his eyes
from the words and picked up the phone. "This is Chastain."
    "You *are* in the office."
    "Who's this?"

"Barnes, Fish and Wildlife Service. Saw the hearing last night. Obviously you've got leads."

Jack sighed. "Nope. Just a lucky guess."

"You're kidding. No evidence?"

"None. I'm about to go in a meeting. I'll call you afterward, give you what I know. When we talked last, your investigator was trying to tie a name to an alias."

"No update. We have intelligence, a fellow we're looking for. We hear rumblings from all over the world, and we think he travels by private jet. We know an alias—a Teague something—and have ideas about names to try to tie it to, but none were on your . . ."

"Hold it," Jack said, cutting him off. "That name. Say it again. Full name."

". . . uh, . . . Here it is. Harper Teague."

"I know that name. I know that person."

"When did you see him last?"

"A year ago, but things have been happening lately making me wonder if he's back."

"Knock, knock," said a voice at the door.

Jack whipped around.

Marge smiled. "Joe's ready."

Jack nodded, and turned back to the phone. "We'll have to finish this later." He ended the call and followed Marge down the hall.

She stopped at Joe's door, let him pass, and closed the door behind him.

"Have a seat," Joe said, motioning to a chair.

Jack sat, glancing at Joe's mementos, his rustic timber desk, his Stetson on the credenza. "You're running late, Joe. That's not like you."

"No it's not, but this isn't easy. The director's on the line."

"Good morning, Jack," the director said, his voice somber.

"Good morning."

"Wish to explain yourself last night?"

"I disobeyed orders. Whatever you have to do, I understand."

"I've said it before. You've got a special talent. You attract trouble, and somehow, strange things happen."

"Didn't plan it that way."

"*Neither did Congressman Hoff. This morning, newspapers across the country are running op eds and commentary, written with the assumption that there was a very different outcome last night. A major effort, orchestrated to underscore something that never happened. And yet, on cable news Hoff is now persona non grata. Yesterday, odds on favorite for president. Today, no one willing to admit they know his name. Surreal.*"

"And somehow, you managed to throw another curve after I left," Joe added. "Senator Tisdale. Caught that on the news this morning."

"*Yes, just amazing.*"

"Just setting the record straight," Jack said.

"*Springing all sorts of surprises, weren't you?*"

"Some of it luck. All of it, I guess."

The phone sat silent.

"So, what are you gonna do?" Jack asked, his eye moving from Joe to the speaker phone.

"*First, I want to know if you realize why I wanted you nowhere near that hearing last night.*"

"I do," Jack said. "Because it was risky, and could've reflected poorly on the agency."

"*True, but that's not the main reason. I ordered that to protect you. Politics is an ugly game. There are people, unscrupulous people, with no qualms about painting a picture of someone like you that serves their interests. They'll destroy you for no reason other than you were the one in the way. You were the pawn. The easy chess piece to knock off the board to advance their cause.*"

"I've encountered plenty of that myself. I'm not sheltered here."

"*No, you're not, but I can't help but think it's my job to protect you from the worst of it. As long as you do things I approve, or that Joe approves, I have no qualms about taking the heat. There are big guns out there. People very good at the games they play. Last night could've turned out very differently.*"

"I know, but I survived. Better than they did."

"*Yes. You may've been lucky, and there will be people wanting revenge. I'll admit, there are people in this town celebrating. That doesn't change that fact that you disobeyed me. People are watching to see what I do.*"

"I didn't disobey out of disrespect. I did, because of something I learned yesterday, and because they shot a friend," Jack said, now angry. "A trusted colleague. I'm not good at keeping my head on straight when someone I'm responsible for is attacked."

"*Like this young scientist you mentioned with Tisdale.*"

"That's what I learned yesterday."

The director sighed. "*Oh, how that sounds familiar.*"

"If you're gonna fire me, fire me. I can land on my feet. I have a job I can go to."

Joe sat up, and picked up his pen. He gave it several clicks. "Where?"

"I don't know. Somewhere in New Mexico. I'm expecting a call, today."

"*Well, that makes this easy.*"

"Hold it," Joe said, his green eyes not leaving Jack's, the lines on his brow now set. He leaned over his desk. "Is that what you want?"

"I don't know, Joe, it's a good offer."

"*Let's consider if you quit today, or the prospect that I start proceedings to have you removed from your job because you disobeyed my direct order. Tell me, humor me, how would you look back on this episode?*"

"Why are you asking that?"

"*Because, I'd like to know what you were thinking at two in the morning. Worried about today? Or no regrets, because it was something that had to be done?*"

"I'm not a rabble-rouser, but trouble sometimes finds me."

"*I know that, but what were you thinking at two in the morning?*"

"Nothing. I was sleeping, and better than I thought I would."

"*I see.*"

"Maybe you don't. I've been awake for plenty of two o'clocks. Last night I was relieved."

"Then tell me what you learned from all this."

"I'm not sure," Jack groused. "Ironically, the politician I thought I could trust most, turns out I couldn't. That's something I learned, but I doubt that's what you're getting at."

"You're right, I'm not."

"For the past few years I've thought a lot about lies. For the last few days I've been thinking about truth. What is it, really?"

"Sounds like you're thinking too hard."

"Am I? We give 'em facts, they shoot the messenger. Accuse us of lies. They're politicians, people who manipulate facts to serve their political agendas. We don't make a habit of lying or being untruthful, they do. They put up images of us, purely for politics, when we're certainly better than them."

"Are we?"

"We may not be perfect . . . some of us aren't worth our salt, but most of us are. But my point is, who are they to provide oversight, when truth for so many of them is a figment of some ideological standard?" He clenched a fist. "Is that what you want to hear?"

"Yes, I want to know what's bouncing around your head."

"Since Montana, I haven't trusted myself. Feared I wasn't good enough to prevent what happened. I feared I'd do it again, here." He sighed. "I'd tell a different story, urge caution, say politicians could come here, play their games, and drive people apart, because that's what politicians do . . . but in reality I didn't believe in myself. Didn't have faith I could work around politics to achieve what the people here deserve. Then, after last night, I said to myself, what was I thinking?"

Laughter bled over the speaker.

"I'm serious." Jack let out a long, slow breath. "You ask what I've learned from this. I've learned truth doesn't shape the politics of politicians. Politics shape what they accept as truth. That's wrong." He let out a bitter growl. "They fail us. The best public policy should be a well-informed public. Information, evidence based. Facts. But no, they shoot the messenger and play politics with the truth. Oversight? Who are they to give oversight?"

Quiet settled over the room.

Jack looked up at Joe. Joe shrugged, and gave his pen several clicks. Nothing to say.

"Jack, I know you're serious. I agree that Congressman Hoff undermined rule of law, and Senator Tisdale fed into society's ignorance, but . . ."

"But what?" Jack demanded.

"There's danger in becoming blinded by our own rectitude. There's danger in being un-tethered to oversight and accountability."

"Are you saying I . . ."

The director cut him off. *"I'm not questioning your integrity. I'm saying you're angry. You're tired. You've been through a lot. You need to step back, regain some perspective. I'm also saying we must always be accountable and open to oversight. And oversight is Congress' responsibility."*

"But they are morally . . ."

"If we let ourselves think we're more honest and morally correct than everyone outside our ranks, then we've set a trap for ourselves. We'll likely justify things we otherwise wouldn't think appropriate, or legal, or moral. We can't assume we're right. We have to be willing to question ourselves. Ask ourselves if we're right. We have to expect and accept oversight."

Jack dropped his head.

"The politicians you've experienced did little to set a good example. But, just maybe the fact that Congressional oversight hung over our heads made you be those things you see yourself as being."

"Did you ask your questions just to tell me that?"

"No, I wanted to know where your head's at. But listen, and closely." The director paused. *"Politics. It is what it is."*

"You justifying them?"

"No, but neither you nor I know what it's like in their shoes."

"Don't want to."

"Neither do I, but theirs is a difficult world, too. Enough said." He paused. *"You have no idea how angry I was watching you step forward last night. I gave you an order. You disobeyed. Everyone knows it. There have to be consequences."*

"Then fire me."

"I don't want to fire you. Not someone who's survived that many battles, honorably. But there must be consequences. People need to see this wasn't swept under the rug." He paused. *"I have no choice but to remove you from your position, at least for a while."*

"I'm not leaving."

"You're not staying."

"I can find a job for him here," Joe said, giving a click to his pen.

"No," the director responded. *"I've made up my mind. Jack has to leave. For his own good. I have to send him where this won't be repeated."*

"Afraid to fire me?" Jack said. "I can quit."

"Yes, you can."

"Jack, listen to what the director has to say."

He crossed his arms.

"I'm removing you from your position. Temporarily, to let things cool down, and prevent conflicts with elected officials. I'm giving you an assignment. Had an email this morning, confirming interest. It's a go." He cleared his throat. *"I'm sending you out of the country. Scientific technical assistance. A place where you can't get in much trouble. Kenya."*

Jack let out a chuckle. "There were things I didn't tell you about Kenya."

"Don't start now."

— · —

Jack returned to his office and closed the door. He walked to the window and took in the canyon, its walls now orange-red from morning sun.

He pulled himself away, looked up a phone number and dialed.

The answer, a gruff, "What?"

"Pug, this is Jack, calling to say . . ."

"You're gonna be stupid, because people now think you're a hero."

"Hardly." Jack turned back to the window. "But this is what I do."

"It's only gonna get worse."

"Maybe. Maybe not. Could get better."

"Don't count on it."

"Thanks Pug, for everything. With things at their darkest, your offer helped me see through it."

"Wasn't doing it for you. I was doing it for me. I'm a greedy bastard."

Jack laughed and said his goodbyes. Then, he sat, and noticed an unfinished email. He reread the words, deleted everything, and started over.

CHAPTER

44

Jack waited on the steps at Elena's, watching Kelly park and climb out of her car. "Much to tell you," he said as she approached, "but it can wait. How was Senator Baca's memorial service?"

She nodded, took his hand, and walked with him in.

They approached the hostess.

"Joining the Trasker party," Jack said.

"Follow me." The young girl led them into the dining room.

At the table nearest the kiva fireplace, Alex waited, sitting with Claire Prescott and Lizzy McClaren. He stood and gave Kelly an embrace. "You were amazing last night."

Kelly blushed.

"You were," both Claire and Lizzy agreed.

"So, what happened, Jack?" Alex asked. "You fired?"

"Banished. Exiled till they call me home. What'll you do?"

"Guess it's home to Ohio. Talk to universities. See if a Ph.D. in economics and experience on the Hill are good for anything."

"It . . ." Claire said, drawing their attention, ". . . it will be. I really wish you well."

They exchanged appreciative looks, then Alex turned to Jack. "Sitting by the river today, I started wondering. What did I say that tied Hoff to Kenya?"

"That saying about favors. A Kenyan ministry undersecretary said the same thing. Said he heard it from an American a few days before. Assumed we all played that game. And, a staffer for the Conservation Caucus mentioned a member being a no-show on a fact-finding trip. Hoff admitted to that. It all fell into place." Jack frowned. "But, Hoff wasn't on Kenya's list of travel visas. I looked."

Alex chuckled to himself. "That's funny."

"Why'?"

"You figure out that he picked up a rhino horn, in Nairobi, from his favorite saying, but you can't figure out how." He shrugged. "House members can travel on private aircraft, if they call it a fact-finding trip and claim there are few options for getting where they're going."

"Why wouldn't he be on the visa list?"

"Someone pulling strings." He stroked his beard, then took a sip of his beer. "If you own a private jet, you know a thing or two about getting what you want. If undeterred . . . doesn't surprise me arrangements could be made. Avoid immigration. A bribe to the right person." Seeing no response, Alex shrugged, then turned to Kelly. "You have no idea what you kept from happening last night."

She scooted closer to the table. "I'm sorry. What was that?"

"You look pale. Everything alright?"

"Yes. You were saying?"

"Something was being orchestrated. Something big, by people with plans. Last night was intended to start a ball rolling. The objective, putting public lands in private hands."

"Come on," Jack said. "Last night was about Manson."

"No. More. But I don't know how deep it goes."

Turning to Kelly, Jack noticed the dazed look on her face. "You okay?"

She nodded.

"I have news," Claire said. "Tendered my resignation, effective the end of the term. Maybe before. Dad could use a little help in his Montana law practice. At least until something else comes along."

"Feel good about it?" Alex asked.

"I do. Time for a change. The river made me realize that."

"By the way . . . the mustangs," Jack said. "Rangers tried catching 'em. Couldn't get close. Kept moving higher, then north, out of the park. They're back in Colorado."

Claire laughed. "I'm glad it's over."

"I feel bad," Lizzy said. "All this change. Maybe it wouldn't be happening if I hadn't invited you all on the river."

"Change isn't bad, Lizzy," Claire said. "You know that. Look at you. Happy on the river." She ran a hand down Lizzy's sleeve. "Silk. Wall Street outfit?"

"Nope, I just bought it."

"Are you sure that's a good investment . . . for here? Must've cost a month's tips."

"I'm not poor. I never said I was. When I came here, my assets were frozen. Things were tight. That's behind me now."

"Then, why life on a shoestring?" Jack asked.

She let out a smirk. "Life of a river guide. They accept what comes, to live the life they love. Gave me a sense of what's important." She paused. "And ideas on taking care of my people."

Claire squinted. "Your people?"

"I bought *Enchanted Rivers*. I'm learning the ropes from Zach. Keep that to yourselves."

Alex threw his head back and laughed. "So you do have money burning a hole in your pocket."

"Sold my shares before it all came crashing down. That's why my assets were frozen. Looked like insider trading, not someone disgruntled with corporate direction."

"So . . . you're rich."

Lizzy flashed a coy smile. "Comfortable. Enough about me." She turned to Kelly. "You made me proud last night."

Kelly looked down.

"You *are* pale. Are you okay?"

Kelly nodded. "I'm fine."

"What's wrong?" Jack asked.

"Nothing." She rubbed her eyes, and studied a ceiling viga she'd seen a million times.

"I don't believe that. Tell me."

"It's nothing. Just a strange conversation I had today."

"With?"

"The governor."

Looks were exchanged around the table.

"About what?"

"He asked me to think about something."

Jack raised a brow. "May I ask what?"

"Completing Senator Baca's term."

Alex's eyes grew wide. He turned to Claire. Her eyes met his.

"What'd you tell him?" Jack asked.

"I told him I'm not a politician."

"What'd he say?"

"He wouldn't take no for an answer. Wants to talk in a week." She stared at an empty wall. "I can't do it. It's not who I am."

"If I had money burning a hole in my pocket," Lizzy said, "which I do, . . . that's an idea I could throw money at."

Alex laughed.

Kelly came awake. "No. No. No. I am not a politician."

"Listen to me," Lizzy said. "A week after I left the firm, I got a check in the mail. Big check. Annual bonus, plus some. They wanted me back. I considered it tainted money. I didn't go back but I cashed it and put it away. Figured someday I'd find a worthy cause." She leaned over the table. "Kelly, you are a worthy cause."

She frowned. "Lizzy, if I were in office, I would not want money being my focus, but that's beside the point. I'm not what it takes to be a U.S. Senator."

"Who is?" Alex said. "Don't do it for yourself. Do it to make a difference. To pull people together. That's what you're about."

"You can do it," Claire said. "You'll have to learn to pander a little. That might be hard, but you can do it."

Laughter spread around the table.

Kelly's face remained stone.

Jack took her hand. "You need time to think. Some place quiet. I have an idea. Lizzy, it can involve you, if you're looking for a cause." He explained.

After dinner, they prepared to go their separate ways. Alex raised his glass and called for a toast. "To the river. To what's real. To change."

CHAPTER
45

The jet touched down in Nairobi and taxied to the terminal at Jomo Kenyatta International Airport. Samuel Leboo stood waiting at baggage claim. After handshakes and introductions, Samuel led them to a Land Cruiser pocked with bullet holes. He drove from the airport and skirted the edge of the city. He turned onto the park road, slowed at the entrance, then continued on, to a destination agreed upon earlier by he and Jack.

Giraffe and gazelle ambled about with a backdrop of sky-scrapers. As the cityscape grew distant, the beauty of the Rift Valley became overwhelming. More giraffe, these reaching high into crowns of acacia trees. Black rhino picked at leaves near the ground. Wildebeest and zebra moved in herds across the savanna, dust kicking up at their feet. In the months to come, some of these animals would begin migrations toward wet season range. For now, they hung close to water holes, surviving the dry season.

At a junction, a second Land Cruiser sat waiting. Samuel slowed and waved the driver to follow. Leaving the park, they drove to high ground and stopped where the view opened to the south and the Athi-Kapiti plains. Farms, their boundaries defined by fences, sat randomly on the landscape.

Samuel exited the Land Cruiser and signaled the other ranger, who stepped from his vehicle and opened the rear door. A woman climbed out and stood, holding her son. Gabriel Kagunda's son. The ranger circled to the other side and opened a door. A boy, actually a young man, stepped down. With the ranger's assistance, he followed, supporting himself with a cane. When the young man saw Jack Chastain, he hobbled in a dash to greet him.

"Mr. Jack," he shouted, nearly in tears.

"Ojwang, it's so good to see you."

"Good to see you, too, Mr. Jack. I . . ." He grew quiet, glancing at the women standing either side of him. "Are these your wives, Mr. Jack?"

The women laughed.

"I would be a lucky man, wouldn't I?"

He nodded.

"Yes, I would, but no." He slipped an arm around Kelly. "This is Kelly. She is very special to me." He put a hand on Lizzy's shoulder. "And this is Lizzy, a very good friend. She is also a very good friend of yours."

"I do not know her."

"Ojwang, you have told me many times that you're smart. True?"

"Yes."

"And you've finished your schooling?"

"Yes."

"Ojwang, did you know if you go to university and if you study hard, you can become a scientist? You can help preserve the heritage of Kenya, forever and ever."

"I have no money to go to university."

"I understand. That's why Miss Lizzy is your friend. She wants to help. A little at first, maybe longer."

Ojwang looked confused, the gravity of it all apparently hard to grasp.

Jack gave a nod to Samuel.

Samuel turned to Njoki. "I've spoken with professors at the University of Nairobi," he said. "They will train Ojwang to be a field assistant. If he has aptitude, he will have opportunity to continue his studies. A gift from Miss Lizzy McClaren." He paused.

Her brow creased.

"We want to continue Gabriel's work. And someday your son will know what his father accomplished. And knowing that, he'll know what he too can accomplish, maybe even following in his father's footsteps."

She looked into the green eyes of the red-headed woman staring back with equal uncertainty. "Mr. Leboo, I do not want my son growing up to think he can change the world. I do not want him willing to put himself where he can be killed by a poacher's bullet. Gabriel's killer could kill my son. I want my son to be there for his family, not gone because of something he could never achieve."

Samuel removed his beret. "Njoki, I cannot make promises on matters over which I have no control. But I know, Gabriel thought his science would make a difference. He believed his science could shed a light. A light others would use to find answers. Answers to difficult questions, possibly providing paths away from age-old ways of conflict, and suspicion, and corruption. Will it be easy? No, but he believed his work would contribute. His work alone? No, society needs too many answers, but his science will help."

She burst into tears. "But his killer . . ."

"Njoki, his killer is dead. He will not kill again, but the need for Gabriel's work continues. To preserve our heritage, something Gabriel dedicated himself to doing."

"His life was too short. His killer . . . " She broke down. "How can you know his killer is dead?"

"I know."

She sobbed.

"Njoki, I want you to support us continuing Gabriel's work. I can continue his work without your approval, but life for you will be hard until you accept that he's gone, and until you begin to believe again in the importance of his work. You deserve that. Your son deserves that. Gabriel deserves that."

She dropped her face into one hand, tears falling, her son clinging to her neck, watching, himself near tears, looking confused. Her sobs began to slow. She looked into the eyes of her son. "Your father, he was a good man, was he not?"

The boy nodded.

"You would like to remember your father for the things that he did, and could have done. Things that were important to him, would you not?"

He nodded.

She broke a teary smile, kissed her son, and turned to Samuel.

"You may keep Gabriel's books until our son is old enough to understand them." She threw an arm around Samuel. The tears began again. She sobbed, then broke her hold and pulled away, slowly raising her head. She put on a strong face, and looked Samuel in the eye. "Mr. Leboo, . . . please . . . continue Gabriel's work."

— · —

Kelly picked up her wine glass, took a sip, and set it back on the camp table. She gazed across the savannah, past fever trees and acacia, into a Kenyan sunset. "It's beautiful here."

Jack tipped the bottle and filled his glass. "Could it make you forget New Mexico?"

She smiled. "That question's not fair to either place. Where's Lizzy?"

"She and Samuel went to set up financial arrangements."

"Samuel Leboo is a good man."

"He is. He and Lizzy will make a good team."

"I wish I'd had the chance to know Gabriel Kagunda."

"Me, too. He was young and idealistic. Wise, in an interesting way."

"How so?"

"Samuel told Gabriel he wanted Gabriel's research to give him the truth. Gabriel said it couldn't. He could provide data, theories, and facts, but truth would have to come from Samuel, in how he used the research. Samuel took that as an insult, and as avoiding responsibility, but it was neither." He paused. "At the hearing in Montana, I defended The Kid's work. I presented facts. I was truthful. I had no idea those same facts had been used to support a lie.

Unaware, I was made to look the liar. But the lie . . . Tisdale's . . . tore people apart as it spread. Had I known Gabriel's words, would they've made any difference? I doubt it. The decks were stacked."

"Then don't think about it."

"Hard not to. Facts take work, but it's truth that's hard. Too many of us whittle a little off here, add a little more there, make it fit our way of thinking, or spin it to mean something to our liking."

"You're talking about lies."

"There's lies, and there's not telling the truth. They can be two different things."

"Is this some sort of message? Because of what the governor asked of me?"

He laughed. "Nope."

"Your feelings about politicians . . . and politics . . . they're complicated."

"I'm working on it. Orders from the director."

"I'm not gonna do it, Jack. I don't want to complicate us."

"You can't say no because of me."

She gave the accommodations a glance, then peered in the direction of other tents. "Interesting camp. Wall tents on wood floors. Luxurious beds."

"You won't believe what they cost a night."

"Do I want to know?"

"Thank your friend, Lizzy."

"Will we see her later?"

"Not tonight." Jack reached for the wine and pulled off an envelope taped to the bottle. He slipped out the card. "Read this."

She read, cracked a smile, then set the card on the table. "Kind of her. She's making lots of assumptions."

"You've been thinking about changes."

"Not that kinda changes. I was thinking about you, babies, our lives together."

He smiled. "I'll go wherever you go, or keep the home fires burning, or take care of the kids. Whatever you want."

"I'm not a politician, and you'll be in Kenya."

"I'll be home before you know it."

"Jack, I'm not gonna embarrass myself, thinking I'm what it takes to be a U.S. senator."

He held her eye. "This wasn't your thinking. It was the governor's, and—according to your father—dozens of people who called him."

"I can't do what politicians do these days."

"Then don't."

"What *would* I do?"

"What most of them don't. Pull people together."

She scowled. "Can't we enjoy ourselves here in Kenya, without thinking about that?" She took a long sip of her wine and stared into the sunset. She appeared to let her eye follow the line of the horizon, then the shadows reaching across the savannah.

Minutes passed.

"What's on your mind?" Jack asked.

"The river trip. The battles among us, the things we went through, including the flood, and how close we felt afterwards. Friends. Then came the hearing, and the prospect of change. Except Lizzy, of course. Change had already started for her. But for all of us, that prospect started on the river. For you, too, and after Johnny was shot, you were ready to act, regardless of consequences. I've never seen you so angry. But in the end, when your banishment's over, you'll go back to what you did before. Look at the rest of us. The changes we could face."

"What're you saying?"

"I don't know. I'm not saying I know what I'll do. I'm making observations. Of all of us, you were the one almost asking for it—for change—you were so angry."

"My own worst enemy?"

"Not that. You were angry, but confident, reconciled, to do what you had to do, whatever the consequences. So, did you? Did you do what you needed to?"

"I guess I did, yes."

"But maybe you wanted change. Maybe you wanted to manage that rich guy's ranch."

"Kelly, I have the chance to finish what I started. Some people don't get that. I didn't in Montana, and I haven't finished what I set out to do in New Mexico, so . . . things are good."

She took a sip of her wine, and set her dark eyes on his. "You feel fortunate?"

"Very much so."

"What more do you need to do?"

"The people there don't yet have reason not to fight."

"But they're not fighting. After the hearing, they came back together."

"Out of respect. Common ground. A sense of community. But some issues they face are difficult. They require solutions to preserve what they value. They need options."

She studied his face. "And you're their champion."

"No. At this point, I'm one of them. There are things I can't do."

"After all that happened, surely you don't question your ability to work with politicians."

He watched a fever tree sway in the breeze. "I'm working on it, but we need legislation."

She appeared to mull the thought. "Remember what Alex said? That eliminating the monument was part of a plan. A plan to put public lands in private hands. Lands that belong to all of us. Could that really happen?"

He nodded. "I'm afraid it's possible."

"Robber barons." Kelly took a sip of her wine. "Could they be successful?"

"Not as long as someone's listening to everyone. Not as long as all are considered."

"Then, the people need a champion."

Jack flashed a knowing smile. "Yes, Senator, they do."

Author's Notes and Acknowledgements

This is a work of fiction. A career's worth of experiences led me to write this story. However, current events made me all the more convinced of the importance of telling it, to give sides of the story rarely told, and provide others a chance to walk in another's shoes. We are in strange political times. All in all, most of my experiences with members of Congress were good, but not all of them. My experiences with their staffs were better. I admit, I've encountered many a young, arrogant, ideological staffer, only to get them into the wild—such as on a trail, or on a river like the Colorado—to see them become cooperative, willing to work with others, wanting to make a difference. The older staffers? . . . my experiences were almost all positive. They had a job to do; I thank those who helped me do mine.

I heard the analogy about traffic lights and rule of law from a man I met while at the Kennedy School of Government. He and others from his African nation (I won't say which) were at the same course. One day while he and I were on a walk, he gave that analogy. He was an interesting man, at one moment wise, the next moment willing to remind a fellow countryman of his place. This was interesting to me. I realized there was much I didn't know about his culture. And, as is described in the story, there was something to be learned from him about ours.

I've had the pleasure of knowing or meeting several Kenyan scientists over the years (they are a capable lot). And, I was impressed with the literature I found for Nairobi National Park. I have no doubt that much of the kind of work proposed by the character Gabriel has been completed, but, nonetheless, the park faces tremendous challenges in preserving migration corridors and the connectivity needed to preserve important species, such as wildebeest and zebra. If migration is stopped, the park could become little more than a zoo.

Nairobi and other national parks in Kenya and continental Africa face other grave challenges. U.S. Park Rangers face dangers, but nothing as routine as the dangers faced by those trying to thwart the poaching of rhino, elephant and other parts of the heritage in Africa. It is tragic that some cultures justify robbing the heritage of another, be it for trophy, superstition, or even unproven medical treatment. Before I jump off my high horse, let me note that Americans contribute to the problem.

Several important voices have written or spoken of the dangers of being blinded by our own rectitude, most recently James Comey, former Director of the FBI. Public servants of all stripes should read his words. They're wise and well worth remembering, especially in these times when things are at their most political.

And finally—Lizzy McClaren. I've encountered many Lizzys over the years. People who stepped away from success, seeking a life more meaningful and real. Some found it in the canyons, others in the mountains, some in places like Yosemite Valley, but the place I saw it most was along the Colorado River in Grand Canyon. River guides and others who were doctors, lawyers, stockbrokers, etc., who left success as the world defines it, and found life in the clutches of the rhythm of the river.

My gratitude to the following: Mary Bisbee-Beek, publicist and touchstone, always there to create opportunities and help me understand how things work. Lynn Stegner, editor (with my background, it's an honor to work with someone with that name and connection), for wanting to know some characters better, and for slowing the pace in places to give readers (and characters) a breather; I like how it turned out. Ann Weinstock, cover designer, for using your creativity to catch the eye and give the story an identity. Kris Weber, book designer, for doing the same on the inside, building a meaningful home for my words, with cues important to me—and, I hope, to readers. To Sue Carter, for giving the book spit and polish. And finally, Phil Zuckerman, Sue Cabezas, and the folks at Applewood Books, thank you for all you do, and for championing the exploits of Jack Chastain.

I also want to thank those who test drove *Killing Godiva's Horse:* John Reynolds, former Deputy Director of the NPS; no one was ever better at showing the men and women of the NPS how much they were valued; I am humbled by your interest in reading the draft and sharing your feedback. David Graber, retired Biologist, Sequoia National Park, and Senior Scientist, Pacific West Region: always the best thinker in the room, and always good feedback now. Geoffrey Koome, Ph.D. student at Clemson and one of Kenya's native sons, for sharing Kenya with me and keeping me from embarrassing myself. Julie Mulford, fellow lover of national parks and spy novels, for reading an early draft and telling me what worked and what didn't. Patrick Ezzell, an old, old friend and backpacking buddy—who, at this stage of life sees how meaningful public service is—for sharing encouragement and the questions one would have if they never worked in a national park. And Cassy, my wife, always willing to read the first draft, and to let me think aloud about plotlines, on those long drives to the ranch.

And now, an epilogue.

EPILOGUE

The cell phone on the passenger seat began to ring. The driver picked it up and checked the caller. "Yes, boss," he said, trying to sound settled, but not quite pulling it off.

"How did Chastain know about the rhino horn, Teague? And why are you not answering your phone?"

Steadying the wheel with his knee, Harper Teague wiped the sweat from his bald spot, keeping the phone firmly at his ear with the other hand. "I don't know boss. It wasn't me."

"It had to've been you. How did he know you were in Africa? How did he learn you met Hoff in Nairobi with the rhino horn?"

"He didn't. How would he know that?"

"He learned about Hoff, you idiot! You're supposed to keep your head down, do your work in the shadows."

"Boss, Chastain hasn't seen me in over a year. I've been here, hiding in plain sight, but he hasn't seen me."

"Why was Tisdale at the hearing?"

"I called his aide, quick as I could, told him to get Tisdale out of there, pronto, and he did, . . . but . . . the senator said you wanted him to help save the horses."

"I did no such thing. Must've been something you did."

"No, he said he got a letter from you. For a favor to your wife." Teague slowed, and listened through uncomfortable silence until he could bear it no longer. "It's a tough crowd, boss. They're not responding to Doc's usual methods."

"Wrong. You were lazy. It's easy to break people apart. Harder to hold 'em together. All you had to do was plant the seeds of distrust, follow Doc's plan. It should've fallen into place."

"It's not working. Not like it did in Montana. Doc needs a better plan."

"You're not the expert. You're the gopher. Figure out what you did wrong. Now, I've got a job for you."

"Yes, sir, what?"

"Find me another member of Congress."

—·—

ELSEWHERE, IN ANOTHER STATE.

"Goodbye."

With a press of a button, a page zipped through the shredder, its heading—*Action Alert, Wild Horse and Burro Babes*—the last line to disappear into the teeth. Then, a copy of a friendly letter, the original of which had been signed with illegible flourish.

"That worked better than it should have. Two birds, one stone. The first bird, retribution. The second? Karma. Someone just as deserving. The score? One more down, two to go."

About the Author

J.M. Mitchell grew up in Texas, now lives in Colorado, and spent the years in between on some of America's most cherished landscapes—Yosemite, Grand Canyon and Zion National Parks. He had a long career with the National Park Service, retiring as Chief of the agency's Biological Resource Management Division, where he worked on the technical and sometimes politically charged issues facing the National Park System. He is the author of two other novels: *Public Trust,* and *The Height of Secrecy*, the latter of which won the award for best mainstream fiction from the Colorado Authors' League, and was a finalist in other regional awards. His writing has appeared in scientific and conservation journals, travel magazines, and newspapers. He serves on boards of scientific, philanthropic, and writer's organizations and remains engaged with the NPS, developing training for natural resource managers. He and his wife split their time between Littleton and their ranch on Colorado's western slope.